HIS MAJESTY'S
Pageboy

Sara Powter

Bible Quotes from the King James Version

ISBN: 9781923097308
Paperback Edition

Pacific Wanderland Publications
ABN 99 768 734 831

Kincumber NSW 2251

saragpowter@gmail.com
www.sarapowter.com.au

1st edition 2026 printed by Kindle, KDP, an Amazon Company.
Also in Paperback, ebook and large print paperback.
Published by Pacific Wanderland Publications.

Graphic Acknowledgements

Background Cover painting
[View of Parramatta], 1838 / drawn by C. Martens
https://www.sl.nsw.gov.au/collection-items/view-parramatta-1838-drawn-c-martens

Inset background
Kew Palace, London 1823.
https://commons.wikimedia.org/wiki/
File:William_Westall._New_Palace_Kew_1823.jpg

Inset
Edward Charles Stewart Robert Vane-Tempest-Stewart,
Later 8th Marquess of Londonderry.
By
Philip de László (1869–1937)
https://en.m.wikipedia.org/wiki/File:Edward_Charles_Stewart_Robert_Vane-Tempest-Stewart,_later_8th_Marquess_of_Londonderry.jpg

Cover by Beckon Creative
beck@beckoncreative.biz

All graphics used are in the Public Domain.

Australian Historical Novels
(All stand-alone books)

A First Fleet Stories (1788+)
Gentle Annie Soames
The Emancipated Potter
Paternity Unknown

The Hunter to Macquarie Collection (1795-1822)
When Upon Life's Billows
The Saddler's Song
Tuppence to Pass
His Majesty's Pageboy
A Fist Full of Holey Dollars (2026)
Far From the Whispering Sheoaks (2026)
Bound Down in Iron Chains (2026)
Buddy's Promise (2027)

Unlikely Convict Ladies Trilogy (1792-1840s)
Dancing to Her Own Tune
(co-authored by Sheila Hunter & Sara Powter)
Amelia's Tears
A Lady in Irons

The Lockleys of Parramatta (1800-1901)
Unshackled Lives - *Prequel novella - free with newsletter signup*
Hands Upon the Anvil
Out Where the Brolgas Dance
Diamonds in the Dirt
The Earl's Shadow
Once a Jolly Swagman
Jonty's Journey

The Convict Birthstain Collection (1820-1840s)
No More, My Love
The Vine Weaver
Scotch at The Rocks
Waiting at the Sliprails
Convict Shadows of the Past
In Defence of Her Honour
I Can't Stop Tomorrow
Madeline's Boy
Jam or Marmalade for Tea

Shelia Hunter's
Australian Colonial Trilogy (1840-1850s)
Mattie
Ricky
The Heather to the Hawkesbury

Author's Note
This book contains many references to King George III
and Queen Charlotte.
All this information is freely available on the web. I have attempted to show a loving side to their relationship, but, of course, there is no evidence to confirm whether this was true. The fact that Queen Charlotte was chosen to care for the ailing king rather than their son is quite telling. She visited often and was furious when she was forbidden entrance when he was ill.
Jack is, of course, a fictional character, as are his mother and many characters in the Australian section of the story.

My thanks to

My husband, Steve,
Thank you for all your support in my writing.
He's my Alpha reader.

To Roby Aiken
for your patience in correcting my punctuation
and to my Beta readers
Noreen Robertson, Linda Upcroft, Lee Boehm & Anna Marie Leffew
for doing the final read-throughs
& Anna Marie Leffew for the excellent advertising she does for me.

And…
Rebekah Robinson for my fabulous cover.
Cover by Beckon Creative
beck@beckoncreative.biz

Table of Contents

The grammar and language in this book are Australian English spelling.

KEY

~   - Time passing in the same locality

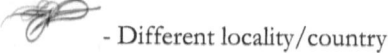 - Different locality/country

Chapter 1   It's a Boy
December 1797, London, England.
John

*L*ady Victoria Templestowe, the widowed Countess of Templestowe-Meade, was still in pain after her protracted delivery. She didn't remember the actual birth as the pain had been so great that she passed out. However, she provided her deceased husband with a son, and this was all she wanted to do. She was determined to be a hands-on mother, even if society would laugh at her.

This child was the only link she now had to her husband. Her beloved Clarence, the Earl of Templestowe-Meade, had died in a stupid phaeton race. He had died needlessly. She gave a huff of resignation. At least she had a son, and her position in the peerage was secure. She was not worried about that for herself, but this was for her boy. She roused after delivering her baby when the pains from the afterbirth hit. The birth had been a breeze compared to the agony of the final stage of childbirth.

Victoria's maid, Rachel, waited until she was cleaned up, then let her cuddle her child.

Rachel swaddled the infant and carried it to the other side of the room, where a crib awaited.

This baby was a surprise to Victoria. She expected to see a red wrinkly baby as her firstborn had been. The child was clear-skinned with a complexion as soft as a peach. Her son was so fair, and she and Clarence were very dark. Their first child had been a girl. Tiny Elizabeth Catherine had also been dark-haired. Sadly, their little girl died soon after birth. Victoria spent days cradling her until she passed away peacefully in her sleep. God rest her beautiful soul. However, this new babe was so lovely. His fair hair was dry, with some curls. This, too, was a surprise as they both had straight hair. Her husband, Clarence, had not even known she was expecting a baby. Now, Clarence was dead.

She now cradled their son tightly and praised God for having given birth to a boy.

Her maid came to tend to her. "What shall you call him, ma'am?"

Victoria met the young girl's timid smile. "I would have named her Jennifer if it were a girl, but I always wished for a baby named John. It means 'God is gracious'. Clarence's middle name was John, so I shall call him that: John Clarence." The girl bobbed a curtsy and nodded.

Rachel looked at the infant and stroked his head. "He's a bonny babe, madam. I'm sure he'll grow up to be a lad you are proud of. He's just like my sister's child: fair and bonny." She snatched her hand away as though burned. She flittered around, grabbing some discarded clothing. The midwife moved the crib into the nursery.

Rachel had been with Victoria through the death of her daughter, Elizabeth, whom she called Bessie, and then she had been her rock when Clarence was killed. The two women had become close. However, today, Rachel was almost flighty. She could not look at Victoria and quickly hurried to tidy the room and leave, ostensibly to prepare the nursery for the baby.

John let out a bellow, and Victoria cuddled the baby brought to her by her cooing maid and put him to her breast. She thought she heard the echo of a cry, but ignored it. She set about satisfying her son's needs.

Rachel stood at the bedroom door, watching the scene before her. Tears welled in her eyes, spilling over and trickling down her cheeks. Her ladyship didn't notice that she was being watched. Rachel dipped her head. She knew she could not stay with her ladyship, having done her and her sister such a great disservice. She left while Lady Victoria was occupied. She had a job to do, and putting it off would not help anyone. She smiled at the beautiful scene before her, then quietly closed the door and left.

~

1806, nine years later, at Buckingham House, London

Lady Victoria Templestowe was recalled to court a year after the death of her husband. As a Lady-in-Waiting to Queen Charlotte, they were often found in or near the music room of *Buckingham House*. Unlike most people who thought the queen had a temper, Victoria adored the older monarch's wife. This magnificent home had been a gift to the queen from her husband, King George the Third. She moved there while her previous residence, *Frogmore House*, which the queen shared with her unmarried daughters, was being refurbished. Colonnades were being built, and an extra floor was being added.

After supplying the king with numerous children, many of whom were grown, the queen sought the company of her lady friends, and those closest to her were lovers of music and literature, as she was. Her favourite room was the music room. Lady Victoria played the harp, and as the queen sat at her harpsichord, they made beautiful music. The queen waved away others who interrupted her peace.

Her Majesty's many daughters had long since refused to obey the strict rules set by a frequently ill father, who happened to be the King. Consequently, the two ladies were often alone in the music room.

Victoria had heard whispers of children born to the unwed princesses, but, to her knowledge, they were only rumours. She saw no sign of any of this.

The two women were working on a duet together and practising each day. So, it was to the music room at *Buckingham House* that they were now leisurely strolling.

The young earl, Lord John Templestowe-Meade, was in the nursery-cum-schoolroom with some of the queen's grandchildren. He had staff there to look after him. He was rarely in any trouble and adored playing with the sand tray and farm figures.

Lord John developed a deep affection for horses and could often be found in the royal stables. When not studying, the queen permitted John to join them in listening to their music. He would lie on a chaise lounge, adoring the beautiful melodies. Victoria's singing would make him sigh contentedly. The young widow had become a firm favourite of the monarch's wife. She had never wished to remarry and loved the quiet life at court with Queen Charlotte. Few of the Queen's Ladies-in-Waiting played the piano as well as Victoria.

At sixty-one, the queen was still beautiful and loved to be surrounded by people with similar interests. Many scientists visited and brought news of new discoveries or places.

The queen's heritage was somewhat ambiguous, as questions arose about the purity of her European bloodline. After nearly fifty years in England, the queen still had the hint of a German accent.

Today, as they strolled along the royal corridors of the immense house, the queen said, "Lady Toria, it's time to choose our tree for

Christmas. When I first thought about celebrating our Yuletide with a Christmas *Tannenbaum*, you thought the children would enjoy it. I remember it was not long after your return to my side, and your adorable cherub, John, could not keep his eyes from the candles flickering on the tree. I willingly admit I was hesitant. Now, they all look forward to decorating the tree with their homemade baubles."

Lady Victoria still found it hard to believe the queen had befriended her. The queen even gave her a pet name of Toria. None of the other Ladies-in-Waiting was given that privilege. She was a widow with a small child, but perhaps that was why. She had no home ties, no reason to hurry away every evening.

Victoria said, "Yes, Your Majesty, I know my John adores the time spent making the paper chains and *papier-mâché* balls. The staff in the nursery and upstairs school room are wonderful."

The queen smiled. "I know it ruffled some feathers when I first suggested that a large fir tree be brought into the palace, but I noticed others also enjoy the festive season this way. Our countries have much in common. I do not doubt that when our sons married, they carried some of our traditions with them."

The ladies had a fair way to walk before they reached the extensive music room, so they chattered about various topics as they moved gracefully along the carpeted hallways. An occasional footman or maid moved aside as they passed. Their bow or curtsy was acknowledged with a nod of the regal head. The servant remained stationary until they had passed out of sight.

The king was currently well and occupied with various state meetings, so Queen Charlotte was content. She looked forward to a morning of music with her friend. She said, "Lady Toria, I think we shall sing some carols today. How say you?"

Victoria was about to reply when they heard voices coming from a room that should have been empty.

The queen put her finger to her lips, and they crept closer. There should have been no one in this area at all. The door was ajar about an inch, and a heated conversation was occurring inside.

An older man's voice sounded angry. He said scathingly, "Clive, I cannot condone what you have done. You cannot permit a peasant brat to take the title of Templestowe. It is yours by right, and you should not have swapped the child."

Victoria did a quick intake of breath.

The snivelling, snide voice of John's legal guardian replied.

4

"Oh, don't worry, I won't, Robert. He won't live that long. I did that for a reason, my friend. I swapped babies so I could remain undercover for a much longer period than otherwise. If I took the role of Earl of Templestowe-Meade now, I would need to be present at too many functions, and having a title would make me a target for every title-hunting parent in this fair city. I ensured that the baby girl, her new parents, and a maid mysteriously vanished. No one will ever look at the bottom of the lake on our estate for their carriage. The Turners are thought to have fled, but they are all dead."

His evil chuckle sent chills down Victoria's spine. She heard that one of the peasant farmers had left about the same time as her maid. No one knew where they went.

The queen grabbed her hand. Victoria chewed on her knuckles.

Lord Clive Templestowe continued his boasting. "We are safe enough. Only Victoria's maid knew of the swap, as her parents were employed on the family estate. I bribed her to stay silent or promised that they would pay. She knew what would happen to them if she said anything. I sought relief with the girl, Rachel, when I visited the child for the first time. I was surprised she'd not been with a man before me." He chuckled. "Well, she has now. I would have used her each time, but on my next visit to check that my orders to get rid of the Turners had been carried out, she had vanished. I presume the ten pounds I paid her was enough to start anew. Her sister was the brat's mother. I suppose I should have checked where she went, but I truly didn't care. Over time, I will do something similar to my so-called nephew, John. He will have a mysterious accident. I shall inherit the title in my own good time."

Victoria recognised the older man's voice as Sir Robert Chesterfield. He was supposedly one of Clarence's oldest friends. He had survived the same phaeton race that Victoria's husband didn't. A tear trickled unnoticed down her cheek.

Queen Charlotte rested her cheek on her friend's shoulder.

The evil conversation continued.

Robert replied. "But Clive, you cannot just up and kill the lad. His mother is a favourite of the queen. There will be a hue and cry."

Clive chuckled evilly. "He's a 'nothing', and she's not his mother! He's merely a pawn in my greater plan. Admittedly, he's not a baseborn love child but a peasant. I am his legal guardian; he must do what I say. Only the king can overrule that."

Victoria was about to say something when Queen Charlotte

grabbed her arm and put her fingers to her lips.

Victoria nodded. She had no idea her child was a changeling. If her second daughter were dead, where would that leave their status? And, who then was John? If she had heard correctly, her son was a peasant's child, Rachel's nephew.

Clive replied, "I was lucky enough to discover that the local innkeeper's stablehand's wife was about to give birth. Thankfully, she delivered a boy on the morning of my sister-in-law's confinement. Lady Victoria had a difficult birth and was unaware that the babies were swapped. I shall dispose of the brat as easily as I have done with others; leave that to me."

Robert said, "Why would you do it, though? What benefit is there to you?"

Clive's evil laugh sent chills down the spines of both ladies. He was obviously walking around the room, his volume changing as he turned and walked towards the door. "Why? Because I could. However, I needed to remain incognito as much as possible. As the brat's guardian, I have access to more than sufficient funds, but as I intend to inherit one day, I am not milking the estate dry. However, I can move around the city's ballrooms and the slums without drawing undue attention to myself. No one suspects me of my nefarious acts and reporting to France. I know for a fact that you have done your share of smuggling gems to Paris; I am only telling you as I have caught your hand in the honey pot. I received word from my latest man with loose lips that you have also been purchasing untraceable gemstones. I disposed of my first courier as he asked far too many questions. I believe my latest ship is now on the way to China with a load that must be smuggled into a small harbour."

Robert gasped. "Clive, did you kill Malcolm McFarlane, as well? Is that who you mean?"

Clive shrugged, then nodded. "Why not? I had to do something to shut him up. My man said he only had cash on him, so I thought he hadn't purchased my order. However, when his daughter returned from her honeymoon, she brought me a selection of fine gems. Her father had passed them on to her before his final trip. She was none the wiser about my actions as to why I wanted the stones, so she's safe enough. She married another merchant. I discovered who Captain Alexander was and befriended him. The only name McFarlane had on him was yours. I took great delight in that, as my men left your order there to be found." He paused and waited for an explosion. He was not disappointed.

Robert knocked over a chair as he jumped up. "You dirty rotten scoundrel. How dare you!"

Clive's evil chuckle was again heard. "That was about a decade ago, Robert, so although you may be a suspect, I presume you have not heard anything more after the incident."

Robert replied with a sulky, "No!"

Clive chuckled. "I have more than sufficient information squirrelled away about you that I can, and will, use if required. I have a new source of gems, but he is equally expendable should he cause me any issues. Now, back to me. Instead of money, I send untraceable gems for the French to trade. They send me brandy and the most exquisite fabrics. I am able to keep whatever lady has taken my fancy at the time in the recent fashions of gay Paris." He paused for a while and took a swallow of his grog. "Did you know that Her Majesty, Queen Charlotte, was friends with the French Queen? I know rumours abounded that it was through our German Charlotte that the French discovered various pertinent bits of information. I will willingly boast to you about my involvement in spreading those rumours. The gems I supply to the French are to purchase ammunition for them with the untraceable stones. However, I also supply information about the military when I can."

Robert gasped. "You're the cursed spy that Parliament has been hunting for? It's you who has been passing on the military information!"

The ladies could not see Clive bow to Sir Robert, but they knew he was cocky enough to do so. Lord Clive said, "At your service, my dear Robert. You forget that my lover was French, and the crown ordered her arrested as a traitor, and then they hanged her. I will never forgive them for that. I was quite attached to Josette." Robert's fist moved fast, but Clive was quicker. He grabbed the clenched knuckles and held them in his vice-like grip, nearly breaking Robert's fingers as he did so.

The ladies could hear a scuffle ensue inside the room. They stepped back a little but wished to listen in on what was going on.

Clive said somewhat breathlessly, "Leave off, Robert. I'm twice the man you ever were and younger to boot. Are you going to hit me again, or may I release you?"

Sir Robert remained silent. Lord Clive chuckled again. "It is a very lucrative business, spying. It's just like cheating at cards, dear

Robert. I have proof that you mark cards with a pin, so I know you will remain silent." There was no reply for a while, then Clive said, "Until I see you nod, I will not release you."

Robert must have nodded. After a few moments, he emitted a rasped, choking sound, then said, "Damn you, Clive! I should have said no, as then you would have to cope with my body, too. You're a blooming mass murderer, and worse, you have betrayed not just your king and country but your family name."

Clive guffawed. "As for my family, Clarence, God rest his soul, he could only produce daughters. Not that I had much time for a man who thought more of his Bible and wife than of his estate. Mind you, if the child had been a boy, he probably would have met the same fate. I've not decided how John's demise will occur, but be assured, it is a foregone conclusion. I will marry some rich innocent one day and foist a hoard of brats on her." He paused and must have taken a deep swig of something as he coughed and then cleared his throat. "And as to betraying 'king and country,' that's a joke; King George the Third is mad, and his heir is a womanising drunkard.

The monarchy is a waste of time. I would have done away with them all, but for the privileges I get. I can have any woman I wish at the snap of my finger, and I may even lay claim to my dear brother's wife. Monty Sharp and I have had eyes on her for some time. She has no idea that I fully intend to cut her off without a penny when the time comes, unless she succumbs to my persuasions. If she becomes my bedfellow, I may indeed relent. It's a pity I am not permitted to marry her, but the law says no. You are welcome to share my bed in a threesome should you wish."

Sir Robert's guffaw joined Clive's evil cackle. "I may take you up on that offer."

This time, the queen gasped and pulled back from Victoria, looking at her whitened face from the shock of the plans they overheard. Victoria shook her head. The seething anger on her face made her look far older than her twenty-eight years. She was ready to deal with the evil man herself. She had refused his many inappropriate advances over the years since Clarence's death and knew that she would have little defence if he tried to take her by force. She would never succumb to either of these vile men willingly. She was determined to sleep with a knife under her pillow from tonight onwards. Her problem was how to keep John safe.

Robert Chesterfield said, "If you can get under her voluminous skirts, you're a better man than I. I've tried for the past nine years. I attempted to make myself indispensable after Clarence's untimely demise, but she shunned me. After her year of mourning, I might have had a chance, but our good Queen Charlotte summoned her back to court as soon as it was over, and she brought the boy with her. The lad is treated as one of the royal grandchildren and given privileges that go with that. For the moment, I cannot get near her unless I make an appointment with both of them. Even then, Victoria insists that either a footman or a maid accompany them. The queen keeps Victoria close. Too close for my liking as I cannot get near her to have my way as I wish." They dropped their voices for a while. There was a chink of glass, and the women presumed they were imbibing more of the king's brandy.

The women heard Robert say, "I challenged Clarence to a race, intending to injure him so I could have my way with her. I forced him off the road to do him a bit of harm, but the stupid fellow up and died. Pity, as he was a nice chap. I had no idea she was with child at the time. However, I would have still had her, but she became a recluse. She even refused my assistance in her time of need. She's a tasty morsel, and I still want her."

Clive laughed out loud. "Take a number, Robert. I have a queue of friends willing to taste what she has to offer. I'll have her one way or another. One day, she'll be mine. I'll see that she turns to me when her boy dies. I would have done away with my dearly beloved brother when it suited me anyway. Now, it will only need to be the changeling brat."

Robert's chuckle was followed by, "And I certainly will take you up on the offer of a threesome, my friend. That is something I haven't engaged in, and it sounds like fun. Doing her together could be delicious."

Clive said, "I have dreams of tying her to my bed and having my way with her, so she can't fight back. I fear she will not come willingly." The scraping of a chair signalled that they were about to depart.

Queen Charlotte grabbed Victoria's hand and dragged her into the next-door room. They had just silently shut the door when they heard voices in the corridor where they had been standing. Not daring to exit, they took a seat on the settee.

A weeping Victoria was drawn into the loving arms of the regal queen.

Victoria's entire world had just been exposed as a lie. She may well be a Dowager Countess, but with her two daughters dead, the boy she had nurtured at her breast was not even her child. She had only been sixteen when she and Clarence wed. She had conceived on their honeymoon.

The fact that Rachel had known also came as a shock. She now understood why Rachel had left her employ shortly after John's birth. The discovery that her trusted handmaiden had been complicit in the swap was shocking. She now remembered the girl's skittish behaviour when she handed John to her. Victoria had been so tired and sore, but she had known something was not quite right. She thought about the beautiful child upstairs. She adored her gorgeous boy.

She turned to the queen and said, "I shall love my boy until we are parted by death. I pray that it will not be for many years yet. He is my reason for getting up in the morning and keeping going. I shall do everything in my power to ensure his safety."

The queen said, "He's not the only one at risk, dear." She looked up at her friend's shocked face.

Victoria said, "I know, your Majesty, but I shall never sink so low that I will sleep with him or the disgusting Sir Robert of that you are sure."

Chapter 2   Heather
1797 Calcutta, India, and London.
Captain Alexander

Willoughby Alexander was a hard-nosed businessman with no time for frivolity or women. His sugar import business kept him fully occupied. He had refused many approaches to branch into the very lucrative world of opium importing, as he had seen the effects the substance had on its users. His sweet world of sugar kept him gainfully employed and away from the possibility of pirates stealing his cargo. Without a wife and family, he could travel to India and other far-flung lands to source the sweet substances that sold so well. He was on a world tour visiting his various plantations. He was trialling a new cane variety on a new farm in Calcutta. He wished to compare the sugar content. Thankfully, unlike tea, this crop could be easily replaced with a different variety the following year if it was unsuccessful. This cane was intended to yield good results for three to five years. He was a happy, single Scotsman, enjoying the warmth of the tropics. His single state allowed him to travel at will.

That was until he arrived in Calcutta. He had been in India visiting his new plantations when he saw the most beautiful girl he could imagine. After being harassed by the hotel manager at the hotel where she had been staying, she sought refuge at the East India Company's head office. She had just received word that her father had been killed on his latest voyage.

Willoughby needed to visit the office to report on the results of the new cane variety harvest. The sugar content of this crop was brilliant, and he decided to continue growing the latest variety. He paused on entering the foyer. Typically, this was a men-only domain, as it served as the city's hub of finance and trade. He expected today would be no different. However, standing in the foyer of the immense building was a well-dressed young female. He went to step around her and complete his business when she turned to him. He did not expect to see a girl who was so astonishingly beautiful that words fled from him. His jaw dropped open, and he stared at her before realising that her eyes were reddened and tears threatened to fall.

They had yet to be introduced, but after a glance at her left hand, he realised she was unwed. He had met his destiny; only she didn't know it yet. He noticed that she was still weeping. "Miss, may I possibly be of assistance to you?"

He saw her swallow and nod. His soft Scottish lilt reminded her of her father. "My papa is dead, and I need to get home to England. I was told that someone here may be able to help. However, no one will talk to me." A tear trickled down her cheek. "Papa worked for the East India Company as one of their captains. My name, sir, is Heather McFarlane."

Willoughby found his hand moving to gently knuckle the drip from her downy cheek. He realised what he was about to do and instead offered her his arm. He said, "How about we go inside where it's cool, and we can discuss this in some privacy."

She nodded. "I have no money, sir. Papa had our funds on his person when he was killed, and they robbed him and dumped his body in a long boat. I've just been informed that our vessel and cargo were also stolen, so I am stranded."

Her Scottish lilt was so musical that he wished she would keep talking. He didn't care what she said; he just wanted to hear her speak. He could listen to her lovely accent for the remainder of his days. It had been a long, long time since meeting a fellow countryman, or in this case, a lady. She could read the price list of essential commodities, and Willoughby would sit entranced and listen to her musical voice. He had never believed in love at first sight until now. He shook his head to clear it. It didn't work. He said, "Miss, I know many of the staff here, so first, let us find you somewhere out of this heat." He covered her hand with his own as it rested on his arm

She nodded and clutched his arm even tighter as they entered the hallowed portal.

~

An hour later, Willoughby had arranged for Miss McFarlane to stay at the consul's house. This edifice was usually vacant as there was no consul in the office. However, the Governor of Bengal was currently in residence with his wife as their house was undergoing repairs. Sir Charles and Lady Helena Oakeley were delightful. Willoughby escorted his instant lady love to the official residence. Willoughby had previously been given an open invitation to visit whenever he wished.

Lady Helena, also Scottish, welcomed Heather with open arms. Sir Charles was not at home, but that did not matter. Miss McFarlane would be safe here.

This nobleman's wife would care for her until Willoughby was ready to return to England.

Usually, Willoughby would stay on his plantation; however, with a new interest in town, he booked a room at a nearby hotel.

~

Willoughby had never courted anyone before, and he found that he was all at sixes and sevens at what to do or how to behave. He knew the rules, but his heart was giving him palpitations, and he discovered that the evenings of drinking and carousing that he usually enjoyed were no longer of interest, but Heather McFarlane was. She was all he could think about. His work suffered, but he didn't care. He made the obligatory visits to his plantation, but ensured he started early so he could spend time with the target of his affection.

He realised that he had even agreed to carry the cargo her father had sourced. Thankfully, it was not opium. He would refuse to do that, even if it were for this delicious woman. He was aware that fellow Scot, Malcolm McFarlane, had tried to create a new lucrative trade route for selling opium. Instead, he was killed.

Heather had the documents for a return cargo to London, and by juggling his own cargo, he could fit the consignment of saltpetre that she had in storage into the space in his cargo hold. Of course, that would also protect the gemstones she eventually admitted she had in her reticule.

When she confessed to carrying a prepaid consignment of gems, she finally showed it to her new protector.

Willoughby gasped. "Miss McFarlane, I thought you said you had no money. These are worth a king's ransom."

She nodded. "That they are, sir, but they are not ours. Papa purchased these for a new client. On previous trips, Sir Robert Chesterfield had Papa purchase gemstones for him. These are for

Lord Clive Templestowe. There are an awful lot of them. I carry them as I'm too scared to leave them anywhere."

Willoughby's eyes flew open. "How many are there?"

Heather blushed. "Over two hundred, I believe. I have not counted them myself. The bag is small, but I dare not leave it anywhere."

Willoughby swallowed, stunned at the volume of gems. "Did your father have a list? You really should know what is there."

Her head shook. "Would you help me list them? I can value them as we do so. I used to do this for my father. It's why he left them with me."

Willoughby's grin and nod inferred that he would. For the next hour, the two heads pored over the table in the official house's dining room. Sitting beside each other, Willoughby could smell her exotic scent but could not identify it. It was sweet but not overpowering, reminding him of gardenias at home.

They sorted the gems into faceted, cabochon, and uncut gem piles, then by colour. They were in an array of shades. There were pink sapphires, supposedly from Madagascar. He had never heard of such stones. With them were sky-blue, dark-blue, and green sapphires from various regions in India and Ceylon. There were multiple piles of rubies, emeralds, diamonds, and a selection of the most beautiful individual pearls.

Heather gasped when she saw these milky orbs. "Oh, I didn't know he purchased these." Heather fingered the creamy globes. "Sir, these are superb. I did not realise Papa had included any pearls in the bag. These are not part of the order. They are my favourite gems of all, if they are called gems."

Her surprise made Willoughby smile. Willoughby watched as she lifted a large pearl and put it to her lips. Rather than kiss it, as he expected, she rubbed the white ball against her front tooth. She smiled, put it down, and then repeated the action with the next ten. When she lifted the last of the dozen large pearls, she frowned. She repeated the action, then twisted it and did it again. She shook her head and set it aside.

Willoughby's interest was piqued. "May I ask what you are doing?"

Heather nodded, then blushed. "Sir, those ones are real, but that one is a fake. I think it's probably glass. If you rub a real pearl on your teeth, it feels gritty. As they are from a seashell, they may look perfectly smooth, but by rubbing them on your teeth, you can feel that they are not. If it's smooth, then it's not real. I have had to test many of these over the years, as some unscrupulous dealers have become proficient in manufacturing glass ones. It's why I used to come with Papa. This was my job. Well, this and valuing them." She met his amazed gaze and blushed. "Papa promised me a strand of my own one day."

If she accepted him as a husband, Willoughby would buy her the most beautiful pearls he could find. He noticed her eyes fill with unshed tears—this time, when one of her eyes overflowed, unable to resist, he did thumb it away. He wished to kiss the tears away and was surprised at himself. She was grieving, and he knew his thoughts were inappropriate, but she did not pull away.

When another tear trickled from her eye, he leaned close and kissed it away. He reached out for her and drew her close.

She leaned against his shoulder and wept. She felt so safe in his arms. He had made no inappropriate moves other than kissing away a tear. She wondered if she dared to lift her chin. Would he kiss her? She had never been kissed and wished him to be the first man to do so. She had grown to admire him in the weeks since they had met. She slowly lifted her chin.

Willoughby was about to kiss her upturned lips when footsteps were heard approaching. Lady Oakeley's tripping gait was unmistakable.

He pulled away but gently brushed his lips over hers. "Later, lassie!"

Heather blushed and nodded. She fully intended to make sure about that.

By the time the esteemed lady joined them, they were packing up the gems into small bags.

Lady Oakeley took a seat at the table while they worked.

They now had a complete list of what was in the parcel, and Willoughby was stunned and thrilled to find that Heather had also estimated the value of each item. The value of the parcel was well over what Lord Clive had ordered. Knowing the cost of pearls, and as they were not on Lord Clive's list, Willoughby suggested that she keep these and some of the uncut sapphires. They could be her inheritance. From what she had told him, this was all the money she would have.

Willoughby asked, "Miss McFarlane, did Lord Clive give your

father money, or did he say the man would buy what he brought?"

Her face lit up. "Oh, I see what you mean. No, sir, he said, 'Buy me about two hundred pounds worth of easily disposable, untraceable gems'. So, although cut and faceted, no stones were to be set in jewellery. Papa always purchased more than required; Sir Robert normally only took what he ordered. I don't know if Lord Clive would have done that. He certainly never mentioned pearls."

They put the last of the pearls in the new small velvet bags he had brought for her, and they carefully replaced the parcel of gems in her reticule.

As they chattered about the astounding collection, Willoughby chuckled and said, "Well, I would say do not show Lord Clive everything you have here. If he complains, then add a few more, but not everything. The more you withhold, the more you can keep for yourself. We don't know how much your father spent on these, but you have valued them at nearly three hundred pounds."

Heather showed her delight by giving Willoughby a huge smile. "We only paid eighty pounds for them, but they would bring more than triple that in Europe."

Lady Oakeley endorsed Heather's smile of surprise. "Yes, my dear, I do agree. You must now look after yourself. The cargo that Mr Alexander will transport for you may take some time to sell. However, I believe saltpetre is a very valuable commodity as the military is experimenting with making something called Congreve rockets."

Willoughby nodded. "I should be able to dispose of that cargo quite quickly, as I have a contract with the East India Company as well. I should be able to sell it on a consignment basis. However, the British army may want to purchase the black powder for those rockets you mentioned, ma'am."

Lady Oakeley nodded and patted Heather's hand. She turned to Willoughby. "Mr Alexander, I came to ask if you could possibly be enticed to stay for dinner. I know we have said to make yourself at home, but one guest has pulled out of the evening's meal. I would dearly like you to stay and even up the numbers."

Willoughby saw Heather give a micro nod, so he accepted with delight. "I would be honoured, ma'am. Although I will return to my room and change first." Under the table, he reached for Heather's hand and gave it a quick squeeze.

She met his glance, smiled and dropped her eyes. Hopefully, after dinner, he would kiss her properly. She was fully aware of how inappropriate that was.

~

The meal was an official dinner for the East India Company. All of the bigwigs and nobility in town came to the dinner. Contrary to the previous meals, the conversation was lively and circled around the embargo of English ships that carried opium into China.

Willoughby smiled to himself. Being Scottish, he sailed in unchallenged under his Scottish flag. He had no intention of mentioning that trick.

Last year, China blocked the entry of ships under the English flag. There were many prepared to turn a blind eye to the smuggling of the drug across the Chinese border, but as the death of Heather's father proved, it was becoming far more dangerous. Not that the Chinese had killed him. Whoever had done the brutal deed had targeted only the captain. It was known that there were pirates who would stop at nothing to make illegal money. Murders and theft were now regularly reported, but McFarlane's name had a price on his head due to his cargo.

Willoughby wondered whether Captain McFarlane had heard whispers of pirates, and that was why he had left Heather in Calcutta. He had his doubts, but no proof. Until he did, he would remain silent.

Dinner that night was a chore. However, Willoughby and Heather sat at the foot of the table and away from the public eye. He saw her tear up as the others discussed the events that led up to her father's death. Willoughby reached for her hand under the fall of the tablecloth. The conversation further up the table was not merely insensitive but downright rude. Admittedly, they did not mention him by name, but even discussing such a topic over a mixed company meal was vastly inappropriate. They should have waited until she had left the room with the ladies.

As Lady Oakeley sat near them, she realised Heather's dilemma and what had upset her. She said to her husband, "Charles, let us talk of more pleasant things. I believe the price of saltpetre is on the rise."

Heather met her smiling face and gave her a nod of thanks. Her tears spilled from her eyes, and she found that she could not stop them. She dropped her head and hoped they would fall unnoticed. She had loved her papa dearly, and now he was gone.

Willoughby gave her hand a loving press, then caressed the back of it with his thumb.

Thankfully, the conversation turned to lighter topics.

They finished the last of the fourteen courses, and Lady Oakeley stood to leave. Rather than just walking out as she usually did, she approached her husband and whispered something.

He looked up, stunned, then nodded. He saw the sadness on their guest's face and blanched. He had had very little to do with the girl staying with them. He had been absent for many of the evening meals, and the ladies usually had a simple midday luncheon. He had not associated their guest with the murder of one of his ship's captains. He felt gutted that he had permitted such a topic at the dinner table.

As the discussion after the meal would be work-focused, Willoughby was excused. Although he had a contract, he was not part of the firm's upper echelons. They would be discussing the nitty-gritty of the company.

Willoughby was delighted. Hopefully, he could spend a little time with Heather.

Lady Oakeley saw that Heather was still somewhat distressed at what she had heard about pirate attacks and murders.

Heather had not known about the violent details of her father's passing. Although he had been referred to as "the captain," she was fully aware that they were discussing her father's murder. The coarse conversation left her in little doubt of what would have happened to her had she been with him. She had intended to accompany her father, but had eaten something that upset her stomach. They were due to leave the following day, so she had remained at the hotel to pack their possessions. He was only supposed to be gone two nights, as the destination for this trip was local. Her father had attended the meeting alone and had been murdered most violently. She probably would have been kidnapped and sold as a white slave to some sultan somewhere if she had lived.

No sooner had they left the dining room than Heather collapsed.

Willoughby swept her into his arms.

Lady Oakeley saw her distress and ushered them into Sir Charles's office away from the other ladies present.

Willoughby lay his precious bundle on the settee and knelt beside her.

As Heather was staying at the residence and Willoughby was a regular visitor, Lady Oakeley decided to leave them alone while she went to fetch a maid to chaperone them before returning to her other guests.

No sooner had she left the room than Heather reached out for Willoughby and drew him close. She interlaced her fingers with his and said, "Thank you for your sensitivity. It was nice to know that someone cared how I felt, even if only a little bit."

Willoughby was still on his knees beside her. Her tears broke his heart. "More than just a little bit, my sweet girl. I wish to be by your side, protecting you forever. I would have declared myself this afternoon, but we were interrupted."

Heather gasped. She gently pushed him away. "So soon, sir?"

Willoughby thumbed away the last tear that fell. "Ahh, well, some weeks too late for my liking. I would have proposed on the day we met, but I believe that is not done. However, you had my heart from that first moment in the foyer at the East India Company office."

Heather's eyes flicked from one blue orb to the other. She shyly admitted, "It took me until that afternoon, sir. However, the feeling is reciprocated."

Willoughby's heart leapt with delight. "Truly? Is it too early to declare myself then? For I wish to. I wish to marry you as soon as can be arranged and spend the rest of our lives together. I wish to keep you safe and make you happy. Will you permit me to court you?"

Heather let out a sob of mixed emotions, a blend of happiness and sadness. Neither of her parents would even meet the man she now planned to marry. She pulled him close.

She was gathered into his strong and welcoming arms.

He said, "So that's a yes?"

She nodded. "Yes, that's a yes if you wish to court me."

Willoughby was aching to kiss her, but he thought he would push her a little more. "Do you wish for a long courtship, or is one minute long enough? I wish to marry you, Miss McFarlane, no, Heather. I wish to marry you very soon. I love you so very much that I can think of no other future but to spend my life with you beside me."

Heather giggled. "I think a courtship of one minute is perfectly adequate, Mr Alexander."

He chuckled. "My name is Willoughby, my love, although my family calls me Will."

As Willoughby slipped his hand behind her neck to draw her to him, she said, "And just to make things very clear, Will, I love you and can't wait to marry you." She lifted her lips for their very first proper kiss.

Lady Oakeley had been standing at the door listening to their declarations of love. She wiped a tear of happiness from her eye. She realised she had to return to the drawing room with the other female guests, but having heard their declaration, she saw no reason to hurry them. However, she cleared her throat and saw Willoughby jump up.

She said, "I heard, dear ones, and I shall be discreet and leave you alone for a few minutes more as you are now engaged. However, Mr Alexander, I would appreciate it if you could bring her into the drawing room shortly. I will let them know congratulations are in order, but I will be the first to offer them to you both. Heather, I know this man to be a good, hardworking gentleman, so I will willingly leave you to his ministrations."

Willoughby said, "Thank you, ma'am," and stepped closer to his fiancée.

Lady Oakeley was about to leave but turned back to Willoughby, saying, "Five minutes, Mr Alexander or I will come and bring in all the other guests to witness your passionate declarations, which I'm sure will occur as soon as I leave." She chuckled at their embarrassment, but she left them to enjoy the moment.

Chapter 3 The "Tidesong"
1802
Martha Alexander

Willoughby and Heather's courtship may have lasted barely a minute, but the wedding that followed was nearly as swift. The service took place ten days later. The couple had known each other for less than a month.

At Lady Helena Oakeley's suggestion, rather than move to the hotel, Willoughby moved into the luxurious residence with Heather.

Lady Helena took Heather aside the night before their wedding and gave the young lady a delightful but thoroughly embarrassing, motherly talk on the act of marriage. She then filled in more intricate details of how to make their couplings enjoyable for both.

Heather was somewhat horrified at the description of what would occur, but sat listening with her eyes wide in astonishment. She was far too embarrassed to ask anything.

Lady Helena chuckled. "Dear, if you wish to have a child, this is how they are made. It is thoroughly enjoyable if you both enter the activity with such in mind. If you lie back and let him do his thing, he may find his enjoyment elsewhere. That is not good, as he could also bring home illnesses to you. Respond as you desire, my dear. It is a delight when mutual satisfaction is achieved. You will understand what I mean later."

Heather asked with some trepidation, "You say it will only hurt the first time?"

Lady Helena nodded. "Yes. That is because you are untouched, dear. It is how he will know you are a maiden. The pain is brief and easily bearable. It is no worse than a cramp during your monthly flow, if that."

Heather grimaced. She usually had great pain each month, but she knew that it was tolerable. She nodded her understanding.

~

On the morning of the wedding, Heather donned her best gown, and Lady Helena's maid attended to her luxurious hair.

As the days were hot, they had decided to have a morning wedding rather than a late evening one.

At ten o'clock, a small group gathered in the chapel in the consul's residence.

Twenty minutes later, Mr and Mrs Willoughby Alexander emerged hand in hand.

Their adventurous life had just begun. The *Tidesong* would take them to ports far and wide.

Heather wore the most amazing strand of pearls that she had ever seen. They were Willoughby's wedding gift to his new wife. He had seen them in town at a top-end jeweller. Most brides donned a small strand of seed pearls.

These half-inch sea gems caught the eyes of the few who witnessed the nuptials. There were over one hundred creamy orbs in the opera-length rope of pearls. They were breathtaking.

For the service, Heather tied the sea-orbs in a double knot, the size of her dainty fist, rather than draped them around her neck in a triple loop.

She could have worn a canvas sailcloth dress, and no one would have noticed her gown, as the unusual way in which she wore the pearls caught everyone's attention.

Willoughby, however, only had eyes for Heather's adorable face.

~

Five years later

Martha Heather Alexander was born at sea, somewhere between India and the Dutch East Indies, in 1802. Her parents had been bound for Calcutta when Heather's birth pains started early.

They had lost two children before this baby and prayed that this child would breathe.

Martha did. She arrived screaming and soon had her parents at her beck and call.

Rather than remain in port, Willoughby and Heather sailed the ocean blue, trading in exotic ports right around the equator.

Their daughter had to learn to swim before being out of flannel napkins. She took to the sea like a fish.

~

By the time she was five, the little girl's life was a series of new places and strange faces; she spoke a little of many languages. As she grew, her language skills did too. They were good enough to purchase what she wished.

One young crewman, Joe, became her bodyguard.

While in every port, Martha had crash courses in piano, grooming, deportment, and the required skills of a young lady.

Heather continued her lessons once they put to sea again, but life on board her father's ship was exciting.

~

The three-masted *Tidesong* safely carried them on many circuits of the briny ocean. Although working for the English East India Company, Willoughby refused to carry slaves or opium. He traded in luxury goods, spices, and valuable gems and pearls, as he had discovered the lust for these sea gems.

Pepper was what he called black gold. That spice was among the most sought-after. Dried chilli also brought top money. He purchased both whenever he could. He paid the pittance the traders asked and made a fortune with each consignment. He answered to no man, but his wife and daughter ruled his world.

~

When on land at a function, Heather's pearls frequently drew the attention and eyes of lustful ladies in the various societies they passed through. He purchased more strands and sold them for an exorbitant profit.

The lovely light-blue sapphires from Ceylon were popular in England, and the diamonds and glittery stones from other places were always easy to sell.

Willoughby intended to buy Heather another string of larger pearls when they had their first child. Sadly, their son had never breathed, and neither had their eldest daughter, who was born eighteen months later. Both babies had the cords tightly wrapped around their necks. They had been perfect, but nothing could be done for either of them. The birth process had strangled both infants. Both babies had been buried under palm trees, on different deserted tropical islands in the Pacific Ocean.

The ship stopped at these tiny atolls whenever it passed by.

Their third child, Martha, was fit and healthy, with a strong will that endeared her to the crew.

Heather had also grown up on a sailing ship. From the time she could crawl, her father, Captain McFarlane, had made Heather wear her kapok life vest when aboard his ship. Heather and Willoughby did the same for Martha as soon as she started crawling.

~

When she was only six, Martha took her first drink of wine when becalmed in the middle of the Pacific Ocean.

They were running out of water fast, but the ship carried a massive consignment of assorted beverages.

For three days, the entire crew and the Alexander family consumed the bottled wine, although Martha's was diluted with the remaining water.

Willoughby and Joe erected a rain sail and then prayed for a miracle.

Empty water barrels were strategically placed to catch any runoff. However, there was not a cloud in the sky.

After four days with not a breath of wind, their water was all but gone.

The cargo of wine was now all that stood between them and dying of thirst. So Martha learned to drink the good drop along with the sailors. Her wine was diluted with some of the remaining boiled water, but she had to either drink it or die.

A week later, an overnight storm broke over their ship, filling the water barrels.

~

By the time she turned seven, Martha had circumnavigated the globe with her parents twice and travelled on numerous short trips to and from India and London.

Once, the ship anchored in Joppa, and they visited Jerusalem, and she and her mother had to cover their faces with hot veils. She learned a few words of Arabic whilst there. She picked up a few more words of Egyptian on the return trip.

She fought a battle against the elements around the southern capes of Africa and South America. She helped hoist the sails when the wind was unfavourable.

Having been born at sea, she loved the feel of the deck bucking under her bare feet. Seasickness had never been a problem for her, but when on land, it took her a long time to adjust to nothing moving around her.

Every journey was an adventure. She never knew what that day would bring from the moment they hauled the ropes ashore in London to the day they dropped anchor in some foreign port.

~

When Martha was eight, they met pirates in the West Indies. They were released unharmed and with the cargo intact. Apparently, one of the crew members on the pirate ship had once worked for Willoughby when he first set sail, and he vouched that he was a good man.

Martha had stomped on the pirate captain's toes when he came aboard. He had snatched her up and tucked her under his arm as he walked around the deck of the *Tidesong*.

Rather than scream or fight him, she demanded her release and threatened him with dire harm should he harm any of 'her' crew.

Her father had taught her how to hold a pistol only weeks earlier, and she saw the pirate had one in his belt. She had managed to extract the matchlock pistol from his holster and cock the trigger without him noticing. Unfortunately, she had no light for the wick, but she didn't know that.

The pirate only realised she had his gun when he felt it poking into his stomach. She pulled the trigger, and he heard the click. Had he owned a flintlock pistol, or if she had been able to access a light for the wick, it would have been fatal at point-blank range; he would have been dead. Instead, he chuckled and removed the weapon from her grasp.

He handed her back to her mother and chuckled. "She will give some man a lively time when she marries."

He planted a kiss on Martha's pouting lips before releasing her to her mother's care. While Heather's arms were occupied with her daughter, the pirate cupped Heather's face and passionately kissed her to gauge her husband's reaction.

The pirate captain had eyed off the very attractive Alexander women but left them otherwise unmolested.

His parting words were, "I have plundered your valuables, Captain Alexander. You have not escaped unscathed, as I have kissed both your women." His raucous laugh echoed through the two ships.

The black-bearded, eye-patched captain kissed Martha on the

forehead again before departing. "Keep this little one safe, Captain, for she is a gem amongst women." He flicked the child's nose, then jumped the gap to his own ship.

Willoughby, Joe, and Heather all heaved a long sigh of relief.

They waved their thanks to Jock, now a crewman on the pirate vessel.

Willoughby was officially carrying a cargo of teak and Chinese porcelain. Thankfully, the pirate captain did not know about the enormous parcel of exquisite gemstones and more ropes of pearls in Heather's undergarment drawer.

Willoughby was sure they would have been pilfered had the pirate seen them. He knew his crew would remain silent, as he promised a £5 bonus per sailor plus a percentage share of the profits. The heavy goods below were a cover for what was of most value in the cabin upstairs. Many of the crew knew of the treasure. They also carried the obligatory spices, such as peppercorns, chilli, cinnamon, nutmeg, and cloves, as well as sugar. These were also worth a king's ransom.

The sugar cones alone were a valuable commodity, and Willoughby had a special area set aside for them. Being very susceptible to moisture, one section of the upper hold was lined with waxed canvas and had shelving built to transport the cone-shaped sweet substance safely.

Heather never managed to carry another child to term, but the young couple adored their little girl, with her pert features, adorable freckles and curls. They had each other, and their daughter made their happiness complete.

~

By her teenage years, Martha could tend to a broken limb, suture a gash, and help her mother cook a meal for the eighty crewmen.

Martha was unaware that her parents had lost more babies.

Joe shadowed her when on deck, but she wore a kapok vest that would float if she fell overboard. She never did.

Being unable to fit a proper piano into a cabin, Willoughby purchased a small virginal keyboard for his ladies to play. This was placed in a small cabin next to Martha's and set up as a sitting room for his ladies. He added an armchair so he could join them and read.

Life on board their sailing home was a delight.

By Martha's fifteenth birthday, she was beginning to turn heads in port each time they landed. Now, two trusted armed crewmen needed to accompany her if she wished to go anywhere ashore without her parents.

One was Ta'nar, their enormous cook, who was from the Pacific Islands.

Joe, Martha, and Ta'nar were often followed by a dozen crew members, shadowing their path to ensure the girl's safety. None had been asked to do this, but they all adored their own 'young lady'.

The food markets were usually their destination. Joe Brand, Martha's shadow, usually carried her shopping. None of 'her' men took liberties, as she was like their little sister.

Willoughby and Heather had often discussed Martha's necessity to be presented in London. They knew their time wandering the ocean was drawing to a close for the moment. They had one more port of call, which they often avoided because of the sweating sickness, which was frequently reported in the area. Their stay here would only be for one night, and the ladies decided not to go ashore.

Martha's needs would and must come first, and that meant heading to England.

~

On their passage homewards, they circumnavigated the globe again, and ten days out of São Luís on the northeastern coast of Brazil, Heather showed the first signs of the dreaded sickness.

With their destination only days away, she struggled to overcome the chills and fever she developed.

A week of tending to his wife exhausted Willoughby, but finally, Heather recovered.

The chills eased, and the sweating sickness slowly abated.

By the time they reached port in London, Heather was well enough to sit on the deck to watch their ship dock as it negotiated the busy, but stinking, Thames River.

Martha remained at her mother's side while the ship was put to sleep.

They owned a warehouse on the docks and had their own small wharf where the *Tidesong* was to remain docked for the duration of their stay.

All the crew were to have extended leave but were to report next week for payment after the saltpetre was sold.

They were in no hurry to land, as the *Tidesong* was their home.

Martha was informed that she would be presented while in port on this trip, but she was aware there was more to this than she was told. It sounded ominous.

~

By the end of the month, Willoughby and Heather had leased a house for the season.

However, with the crew at a loose end, Willoughby promoted his first mate to captain.

Bradley Scott was to take a short trip to the Mediterranean Sea to buy a cargo of wine and return before the trio joined them for the next voyage at the end of the season.

However, that was not to be.

Chapter 4   His Majesty's Pageboy
Buckingham House, London, 1806
John

*A*fter the overheard conversation, the queen ushered her friend into the music room. "We shall keep him safe, Toria. I shall ensure that the king will keep John close."

Victoria's glazed eyes were nothing compared to what her heart was feeling. Clive had planned this since before she gave birth. He had stolen her daughter and replaced her with John. She turned to her friend and said, "Your Majesty, Clive killed my baby, and Sir Robert all but killed my husband." She was still in a daze. She gasped and asked, "How could Clive have changed my baby without me knowing, and I never even realised? Why did he bribe Rachel? Did he have something against her?" Queen Charlotte sat beside her friend and slid an arm around her shoulders.

Victoria found speaking difficult. After some time, she said, "What is worse, who are John's parents, the Turners? How do I tell him he's not my son but the child of a stablehand from an inn? How do I keep John safe from his uncle, who is now not even his uncle? What do I do? My beloved boy is not even entitled to be the earl, so what about me? Where will we go, for I will not leave him alone? I should not even be here with you. I love him so much."

Queen Charlotte saw movement on the other side of the room, "Toria, look."

Unbeknownst to the ladies, John had come searching for his mother. He had known she was coming to the music room, and he was going to read while she played the harp. He loved music and was often permitted to sit and listen while the ladies played their instruments. He had his favourite wing-back chair, where he could curl up and listen quietly. He had fallen asleep while waiting and woke when they entered. He now moved from his sanctuary and came towards his mother. He had heard her distraught words and initially frowned until the meaning sank in. When he saw her weeping, he ran to her, saying, "Mama, I love you anyway. Even if I'm not your boy."

Victoria reached out for the adorable fair-haired child. Though his locks had darkened as he grew older, he was still fair. It was now halfway between blond and light brown. His honey-coloured brown eyes were vastly different to her bright blue ones. Some had called them hazel, but they held no hint of green. They were golden, the colour of light amber. Rachel's had been similar, but Victoria had never associated the two before. She cupped his face and said, "Johnny, my darling boy, you will always be mine, even if you didn't grow in my tummy. You have grown in my heart. Your parents are dead, just as my little girls are. We only have each other."

Sitting beside her son, she cuddled the confused little boy in her arms. She had no intention of him finding out like this, but now he knew. He knew everything. "Darling John, the first thing is, we must tell no one we know, not a single soul. Do you understand?"

John nodded. "But why, Mama? What did I do wrong?"

She could see confusion in his hurt face. "Nothing, my darling child, Queen Charlotte and I overheard Uncle Clive boasting of horrible things to Sir Robert Chesterfield. Whenever you see either of them, stay silent. They are in this together. Do not trust either of them, or Lord Montgomery Sharp."

The nine-year-old boy climbed onto the lap of the only mother he knew. He nodded against her chest. "But will he try to hurt me? Why? I never did him any harm."

Queen Charlotte answered. "Sweet boy, it's because you are a living boy. We are both pawns in his wicked schemes. For the moment, you are safe, as he is unaware that we know all. However, you must be aware that things in the palace are not as they should be. Lord Clive is a spy for the French and probably any other mercenary who will pay for information. Be careful, my darling boy. Be oh so careful."

John's head nodded back and forth again. His world was in turmoil. His uncle, whom he now discovered was not his real uncle, was trying to kill him. His mother was not his mother, yet he clung tightly to the only woman he had known as such. She still wanted him and loved him. That was all he cared about. He clung to her like a limpet. "Can I still call you Mama?"

Victoria said lovingly, "Of course, my darling. It is important that you do. We are all each other has, and you are and will always be my special boy. I will keep you safe for as long as I live."

The queen said, "John, I shall tell His Majesty, but I shall also write a letter detailing what we overheard and keep it in my personal journal. I shall sign and date it, as shall your mama. I will ensure the conversation is fully recorded in my diary pages. We will have a dated written record should it ever be required. I will also ensure you know where it is. My personal journals are not read by anyone other than me, so the letter will remain safe."

Nine-year-old John snuggled closer to Toria. Fear etched on his young face. He could not help the tears that flowed. His world had just shattered. Queen Charlotte was not immune to the confusion. She had no idea there had been whispers about her friendship with Marie Antoinette. However, the French queen had passed away some time ago. Queen Charlotte knew the French were still receiving information they should not have access to, but she had no idea that there were whispers she was involved. The king had asked her to keep her eyes and ears open for a spy, and now she knew who it was. Had he guessed there was some connection with Lady Victoria's husband's family? Lord Clive Templestowe was the channel through which they ran. Sir Robert was also somehow implicated. Who was the man Clive ordered to be killed? They had not overheard how. Who were the other people they discussed? They overheard that Lord Montgomery Sharp, Viscount of Rathsharp, was used as a courier, but they were sure there were others. Someone had performed the dastardly deeds.

~

Even though King George was unwell, Queen Charlotte sought him out to say goodnight. She had changed into her bedtime garb and donned a brocade dressing gown that covered her more than a ballgown would have done. The royal couple had separate bedroom suites since a few traumatic incidents some years earlier; however, the affection between the two never waned.

After the severe illness the king suffered in 1789, they lived almost separate lives. This was not because they didn't get on, but because his bouts of illness were becoming more frequent. For the moment, his majesty was well, but he lived in an almost silent, darkened world, whereas Queen Charlotte loved people, noise and activity. She adored having her children and grandchildren at hand. Sadly, her sons lived elsewhere. The royal couple appeared together in London whenever possible, but their life in Windsor was far more peaceful than living at *Buckingham House* in London.

Queen Charlotte was somewhat upset as the king had not permitted their daughters to marry, and they rebelled by disgracing themselves with some of the palace courtiers. She rarely saw them now as they remained at *Frogmore House*. Their eldest son's morals were no better.

As she approached her husband to say good night, she waved away the attendants for private time with him. She snuffed all but one candle. The king could only relax once the room was darkened. He held his hand to his wife, and she came to his side. They lay curled up in the dim light, chatting.

Queen Charlotte relaxed into his arms. After giving birth to fifteen of his children, they often used this time to talk about their family.

Their private conversations were often about their eldest son, George Augustus, and his social antics. His nickname, 'Prinny,' was as common as his morals. He willingly declared that he liked wine and women far too much. Once considered extremely attractive, his physique was already beginning to show the effects of his excessive eating and drinking.

Tonight, Charlotte wanted to discuss another child. One that was not theirs. She cuddled up to her husband on the big feather bed and said softly, "George, we have a problem. Lady Victoria and I overheard a plot to kill her son today. The man speaking admitted he had already killed at least three other people, and probably more."

King George gasped. "Tell me all, my dear."

Charlotte did, but they kept their voices low. She related the conversation and explained that Lord Clive was the spy they had been looking for within the palace and court. "George, Lord Clive Templestowe is the French spy we have sought for years. He is also a murderer. His friend, Sir Robert, is not much better. However, from what we overheard, we doubt Lord Montgomery Sharp knows much of their doings, but he is often used as a courier. He's only the mule. Sir Robert challenged Toria's husband to a race, hoping he would be injured so Sir Robert could force himself on her. He had no idea she was with child at the time, and therefore she had withdrawn from society. Thankfully, I have kept her close to me. I did that as a favour to myself, as I adored having little John nearby. However, I now believe that by doing so, I may have accidentally foiled Lord Clive's plan to do away with the lad."

King George growled angrily. He knew that he had given Clive some information that should never have passed his lips. "What can we do to keep this woman and child safe?" He liked Sir Robert and Monty Sharp.

Charlotte gave one of her delightful chuckles. George always loved the tinkling sound of her laugh. He didn't hear it often now. But they had grown old, happily content with their arranged marriage. They married when she was seventeen, and he was twenty, and surprisingly, they liked each other. He knew she would already have an idea about what to do with the boy. He only had to agree for it to be set in place.

His beloved said, "Well, my dear, you are King George, and this is where you come in. I feel that you need a new pageboy. A very young one who can run your errands and pick up things when you drop them. One who will love you and obey your every word. He reads well and can entertain you."

George drew his belovéd Charlotte close, more to drop his voice than anything else. "Is he really in that much danger?"

Charlotte nodded against his chest. "I shall do the same for his mother. I have a spare room beside mine, and she can move in there as my handmaiden. I am determined that we shall thwart Lord Clive and ensure he cannot harm the lad or his mother."

George heard a noise outside his room. "Shhh! Wait here." He pulled himself off the bed and shuffled over to the door. He threw it open, but he was not fast enough. He saw someone vanishing into the darkness of the corridor, but could not identify who it was. He huffed with frustration that he was unable to move fast enough.

Charlotte watched her somewhat feeble husband as he moved across the room. King George III returned to stand at the end of the bed and said, "I feel that we may also add guards outside our rooms. If Templestowe-Meade is our spy, he remains hidden for a reason, or he would have disposed of the child already. If James Hatfield has any connection with Lord Clive, they may try another assassination attempt. What about the other men mentioned? Would I need to banish or arrest them all?"

Charlotte sighed. Only they knew how much that attempt on

her husband's life had affected him. He acted as though nothing had occurred, but it shook him dreadfully. She was fully aware that his mind was not as it should be, but he was still the king. If her idea worked, then Lord Clive would be unable to get close to John. "George, come back to bed! I have more to discuss."

The king shuffled towards his side of the big bed, muttering, "This is not the first time I've heard someone at my door. I don't like it, Lottie."

Charlotte loved it when he used his pet name. She smiled in the near darkness. Tonight, she had an idea. "I have an idea that will stop you from needing to check for yourself. The little boy, John Templestowe-Meade, is the only one I would trust. Although he is known as an earl, he has no right to the title. Lord Clive has something up his sleeve that jeopardises the child's life. You would care for him by keeping him close. This would keep him safe while he becomes your legs and ears. He's nine and is an adorable boy. Lord Clive will not be able to get at him if he is your shadow."

George crawled back under the blankets. He was cold, so he drew Charlotte to him to warm up. After a few minutes, he said, "I'll think about it, my dear, but it is possible. I'm getting on, and, as you know, my health isn't good. Our George is unfit to step into my shoes, but he will anyway, as he is my heir. Our nickname, Prinny, has become a byword for excess. I fear he will do the country great harm. I'm sure he will run up debts that he cannot pay. He will take no counsel from me, and I am his monarch, as well as his father. It's why I gave you my royal authority, should I have another bout of illness. Even if Prinny becomes Regent, you would still wield power until I die. Now, about this boy, I don't want an undisciplined child in my presence. Is he like George?"

Charlotte reached out for her husband's hand and stroked it comfortingly. "Husband mine, our George is forty-four, John is nine and very well behaved. There can be no comparison between the two. John will be a page boy for you. He will be at your beck and call, but you will be doing him a favour. By keeping him close, you will be keeping him alive. Will you consider it?"

The king mumbled a reluctant agreement. He certainly could do with a young runner at his beck and call. He adored his children when they were young. If nothing else, he could further the lad's education. The boy probably needed a firm hand to behave. His own children certainly did.

~

John moved into the dressing room of the king's quarters at *Kew Palace* the following week. As a child, he had been told to be seen but not heard. Therefore, he had seen the esteemed gentleman around the palace for most of his young life, but had rarely been so close to him. To find that he was now to shadow the monarch and be at his beck and call was a delight. He adored the king.

King George was a delightful but stern man. He adored his own children, but he was a strict father. John discovered that the monarch was, in reality, just a grandfather. Something that John had never had before. Most of their time was spent at *Kew Palace*. This residence was a child's delight if one liked outdoor life. John did. The king loved gardening, as did Queen Charlotte. The gardens were extensive and kept expanding.

John was permitted to climb up some trees and discovered a very old treehouse. It had been built for the princes when they were young, and a single comment of delight saw the gardeners repairing it for him. King George adored his young shadow, and they were often seen together enjoying the gardens or the fancy pagoda.

~

John quickly learned that if he were quiet, he would often be forgotten and, therefore, overhear the workings of the empire. He was still attending to his lessons, which would be completed when the king was resting. His tutor also assigned him schoolwork while the king was holding an audience with various peers of the realm or his politicians. John's delight was when his friend William, whom he called Bill and who was a year younger, came with his father. The boys were permitted to study together when Bill's father, William Wilberforce, was in conference with either the prime minister or the monarch. The boys had met when they were younger in the palace nursery. Until recently, they found little time to be together. However, the Slave Transportation Act was passed into law a few years ago, and it was through this legislation that John and Bill met. An amendment needed more work, so they relished the time they could spend together.

Occasionally, the boys sat and listened, but more often than not, the nine and ten-year-olds snuck away to a nearby room that had been a military planning room to play soldiers in the huge sand-pit with lead figurines. Since the Napoleonic wars were ongoing, the boys had to ensure they put everything back exactly as they found it.

John was permitted to bring some books, a chess set, and some toy soldiers. These occupied the boys for hours and forged a close friendship.

Bill had a sister who was a year or so younger and two baby brothers, so his father, William senior, was permitted to take his older son along to spend time with his young friend.

Chapter 5   Monarch to Manic
September 1810
John

*J*ohn shuffled between the Windsor residences, *Kew Palace* and *Buckingham House* in London for four years as the royal households moved from palace to palace. He accompanied the king and queen wherever they wished to go. He knew the royal couple had their separate rooms in London and residences in Windsor. This came about due to the king's illnesses and state of mind. However, John was also aware that the king was often in a state of borderline madness.

John occasionally heard the queen's voice raised in anger. This was very unusual. Lady Victoria was always part of the queen's entourage, and she remained close to Her Majesty, but John remained with His Majesty whenever possible. However, after the death of the youngest of the royal couple's children, Princess Amelia, the king's behaviour spiralled out of control. His moods swung, and when they did, John was sent to his mother for safety.

When the king was well, John shadowed his every move. Now, the monarch never moved from *Kew Palace*. John still slept in the king's antechamber and trained himself to stir at every murmur by the regal gentleman. These disturbances became more frequent over time. These ranged from issues with his vision to bouts of hallucinations. However, King George also suffered from severe abdominal pain and seizures.

During these episodes, John was barred from the king's rooms because several royal attendants had to restrain the king.

One other strange symptom of the king's malady was the blue colour of his urine. John had overheard the physician discussing this and mentioned that his new medication, gentian violet, would cause it. John had watched the doctor make up this medicine. When mixed with water, the fine dark crystals turned a bright pink-purple, and the king had to consume the concoction. John had to hold the chamberpot for the king, and the vibrant colour of the fluid initially shocked the young man.

The king turned to his young friend and said, "Laddie, never fear; this unusual occurrence started when the medics made me drink that purple medicine."

John gulped and nodded. He had seen the doctors in consultation about how to treat the king's various illnesses. Blue pee was something he had never seen before or expected to see.

~

Over the years, John had fetched and carried everything from the royal crown to the official robes at the opening of Parliament. Everyone in the parliamentary building knew him. He had free passage to all areas of both houses, Lords and Commons, as he was often sent to collect something from somewhere. John felt safe as his 'uncle' was not permitted entrance to the royal abodes or to either house of parliament. His life was one of privilege and luxury, but John was bored. Totally and utterly bored.

When in London, he wandered through the rooms of *Buckingham House*, learning about the paintings on the walls. One painting in particular caught his eye. John used to stare at the Allan Ramsay portrait of the king in his coronation robes, made by Ede and Ravenscroft. This magnificent painting hung in the Green Drawing Room. When the room was unoccupied, John would sit and gaze at the intricate details of the masterpiece.

Queen Charlotte had caught him gazing adoringly at the painting on her last visit. John was informed that the robe was in storage.

With the queen's blessing, he had been permitted to stroke the colossal ermine cloak and the golden suit the king had worn for his coronation. He knew the complete outfit would have been awe-inspiring when his majesty donned it. Having seen the original, the painting meant so much more to him. A matching portrait showed the queen in similar attire. He was permitted to see that as well.

John realised that soon he wouldn't be able to remain in the king's presence, as his monarch grew increasingly unwell. Hopefully, his illness would be brought under control once more.

John needed something to occupy his time during the king's periods of seclusion. He knew he needed to be around as many people as possible for his own safety, but where could he go? An overheard conversation about the lengthy sessions of the House of Commons gave him a solution. He was granted access to the gallery, where he could listen to the political minds discuss the wheels of reform turning. He kept the security guards informed of his destination.

One of the regular topics of discussion was the follow-up debates on the Slavery Trade Bill. John had sat through many discussions about the abolition of slavery and fully supported his friend, Bill's father, in his work. When possible, after listening to a rousing speech in the House of Commons, the boys would debate the pros and cons of owning slaves. Mr Wilberforce was an engaging speaker, and his powerful voice gave an impassioned plea for the abolition of slavery.

The sessions in the House of Commons usually started in the late morning and continued through the afternoon. These interesting debates often went on into the night. Many fell asleep during the early morning question times.

During one of these lengthy days, John met the court reporter, T. C. Hansard. The man could take notes as fast as a person could speak. This intrigued John, and he watched him with great interest.

Mr Wilberforce often brought one or two of his younger sons, and they were left in John's care if he was near. However, John missed his friend, Bill, who was now at college. He wished he could study with him, but knew it was too dangerous even to suggest it.

Mr Wilberforce also endorsed other reforms under debate. The Church Missionary Society was formed to spread the Gospel of Christ. This was fascinatingly interesting to a young man on the cusp of adulthood. He had always believed in God; that was a given, but was it a personal belief? Who else could make the world so beautiful but a creator like God? But Mr Wilberforce also spoke of a personal faith. His words challenged John to think deeply about his beliefs, and a very small question asked by Bill's papa made him stop and think.

Mr Wilberforce spoke about the 'Great Commission' that Jesus mentioned, but John had no idea what that was. For all his life, John had said his prayers religiously, but did he mean them? Who was God? Did God care about a young peasant lad like him? Were his prayers personal, or were they said by rote? So John listened to the older man's wisdom.

Whenever the topic of conversation came up, John moved closer to glean what information he could.

After one session, John dared to ask Mr Wilberforce when he came to collect his sons. "Sir, you speak of 'a great commission,' but may I be so bold as to ask what exactly that is?" John was nervous. This man was famous, and he had no right to approach him.

Mr Wilberforce smiled and then sat next to John. "Son, the Great Commission is a challenge from Jesus. The disciple Matthew, who was formerly a tax collector, records them in his Gospel. In chapter 28, verses 16 to 20, verse 19 is the charge to us all. He writes,

Then the eleven disciples went away into Galilee, into a mountain where Jesus had appointed them. And when they saw him, they worshipped him, but some doubted. And Jesus came and spake unto them, saying, All power is given unto me in heaven and in earth. Go ye therefore, and teach all nations, baptising them in the name of the Father, and of the Son, and of the Holy Ghost: Teaching them to observe all things whatsoever I have commanded you: and, lo, I am with you always, even unto the end of the world. Amen'."

John was stunned. "Do you mean the challenge comes directly from Jesus?"

Mr Wilberforce said, "It does indeed, son. We are each asked to share our faith with others. It's what my new society is all about. The Church Missionary Society is an extension of the Great Commission given by Jesus. In addition to that, there is the abolition of slavery, and another aim of mine is to form a group for the prevention of animal cruelty. However, even that is a drop in the ocean for what is required. The world would be a better place if we managed to get these three Bills passed."

John nodded. "It would indeed, sir."

Mr Wilberforce turned to the budding man and said, "Laddie, I have known you all your life. You are now what, fifteen?"

John nodded and shrugged. "Nearly, sir."

The gentle voice continued, "I know that you are aware of the immorality creeping into the upper echelons of society, but stay well clear of such action and stand firm in your faith."

John nodded again.

Mr Wilberforce continued. "If you feel God is speaking to you with an urge to speak up or out, grasp it. Joshua chapter 1 verse 9 says,

'Have not I commanded thee? Be strong and of a good courage; be not afraid, neither be thou dismayed: for the LORD thy God is with thee whithersoever thou goest.'

But, John, if the Lord speaks through you, be prepared to be ridiculed and persecuted. Those who stand firm in Jesus may well have eternal life, but life on earth can be difficult. Stay away from the temptation put before you in the palaces that you inhabit. Strong drink, immoral women and corruption are rife and destroy a man quickly. Stand up for what you believe and protect those you love. Let no man tempt you with such corruption. They may claim to be friends, but they are not. Flee from such men and resist the temptations thrust before you."

"I will try, sir." John was in a quandary about whether to mention his background and decided against it. The fewer who knew, the safer he and his mother would be. However, the conversation set John thinking. How could he tell others about the faith his mother and Queen Charlotte had taught him when he still knew so little about it?

Mr Wilberforce said, "John, the idea of a denomination-specific mission agency would mean that there would be less bickering about the focus of our outreach. The London Missionary Agency is well-intentioned, but too many of its members cannot agree on where to focus their work. However, they have a true faith, so if you find someone to speak to from there, do not hesitate to question them."

John set out to discover whom he could approach to ask.

Many studied how to become missionaries through the London Missionary Society, but they were not from the Church of England.

~

Three weeks later, through Bill, who was home from college on holiday, John found just the man he needed in Charles Blomfield. He was the newly appointed private chaplain to William Howley, Bishop of London.

Mr Wilberforce recommended this man. The Wilberforces knew Charles from Trinity College, Cambridge. Charles was the son of a grocer and not from the upper ranks of society. He felt a call to join the church and had a genuine faith. He studied Classics at university and won more awards and letters after his name than John could remember. Charles taught John about personal faith, how to share it with others, and how to live a Godly life. His birthday gift to John was a well-worn, leather-bound bible. Although the numerous palaces had exquisite illustrated bibles, many were never used. This book was his very own. John spent many hours devouring the words of his Christ and Saviour.

~

Kew Palace, early in 1811

John was pushed aside as the doctor entered the royal bedchamber. John had notified the attendants that the king could not see at all when he woke. Knowing he would not be needed for some hours, John went to seek his mother.

On arrival at *Frogmore Cottage*, he saw she was with the queen and waited patiently until he caught her eye.

Toria moved toward him, and they managed to have a quick word. The queen had asked for this to occur when the king had another turn. As John knew the royal couple were close, he willingly brought news of His Majesty's most recent illness. Last year, they were unsure whether His Majesty would survive. The king had remained ill for some time.

John may well be a young man in the making, but he still hugged this beloved woman every time he saw her. This morning, he whispered, "Mama, His Majesty cannot see. His eyes were open, but he could not even see me in front of him this morning. They are normally cloudy, but still. This morning, the king's eyes were darting everywhere, and he could see nothing but blackness, even with the curtains open."

Toria gasped. "Oh, my beloved boy, King George will need you closer now. Your role of protecting him will be more against himself than any enemy. What other symptoms has he exhibited?"

John flicked his eyes around to ensure they could not be overheard. "I may not be permitted to stay near him any longer. Mama, he has exhibited anxiety, hallucinations, severe pain, nausea and vomiting, and has had palpitations. The doctor said he also has high blood pressure, numbness, and muscle weakness recently, as well as blue urine. However, the king explained that that was from one of the strange medicines he had been given. I read to him and even sing, but he loves to watch, but if he is blind, he will be unable to walk in the gardens any more."

Toria brushed his fringe out of his eyes. "John, you need a haircut."

He chuckled. "I have not had time to have it done, Mama."

Toria flicked his nose lovingly. "Son, you are the king's attendant. You need to keep yourself looking immaculate. As to walking in the gardens, when he's well enough, I'm sure he will still wish to sit in the sunshine and smell the glorious perfumes of his flowers. He will learn to use his other senses. Use your eyes for him and describe them to His Majesty. Be his eyes as well as his feet and ears. You must encourage him to do so. You must become his sight."

John nodded. They were still alone, so he asked, "Mama, have you heard from Uncle Clive? I turn sixteen soon and... well, you know."

Toria had recently had a run-in with the man. He had tried to force himself on her once again. She said, "John, if the man is going to act, I believe it will be just before you attain your majority, so we have some years up our sleeves. While the palace needs Clive to feed information to Napoleon, you are safe. Clive won't reveal his hand until he can no longer make money from his evil ways. We must be on our most intense guard over the next years. When Clive acts, it will affect not just us but the entire palace. Their Majesties well know this scandal, and it will have major international ramifications." She cupped his clean-shaven cheek and said, "Whatever happens, you are the son of my heart. Remember that I love you more than my life itself."

John's voice broke last year, and he was learning to shave. He hugged the woman he had called "mother" for all his life. "I'll be careful, Mama. It won't be just me that he's after, so watch your back as well. You are all I have in this world. If something happened to you..." He couldn't finish his statement. His voice dropped. "You must be careful as well, Mama. You are also in danger." He now understood the threats to his beloved mother were also dire. "I've been boxing and fencing to stay fit. I will protect you, Mama." The pair hugged each other in farewell and were caught by the queen. Both fell into a deep bow and curtsy.

Queen Charlotte walked to her friend's side. "Good morning, Little Lord John; is all well with His Majesty?" With a gentle flick of her wrist, she told them to rise.

John saw two other ladies-in-waiting some distance behind her. "Your Majesty, I came to let you know that the king seems to have lost his sight. It's not the usual blurry vision, but a total absence."

Queen Charlotte gasped. "He can see nothing at all?" John shook his head. The queen swallowed and dropped her voice. "Were you asked to come?"

Again, John shook his head. "No, ma'am, but you asked me to let you know if his condition worsened. I was told to leave when the doctors entered. I came directly here before I was silenced." He noticed her eyes were now glassy.

She said, "Oh, John, how my George will hate this. I know it's a lot to ask, but take care of him for me, won't you?"

This time, John nodded.

The queen thanked him. "Keep your mama informed if there is any change. I dare say I may not be told officially for some days. I am being kept away from him now, and I hate it. I write to him daily. However, if his eyes are gone, I will need you to read my letters to him. Would you be kind enough to do that? There is no one else I would dare ask, but you know of my deep love for your king."

John bowed. "I would be honoured, ma'am." John was aware of the awkwardness of the situation. He was also fully aware of the affection between the regal couple. Not that his mother ever spoke out of turn, but he knew that when the queen entered the bedchamber, he had at least an hour to himself and usually went to visit his mother. As a teenager living in a royal palace, he knew that not all unions were so happy. However, the queen's affection for her ageing and ill husband was apparent, as was the trust the king had for his wife. John didn't move until dismissed.

The queen said, "John, when things get too difficult for you with him, please know that you are welcome to join your mama here with me. I fully intend to keep you safe, which means keeping you close to me. As his illness progresses, you may need to leave there permanently. Your background is irrelevant, as your behaviour is far superior to that of those who should know better. You have proven yourself many times over."

This time, his eyes glistened with unshed tears. He was an orphan with no known family. His maternal figure was no relation, and he only knew his real surname because it had been overheard. For the queen to care for his well-being was incredible. "Thank you, Your Majesty. I will stay as long as I'm permitted."

The queen nodded graciously and said, "Just know you have a home here with us, Little Lord John. I shall make you a footman of my royal chamber. Your mother can't lift me, and I will soon need the assistance of a strong arm or two." She swallowed, lifted her head and with a minute shake, said, "Thank you, John. I shall try to visit my husband later and tell him you have my permission to read my letters aloud to him."

John knew he was dismissed. He bowed low and moved away from his mother's side. At least he had somewhere to go when that time came.

~

The king was moved permanently to *Kew Palace*, and Prince George assumed the role of Regent. Queen Charlotte still held power over many things. As the king's illnesses now manifested in multiple complications, John was at a loose end. When the monarch was well enough, John would be summoned to his side to read to him and occupy him. When the king was ill, John would return to the queen, who now lived in *Frogmore House* on the Windsor Estate. The fifteen miles were done on horseback. John had free access to the royal stable and would often head out for a ride to exercise the horses. If he were to stay at *Frogmore House*, another groom would return his steed. He had clothing and a room at both residences.

As the monarch was now virtually locked away, it had been many months since John had seen him. He wondered if he would ever be recalled to duty.

~

Years passed. 1816 was a year without summer. The sun had hardly been visible all year, and many felt the oppressive effects of the unusual weather. John could not wait for it to be over. Although it was summer, the sun had hardly put in an appearance. Each day was dark and dreary.

The queen's ailing condition didn't help. She rarely went for her long walks, as she could hardly hobble to the front door.

Now age nineteen, John was no longer needed by the king. He felt useless but had no idea what to do about his situation. He was aware that his uncle's guardianship would soon end and that he needed to be even more vigilant about the potential danger.

~

The following year, John turned twenty. He was too old to be a pageboy to the ailing king, although that was still his official title.

To put it bluntly, he was bored. He responded to the title of Earl of Templestowe-Meade, but he had never seen *Meade House* on the Templestowe Estate, as Lady Victoria had left soon after he was born. He remained in the palaces and *Frogmore House* and worked as an upper footman, but he was not a servant, nor did he have the benefits of other peers. This was because he had not reached his majority. He was between a personal footman and a valet, but no longer served anyone. He was a Lord-in-Waiting with no one to wait on, as he was no longer permitted to visit his monarch. Servants bowed to him as he passed, and he had free range of every room in the various palaces, unless there was a function in progress. Even then, he was often kept near the Prince Regent, should he be needed to run a message. John floated for a while until Queen Charlotte made him her personal footman. She was now his employer as she was the king's legal guardian. When the parliament enacted the Regency Act, Her Majesty became the king's custodian, not the Prince Regent. Under the Act, the monarch was suspended from personally discharging royal functions.

His Majesty, King George III, had this Act drawn up in 1789 when the first major bout of illness struck. He recovered before the law had been passed. Knowing how ill he had been, the king approved the parliament's actions. He trusted his wife, but not his eldest son.

Eventually, the Prince Regent did not want John in his retinue as his friends were older and worldly-wise. The prince preferred to be surrounded by his own circle of friends and acquaintances. This large and somewhat immoral group of upper-class nobility were the same peers John tried hard to avoid. Having spent much of his youth in the presence of the king and queen, his eyes were opened to the licentiousness of the court under the Prince Regent. He did not like what he saw.

John was not of legal age, but had been officially presented at a Levee to the prince. Both men knew he was not entitled to this privilege, yet other earls his age received it, so he was not left out. To waylay suspicion, John, supposed Earl of Templestowe-Meade, was garbed as an earl and presented to the Regent. The prince's whispered words to John were, "Thank you, Little Lord John, continue to keep your head down."

Both men knew things would change dramatically when John came of age the following year, if he were still alive. With the evening festivities over, John was once again returned to *Frogmore House* in a royal carriage with six armed footmen to oversee his safety.

John needed to attend a few official functions at the palace, and a ball often followed these. Women wore disgracefully indecent gowns, and some even dampened the undergarments to encourage the flimsy fabric to cling to their bodies to attract him. It didn't work. John walked away in disgust.

Some tried to brush against him, and one even suggested that he take her for a walk in the garden. Thankfully, he was called away. The Regent had noticed him cornered and sent a footman to rescue the inexperienced young man. After that fiasco, the prince ordered the young man to stay by his mother's side. This left John free for the occasional social outing with Bill Wilberforce. Not that he dared go far from safety.

Queen Charlotte permitted him to attend a society presentation ball of less well-known members of society. He was advised not to step outside unattended. At the ball, John met and danced with one of the most beautiful girls he could imagine. Miss Martha Alexander was the epitome of his ideal lady. She was fresh and natural, rather than the over-fluffed and painted giggling females he had been surrounded with at court. Her gown certainly did not show much of her décolletage, nor did it appear dampened to accentuate her superb figure. Her dress was almost puritan amongst a room full of social butterflies. She was purity personified in a room full of pimped and preened toffs. John was instantly drawn to her. He wished the night would never end. She stole his heart when he had not even realised he had one. Miss Martha's only adornment was a long rope of breathtakingly perfect, large, pea-sized pearls around her elegant, slightly freckled neck. Although the young couple were permitted only two dances, John's eyes remained fixed on her. He chose dances where he did not need to change partners.

Countess Lieven and the Prince Regent permitted a debutante to do the German Waltz, and it was two of these that John chose. When both dances were over, he should have floated off to chat with other friends, but he remained close to this girl. For nearly an hour, he hid behind a huge floral display and chatted to her through the plant's leaves. Martha remained in full view of the ballroom, and no one realised she was talking to anyone. When she spoke, she hid behind her fan. She was no simpering miss, and her life of travel and adventure was what John dreamed about. John mentioned that he was His Majesty's pageboy, and rather than fawn over him, she chuckled.

No one else had asked her to dance, so John learned a great deal about her wonderful childhood, including sailing the globe with her parents and even being held up by pirates when she was young. He was somewhat jealous as he hardly left the luxury of various royal palaces, while she had travelled the world. John was pleased that the prince was not here tonight, as this girl would have attracted his attention, being so different from all the other debutantes present. Her adorable face and the simplicity of her garb caught his attention; however, he knew that should the prince notice her, she would be a challenge to conquer. It was as well that the regent was absent. He knew the Prince Regent permitted indiscretions, at which Miss Martha was verbally irate and unwisely voiced her ire to John. This occurred after John admitted his role as His Majesty's pageboy but explained that he served King George, not the prince. He quietly mentioned that the prince's lavish parties were a blot on his parents' good names. They would vehemently dislike such behaviour, but now, they had no say.

~

For weeks after the ball, John could not get this lovely girl out of his thoughts, but he didn't have the chance to meet with her again. Although he attended more functions, she did not appear at any. He had hunted for her but, sadly, had not discovered where she lived. Her smiling, freckled face never left his mind. Had he found her, he was unsure what that could achieve. He knew he had nothing to offer her, as he was not the rightful earl, but that did not stop him from thinking about her and pining for her. If only he were free to pursue a relationship... but that would never happen.

Occasionally, over the weeks since the ball, John had to follow the now cumbersome prince like a trained mouse as the queen was ill. John was privy to very little of the political nuances of the day, but through his friendship with Bill, he could keep up with the discussions about slavery. He absented himself as quickly as he could from the regent's presence.

Mr Wilberforce often sought out John to keep an eye on whatever offspring he had in tow. John was delighted to do this service, as it always ended with a lengthy conversation about faith.

With the assistance of Mr Wilberforce and Charles Blomfield, John's faith grew. He discovered that each residence had a small chapel, and he spent some of his spare time praying there.

Chapter 6   Miss Martha's Rebellion
London 1817
Martha

The irate young lady paced the room. She was furious. "Papa, how could you sell me? What do you think you were doing?"

The gentleman held his head and groaned. "Keep your voice down, Martha. My head is nearly ready to explode." His daughter had spent the morning playing the piano in the music room, and the notes floating through the closed doors were loud enough to make his head pound even more than his regular hangover. Willoughby had reluctantly summoned her to his office late in the morning.

The furious girl said, "You're nearly ready to explode? What about me? You lost me in a game of cards? What were you thinking? I'm not a chattel to win or lose in a game of chance." She stormed about the room, looking for something to throw.

Her father said, "I wasn't thinking, sweetheart. I was blind drunk and didn't know what Lord Edgar had me sign."

"Drunk! That's your reason for everything now, but it's no excuse, is it? It just shows your lack of responsibility." She spun around and faced her father. "You've been constantly drunk since Mama died last year. What about me? I was presented at court last week, and was supposed to be looking for a husband I liked. Lord John Templestowe-Meade showed interest, and I like him. He's close to my age and not a filthy grandfather who lusts over anything under the age of twelve, as well as any pretty man or boy who catches his eye. Did you know that Lord Edgar was one of those sorts of men?

My problem is that I don't look nearly sixteen, so I attract a child-loving rogue. Lord Edgar is nearly sixty and has already been married three times, all to girls under sixteen. I will not be lost as a payment for a bet on a drunken whim over the turn of a marked card." She thought of the handsome young man who had laughed at how she wore her pearls.

Willoughby Alexander cringed. He knew she was right. He had hardly had a sober day in the past ten months. He couldn't face life without his beloved Heather. She had been his life for nearly two decades, his reason for getting up in the mornings and his reason to live. He had managed to remain sober and upright through Martha's presentation ball, but things had gone downhill since that night. Without Martha or Heather in his home, he didn't want to exist. Now, Martha was soon to be gone. "It's done, love. Lord Edgar, the Earl of Oxenborough-Thorpe, has written to say he would send the notice of your engagement to the papers today."

Willoughby lifted his bloodshot eyes to his beautiful daughter and murmured an apology: "I'm so sorry, love, so very sorry, but what is done is done. It's a debt of honour, and I cannot withdraw it, even though he got my signature by stealth. Had I known what I was signing, I would have walked away. As you say, I'm sure he was cheating with marked cards."

The irate girl continued pacing the room. "I won't do it, Papa. I will run away, or I warn you, I will jilt him at the altar in front of the peers of London. He cannot marry me without my consent. No church in the land would allow that. I absolutely refuse to be sold to such a man as he. Yes, I shall shame him at the altar."

Willoughby cringed as she threw open his office door. It crashed into the bookcase on the wall. A vase on the top shelf wobbled and then fell to the floor with a crash. The contrite gentleman knew he was in the wrong. He put his head in his hands and wept. Pleading to his dead wife for her forgiveness. "Oh, Heather, I'm so sorry!"

Martha turned in the doorway and gazed at her sobering father. Her voice almost dripped venom. "And what about me? You betrayed me." Martha turned on her father again. With her voice lowered, venting her loathing at what he had done, she said, "Mama trusted you! Your last words to her were that you would care for me. Now, you have sold me to a man who has a penchant for children. You know that, don't you? He frequents the Rookeries to hunt for his innocent victims. The younger the better, and he's none too fussy about their gender."

Willoughby groaned. He lifted his head again to look at her and moaned. "I didn't know, my darling one! I had no idea that those stories about him were true."

Martha stood with her hands on her hips. "Well, Father, I will not stand by and be sold like a lamb to the slaughter. I'm going to retrieve that document. I don't care how embarrassed you are; I refuse to be your sacrificial lamb. Sober up and be the man Mother used to be so proud of."

With those words, she stormed out of the room. The door slammed behind her, and her father clutched his aching head. It was no use trying to stop his daughter. He had tried to do that before, but she was too headstrong for him. Only Heather could talk reason into her, but she was gone. He rested his head on his arms again and wept. "I'm so sorry, my belovéd girls." His heart and his head hurt so much. Heather had been his life; she was his reason to wake in the morning and work as hard as he had. When he travelled, Heather and Martha accompanied him. The three were close. Then, nearly a year ago, Heather had fallen ill on their last trip to Asia. She had contracted a shaking, sweating disease, and although she had survived the first two rounds of this illness, each had sapped her strength until she was but a shell. The final bout of this debilitating sickness had taken her from him. She had died in his arms, with him pleading for her to keep fighting. It had been to no avail. Heather was gone, and he alone was to care for their only surviving child.

Although Martha revealed her plan to her father, it was somewhat risky, but she had little option. She refused to marry the debauched, aged earl. She planned to break into his house to find the forged marriage settlement document that her father had been tricked into signing. She set about planning her revenge.

On board her father's ship, she wore a split riding habit instead of a dress. It was this outfit that she extracted from her wardrobe. She coupled it with a dark-coloured cloak. She then sat and considered where the man would keep his valuable documents. His office was the obvious place to start her search. It occurred to her that she may need more than one visit to find the document. If she failed, then she would jilt him publicly at the altar. Either way, she would succeed.

Night fell, and at midnight, Martha crept out of their house.

She knew where the earl lived and walked the two blocks to his residence. She managed to break into Lord Edgar's townhouse through an unlocked window that led into his den. With a grin, she struck a light on the tinderbox and lit a candle. She hunted through the papers on the desk and only found the engagement notice. There were no other official papers on his desk. She bent her head and quietly opened the drawers when she felt she was being watched. She looked up and gasped.

The earl stood on the other side of the desk, watching her every move. "Hello, my beloved. Can't you wait until the service tomorrow, eh?"

Martha had known fear on an angry sea, but the emotions washing over her now made that pale into insignificance. "Tomorrow? What is happening tomorrow? No, sir. I have come to take back the document. I will not be bought, sold, or won by anyone." She backed away towards the open window.

Though the earl was older than her, he was not feeble. He moved quickly and caught her before she could make good her escape. "I like this game, my dove. It's one I'm used to playing. The more you fight, the better I like it."

Martha tried to suppress her fear. "Unhand me, sir! My father has changed his mind and will pay you instead of this bribery."

An evil chuckle stole her bravery. "He has nothing left. I own it all. He should have stopped playing hours earlier. This is no game, and a debt of honour cannot be undone. You are mine already."

"He said you cheated." She realised that he held her so tightly that her arms were pinned. However, she had not spent time on her father's ship without learning how to immobilise a man. Her action was so swift that it surprised her captor.

His excitement at the chase and possible relief of his raging needs was short-lived. His trousers were becoming uncomfortably tight. "And why not, my dear? How else could I claim you?" He reached to unbutton his flap. At that moment, she kneed him in the groin as hard as she could.

The howl of pain to his engorged manhood made him crumple to the ground. She had missed a full-force kick, or he would have been insensible. His anger was enough to rouse him, though in great pain. He saw the girl intended to make her escape, but he grabbed her ankle and dragged her to the ground. Even though his groin throbbed in agony, he managed to hold fast to her.

The more she struggled, the tighter he held.

Through his agony, he said, "You little whore, you will pay for that. No one does that to me and survives unscathed." His breathing was still ragged, and he was still in pain.

His grip on her arm was like iron shackles. She could not escape, but she did not stop trying. She twisted and wiggled, but to no avail.

He pulled her closer until she was wrapped in his arms under him.

It seemed like an eon had passed, but eventually, his breathing returned to normal. "You will be mine, even if I have to take you now. I shall ruin your father's name if you cross me. You will marry me, and I shall ensure that right now."

Martha was angry at herself, her father and this filthy-minded man. She was furious and spat in his face. She said, "So much for being a gentleman; I wouldn't marry you if you were the last man on earth."

Again, she heard his evil laugh. He had now recovered from her attack and was battling to access her gown. Thankfully, the split skirt riding habit made that endeavour far more difficult than he expected.

Eventually, he backhanded her. The heavy slap snapped her head sideways and made her dizzy. She must have lost consciousness, as when she roused, she realised that he had ripped off her split skirt, as he had been unable to lift it.

Within moments, he had the fall of his trousers fully unbuttoned and quickly pinned her arms with his own. His engorged manhood punctured her maidenhood. As he forced his way past her virginal block, he chuckled with delight as she screamed in pain. He gave her another backhander, and she blacked out. He used her body as he wished while she lay on the floor.

His painful actions roused her after a few minutes. She resumed her fight and struggled again, but his weight held her captive. Her actions only made him pump into her harder. His evil laugh sent chills down her spine. He now had her arms pinned above her head.

As he pleasured himself, she realised she was ruined. However, she would still refuse to marry him. Life with him would be sheer hell. She would not relent. She may be forced to the altar, but he would not win. She would refuse to say the vows. No one could force her, not even her father. She would do anything rather than marry this debauched earl. She would flee to sea with her father and never return to England again. They would leave for India or one of the other exotic places they had been. There were far more welcoming lands than this cold place.

Eventually, the earl rolled off her and sat up. She caught sight of the earl's bloodied manhood and was horrified at what he had just done to her.

Martha tried to cover her private areas only to discover that her outfit was no longer decent. He had not just torn her clothing but shredded it as he ripped it from her body. She was unable to hold her garments together to cover herself.

He chuckled at her discomfort. He said, "I shall drive you home. Even as my future countess, you cannot be seen in public in the condition your clothing is in. Stay here while I bring the carriage around."

Martha sat meekly on the floor and waited until the door closed. She would not stay. Moments later, she slipped out the window and cut across his lawn.

Unbeknownst to him, she had left her cloak in the bush near the window. She grabbed it and covered her nakedness. Her nether regions hurt, but thankfully, she was due for her monthly flow tomorrow, so it was unlikely she would conceive a child.

Five minutes after escaping, she entered through the French windows of her home's library. Although she crept in silently, her father was waiting for her. For once, he was sober.

Surprisingly, he was not angry at her escapade. His voice came out of the darkness. "Did you get it?"

She had not noticed him, and she jumped. As she did so, her cloak parted.

Her father saw the state of her clothing and asked, "Did he do this to you? Did he...did he...?" Willoughby was unable to finish his question.

Martha said the words for him. "Did he ravish me? Yes, he did, and he still wants to marry me. He hurt me, and I shall have a bruised face and arms tomorrow as his fist or hand will have left its imprint. I'm not quite sure what he hit me with, but that's the least of my worries." She turned to her father and said, "This is the man you sold me to on the turn of a card, Papa. I will not wed him, even now. I am ruined, but I am alive to fight him another day. Why could you not have sold me to Lord John?"

Her father was speechless. What had he done? How had his life fallen apart so drastically? His beloved daughter was ruined.

Martha watched the emotion play on her father's face. She said, "I shall leave at first light. I don't care where I go, but I will not marry that animal." It was daylight in mere hours.

The realisation washed over him that he was responsible for her shame. Her father gagged. His drinking had brought his daughter to total ruin. He swore never to touch the grog again. "I shall come with you, my love. We shall leave the country never to return. We will go to the ship at first light."

Unfortunately, life was not that straightforward.

~

At dawn, Willoughby and Martha headed down to his ship. When they reached the dock, they found it empty.

Joe Brand, once Martha's shadow, one of Willoughby's crew, was on the wharf. He said, "You could have at least told us that you had sold the *Tidesong*, sir. The new owner sacked us all yesterday and brought in his own crew. I got nowhere else to go, skip. I s'pose I gotta find another ship to take me on."

Willoughby felt ill. He had no recollection of signing away his ship, but as he had signed his daughter away, he presumed that his ship had already been lost. They had no escape due to his evil deeds. His money was forfeited, and Heather's pearls were all he had left. They were in his coat pocket. He realised he would need to sell them to buy a passage out of London.

The three stood gazing at the empty berth, all wondering what the future would bring. Willoughby had no idea what they would do or where they would go. They turned to head to a pawnbroker's when a carriage drew up behind them.

The Earl of Oxenborough-Thorpe alighted and stood watching them with his arms folded. "Going somewhere with my future wife, Alexander? You are not trying to renege on a debt of honour, are you? I have booked the church, and I shall marry your adorable daughter at two o'clock today." His evil cackle sent chills down the spines of both Alexanders.

Martha turned and said, "I shall never marry you."

Willoughby took her hand and said, "Silence!" He then whispered, "We'll find a way to escape."

The earl laughed. "Oh, you'll marry me, my girl. I have

already deflowered her; did she tell you that? A delicious morsel she was, too."

Willoughby felt like thumping him, but knew that if anything happened to him, Martha would have no choice but to do as the evil peer bade. He grasped his daughter's hand and drew her close.

The earl approached and took Martha's arm in a painful grip; then, he forced her towards the waiting carriage.

Her father had little option but to follow in their wake.

Joe watched on in horror, but there was nothing he could do to help but pray. He didn't often talk to the Great Man above, but tonight, he bowed his head and begged for her to remain safe. "God, help her." He had known Miss Martha since she first crawled. He had kept her safe all her life. The earl's words horrified him.

Another set of unseen eyes stood in the shadows. He was unable to intervene, as he should not have been on the docks. Mr Wilberforce was here to check on the arrival of a suspected slave ship. He wondered if Lord Clive was the owner of the said vessel. He suspected he was.

~

At a quarter to two, Lord Edgar waited outside the room he had forced her into. On the bed lay an extraordinary gown that would usually have made Martha drool; however, she refused to put it on.

She stood in her drawers and camisole, arms folded. She figured that he would not take her out of the house if she were unclad. How wrong she was.

When the knock came, she refused to answer the door. She had locked it and would not even let a maid in. She did not take the earl's stubbornness into account.

The man's shoulder made short work of the flimsy lock.

The door crashed open, and splinters of the frame crunched under his boots as he entered uninvited. "As I suspected, you are not dressed, my dear. I will manhandle you into the gown myself."

Another slap to the back of her head sent her reeling against the bedpost. He obviously had experience dressing a semiconscious woman.

He quickly had her in the gown, and he was soon buttoning her crystal beaded dress as she lay face down on the bed. Martha realised that the gown would have cost him a fortune.

Still groggy, she could hardly stand unaided as her head was still ringing. She fully roused as he swept her into his arms and carried her downstairs. She protested and kicked all the way. Only when she saw her father in the carriage did she quieten.

Willoughby took her hand and drew her to him. "I'm so sorry, my darling girl."

Her only response was to glare at him.

Willoughby deserved her wrath, so he was surprised when she squeezed his hand lovingly.

The drive to the church was done in silence.

The earl sat facing forward, and Willoughby sat opposite him and next to his daughter, attempting to comfort her.

The journey was far too short for Martha's liking.

The earl alighted and grabbed her hand, pulling her quite literally from the carriage seat.

Not trusting them to walk up the aisle, the earl's fingers curled around her arm, and he marched her to her doom.

Martha walked meekly with her eyes down, determined to carry through on her threat to jilt him at the altar. He would pay for what he had done to them, and she fully intended to shame him publicly, exposing his deviant lusts. She noticed the church was packed with toffs. The same immoral creatures she detested. A smile flickered across her lips, and she stood a little more upright.

Unable to stop himself from gloating, the earl had invited everyone he knew. The church was filled with the cream of society and the realm's top-ranking peers. "Perfect!" She thought and smiled, but she was livid.

The minister could not see the ire on her face, but he did notice a hand mark on her cheek. He was unaware that he would soon be challenged about keeping his vows and not marrying an unwilling bride. This would be a service he would never forget. The service started. Lord Edgar had not released his vice-like grasp on his bride's arm. The compressed circulation was now impeding the movement in her lower arm, and her fingers tingled. Martha plastered a false smile onto her lips, but she was seething. When the minister reached the words of acceptance, she took her only chance. She turned to the earl and shook off his hand. In a loud voice, she said, "No, absolutely not! I will never marry him." She turned to the earl and almost yelled, "You forced me here today. I have the bruises to prove you physically harmed me. I told you I would not marry you if you were the very last man on Earth. Send me to the Antipodes, as you will never get into my drawers again."

The earl turned to hit her and remembered where he was. Instead, he grasped her arm again. He could not shut her up with a slap or punch in a church. He insisted that many of his peers attend the nuptials to this beautiful, wilful girl; now, he knew he would pay dearly for that gloat. He swallowed nervously, but he was keen to bed her again. This filly would be fun to conquer.

She turned to the congregation and said, "Do you all know that he ravished me last night when I broke into his house to get the illegal document he made my drunken father sign? The earl cheated at cards and tricked my father into signing over all his possessions. This was to ensure I would turn up today. Well, I'm here, but I still will not marry him. I refuse! I would rather die than be shackled to him for life. I will freely admit that I am ruined, but I don't care. I will not wed this devil beside me, for at least I shall be alive." The horrified gasps were about to get worse for the earl. Martha ripped her arm from his shocked grasp. She backed away from her groom and toward her father, then turned back to the earl's peers. Continuing to speak loudly to the congregation, she said, "Did you know he likes bedding little children? He doesn't even care about their gender. He takes pleasure in causing pain to anyone who displeases him. He is a deviant and should be arrested as well. Do you know that he is a Molly boy and likes men, too? I believe that's what you call a man who likes men and boys. Did any of you know that, or perhaps you joined him in his perverted activities? I'm not even sure that he doesn't force himself on animals as well. This man's debaucheries know no bounds. His three other wives were all under eighteen years old when they died. Did you not care about them?"

The earl knew he could not live down these accusations. Far too many people had heard of his twisted proclivities toward young children. Although he would deny them, the mud would stick, especially about the bestiality. She was correct; he was not fussed if they were boys or girls as long as they were young. How did she know about his other proclivities, though? Also, her accusation about cheating would see the end of him in society.

Her father had been warned she would do this, but her crass words shocked him. He had no idea that his meek-mannered daughter had this in her. However, she had grown up with sailors and knew all about life on the docks. Willoughby took his daughter's hand and started to leave the church. The poor minister was unsure what to do. He stuttered and almost dropped his bible.

The earl suddenly realised she was leaving. He chased her halfway up the aisle and tried to snatch her from her father's grasp. "You shall marry me!"

The minister cried, "No, I won't perform this marriage." He tried to grab the peer.

Willoughby defended his daughter and tried to push Lord Edgar away. The earl swung at him, and the sickening crunch of a fist on Willoughby's jawbone echoed around the church. The earl's elbow caught the minister in the nose. Blood flowed.

The congregation gasped in unison.

Willoughby collapsed in a heap. As he fell, his head hit the raised step on the side of the aisle. As he had not released his grip on his daughter's hand, Martha dropped to her father's side. His eyes were open, but he did not see or move. His fingers loosened. She noticed blood beginning to seep down the timber step and onto the carpet. She knelt at her father's side and tried to rouse him. She slipped her hand to the back of his head and realised that his skull had caved in. He had died the instant he fell. She threw back her head and released a howl of grief as she drew him into her arms.

The congregation sat frozen.

One man stood, but only to see better. Her father had introduced her to Lord Clive Templestowe as one of his business partners. Aghast, she turned and screamed at the earl. "You've killed him. You beast! Is this how your other wives died? Did you murder them all?" Now standing, she addressed the congregation while holding up her bloody hands and said, "Are you all willing to have me led to the slaughter to save my reputation. I'd rather kill myself than marry such an animal as him." Her beautiful gown was now covered in her father's blood. She turned and growled at him. "Murderer!"

The earl was aghast at what he had done. Willoughby Alexander was dead, and it was his fault. His eyes were fixed on the growing pool of blood, and he did not see his angry ex-bride approach him. He did, however, feel the kick she aimed at his groin. Her almost gentle kneeing of him last night was nothing to the agony he felt now. Her pointed-toe shoes, which he insisted she wear, connected with the most vulnerable part of his anatomy and forced at least one of his wiffles up into his body. He collapsed to the floor and cried out in agony. She would pay for this.

The sound of smirking rippled through the church.

Martha was not finished with her groom. "You think you are so high and mighty because you are rich and have a title. You got my father drunk, and then, as you have with others, you cheated at cards until he had lost everything to you. You stole his business and his ship to try to get me." Her eyes scanned the congregation. She drew a breath and turned to the only person in the congregation standing. He was her father's silent partner. "Lord Clive, Papa has nothing left, so I hope you are well-heeled to pay his outstanding debts."

The man sat down hastily. So much for him remaining anonymous. He cursed her silently.

One man silently cheered at her outburst. William Wilberforce had been the man on the dock last night. He had stolen into the church service late, sure that she would do something dramatic, but he had not expected this. He would do what he could to help her. For now, he left to get the constabulary.

Martha wasn't done yet. She addressed the congregation while gazing at her prostrated, groaning groom. "Well, this miss will be owned by no man! I'd rather live my life ruined, with no reputation, than to die by your hand as your other wives did."

The only person who moved now was the minister's wife. She had been sitting in the vestry and came to Martha's side. Martha was reeling. Her father was dead, and his business was gone. It had been stolen, no, embezzled, by Lord Edgar, and now she had nowhere to go. When nearly at the vestry, she screamed at him, "I mean it. I would never marry you if you were the very last man on Earth. Send me to the Antipodes, but you will never get into my drawers again." With that comment, she left with the minister's wife.

The earl groaned from his place on the ground and said to the minister, "There will be no wedding today, reverend, but I want her arrested. She broke into my house and now has physically assaulted a peer of the realm in public."

Chapter 7 Death, Murder, and Mayhem
November 1817, Windsor.
John

*A*fter the king's blindness struck, young Bill Wilberforce came to say his farewells to his friend. At age nineteen, he was going to King's College in Cambridge.

John's life at court once again became lonely. The regent and his entourage now occupied *Buckingham House* in London.

John now lived permanently at *Frogmore House* with his mother and the ailing Queen Charlotte. He had become vital to the queen's comfort. She trusted none of the other footmen to tend to her. John knew just how to place her pillows and ease her pain.

His mother's soothing voice was easy on the queen's ears, and Toria read beautifully, as did John.

The king was wasting away on the other side of the same estate. John was now blocked from his side. His majesty was now a recluse; even the ageing queen was forbidden in her husband's presence.

When the news about the king's debilitating illness arrived some years earlier, Her Majesty almost exploded in anger. Not because he was sick, but because the courtiers delayed telling her and forbade her from visiting her husband.

John had never seen her angry before and was shocked by her vehemence. He knew the king's temperament was unstable, as he had witnessed various incidents over the years. He managed to slip into the king's bedroom and deliver a loving message from his wife. He was permitted entry with the excuse of collecting his things, which he did.

Now, one of his daily duties was to read the news to the queen. While his mother read the personal correspondence, John was digesting a shocking story in the newspaper. He would not read this article to Queen Charlotte. Today's story occurred earlier that week.

One of the peers had violated a young girl, and she jilted him at the altar. She chose to live in shame rather than become the peer's wife. The story continued with graphic details. John frowned.

William Wilberforce would surely know who it was. Only the initials Miss A. were used. His stomach hit the floor. Was it Miss Martha Alexander? The rest of the details fitted.

The paper said the earl had hit the girl's father whilst in the church, and the man died where he fell. He knew that Captain Alexander had died that week. Was that Martha's father?

The story said that the earl then had her arrested for breaking and entering his property, attempted theft and assaulting a peer. The bride had been charged and was being held in custody.

John read the story, noting that no other initials were mentioned. Lord Clive's name was there as he knew the unwilling bride's father as a silent partner.

He read that his uncle arranged for the removal of the man's body and for his burial. When the deceased man's name was mentioned, John gasped again. Surely there could not be two men with the rank and initials of Captain W. A. Was the man Captain Willoughby Alexander, Martha's papa? Was the jilted bride the beautiful girl he had met at the ball? If the story were true, then the earl had violated her.

John gasped; everything fitted. It must be Martha. His heart grieved for her.

John gazed unseeing out of the window. His heart hurt.

He told his mother the story when they were off duty and explained how he had met her. He mentioned the ball and their long conversation.

Victoria also read the story. She was surprised that Lord Clive was doing something good for once. He would surely have a motive. Had this Captain been the way he sourced the gemstones he traded with the French?

John was sure there was more to it than what was reported. Was Captain Alexander the man buying gems for his uncle to give to France, as Martha suggested? He would try to find out.

~

The once beautiful queen aged dramatically after her husband's illness struck him down. Now in her seventies, she was still regal, but the onset of dropsy had curtailed her activities. Her grey hair was still beautifully arranged, but her once smooth face was now wrinkled with age.

Gone were the visits from notable persons such as Sir Joseph Banks, Daniel Solander, John Lightfoot, and the geologist Jean Andre de Luc. Even the likes of Fanny Burney, Elizabeth Harcourt, and Margaret Cavendish, the Duchess of Portland, all stayed away. The last two women were, like Queen Charlotte, enthusiastic naturalists.

John was present when Sir Joseph suggested a penal settlement in the new south land that Lieutenant James Cook charted.

John had been on hand for many of their collecting expeditions around the extensive *Kew Gardens*; now, the queen never left her suite, let alone her bedroom.

On the rare times she was well enough, she would ask to be carried to the small cottage she had built on the estate.

Victoria and John remained with her during her stay. This cottage was known as *Queen Charlotte's Cottage*. It was a place where many happy hours were spent when the royal children were young. Now, it sat empty. Her heart was heavy.

The queen's illnesses meant that even two royal weddings had to be held in her residence rather than in London.

When William, Duke of Clarence and Edward, Duke of Kent, married, the weddings took place at Kew in a double ceremony. An altar was set up in the Drawing Room of *Kew Palace*, and afterwards, the queen retired to her bedroom while the wedding party enjoyed a sumptuous meal in the dining room before travelling to *Queen Charlotte's Cottage* for tea.

John had been witness to it all. The royal family knew him by his first name, or more often, they called him "Little Lord John," as he had refused to use the title of earl while with the royal family. As he had grown up with some of the monarch's grandchildren, he was treated much the same as they were. The king knew he had no claim to any title. He was far more to the princes and princesses than mere staff. He was a trusted friend.

Victoria and John tended to Queen Charlotte with the help of other Ladies-in-Waiting, but John now took the role of Her Majesty's personal footman. She would trust no one but him to move her from the bed to the chair and back.

On the rare occasions that she could not walk, John had the strength of youth to carry her from her beloved black reading chair to her bed.

He was due to turn twenty-one at the end of November; as such, he was aware that Lord Clive would be panicking to grasp any opportunity to end his life. He was sure he was only alive because of the royal couple's protection, but what would occur once they were gone? In the royal chambers, he was safe, but for how long?

~

17 November 1818

The queen sat in her favourite chair, dying.

John stood silently just inside her bedroom door. He was part of the furniture, a shadow that moved. Someone to attend to the needs of the grieving family, but he also wiped away his tears.

He adored the beautiful lady who was like a grandmother to him. He wished to go to his mother and cry like a baby, but she was finding her friend's illness difficult as it was.

His mother had sat up with Her Majesty all night, then dressed her in her dressing gown when morning came. Only then was John permitted to enter.

He carried the elderly lady from her bed to her beloved black chair at the foot of her bed.

Once Queen Charlotte was settled, she permitted her children to enter. She did not wish to die prostrated.

The queen's weak voice said, "Thank you, John. Stay with me, but let the others in. I have loved having you by my side during my last days. Care for Lady Victoria, lad."

John bowed and nodded. He let the family in and then took his place beside the door; on guard, but at hand should he be required for messages. The queen caught his eye and smiled her thanks.

The slim bookcase held tomes of her journals, one of which enclosed the document she had written in 1806 when they overheard the plot to kill him. He knew which book it was. He had placed her journals on this shelf many times over the two decades.

He rested his hand on the timber shelf beside him. He didn't want to see her die. Yet, he had to remain in her room. Hopefully, she wouldn't linger in pain for long.

Today, he had placed a sheepskin rug on her chair to make her more comfortable. Moving her to use a chamberpot would not occur today.

His eyes took in the room's simplicity. The blueish-green colouring above the black dado rail provided a beautiful background for the paintings that hung there. One large painting was an angelic cherub of a child, and the other was a girl.

John had never asked who they were, but had presumed they were two of the royal children, possibly Princess Amelia.

The canopied bed was not overly ostentatious. The furnishing was simplistic at best. They were white, with a leafy green highlight. A colour scheme that reflected the queen's love of the outdoors. The lower section of the walls was painted white and featured simple panels. The floor was wall-to-wall carpet, and the geometric pattern made the colour look brown. This was a luxury that the queen deserved.

The staff quarters mainly had bare timber floorboards or something equally as cold.

John smiled to himself. As they were not regular staff, the queen kept them close to her. Since he moved in, they had a royal suite down the same corridor as the queen. His mother was the chief attendant and the regal lady's main confidante. Though still a Lady-in-Waiting, she was now the senior Maid of the Royal Chamber.

John tried hard to keep his mind away from the dying lady, and he had managed to do so.

The sound of weeping broke through his reverie.

John's eyes now fell on the queen.

Her aged head had dropped forward. Her son, the Regent, was closing her eyes.

Her Majesty, Queen Charlotte, was dead.

The two princesses who had remained by Her Majesty's side now turned and wept in their brother's arms.

Queen Charlotte had died sitting in her favourite black armchair, just as she wished. She was surrounded by her two daughters, Augusta and Mary, as well as the Prince Regent and the Duke of York.

With a nod to John, the Regent, Prince George, sent for the doctor so that the man could pronounce that Her Majesty was gone.

Knowing that her death was imminent, the doctor was outside

the door.

Now dismissed, John did his duty, then went to tell his mother.

~

Less than an hour after Her Majesty died, the Regent ordered his mother's journals and private papers to be packed for his collection later that day.

John had to remain on guard until they were moved. He had returned to Her Majesty's room as soon as he informed his mother. He waited until the doctor departed before entering the room.

He knew the queen's journals had been locked away securely, as evidenced by the now-empty shelves. He was surprised that this had been prioritised over the queen's death.

John remained with Her Majesty until she was placed into her coffin.

The prince sent his brother to collect the journals, but he had already removed one in particular. He tapped the cover as he passed John.

John bowed in acknowledgement. The report was safe. John was aware that the prince had read the letter the queen wrote twelve years earlier, when she and his mother had overheard the plot to kill him. Keeping this journal safe was to protect the crown. This was about treason, not him.

~

The remainder of the day passed in a blur of activity for everyone.

John hardly saw his exhausted mother as she was busy washing the queen and dressing her in her funereal garb.

John stood guard outside her room.

Once gowned, the queen would lie in state until her burial.

John and Victoria took their shifts, sitting with her for the final time.

The long night was cold, but the mood was even colder.

Death sapped all joy from their usual existence. The front knocker was wrapped, and the curtains were kept closed.

Frogmore House fell silent.

To keep from falling asleep, John thought about his exciting conversation with Miss Alexander at the ball. She mentioned so many wonderful places that he wished he could visit, and her descriptions were so vivid that he could picture them.

Mr Wilberforce had been suspiciously absent for some time.

John was sure he would know where she was, but he had not had a chance to confirm the newspaper article. Another article followed, mentioning she had been arrested and charged. There had been no follow-up article to that. He wished he knew where she had been sent.

The night blurred into a flurry of activities for the following day.

~

Queen Charlotte's coffin lay in the dining room at *Kew Palace* under a canopy, lit by six candles in large silver candelabras, before being taken to *Windsor Castle*. Victoria, John, and others took turns sitting with her body. John comforted his beloved mother in her grief, but his heart hurt too.

When the evening of the funeral arrived, the cobbled courtyards were covered with straw to prevent the gravely ill king from hearing the sound of his wife's funeral procession.

The funeral service started at eight o'clock at night.

The Regent decided not to tell his father that his beloved wife had died.

The queen left her home for the last time.

John was to precede the queen's coffin into the church, holding her crown.

~

Returning to *Frogmore House* after the funeral, at a quarter to ten, the house was eerily quiet.

Distant noises came from the kitchens.

John intended to find his mother. He had expected to see her leading the procession of Ladies-in-Waiting, but she had not been amongst the other attendants. As part of the disreputable collection of peers that usually clustered around the Regent, John was surprised that Lord Clive was also absent from the service.

John shrugged the thought away. He wondered where they would go now that the queen was dead. He presumed that *Frogmore House* would be closed and that the staff would be dismissed. Would he return to the king's residence?

For most people, this was almost a relief. They had other homes to go to, but *Meade House* on the Templestowe Estate was unsafe for them. John was aware that the royal residences had been used as places of safety for the pair of them for decades.

He walked along the hallways and moved leisurely towards their quarters. Had the queen made any arrangements for them?

Maids were already at work stripping the personal effects from the queen's suite.

He finally reached the end of the long corridor to find his mother's door slightly ajar. He knocked and waited. Silence! He gingerly pushed the door of his mother's room open and called his mother's name—still silence.

John moved inside and noticed the dressing room was a mess. This was not usual. Her quarters were usually immaculate. Today, dresser drawers were open, and items were strewn everywhere. Her jewellery box had been upended on the dressing table. She was never this untidy.

Something was wrong.

He ventured further and moved towards her sleeping chamber, picking up one of her best slippers as he walked. He figured she must have lost one and gone looking for it, but where was she? He had never seen her room in such a state. "Mama, are you here?"

The bed was rumpled, but she was not there.

He was about to turn and leave when a slight sound caught his ear. It came from the far side of the huge canopied bed.

John followed the noise and was horrified to find his mother on the floor, covered in blood. Her attire was torn, her skirts lifted, exposing her private area, and her face was swollen almost beyond recognition. He could see that some of her fingers had been broken, and they were also bloodied. She had been ravished violently, and her face had been slashed, probably by the knife she kept under her pillow. Her upper thigh was covered in bruises and scratches, and had a long cut on it as well. "Oh, Mama! What happened?"

Victoria was groaning and mumbling incoherently.

John slid to the floor beside her. He lowered her skirts. He was about to cradle her when he noticed that one side of her chest was hollowed, and a footprint was on the bodice of her gown. Still, he drew her carefully into his arms. Her breathing was laboured, but she roused when John held her.

Victoria realised someone was there, but she could not see through her swollen eyes, so she didn't know who held her.

Her words rasped out weakly. "Tell my John... Clive did this." She took a breath. Bubbles of blood oozed from her mouth. The following words were equally heartbreaking. She rasped, "Tell John, I love him."

Her sunken chest and the bubbling blood showed that she had broken ribs and one had pierced her lung. He gasped. "Mother, I'm here! I love you!"

Her head turned towards him. "Danger! John…flee. I love you."

She drew a breath and exhaled with a sigh.

No more came.

Her exhale seemed never-ending as her life force ebbed from her earthly body. She was now in the heavenly realm.

John shook her gently, but she was gone. He embraced her tightly, sobbing into her neck. "Mama! Don't leave me," but he knew she was dead. Pain could hurt her no more, so he crushed her to his chest in his final hug.

He was grief-stricken; his following words were strangled and bitter. "I'll make him pay. I don't care if it costs me my life." He had his last long hug, and then he sat up and released a long, tortured howl of pain and grief.

The sound echoed across the room, down the corridor through the open door, and reached the staff's ears.

Within moments, the room was filled with worried people.

Lady Victoria's maid, Kitty, was the first to arrive. She stood gazing at the room's carnage.

Others stood and paused at the scene of chaos, while others came into the bedroom in answer to John's wailing.

Ignoring the stares of the staff, he lifted his mother onto the bed. As Victoria's private parts were now covered, she was decent again, although covered in blood. He caressed her beloved face for the final time and kissed her farewell. He called Kitty to her side. "Stay with her, Kitty." The maid nodded.

Tears streamed down his face as he forced his way through the staff who filled the outer room, oblivious to the stares of others. He marched towards the official reception rooms downstairs. Today was the day that he would face his nemesis. His bloody hands were clenched in anger. If the prince happened to be in earshot, then all the better. John didn't like the man's morals, but the prince had been made aware of the situation years earlier. He knew why they had been kept close to the royal couple.

As the queen's funeral was over, many official guests returned for an intimate supper with the Regent. John knew that Clive had somehow managed to wangle an invitation to the evening event, but he had not seen him at the funeral; now he knew why.

The official stateroom for the function was on the lower floor just inside the main entryway. As he was covered in blood, the staff moved out of his way as he strode angrily along the hallway and down the main staircase. With his fists still balled, John stormed across the foyer and marched directly into the stateroom.

On entry, the door crashed against the wall as he flung it open. A Ming vase wobbled dangerously, but one of the maids caught it in time.

Lord Clive stood in the centre of the room as others dribbled in slowly. He had obviously changed, as he was immaculately attired. The peer's smile vanished as he realised who had entered and that John was covered in blood. He blanched but remained silent. Clive took a step backward as John approached him menacingly.

John didn't notice anyone but his quarry. If Clive had spoken, John would have grabbed the closest item and smashed it over his so-called uncle's head. Without a word, he marched up to his nemesis and gave him an uppercut with his clenched, bloody fist, catching his 'uncle' on his square chin. A left hook to his stomach followed this. Clive hardly had time to react before another blow landed on his solar plexus. He could scarcely draw a breath. He still didn't fall.

As each blow fell, a diatribe of bottled-up vitriol escaped from John's lips. "You maggot pie, scum-sucking, murdering, cock-teaser!"

Crunch, another punch was thrown to his face. "You have wanted to grind your wiffles into Lady Victoria since her husband died. Well, now you have, but she was no whore. She fought off you and your crony, Sir Robert, for two decades, but you couldn't keep your hands off her, could you?"

Lord Clive tried to defend himself, but the boy he knew had become a man. They were now the same height, and John's physique had matured; his hours spent boxing and fencing had built his muscles. Clive had no hope of fending off the angry young man. His dissipated lifestyle had rendered him unfit and overweight, while John was in the peak of his physical fitness.

Another punch connected with Lord Clive's chin. John said, "I say 'was' because she is dead. You killed Lady Victoria Templestowe as sure as if you had strangled her yourself. You slashed her hips and her face and kicked her so hard that her ribs punctured her lungs. She drowned in her own blood. Does that make you happy?" John's anger overflowed.

Clive managed to utter, "I did no such thing. She was alive when I left her." He gasped, realising what he had just admitted in public.

John was livid at his words. "So you admit that you were with her and violated her violently while our late queen was being buried? You scum! You, who had been banned from Mama's presence since your friend Sir Robert murdered her husband so he could light-skirt her himself. You must be 'dicked in the nob' if you think you can get away with such an obscene transgression against a titled lady. To do it on a day such as this is appalling. She was a royal Lady-in-Waiting and a Countess under royal protection, and you offered to use her with him in a threesome with Sir Robert. You disgust me!" This time, Clive's nose was John's target. John's aim was true. Blood now streamed from the smashed appendage on the once-handsome face. "You are a murderer, Lord Clive, and one who killed my real parents, the Turners, their coachman, as well as Lady Victoria's legitimate daughter, whom she would have named Jennifer, plus a sea captain for the East India Company, Captain McFarlane, amongst others. I suspect you killed Mama's maid after you used her."

A look of horror washed over Clive's face. How did John know all this? How long had he known? Did Sir Robert or Lord Montgomery tell someone? Who else knew? How did John know of his association with Sir Robert? How had Monty's identity been revealed? Clive hardly had time to draw a breath before the next swing from John crumpled him. The punch that came sent him to his knees. He could scarcely defend himself because his hands still hurt from knocking Victoria around. She had dodged many of his punches but had not been fast enough to avoid his boot. He had violated her as she lay on the floor, immobilised and weeping. The fight had gone out of her, but she was still breathing when he left her. Relieving his lust, he kicked her again when he finished with her because she had rejected him for the past two decades. The shock of being caught with his own words had thrown him completely off guard.

John saw the Prince Regent arrive, but he continued his tirade. "If you think you have been sneaking around our realm as a spy without being noticed, you are wrong. You have been tailed for the past sixteen years. You will pay for your traitorous and treasonable acts. Not to mention all the Englishmen who have died because of the information you passed on to the French while working as a spy before you were discovered. Another friend of yours, Lord Montgomery, Viscount Rathsharp, was caught with incriminating evidence on him. He's not here today but will soon be arrested. You can be assured that he will sing like a bird. Your goose is well and truly cooked." Mr Wilberforce had mentioned this to John as they left the church after the funeral.

Clive realised his clandestine activities were now fully exposed. He wondered if the boy knew of his plan to dispose of him.

While still on his knees, John pushed his shoulder and set him off balance, but he didn't collapse. The young man continued. "Planting me as a changeling to feather your nest so you could remain undetected was used to our advantage. You have been played as a pawn to feed false information to the French, while I was kept safe by the royal family. Your friends, Sir Robert and Lord Montgomery Sharp, will be tried with you. The courts will have the final say over their involvement. You were duped and have been passing false information to the enemy, to the point where we laughed behind your back. You have been fed fabricated deceptions for the past fifteen years and were too stupid to realise. Why do you think the French lost?" John's arm pulled back and then landed another blow on his 'uncle's' face.

The punch following this comment was so hard that Clive collapsed backward and now lay sprawled on his back. His face was mangled and hardly recognisable. He groaned where he lay but was not unconscious.

John wasn't done yet. He realised that many others in the room, other than the prince, were witnessing his actions. In a loud voice, he said, "For you to violate and then murder Lady Victoria while Her Majesty was being buried is despicable on so many levels. I shall ensure that you will be charged with her murder and never again have access to the Templestowe Estate or the funds it holds. I never wanted to be an earl anyway; I don't care if it reverts to the crown. You can have the damned title and everything that goes with it, but I feel that will be short-lived. I foresee a quick end for you, as treason, betraying the crown and the monarchy, and country are each life sentences, not to mention the numerous acts of murder, betrayal, sedition or violating a peeress, take your pick. You will die, and I will watch you dance at the end of a hangman's noose."

John's final action was a kick to the prostrated man's side. He heard the crunch of a rib or two as his foot connected with his nemesis's chest. It was over. He felt a presence beside him. Through his tear-filled amber-coloured eyes, he turned to see the Regent.

Prince George's face was unreadable, but he obviously sympathised with John, not Clive.

John was told a decade ago that the prince had been made aware of the situation and was using Clive to trick his enemies; he was just about to find out whether that was true.

Clive lay groaning on the floor, and no one came to his aid.

The prince laid a restraining hand on John's shoulder. "Enough, lad!" The prince's eyes fell on the prostrated figure before him. However, he asked, "Little Lord John, is Lady Victoria truly dead at this man's hand?"

John nodded. His anger had not burned itself out, but the pain of her loss now threatened to overwhelm him. "Yes, Your Royal Highness; her final words were naming Lord Clive as her attacker. She died in my arms less than ten minutes ago. She was so badly injured that I have no doubt his bloodied clothing will be found in his rooms." John opened his arms and motioned to his blood-spattered garb and hands. Another person came to his side. A caring arm slid around his waist, drawing him away from the stricken man. John didn't look who it was. His gaze was fixed on the traitorous murderer.

The prince gave a nod of thanks to the man and motioned for some of his guards to remove the offending person, who was now groaning on the floor in a pool of gore.

The Regent's words sealed Clive's fate. "Take him to the tower and lock him in chains. We shall deal with him later. Please do not send a doctor, as he does not deserve one. He is a traitor to the crown and shall be treated as one. If he dies, then so be it; it will save us the trouble of a trial. It's a pity we no longer hang, draw, and quarter prisoners, as this scum would be an apt candidate. Even that would be too good for this man, who is the dregs of humanity. He deserves to be keelhauled. I have been aware of his crimes for many years and have used him as a fudge spreader. His usefulness as a pawn is now at an end." His guards roughly lifted the felon. The prince smiled wickedly. "Ensure that Viscount Montgomery Rathsharp and Sir Robert Chesterfield are arrested and kept well apart from this traitor. They were at the funeral, so they will not be far away. They are part of this intrigue and are equally guilty. I have enough evidence to hang them all. Until rescinded, their estate and possessions will be frozen, and their estates will only have access to an allowance that covers bare sustenance. The crown will revisit this at some later date." The Prince Regent gave a flick of his hand as his orders were carried out.

Clive managed to sit up. There was now a large pool of blood on the floor where he had lain. The maids set about cleaning up the mess while the stunned gathering watched in silence. John remained gazing at the gore while the man who had called himself 'uncle' was roughly removed from the room by palace guards.

Before leaving, Lord Clive, although groggy from the beating, managed to say, "As the rightful Earl of Templestowe-Meade, I want John charged for assaulting a peer of the realm."

John was numb, but he didn't care. With Lord Clive arrested, the king declared insane, and the person John had called mother now dead, he realised that he was bereft of place, purpose, and family. He didn't care if he was charged with whatever the courts threw at him. He was done with this immoral place and done with this life; he would rather work in a stable as his real father had.

John was about to turn and leave when William Wilberforce spoke beside him. "John, keep your faith. Some good will come from this. Trust the Lord will see you through. These may be your darkest hours, but know you are never alone."

John had not realised that his best friend's father stood beside him in his great time of need. Where had he been? He was now sad that he had never confided in Mr Wilberforce, but he had wished many times that he could. Now, when he had nothing to lose, it was too late. He merely nodded at the advice. His eyes were awash with salty tears, and his hands were hurting and bloody from the belting he had delivered. The tears now cascaded down his cheeks, but he stood mute. What would happen now? He huskily asked, "What now, sir?"

William said, "Come, John, we will get you cleaned up. I will stay with you and be there for you."

The Regent knew of the loyalty of this lad who served at his parents' side. For nigh on twenty years, Little Lord John had lived with them in the various palaces. The prince took pity on the young man, who was like a little brother. From near the maids cleaning the floor, the prince said, "John, I'm sorry about this situation, especially as it came to a head today of all days. Until Lord Clive is charged and found guilty, he has the right to have you held for assault. As you publicly acknowledged that you are a changeling and he is the rightful Earl of Templestowe-Meade, justice must be done."

John nodded. He was fully aware that he would have to pay the consequences of his actions. "I understand, sir, and thank you."

The prince came to his side and said, "I will vouch for you, lad, so transportation will be your sentence. I will ensure you are not locked up near him. John, the law says, 'If a noble is found guilty of treason or murder, he would be served with a Bill of Attainder, an act of legislature that declared the peer guilty of his crime and affixing him with the verdict of 'corruption of blood,' a metaphorical stain on his peerage, whereby he would lose not only his life but his property and titles, for it will be stripped from him of the right to pass them on to his family or heirs. However, if he has none, they will revert to the crown, rendering the title extinct'." The prince paused as various members of the aristocracy and older family members entered the room, gasping at the carnage they saw. The Regent continued. "I shall enact this law as soon as his case is heard. Lord Clive will be charged with the murder of Lady Victoria and others you mentioned. As you know, I have in my possession the document in the queen's journal, and this will be enough to see him hanged. His guilt is merely a technicality, as I heard his confession to you. However, we must gather more evidence of his guilt for the murders, as neither of the two ladies is present to testify at the trial. I don't suppose you have proof of any sort?" By now, other peers had drawn close to the bloodied young man.

John nodded. "I don't personally have proof, but I know where there is evidence of a quadruple murder. The lake on his estate holds a carriage with at least four bodies. They are my parents, their coachman, and Lady Victoria's infant daughter, Jennifer, who was swapped at birth for me on Lord Clive's instruction so he could remain hidden as a French agent."

A gasp echoed around the room. They had missed that first accusation.

The prince's filthy look silenced them. "Go on. Is there more?"

John nodded. "There was also a man whom Lord Clive ordered killed. That was in Calcutta, the year I was born, in 1797. I believe that the man's name was Captain Malcolm McFarlane. His daughter lived in London with her husband. Their names were Willoughby and Heather Alexander. She died last year, but I know that he was with the East India Company. You may be able to obtain more information from Sir Robert Chesterfield. I believe Lord Clive was a business partner of Captain Alexander. Captain Alexander is also dead now, but his daughter, Martha, isn't. That was the case a few months ago about the reluctant bride and the groom who killed her father."

The prince looked at John, astonished. "He's tied to that story?" Mr Wilberforce had revealed the entire incident to the prince. Miss Martha's accusations during the service had condemned her groom to banishment.

John nodded. The newspaper article hinted that Miss Martha Alexander was the daughter of Captain Willoughby Alexander. John had no intention of passing on the information to her at a ball, but it was now time for some justice. He would see fair play for her grandfather's murder. If only he could find out where she was.

Chapter 8 Journey into the Unknown
1817 London
Martha

Once the church emptied, the congregation milled outside.

The reverend saw Lord Clive Templestowe frisking Willoughby's pockets. When he saw the peer pull out the long strand of milky pearls, the minister demanded that they be handed over for safekeeping along with her father's watch, coin fob, and a billfold full of money. The minister said, "Sir, these belong to Miss Alexander, not her father. Therefore, they are not yours." His bloodied fingers wiggled impatiently, and the pearls landed in his outstretched palm. The other items followed. The reverend's nose was still smarting.

Clive reluctantly dumped them in the clergyman's bloody hand, accompanied by a filthy look. The yard-long strand of milky pearls was perfect. The queen herself would have been happy wearing such perfect gems. He watched with frustration as the opera-length strand was wound around the minister's bloodstained fingers. He had never seen such perfectly matched globes until the day of Martha's presentation.

Most young girls wore a single strand of tiny seed pearls. That night, Martha was unadorned but for her magnificent sea gems. They were priceless, and he wanted them. However, she wore them in a very unusual way. Instead of winding them around her neck in a triple or quadruple loop, she draped them around her slender neck and tied them in a double knot larger than her fist. Her gown had the palest of creamy sheens to it and was made from the most exquisite sheer silk that he had ever seen. Willoughby must have purchased that fabric for her in China. Her underskirt was a gorgeous, embroidered, floral, soft-pink fabric visible through the gossamer-thin silk. The simplicity of her gown was exquisite.

The night of her debut, Clive gazed at the girl he had known since she was little and decided to make a play for her hand. He knew he must wed at some stage, and if she came well-endowed, then so be it. Now, his opportunity was gone.

~

That afternoon, the now-shunned Lord Edgar pressed his case to the magistrate, and Martha was taken from the safety of the minister's home and escorted to Newgate prison.

She demanded a change of clothing and was permitted to access her luggage. She then changed into a brown riding habit and a warm cloak, which consisted of a dark skirt and blouse. She chose this outfit as it was made from a more durable fabric than the muslin gowns she normally wore. Thinking of what was ahead, she thought she could sell the beads on the bloodied wedding gown. She rolled it into a ball and carried it with her.

Knowing that she would not be permitted anything else, she asked the minister and his wife, Reverend and Mrs Tuddenham, if they would store her possessions until she knew the outcome of the trial.

They willingly agreed and also mentioned that the pearls that had been in her father's pocket had been returned to them for safekeeping.

~

Summer faded into winter, and Martha wallowed in self-pity in the squalid conditions of Newgate prison while awaiting her trial.

The Tuddenhams wrote to her and assured her that her and her father's possessions were safe. They had cleaned out the rented house and packed everything that belonged to the Alexanders. Even her mother's gowns were placed into storage.

Their latest letter mentioned that a friend would seek her out when she next visited the gaol. Her name was Mrs Elizabeth Fry, and she, along with a group of other well-meaning women, visited the female prisoners and supplied some of the necessary items for their survival.

Martha had been arrested before her monthly flow started, so she had forgotten to get her menstrual bag. With a chuckle, she looked at the expensive gown. She tore the fabric of her crystal-beaded wedding dress, which she had worn on the day that the earl had forced her to wear it for their failed marriage. After removing the faceted beads, it would be used for her menstrual rags. She laughed at that thought. The crystals from the gown would be used to purchase items while she remained in prison. She was thankful she had not conceived a child.

Reverend Tuddenham sent news of her father's burial.

As a business client for many years, Lord Clive Templestowe had the decency to ensure that Willoughby Alexander was buried next to her mother.

The reverend did the service himself and waived all the fees, though he accepted a hefty donation from Lord Clive. He held back enough to pay for a matching headstone for the burial plot.

Martha wept with relief that her father was not placed in a pauper's grave. She found that the brief time spent with the minister and his wife revealed another side of the church to her. These people were loving and caring, and Mrs Tuddenham explained that they were doing the work the good Lord wished them to do. They planted a seed of faith.

As Martha had spent little time on land, she had little experience with the church as an organisation. Her parents certainly took her to church with them whenever possible, wherever they had been, but since her mother died the year before, they had not darkened the door of one since her mother's funeral. For some reason, it comforted her to know her parents were buried in consecrated ground, although she didn't fully understand what that meant.

~

Winter came and went, and by April 1818, Martha was shivering in the filthy cells of Newgate prison.

Her cloak had worn thin, and the conditions were horrific. Thankfully, the genders had been separated nearly four years earlier, but the warders still caused problems for some women.

If any women wished for extra food or clothing, the guards accepted payment as they saw fit. Their carnal activities were often in full sight of the inmates, though some younger women were still taken by force. Many girls found themselves carrying a child and not knowing which guard was the father.

Thankfully, Martha was not violated, as she managed to extract the crystals she had taken from her wedding gown and sold them to supplement her food supply. She still had some left.

The common women's felon ward backed onto the passage leading into the courthouse, meaning she was housed very close to the courtrooms. She presumed her case had been forgotten.

Mrs Tuddenham was her only visitor, although she had received a note from William Wilberforce, and he reassured her that he was watching over her case.

~

Eventually, her name was listed for her court appearance.

Mrs Tuddenham brought her a clean gown and washed and dressed her hair. "I shall be in the gallery, dear, but the reverend will be permitted in the seats nearby. Stand firm, dearie. I know that your faith is challenged, but I believe that some good will come from this."

Martha nodded, but she didn't believe the lady's words. What good could possibly come out of this mess? She was now alone in the world. Neither parent had siblings. She had no extended family to turn to.

Mrs Tuddenham waited with her until the turnkey came for the women facing trial that day. Mrs Tuddenham held Martha's hand, and this simple act gave her strength. As they arrived at the courtroom door, the minister's wife said, "You can do this, lassie. We will be here for you. Hold your head high."

The courtroom was packed.

Martha wondered why until a cheer erupted when she entered.

She received a standing ovation from the gallery, and she froze in shock. "Why?"

Mrs Tuddenham said, "You have supporters, dear. Many of them are the poor from the Rookeries. This man and his vile friends have harmed them and their children. Since your actions to his, um, wiffles, the earl and his friends have not visited there; they have now been ousted from society; it is no longer a safe place for them to visit. Some peers have even left London." She gave a small chuckle. "Your words as a gentlewoman carry much weight. These folk know that the court will listen to you and your claims. So hold your head high, as you speak for many people here. Today will be his first public appearance since your failed wedding. He is now *persona non grata* to all in London. His proclivities make him shunned. Doors have closed to him." She shuddered in disgust.

Martha smiled to herself and raised a hand to wave to the massive gathering of supporters. As she did so, another enormous cheer erupted. She stood up a little taller.

Mrs Tuddenham said farewell and left to join the unwashed masses above them.

Martha sat through two cases where the poor woman did not even have a chance to respond to the charges against her. Forewarned, she knew what to expect. She knew she would be found guilty, even though she stole nothing.

When her case was called, she expected the same treatment. However, those in the rogues' gallery demanded justice for her. The calls started as soon as her name was called.

How did they even know what she said in the church, and why were there so many here to support her?

With over two hundred angry peasants calling for her release, the judge was flummoxed about how to react. He was fully aware that he needed to continue with the case, and that meant he would not throw the book at this slip of a girl. His notes said she was only sixteen when arrested and that her groom had killed her father in the middle of their marriage service. No wonder she refused to wed him. This would not be a simple case of theft. He smiled. This case would be one he would remember for some time.

The white-wigged judge called the court to order. When all was silent, the judge checked to see that both parties were in the courtroom.

Happily, they were both present.

He motioned for proceedings to begin.

The Earl of Oxenborough-Thorpe stood and called for the charges to be enforced.

The gallery erupted with jeers of hatred towards the shamed peer.

The judge banged his gavel on the small sounding block and called for order. It didn't work, so he smashed his hammer onto the timber ledge of the dock.

The echo of the loud sound did the trick.

When everyone was settled, the judge began this unusual case.

Martha had not seen Lord Edgar until he spoke. The now-overweight man hardly looked the same debonair lord she had last seen nearly a year ago, when he was dressed in his wedding attire. He was now flabby and dishevelled.

As she listened to his voice, she shuddered.

The earl's lawyer read the charges.

Martha had not even met the man supposedly representing her.

The legal fellow looked at her, and she shook her head and waved him away. He sat down and shrugged.

When the judge asked if she had pleaded guilty, she replied for herself. She stood and spoke loudly. "No, I'm innocent. I stole nothing, but he stole my innocence."

The judge accurately understood the meaning of this comment: "Miss, do you mean to say you were alone in his house at night?"

Martha nodded and said, "I was your honour. I was there to find a document that my father had been forced to sign in a drunken stupor. I am no pawn to be bartered over the turn of a card. What is more, Lord Edgar cheated while playing cards with my father, who was rolling drunk." She pointed to the earl. "He boasted to me that he marked the cards."

An audible gasp came not just from the judge, but also from all the jury and many in the gallery. Someone upstairs called, "Wot ya expect from the lying, cheating, bugger like him? I hear he does animals, too. Did ya know that?"

A missile followed the words and caught the earl on the back of his head. The raw egg hit its target.

The earl swore and turned to look at the gallery, giving them a filthy look.

Someone up in the gallery cackled with laughter at his discomfort.

The judge called Martha to his bench. He wished to question her privately.

She came reluctantly but would not answer his questions quietly.

When he asked if the earl had violated her, as he took her comment to mean just that, she turned and spoke to the gallery, repeating his question.

She addressed the multitude in a loud voice. "The judge asked me if Lord Edgar deflowered me; he did, and yes, I am ruined, but

I still refused to marry him when he quite literally dragged me to the altar. My father came to my rescue, and so my groom punched my father during the church service." Pointing to the earl, she said, "That man killed my papa in the church and then had the nerve to charge me with theft. I would rather live my life in the Antipodes as a fallen woman and convict than be wed to that murderous animal." Her years of reading now paid off. "According to the case in 1811 of William Hodgson, who was found guilty of the 'ravishment' of nineteen-year-old Harriet Halliday, I could press my case against him. However, I know he would win as he's an earl, and I'm now just a fallen gentlewoman. It was because of the earl that I now have that stigma. If I'm sent away as a convict, at least he would never get his grubby hands on my person ever again."

She didn't even turn back to the judge. Without waiting for permission, she flounced back to the prisoner's dock.

The judge admired this girl's spunk. She had spirit and would take no nonsense from anyone. "Miss, I understand you have been mistreated, but the law must be upheld. Your action in the church of applying untoward upward pressure to the earl's um..." his cocked eyebrow showed that he was amused. He crossed his own legs protectively behind his bench.

Martha, now back in the prisoner's dock, finished his sentence. "Crotch, sir, or better still, wiffles, is the word I believe you are looking for, Your Honour. Yes, I kicked him in his private parts as hard as I could, with my pointed-toed shoes that he insisted I wear. This was in response to..." She pointed to the earl, "...him murdering my father in the church on what was supposed to have been my wedding day, not to mention his forced violation of my person. The pointed tips of my shoes drove home my refusal to wed him. He ravished me the night before to try to force my hand. I would kick him again in a heartbeat if you will allow me to, as I'm sure many upstairs in the gallery would approve of said action."

Again, the courtroom erupted in laughter.

Martha stood and waited patiently for the judge to regain control of his court.

Her butter-wouldn't-melt-in-her-mouth expression nearly made him smile. The elderly, be-wigged man bit his top lip and made a concerted effort not to laugh aloud. He had seen many men in the room cross their legs protectively. Some on the jury were not as successful at muting their jocularity as they covered their mouths with handkerchiefs.

Eventually, he succumbed. Chortles erupted from that area of the courtroom. Her wide-eyed look of pure innocence eventually made the judge nearly double up in laughter. Oh, how he wished he could release her, but he must uphold the law. He tried to cover his mirth with a false sneeze. However, he needed to keep her away from her attacker. He wished he could charge the unscrupulous earl, but no one had brought charges against him... yet. Lifting his eyes to the gallery, he wondered how long that would last. He could act on her accusations, and may do so after her transportation. Her words had been issued in court and had been recorded. He wrote a note to charge the earl if he confessed to his actions. He knew such a vile charge carried the death penalty. He hoped the earl would trip up in his comments.

After brushing his hand across his nose a few times to hide his smirk, he said, "Yes, those, miss. However, as I said, the law must be upheld. You attacked a peer of the realm, and the punishment for that is up to twenty-five years of imprisonment. But, miss, you have not been charged with that. The charge against you is break and enter with intent to steal."

Martha gasped. "Twenty-five years for defending myself?" She was horrified. "Where are my rights? I was only trying to take a document that was ours. I stole nothing."

The judge shrugged. He cleared his throat and continued. "As you admitted that you were definitely in Lord Edgar's house with the intent to take something, I have no choice but to find you guilty. However, because of extenuating circumstances, which include the death of your father, I will give you a minimum sentence of seven years. I will also instruct that you are to be transported on the next merchant ship departing from London and taken to Sydney in the Antipodes, where you will serve your sentence. This means that you will not be incarcerated with the other unfortunates who would travel on a convict transport. You will be assigned to a family travelling to the colony and serve as a maid to them until you arrive. Reverend Tuddenham, can I leave that in your hands? Mrs Fry will be able to assist you in choosing such a family."

The minister stood and nodded. "Willingly, Your Honour," he said with a smile. This was the best outcome possible for Martha.

In essence, she would be given free passage to a new life. She had no future here anyway, as her violation had been made public.

She was ruined, but he had set aside some money, her pearls and her father's valuables for her to establish herself in a new life. Martha smiled. She had been sentenced to seven years for break-and-enter, but not theft or assault. She almost danced with delight. However, she politely said, "Thank you, Your Honour." Then she bobbed a curtsy.

The judge nodded his approval, his brows lifted in astonishment at her polite acceptance of his judgement. He dismissed the case. Sadly, she did not give him a chance to question the earl. His eyes followed the slim figure as she walked towards the exit door to the gaol.

As she arrived at the door out of the courtroom, she turned to the gallery and gave them a curtsy. Another cheer erupted.

She heard a masculine gasp, followed by an angry shout.

She and the guards turned back to see what had caused it.

The guards were unsure if this was a plan to escape, so they took her arms and held her.

In sheer amazement, the three watched as the gallery began to rain eggs aimed at the disgraced, dishevelled, now obese peer.

The earl was pelted by dozens and dozens of raw eggs, many of which were rotten. The stench was overwhelming. The earl was drenched in the gooey substance and was cursing and abusing the crowd.

Martha giggled, then twisted and loosened the guards' arms to see the judge and jury's faces. They were all trying hard not to laugh. However, the courtroom would need to be cleaned before more cases could be heard.

Before she was out of earshot, the judge adjourned the court.

Wiggling free from the guards, Martha all but skipped back to her cell.

~

In May 1818, a laden merchant ship was departing for Sydney, and a family with three children was *en route* to the same destination. Martha was assigned to this family.

Two days before sailing, one of the guards from the gaol escorted her to the vessel.

The Tuddenhams met her at the dock where the ship was waiting. Mrs Tuddenham introduced her to the lady of the family, Mrs Louise Beattie. Her children ranged from six to twelve.

Four other convict girls were to travel on the same vessel.

Another family, the Johnsons, had some of the girls assigned to them.

Mrs Tuddenham took Martha aside before leaving and said, "Dearie, I asked if I could send along your possessions on this ship, but they will not permit us to include them. I shall send them when I can find a vessel to take them as cargo. Write and let me know where you are. I will need to use some of the money in your papa's billfold to pay for the passage."

Martha nodded. In the short time she had known this woman, she had learned to love her. "I will write if I am able. Thank you, Mrs Tuddenham. Could you sell Mama's pearls and use that money to send my things if there is not enough? Keep the rest for your work in the parish." With that, Martha hugged her.

The guard escorted the Tuddenhams from the ship.

Martha was not permitted on the deck until the ship was out of the river. She and the other four girls sorted the cabins and occupied the children.

~

A week after setting foot on the ship, they hit the open water of the English Channel. It had taken that long to coast down the Thames River with the ebb and flow of the tide.

Martha explained to her companions why the anchor was dropped and hauled aboard every six hours. She was delighted to feel the deck move under her feet again.

Once at sea, while the others were prostrated with seasickness, Martha stood on the foredeck as close as she could safely get to the bowsprit and felt the salt spray on her face once more.

The salt of the waves mixed with her tears as she remembered how many times she had stood in this spot on her father's ship.

A voice behind her made her jump, and the sound of a familiar voice made her spin around. "Now there, Miss Martha; no more tears from you. Your papa would not like to see you weep."

She gasped. "Joe, what are you doing here?" She had last seen him on the dock on the day before her father died. She greeted her shadow with a hug. His visage was enough to scare a pirate, but she knew him well.

Joe gave her a toothy grin. His teeth were like a picket fence, as every second tooth was missing. "I could ask you the same thing, Miss Martha. Where's your papa?"

Martha's face almost melted. "He's dead, Joe. The man who collected us on the wharf killed him the next day. It was accidental, and it occurred in church, but dead is dead, and I'm now alone." She released a long sigh.

Joe was shocked. "Oh, Miss Martha, that's real bad for you, so you are completely alone? 'N' I heard your mama died last year."

Martha nodded again. "She died of the sweating sickness she picked up on our last trip. That's why we didn't go on the last journey with you. Captain Scotts was a good man. I was sorry to hear of his death on his first voyage. Papa didn't cope with Mama's death and started drinking. Things went from bad to worse, but they are together again."

Joe grabbed onto a rope as a large wave approached. "Brace, miss."

Martha had grown up hearing this call. She realised a big wave was about to hit. They would probably get wet.

They rode out the subsequent three waves before continuing their conversation.

Now drenched, Joe asked, "Wot are you doing here then, miss? Is you a passenger?"

Martha shook her head. "No, Joe, I'm a convict on my way to Sydney. I was sentenced to seven years for breaking and entering the earl's house. Things went crazy the day after we met you on the dock."

Joe was more than shocked. "Cor, Miss Martha, that's rotten for you! Well, just know I'm on board if you need me at all." He looked around him and said, "I'm about to go on watch, so I gotta go. I'll see you later, and we can chat about old times." He tipped his cap and returned to duty.

Martha remained at her favourite spot for about half an hour until the seas became too rough. She could feel a storm brewing, so she decided discretion was needed and headed indoors.

~

The journey southward was pleasant for Martha. She had hardly anything to do as the family lay moaning on their bunks. Having spent much of her life on a ship's deck, she relished the wind in her hair.

During one stormy day, she was in the right place at the right time.

When another rogue wave approached, the cabin boy had just

delivered a snack to the captain at the helm.

She heard a call of, "Brace, brace, brace," and grabbed a rope to hold tightly.

The wall of water approaching was enormous.

The young lad was caught out on the open deck and would have been swept overboard but for Martha's quick thinking. Young Charlie Green was washed off his feet and heading for the gunnels.

Martha was on the main deck in front of the cabin doors when the wave hit. She reached out and grabbed his shirt as he slid past her position. She then grasped his braces and held them tightly.

Once the wave had cleared, she flung open the hatch and slammed it shut behind them. Both were safe. Drenched but otherwise uninjured.

Eight-year-old Charlie was sheet-white with fear. He threw himself into her arms. But for her fast thinking, he would now be wallowing in the churning seas and on the way down to Neptune's Grave.

That particular storm blew itself out four days later.

~

The families finally emerged from their cabins two weeks after a stomach-churning start to their trip. All had lost a significant amount of weight but were otherwise none the worse.

The five convict girls set to work cleaning their cabins and entertaining the children. Sarah, Kitty, Vicki, and Milly rounded out the five convict passengers.

For the next fifty days, the seas remained calm.

Sarah Hallowell was the eldest of the convicts, and she and Martha worked with the Beattie family. She admitted that she had not been seasick but was expecting a child. She was a few months along, and the baby was due soon after they docked in Sydney. She didn't know who the father of her baby was, as she had been violated in the dark while awaiting transportation.

Martha comforted the frightened girl, knowing full well that she could have been in the same situation had she conceived when the earl had his way with her; she would have been due in a month if that had occurred.

The pair admitted her condition to Mrs Beattie, who then comforted the weeping maid. "Dear girl, I gather this was not consensual?"

Sarah shook her head.

The kind lady continued. "Does the father know of your condition?"

Sarah shrugged. "I don't know which one he are, missus. I got took by a mob of young maggot-pie, cock-teasers, and they each did their thing on me. I got done over proper like, and they left me for dead. I don't even know who took me to the doctor, but I'm mighty glad that I was found."

Mrs Beattie drew the weeping girl into her arms. She looked at Martha for an explanation of the unfamiliar terms.

Martha knew many worse names for such disrespectful men. "Ma'am, being called 'a maggot pie' means they are the lowest form of fellow. A 'cockteaser,' well, there's no polite term, but suffice it to say they use their male appendage on whomever they wish, regardless of the female person's status. The word is often accompanied by a phrase like 'grinding your wiffles into a whore'."

Mrs Beattie swallowed in shock. "How do you know such vile terms, if I may ask?"

Martha chuckled. "My papa was a sea captain. I was born on board Papa's ship. Mama and I used to travel with him wherever he went. One of our crewmen, Joe Brand, is on this voyage as crew. I love the sea, but I came to know our crew well and all their cant. When I was old enough, I assisted our cook in feeding our crew. I love the wild and angry moods of the sea, as well as the tranquil nights when the lights play in the water and the stars in the skies above. Having said that, my father was a gentleman. I have all the usual ridiculous skills a young lady in society should have, and I was presented at court. I play the piano quite well, sew, and sing, and I have even dabbled in watercolours. However, I can also feed a hungry crew of one hundred and fifty."

Sarah's mouth was open in shock. She'd been far too sick and frightened to speak much to any of her cramped bunkmates.

Mrs Beattie asked the question she had been far too afraid to voice. "Dear girl, with such a background, how did you end up here?"

Martha was tossed by the roll of a wave but hung on until the ship steadied. She said, "Ahh, yes, well, that is a tale in itself." She proceeded to retell her saga.

The listening pair gasped at the end of her tale.

Sarah said, "He... he... did you over too?"

Martha nodded. "Then he had the audacity to charge me with

attempted theft, break and enter. I received a seven-year term for my crime rather than the assault of a peer. The judge seemed to pity me and sent me on this ship rather than wait until next year for a female transport vessel. Thus ends my saga." She gave a pert curtsy and chuckled.

Sarah almost whispered her question. "How do you cope with knowing you are ruined?"

Martha caught the nod from her mistress. She wanted to know as well. "Well, it's like this. I'm alive; my father and the earl's first three wives are not. I'm a survivor, not a victim. It's all in your attitude, Sarah dear. Believe me, I felt remorse for venturing out that night, but if I had not, the ending would have been the same. The only other outcome was for me to be married to the filthy, murderous man, who liked both little girls and boys, and some said animals, as well. As I told him in court, I would rather live my life ruined than be killed at his hand. That was the alternative. Papa and I had tried to escape, and that failed. Ask Joe, he was there and tried to help us."

Mrs Beattie turned back to Sarah. "Dear, when do you think you are due?"

Sarah shrugged. "About Christmas or a bit after."

Chapter 9   Scrubbing out the Past
John becomes Jack
1818

With the queen's passing and Christmas shutting things down in London, John's court case was delayed.

Once the festive season was over, justice was administered swiftly to John and his so-called uncle.

John was tried and found guilty of assault. Clive didn't appear in court, but his letter was damning. Witnesses were called, and John was sentenced to fourteen years with transportation. Considering the usual sentence for assaulting a peer was twenty-five years, his sentence was light.

Clive's trial followed a few days later.

As the prince revealed on that fateful day, he held the queen's letter reporting the treason, but that was not enough, as it was only hearsay. The courts needed more evidence to find him guilty.

Chesterfield and Rathsharp sang like birds. They each supplied the information on where to find the required evidence that eventually convicted Clive. The lake at Clive's home was drained, and the remains of the coach, two horses and three adults and two small children's bodies in the coach and also a driver, were discovered in the mud.

Rathsharp told the prince who they were. Jack's family was dead. A newborn baby's skeleton had been found in the arms of a female body, plus a small child's skeleton sat huddled in the arms of another female passenger. The maid's uniform identified her as Rachel, Lady Victoria's missing maid. The doors of the coach had been nailed closed, and the driver had a head injury.

The discovery of the bodies, along with Queen Charlotte's letter, sealed the earl's fate. Clive was found guilty of multiple murders and sentenced to be hanged. Due to his co-conspirators' information, Sir Robert and Lord Montgomery were banished to their estates for the terms of their natural lives. All their funds were frozen, and the crown administered their estates. They had to grow their own food. Most of their servants left. Each estate had only minimal staff willing to remain working with traitors.

John had not known about the older child found with his parents and realised it was probably his sibling. That knowledge knocked him off kilter. However, he was not surprised to hear the extra person was confirmed to be his mother's missing maid, Rachel. Her monogrammed uniform revealed her identity. Clive confessed that she had been John's aunt.

John was reeling at this news. He was taken from his solitary cell on the day of the hanging. He promised on the day of the queen's funeral that he would watch Clive dance at the end of the hangman's rope. The prince permitted him to fulfil that promise.

Lord Clive saw John's arrival from up on the scaffold and sneered at him. However, he remained silent.

John's face showed no emotion. His heart hurt as the last person he loved was gone. Clive had personally murdered the woman whom he called mother, as well as the woman who had given birth to him. He was numb, having only discovered the entire truth about his family that morning.

The noose was placed around Clive's neck, and John closed his eyes. He didn't want to see Clive die, even though he had caused so much destruction.

William Wilberforce and Bill stood on either side of John as that part of the young man's life drew to a close.

John expected to feel something, but he didn't. He still could not believe that one man's lust and greed had caused so much damage to so many. The countless numbers of English soldiers who had died because Clive had supplied battle movements to France during the war ate at him.

John and now everyone else knew that Clive Templestowe, Earl of Templestowe-Meade, had blood on his hands for at least seven deaths. The one death he was personally responsible for was that of Lady Victoria. However, Clive received only six life sentences, as the seventh death could not be proved, even though Sir Robert had corroborated the rumour of his involvement in Captain McFarlane's murder; it occurred in a foreign country, so the crown did not press charges for that murder.

Then came the sentencing for the treason. All the murder terms were as nothing, as he was to be taken out and hanged that day for the betrayal of the crown and country. His official crime was treason.

John waited until the body stopped jumping like a puppet before turning away silently. It was over; he was safe from his uncle's ire, but at what cost? After a few steps, he paused, bent over double and took a deep breath. He did not wish to be reminded of the man he had just watched go to face his eternal judgement. God could deal with him now.

John could walk no further as his eyes filled with tears and his heart thumped. He stumbled and found his arms instantly grabbed. A Wilberforce male firmly held each arm.

Mr Wilberforce said, "Come, lad. We have the prince's permission to walk before we return you to your cell in the Tower of London. Call it a leave pass."

John nodded. This man was the father figure he missed; Bill was like a younger brother. As they led him away from the grizzly sight, John's eyes swam, and he stumbled often.

Mr Wilberforce led the way and, after some distance, said, "In here, lad." He opened a door and led him into what looked like a dark hole.

John trusted him, so he followed him inside, unconcerned about where he was. He never had the time to discover London, so he knew nothing of the warren of parliamentary apartments. He knew many of London's peers by sight and their names, but he had never socialised with any of them. John was all but a ghost; seen but never heard. At the palace, he was almost a servant. Nearly everyone ignored him but the royal family. To them, John was much closer than the staff; he was almost family. Always on hand, should they need him.

Many peers, such as Lord Charles Lockley, His Grace the Duke of Gracemere, were kind to him, but he was kind to everyone. His beautiful, much younger wife was often at his side. Lord Charles would often stop to ask how Lady Victoria was and never failed to smile at him as though he were an equal. Her Grace, Susanna, was a close friend of Lady Victoria's. Lord Charles had spent many years at the king's side as Lord in Waiting. John knew that about the time he was born, Lord Charles married and retired to the country, though he still appeared in London for Parliament. John met him because of his friendship with Mr Wilberforce. His Grace was another close friend of Mr Wilberforce, so they had met often. Both were men of faith.

Another door opened, and John followed his mentor into what was obviously a man's den. Mr Wilberforce said, "I don't belong to any of the popular gentlemen's clubs; therefore, I keep rooms here, so I have a central place to stay. Bill often sleeps here."

John was still somewhat dazed with the day's outcome and nodded in reply. He was beyond words, so he just stared at his friends.

Bill handed him a glass of some brown liquid.

Without even sniffing it, John tossed it back. It burnt all the way down, but he held his glass out for a refill. The chink of crystal on glass echoed around the room. The contents vanished, and another one followed.

John rarely imbibed, but today was not a usual day.

Once gone, John sat gazing into the empty glass. After some minutes, he raised his eyes to meet his friend's father's loving face. "Sir, what's to happen now? Have you heard when my transportation is to occur?"

Mr Wilberforce shook his head. "No, laddie, but that's not what this is all about. I know today will have rocked your faith. For the man you have known all your life as 'uncle' to meet his maker on the day you gain your majority is not forgotten by us. We know it's not a day to celebrate, but it is remembered. Acknowledge it, and then you hopefully can move on."

John nodded. "I no longer have Lady Victoria, a home or a job, but I still have my faith. I shall not let you down, sir. I shall stand strong. However, I must confess that I have been aware of Clive's duplicity for most of my life. I was never permitted to tell you for security reasons. I was nine when the queen and Mama overheard the plot." After revealing what he knew, John wished to put the past behind him; the only way to do so was to leave himself behind. An idea was slowly taking shape in his mind: "Sir, I need to reinvent myself, but how? Would a name change work? My real name is John Turner, and I no longer wish to be known as John Templestowe-Meade. Jack is a common derivative of John. How about that?"

Mr Wilberforce was surprised by the smile and said, "Jack is a good, strong name, one that can mean 'may God protect'."

John teared up again. "He's done a great job doing that so far for me, but He failed both Mama and my parents."

Mr Wilberforce's head shook. "No, lad, He didn't fail them; an evil man did. God doesn't kill people; bad people do."

John frowned. He didn't understand.

Bill came and sat beside him. "Did Charles Blomfield not explain things to you?"

John frowned and shook his head. "Explain what?"

Bill chuckled. "About sin and the fallen world! You know the Bible stories, and putting them in context. I shall ask Papa to put it together for you. It's why bad things happen to good people. Lady Victoria was a good woman with a strong faith, and she certainly did not deserve to die. Do you really think she will end up in the same place as Lord Clive?"

John shook his head. "No, but I'm not God. I don't have to judge them. I would condemn him to eternal damnation if I could."

Mr Wilberforce's face showed just how proud he was of his son. "Okay, fine, I will start at the very beginning. Settle back, as you are in for a story that has taken thousands of years to get to where we are today."

John nodded. "I believe in God already, but I'm no theologian. You'd better simplify things for me. You know, dumb things down."

Mr Wilberforce chuckled. "I won't need to, lad, as the story is simple. Theologians only complicate things. We'll start at the very beginning." He inhaled and made himself comfortable. "Two words sum up the first chapters of the Bible, and they cover much." He saw a surprise cross John's face. "No, don't worry, I will not go through the Bible word by word. But the first few chapters of Genesis need explanation. You see, the Bible is not numerous separate books but only one book written by many authors over thousands of years."

John gasped. No one had ever told him that before. However, he remained quiet other than murmuring a soft, "Okay, go on."

Mr Wilberforce gave a nod. "Fine. Those two words are 'God made,' and He did make everything: the stars, the heavenly realms, the earth and everything under the earth, including the angels and mankind. Not only did He make them all, but He made them perfect. Verse one says,

'In the beginning, God created the heaven and the earth'. But at the end of that same chapter, in verse 31, it says,

'*And God saw everything that he had made, and, behold, it was very good. And the evening and the morning were the sixth day. However, that's when things started going wrong*'."

Mr Wilberforce looked for a reaction and saw John gesture for him to continue. He did. "In the next chapter, in verse seventeen, we see Adam and Eve living in a beautiful garden where they do not have to work for the food they need. God had given them just one rule.

'*But of the tree of the knowledge of good and evil, thou shalt not eat of it: for in the day that thou eatest thereof, thou shalt surely die*."

Mr Wilberforce raised eyebrows and made John smile.

John said, "I could cope with just one rule."

Mr Wilberforce and Bill chuckled together. "If only it were that simple, but another character enters the story. Lucifer was one of the angels that God made in the first week. Like us, the angels are given Free Will. Lucifer challenged God, and then he, along with one-third of all the angels, was cast out of the heavenly realm. They were banished to what we call the underworld. This was the first sin: thinking he was better than God."

John gasped. "I thought Eve's disobedience was the first sin?"

Mr Wilberforce shook his head but then said, "No, that was humanity's first sin. Lucifer's was pride. Anyway, jumping ahead to that bit… Eve was tempted by Lucifer, who took the form of a snake. She gave the fruit to Adam, and both had their eyes open to the world around them. They could have eaten from the Tree of Everlasting Life, but they didn't. Mankind sinned and shut the door on God. God didn't shut them out; it was the other way around."

John's eyes were as big as saucers, and he listened intently. He'd heard the Bible stories, but no one had ever put it all together before. He asked, "Then what?"

Mr Wilberforce said, "Then God gave them a way back to Him. He promised a pathway back to Him and a way to restore the perfection they had broken in the garden. Can you guess what that pathway was?"

John's brows furrowed, then cleared. "Jesus! That's how He fits in."

Mr Wilberforce nodded. "Yes, God sent His only Son to make a pathway back to Him. But to do that, Jesus had to deal with sin. He could do that because Jesus is not only God's Son as fully man, but He is also fully God. Only by a perfect man dying and taking our sins upon Him could that door be unlocked."

It was as though the scales on John's eyes fell off. "That's why Jesus died! I had no idea that the Bible books were so closely linked. I knew it was more than a story. I never doubted that, but Mama never tied them all together for me. I pray, but really had no understanding of the entire meaning."

Mr Wilberforce said, "Ahh, but we're not finished yet. You see, we now come to us; not just you, me and Bill, but all of humanity. We have a decision to make. It's not really two questions but one with two options. This is where it becomes personal. It's our turn to be involved. We must decide for ourselves whether to follow God's path, believing in our forgiveness through Him. Or, we reject God's offer and follow our own will; that is, following the devil or Lucifer. That is what Lord Clive did. He rejected what he knew was right. By doing that, he took good people down with him. That's why Lady Victoria died. It's why many Englishmen died in the French wars. We knew there was a spy before his identity was revealed, but the aristocracy never guessed that it was one of their peers. I now know that. Through Clive, their majesties fed the enemy false information. I'm quite sure that after many conversations with Lady Victoria that she is now in the Lord's presence."

John murmured as though to himself, "Mama was a victim of sin."

Bill nodded. He had sat listening to his father beside his friend. "Yes, my friend! Lady Victoria was a good person. She had true faith and lived a good life, but I think her life would have been different if Lord Clive had lived and become the rightful earl. Everything he owned is now forfeited to the crown. Her husband died before he could settle anything on her, and Clive certainly didn't make any provision for her. With the queen dead, neither of you had a home. John, Lady Victoria had nothing except you."

John nodded. He knew that. It had bothered him. It was why he had gone to see her after the queen's funeral. He was going to ask where they would go.

Mr Wilberforce continued, "Well, my young friend. It's not just about believing in God and Jesus. Satan, as we call Lucifer, believes in God as well. He knows God exists but refuses to obey Him. No, we must live our lives for God, resisting temptation, just as the Lord's Prayer says. Remember, we also must repent of our sins; only then will we be forgiven."

John nodded again. "I can do that. I believe I've tried to live a good life, but I will now understand my decision-making."

The older man said, "You need to ask for forgiveness for the other things, too. Lad, you did belt Lord Clive to a pulp. The kick at the end was unnecessary, as he was already down. A few of the other blows should have been avoided, but he certainly deserved most of the other strikes."

John blanched. "Should I not have challenged him?"

Mr Wilberforce said, "Oh, John, I'm not saying your anger was wrong. It cleared the air in such a way that Lord Clive received instant justice. His comments, or lack thereof, condemned him. His admission of violating Lady Victoria was enough to seal his fate, but the queen's journal that the prince produced condemned the traitor. Remember that even Jesus exhibited justifiable anger, so there is no problem with your anger. Jesus cast the moneychangers out of the temple as they were desecrating the house of God. Another time, a fig tree perished because it bore no fruit, but you must keep your temper under control. You must continue to stand for what you know is right, even if it threatens your earthly existence. Your heavenly reward will await you even if your life on this earth is unjust."

John released a long sigh of relief. This last comment made him think deeply. The older man's eyes settled on John's. "If you had not stopped when the prince put his hand on your shoulder, then I would question your motives. But you held your blows when told and left the guilty man to be judged by the authorities."

John nodded. "But where does that leave me now? I still have nothing, not even my name. Hence, my wish to change who I am." He grinned. "I presume John is my real name, but today, John Templestowe-Meade will die. Jack Turner is my name from this day forward. Do you think I could write to the prince and arrange to have my name changed before I'm shipped out? It will be a completely fresh start."

Bill nodded his approval. "Jack, yes, it suits you too. And so you shall be known. You are of age now, and I think a new start is in order. Put your old life behind you, my friend."

Mr Wilberforce relaxed into his winged armchair. "Fine, then, Jack, I want you to remember this. When the doors close on you as they have, that's when God works best. When you have nothing else left in your life, God is still there, working hard for you. He is up to something. Trust Him. The Regent said that you will not be hanged, as many others have been for a similar crime. He was correct. Getting only fourteen years is amazing. However, as you know, the judge said, it's unlikely that you will remain in England, so think of what you can do in the new colony, as that is probably where you will be sent."

The confused young man asked, "But what can I do? I've been a royal pageboy most of my life. I can fetch and carry, but I lack the necessary skills to do anything else. Oh, I do love horses. I spent a fair bit of time in the royal stables."

Mr Wilberforce smiled and said, "Then work with that, young man."

"Huh?" John said.

Mr Wilberforce shrugged. "What about an inn? I mean, running one as your real folks did. I believe the prince owes you back pay, and he mentioned to me that you will receive some compensation for your tireless service to his parents. I believe he wrote to the governor of New South Wales as soon as the sentence was handed down. Accept it gracefully and make a new life for yourself. Having lost the bible Charles gave you, I shall ensure you have a Bible on whatever ship you travel on. Teach others the faith. If nothing else, that will bring purpose to your life."

John nodded and replied, "I will, sir. I also promise you that I will keep up my prayers, seek the truth, and live my faith."

Mr Wilberforce slapped his thighs. "Do that, laddie! Now, we must return you to your current abode before we, too, are arrested for harbouring a felon." He chuckled, then added, "I do ask that you keep in contact and let us know where God leads you. I believe that you will have an interesting life, and I know my Bill wishes to keep in contact. Letters to the Antipodes will not be frequent, but our prayers will be constant. Will you do that for us?"

Now spiritually refreshed, the overwhelmed young man nodded. "I will, sir. If I have access to writing materials."

The three stood to leave, but before they did, John was enfolded in two bear hugs.

They had to walk a few blocks back to his cell in the prison. As they meandered, Mr Wilberforce said, "Oh, I forgot to mention. The prince had all your possessions packed up, along with a few things that Lady Victoria loved. Once you are settled, please let me know, and I'll ship them to you. He personally oversaw the packing of certain items, like Lady Victoria's diaries and other personal mementos. He wished you to have them. As she had no other family, he thought you would want them."

John knew of those small leather-bound tomes, and he would value them. They contained a journal of his young life. "Thank you indeed. I will value those greatly. She was an only child, and neither of her parents had any siblings. She had no other family. It's why we were so close. We only had each other. Lords Clarence and Clive were the only two in their family. They were also the last of their line. The title would have died out if Clive had no legitimate sons, which he didn't." John, no, Jack, sighed pensively. His so-called uncle was dead. He hoped he was finally safe, but it was all too late; he was alone.

Lord John would never be spoken about again. Jack Turner returned to the cell with a few other better-class prisoners who were debtors rather than criminals. He had been tried in a private court and convicted without a public presence. He was sure the prince would have the records updated to reflect Jack Turner's new name. Newgate Prison's reputation was mild compared to the squalid conditions in the overcrowded cells, and it was there that Jack awaited his transportation.

~

Weeks turned into months until one day in September, Jack Turner's name was called to board the convict ship that would carry him to a new life. Lord John Templestowe-Meade was officially dead. According to Mr Wilberforce, the Prince Regent had expunged the Templestowe-Meade's name from the conviction record and had it recorded under a new moniker. John had already served nearly eleven months in prison.

Chapter 10 Unscheduled Stopover
Martha's Journey

*T*he merchant vessel sailed southward, taking Martha far from all she knew. Only days before reaching Cape Town, sickness hit both families. June in the south was cold. One of the Beattie children died, and the two free settler families decided to remain in Cape Town until everyone was well.

This, however, left the five girls in limbo. The girls had to complete their journey to Sydney regardless of whether the families remained in Cape Town or recommenced their journey at a later date.

Unable to travel on the merchant ship without the two families escorting them, Martha only managed to say a quick farewell to Joe. Now, he was gone, and she was alone once more. Her last tie with her past had sailed away.

The five prisoners were taken into custody on landing and held in a small room at the East India Company's headquarters in town. This was as much for their own safety as for anything else. There were no cells where white women could be incarcerated, but their safety could be assured here. They had beds, food and company, so they relaxed and enjoyed the stay. One of the employees knew Captain Willoughby Alexander and ensured that Martha and the girls had more than adequate food, clothing and bedding.

With no information about what was to happen to them, the girls waited... and waited. Days turned into weeks. These weeks turned into months.

~

In July 1818, the transport vessel *Hadlow* was fitted for housing convicts at Deptford Dockyard, Kent. The guard consisted of a lieutenant and thirty-two members of the 48th Regiment of Foot. It embarked on 17 July, along with six women and four children. The vessel sailed to Woolwich in Kent on 30 July and collected fifty male convicts from the prison hulk *Justitia* on 1 August. The following day, she sailed for Sheerness, where she took on board another ninety-seven convicts from the prison hulks *Bellerophon* and *Retribution*.

The *Hadlow* departed for New South Wales on the 22nd of August under the command of Captain John Craigie.

~

Martha had no idea what their trip to Cape Town had been like, but in mid-September, the *Hadlow* was tied up to the wharf in the harbour. She and the other four girls had been incarcerated for over ten weeks. The expectant Sarah needed exercise, and the others were bored out of their brains. Martha requested some books, but the selection of reading material supplied was limited. They were given a tatty Bible without a cover, two novels that a lusty man would have enjoyed, and the written history of the Dutch East India Company; she enjoyed this. There were many books in Dutch, but as England had occupied the town for only twelve years, much needed to be done to improve the library.

~

One of the rare interactions with the admiralty came in the middle of October. A man in a red uniform came into their room without knocking and said, "Well, ladies, your transport has arrived. You will be taken to Sydney on the *Hadlow*. Pack your things, as you will be moved on board this afternoon."

Martha smiled. "Thank you, sir. Are the Beatties and Johnsons travelling with us?"

He chuckled. "No, you are convicts, and you will be travelling with the one hundred and fifty lusty men who are already on board, not to mention the same amount of equally female-starved crew. I'm sure you will enjoy your journey as much as they will enjoy your company." He gave an evil laugh as he left them alone and locked the door.

The girls gasped.

All realised what the man meant. They would be incarcerated with more than three hundred uncouth men, not to mention the soldiers acting as guards. All blanched, and silent tears flowed from each.

At four o'clock, the door opened again.

Mrs Beattie came in and embraced each girl in turn.

She left Martha until last and stood holding her hand. "My dears, I have come to tell you that since the loss of our little one, we are returning home to England. However, this means you must continue your journey without our protection. The major here will escort you onto the ship. When they have finished restocking, you will set sail. I believe that will be on the afternoon tide tomorrow." She paused and swallowed. "I also must break the news that the only place for you is in the sick bay; otherwise, you would be in a cell next to the convict men. The problem with this is that the major cannot ensure your safety."

Martha already realised this. She brushed away a tear and reached out for Sarah's hand. Both girls had already been ravished, and she was well aware of the ordeal that faced them.

Martha doubted that they would arrive in Sydney unmolested. However, they had no option. They were convict women and should have been in irons all this time. They could not refuse passage.

~

That afternoon, they were ushered unceremoniously onboard the *Hadlow.*

The doctor, Thomas Roylance, met the five women at the top of the gangplank. He demanded that they be unshackled and escorted them to the sick bay.

The guards remained behind them as the doctor led them through the cages of sex-starved men. Arms reached for the girls as they passed the locked iron cages.

The doctor opened the sick bay door and stood aside to let them enter. He wished he had taken them through the other passageway, but the captain had refused.

Now safely out of earshot of the male convicts, Martha spoke. "Thank you for your care, sir."

Once inside the sick bay, Doctor Roylance shut the door behind them. He said, "Now, ladies, we have a problem. I insist that you remain in this area unless escorted by one or more of the armed guards, the captain or me. It will be hard enough to keep you safe, as once we are at sea, the cells will be unlocked." His gaze was fixed on Kitty. She was the youngest girl in the group. She looked only fifteen or sixteen. Thomas wondered about their backgrounds. He presumed all female convicts were of loose morals, but one could never tell.

Martha spoke again. She met his look with understanding. "Sir, two of us have already been recipients of such vile action. Sarah is carrying a child after her ordeal, but thankfully, I did not conceive. The three younger girls are still innocent."

Thomas was stunned. This girl's voice was cultured and refined. "Who are you? I can tell you have some education."

Martha shrugged and nodded. "Who I was does not matter. I'm now a convict, but I'm a gentleman's daughter who fell foul of a vile earl. My companions were all caught stealing because of hunger. It's why we were sent on a merchant ship rather than a convict transport. We were supposed to be kept safe until we arrived."

Her eyes were salty pools of misery, and it broke his heart.

He realised that being ravished by the earl was bad enough, but if the convict men, *en masse*, overpowered him, even the expectant Sarah would not be safe. Doctor Roylance said, "We have no option but to house you five here, but I shall ensure the door is locked when I'm not here. I shall add another bolt to the door. I don't suppose any of you know about nursing?"

Martha and another girl put up their hands.

The doctor smiled. "Good! If you are happy, you can assist with my treatments while you are here."

Martha had done her share of helping the ship's sawbones when on her father's vessel. She could suture a wound neatly and cleanse a deep wound of shards of splintered wood without her stomach turning. She explained her experience on her father's ship.

Again, the doctor gasped. "How old are you, miss?

Martha stood up straight. "Nearly seventeen, sir! I have sailed around the globe at least six times with my father and have assisted on board with my mother for my entire life. I know the running of such a vessel as this and will assist where required."

The doctor's head nodded. He was rendered speechless at the confidence of this young lady. For a young lady, she certainly was. He had much experience with convicts, and these five were not the run-of-the-mill, slovenly women who typified the reputation of a convict wench. He swallowed nervously. Could he keep them safe? He wasn't sure, but he would try. No, he would do his very best. He said, "Fine, then settle in as best you can. I'm sorry, there is only the patients' slab bed for a sleeping area. The single timber slab allows me to fit more in if required. Blankets are on the shelf over there, and there is a chamber pot in that cupboard." He pointed to the various places, then frowned. With the information given, he departed. He would get the carpenter to add an internal bolt to the door.

They faced an uncertain future for the voyage. The kind doctor left them to settle in.

They heard the snib of the lock as he locked the door behind him, which was comforting rather than upsetting. They wished there was a bolt inside, but alas, there was nothing. He said he would fix that.

The girls had very little luggage, and the large timber slab would be the shared sleeping area.

Although it was big, about six feet by ten feet, it was filthy.

The first thing the girls did was scrub their sleeping area. The bed base had congealed pools of blood on the timber panels, and the five girls refused to sleep on such a dirty place.

They placed their scant items on a chair while the bed and central operating table were scrubbed clean. They took the scrubbing brushes, a cake of hard, yellow soap, and a coopered bucket, filled it from the keg of seawater that sat off to the side of the room, and scrubbed everything they would be using.

By the time they finished, the centre operating table, side bench, stools, chairs and operating utensils were all clean. The floor was their next target.

After scrubbing, each surface was doused with alcohol to sterilise it.

All wooden surfaces had shown signs of recent use.

Martha knew her father insisted that their sickbay was kept scrupulously clean.

By the time they had finished, an hour had passed. Their large sleeping area was now fit for use.

The girls were aware that if there were patients, they would have to sleep on the floor. As the bed had no mattress anyway, this was no hardship. It only meant the ship's rats could nibble them while they slept.

~

The anchor was hoisted, and the ship exited the harbour on the afternoon outgoing tide.

Sarah was anxious.

Martha could tell she wished to say something, but was afraid to voice her words. "Sarah, what's wrong? Is the baby becoming uncomfortable?"

Sarah shook her head. "No, it's not that." Her eyes flicked to the other three girls. "I need to say something, and none of you is going to like it." She patted the bunk, and the four girls clustered around her.

They had become close over the past months and had learned to trust each other.

Once settled, Sarah said, "As you know, this babe is the result of a group of young men ravishing me. I learned that to fight back only egged them on. If you are attacked, lie as still as possible and let them do their thing. Men seem to like you to fight back, so don't do it. I tried and was kicked until they knocked me out."

The four girls gasped in horror.

The other three girls were younger than Martha and had never been with a man before. Martha was fully aware that it hurt and told them that. "She's right, girls. I fought back, and it hurt so much. My attacker thumped me and knocked me out because I resisted. I came around while he was doing his stuff. I think Sarah is correct, as we must prepare ourselves for such a thing to occur. I feel that at some stage over the next weeks, we will need to fend them off. The doctor can't always protect us, and even if he tries, he could easily be overpowered by them, given that he's just one man. Once we are at sea, the convicts will be released from their cells, and we will be vulnerable to both groups. The crew sound worse than the felons."

The youngest girl sobbed softly. "I dreamed of finding a man and keeping myself for him."

Her friend said, "Me too. I wanted to leave London and live on a farm with chickens and pigs and have babies with a man I loved."

Sarah and Martha hugged their friends. Their eyes met over their heads.

Martha said, "Then we shall do our best to fend them off." She sounded a lot more convincing than she felt.

~

By the time they lost sight of land, a storm was rolling in.

Martha was thrilled as it meant the men would not be permitted free rein of their deck. The girls were informed that the men's cells were unlocked in case the ship pitched too far and turned turtle; however, the hatch to the convict deck was kept closed and guarded. There was a locked door between the convicts and the sickbay. They had food and water below, but were not given the liberty of any upper deck time.

Once again, Martha did not succumb to the ravages of *mal de mer*. She assisted the doctor in stitching the crew's minor cuts and scrapes. The four other girls were prostrated by seasickness. They remained huddled in a small side store room while the sick bay was in use.

One poor young crewman lost three fingers when caught in the rigging. She had to help amputate the mangled digits and sew up the stumps, but persuaded the doctor that the boy should keep his remaining fingers. The young lad's name was James.

Before they finished, the doctor had another crewman to treat, and his wound was severe. He had a bone sticking through the skin on his arm, and the doctor had no time to reset the bones, as he was sure more injuries would be brought in.

Martha was working on James's hand, sewing the final finger stump.

He lay still on their slab bunk. His eyes followed her as she worked. He was obviously in great pain, but he didn't even yell as she pushed the needle into his skin. He clenched his teeth and groaned occasionally until she was done. "Thanks, miss. That wasn't too bad," and proceeded to pass out.

When he did, Martha doused the stumps in brandy and bandaged his hand. That roused him. Only then did he scream in pain.

The doctor glanced at his first patient and saw that Martha had finished her work. He watched as she bandaged the hand like a professional and shook his head in astonishment at her skill. She was barely out of childhood, and life had thrown her a rotten deal. Once she was finished, she tied the bandages with a neat bow.

He chuckled and called her to assist him. His patient had also passed out, and he was getting ready to amputate his arm.

Martha washed her hands and set aside the used equipment, planning to wash it later. She was aghast at what she saw. The doctor had the bone saw in his hand and was about to amputate the arm. "Please, sir, can't you save his arm? He's only about my age."

Her beseeching eyes penetrated his tough exterior. "No, I'll have more patients arriving at any minute."

Martha tried again, "Sir, I can deal with most small injuries. I can help with this until they come."

He gave an exasperated sigh and said, "Oh, fine then. Hold him while I reset the arm."

She shook her head. "Can I dig out the shards of wood and bone first? He'll heal better." She had seen the state of the sickbay and realised he did not associate the filth with infections and patient healing.

He huffed and said, "You have only until I get the splint sorted."

Martha set to work cleansing the bone. She picked out the shards of timber and bone fragments with a pair of tweezers and then doused the ends of the bone with brandy. She had just finished when the doctor returned, ready to reset the bones.

His face wore a frown. "Do I smell my brandy again?"

Martha nodded. Embarrassment washed over her.

His expression did not change. "Why?"

She explained, "It helps to prevent infection. That's why we scrubbed the benches and table on the day we arrived."

This time, his face showed astonishment. "You really think that helps? I saw you wash your hands after treating the other sailor. I suppose you are going to tell me it's what they did on your father's ship."

Martha nodded. "Yes, sir, and then we used a slosh of rum or strong brandy on our hands between patients."

With a cocked eyebrow of intrigue, he asked, "Did it work?"

She nodded. "No one died from infection."

"No one?" With a shrug, he returned to his work. He had heard rumours of this theory.

She shook her head.

The doctor was surprised. "So, I'm to scrub between patients and just give my hands a slop of alcohol?"

She nodded. "Yes, sir, and instruments are to be boiled between uses, and if you can't boil them, dousing them in alcohol will work. Mama used to boil them in a pot for four minutes. We also used various medicines collected from a wide range of sources. Many countries had home remedies that work brilliantly."

When he heard that, both eyebrows shot up. "Talk to me while we work on the sailor. He'll be in pain for a while, but at least he'll have his left arm."

Martha chatted about the various medicines they had discovered while travelling. "Sir, the most interesting ones are the seeds from the paw paw or papaya fruit. They are eaten when you have worms; it is as good as, if not better than, wormwood, as it has no side effects. However, the fruit, mixed with coconut flesh from a green nut and mashed with some cooked fish, is what is fed to babies in the islands when their mother dies in childbirth."

The doctor chuckled. This was not the conversation he ever expected to have with a teenage female convict. "Go on, tell me more."

Martha was working on a large splinter of bone that had cracked but not broken off. She managed to put that chunk back in position. The doctor was now ready to reset the arm. Martha cleaned the instruments with brandy and insisted that the doctor wash his hands with soap.

Once that was done, she doused the entire area with alcohol before the doctor sutured the injury.

They fell silent as they worked together. Soon, the young sailor had his arm bandaged and splinted. He had groaned as they eased the bone back through the hole in the skin, but he did not regain consciousness.

While bandaging the arm, Doctor Roylance said, "Tell me more of your fascinating discoveries. What else do you know about childbirth, for instance?"

Martha smiled. "I helped my mother deliver a baby in a village in the *Islas Salomón*, which is known as the Solomon Islands to us English speakers. I learned that they deliver squatting and that this is much quicker for the mother, although more uncomfortable for the midwife. They have no medical doctors, only witch doctors. However, those men are more likely to dish out punishment than to administer medicine. This poor girl had a backwards birth. You know, feet first. What are they called?"

Dr Roylance hated those deliveries. "Breech birth. Did the child live?"

Martha nodded. "Yes, but the mother did not. It's how we learned about the baby formula. There were no other nursing women available to feed the new child, so the girl's mother-in-law took the infant and prepared this concoction. The baby thrived. We had broken a spar, and while the men fixed the ship, we got to know the locals. In this particular place, Laulasi Island, they worshipped sharks. The strange islands were man-made, built from reef rocks, in Langa Langa Lagoon on Malaita Island. There were men's huts and women's huts. Mama and I only saw into the latter. Papa said the men's one was full of skulls. When I heard that, I wished to get back onto the ship and stay there. Papa was determined to help me learn and see everything I could. That was one lesson I would have willingly skipped." She glanced up at the doctor. Was she talking too much?

He chuckled, "Go on, I really am interested. I've not been to these islands, but I have heard of them. They are apparently headhunters."

Martha nodded. "They are, but we didn't know that then. Anyway, as Mama and I arrived, a bloodcurdling scream emanated from this tiny thatched hut. Mama had delivered babies often, and she could not ignore the travail of the poor girl. Papa spoke Spanish, and they knew a few words, plus we used sign language. Soon, Mama and I headed into the birthing hut. This consisted of a shelf surrounding the room, and one section of it had a hole in the bench. This was for birthing."

Martha started scrubbing the centre table while she spoke.

The doctor now rested against the freshly scrubbed side bench. The room reeked of brandy. Intrigued, he asked, "What did you do?"

Martha explained. "When we entered, one foot had emerged, but the other was stuck. We had no forceps, so Mama had to use her hands to find the other foot. She worked it loose, and soon, the healthy, large baby boy arrived. The poor mother expired soon after the birth. She had been cut with a bush knife long before we came. Her death set the women of the village wailing and covering themselves with dirt. The baby was the chief's grandson. Because we delivered him and he was alive, we were not harmed. It was only after Papa was taken into the men's hut and saw all the skulls that he realised they were headhunters. We fixed the broken spar with timber from the main island and left as soon as we could, just in case we did something to annoy them."

The doctor was laughing by the time she finished her description of their voyage. The adventures this girl had experienced in her short life made him determined to keep the five girls safe if he could. She had just finished telling him that a week earlier, they had crashed a village wedding feast. He was fully aware that very few white people dared to set foot in the Solomon Islands. This brave family had called in by necessity as the islanders had not seen white women before. The visit brought its own problems. As whaling ships called in often, white men were not unusual. However, Martha and her mother needed to strip in front of the village women for them to realise that they were indeed females.

He was somewhat in awe of this girl. She was only a convict, but she had already challenged him and his beliefs, let alone his understanding of hygiene. He had often wondered if blood carried any infection, but he wasn't sure if it was true. He usually washed his hands between patients, but never his instruments. If this lad lived, then he would follow her advice. Usually, a wound such as this would lead to immediate amputation. He had no intention of admitting to her that amputation was his usual treatment. He had even amputated a leg because of a huge but jagged splinter. The rotten timber had disintegrated as he attempted to remove all the shards of wood. It had taken two days of treatment before the skin showed signs of dying. The edges of the injury went from red to pus-filled to black within hours. If alcohol helped, then he would use it.

The lad with the amputated fingers returned to his hammock as soon as he roused. The sailor with the broken limb remained unresponsive.

As the storm eased, the exhausted girls crawled into the extra-wide bed near the unresponsive injured crewman and slept soundly.

Martha checked that the bolt was locked before surrendering to sleep.

~

Some hours later, the door opened, and each of the girls had hands clamped over their mouths.

Their worst fears had come true; however, it was not convicts but crewmen who had broken in.

Somehow, the new inside bolt on the door had been unlocked as they slept. A dozen of the crew were now circling their bed.

The girls had no idea what happened to the soldiers supposedly guarding them, but they knew that they had no hope of fighting back.

Even Sarah was not exempt. She was forced on her hands and knees and violated backward.

One by one, the men lined up and slaked their lusts on the girls.

Kitty, Vicky and Milly hardly noticed the patient from the other end of their bed had moved. He was sitting on the other side of their room, watching the activities with a toothy grin. He claimed his turn next.

Martha wept in disgust and disappointment. She had helped him, and this was how he repaid her. He had obviously unlocked the new bolt the doctor had installed on the door and let his friends in. While one man had his way with her, her gaze remained fixed on the patient in the chair on the other side of the room.

He was about to take his turn when the doctor entered with

Captain Craigie on his heels. The two men had come to check on the injured crewman. Instead, they found the women in a state of disarray and distress and some of his crew in the act of violating them.

The captain's ire exploded from him. "Get out, you filthy dogs. I'll deal with you later." He knew his crew well enough to recognise each man.

The girls extracted themselves from the grasp of more than a dozen lusty men. They scrambled to the far side of the large sleeping platform and remained huddled together.

The captain waved in military guards, and the thirteen men were clapped in irons and confined to the brig. They would be dealt with later that day.

Sarah was a mess. At over eight months along in her confinement, the vicious actions of the men had made her bleed.

All the girls followed her instruction not to fight back.

Martha knew that sadists existed in all walks of life. One man had used something on Sarah other than his male appendage. Why, Martha didn't know. They had caused them no harm; just the opposite. They had helped them.

Captain Craigie promised that the men would each receive their just punishment.

There were now only three weeks until they were due to arrive in the colony. Because of the various storms and extremely rough seas, they survived for five weeks without molestation. That had ended today.

Martha counted three men doing vile things to her friend. She knew that two had attacked her, and the other three girls also had two each.

Thankfully, not all of them had managed to get a turn satisfying their lusts before they were interrupted.

A few men turned to them in disgust as they were led away.

The sailor she had helped operate on said, "We'll be back, and I'll get my turn."

Patient or not, Doctor Roylance gave him an uppercut, sending him flying.

The crewman hit his injured arm and howled in agony.

The doctor waved for him to be taken from his sight. As the young man reached the door, the doctor said, "But for her, you would have lost your arm today." He huffed, "Get him out of here! I will not treat him again."

The young man turned and looked at Martha. He gave a rude bow of thanks and departed with a chuckle. His smile showed blackened stumps of teeth. While being clasped by guards, he muttered as he passed her, "You'll keep."

Captain Craigie said, "I will ensure that those men remain under lock and key until we dock. We must work out a way to keep you safe until then."

The doctor said, "If the girls are happy, I was planning to sleep in here, on the floor."

The bushy eyebrows of the skipper flew up. "Really? Do you think that is wise?"

The doctor shrugged. "I don't see any other options. Even if we moved them into a cabin, they could not be protected unless someone slept across the doorway. Your cabin is not even safe for them, as you must be at the helm. Here, I can keep them protected as this is where I work. As you know, the perpetrators were not convicts but some of your crew. They come and go at their pleasure."

The captain smiled. "Fine, then I shall arrange a hammock for you."

The doctor chuckled. "Thanks, captain, but I'll move my mattress from my cabin."

The captain smiled at the medical man. "If you are sure, I'll sort that for you. The soldiers can move it in."

The doctor nodded. "Thank you, that would be good."

The captain turned to leave. At the door, he turned back to them and said, "I'm sorry this occurred, girls, but we shall endeavour to keep you safe." With those few words, he was gone.

Martha sighed with relief. They should remain safe, with the doctor sleeping in the sick bay. None of the girls was promiscuous, and they had not encouraged any of the crew. Circumstances beyond their control had caught the girls. All were from a better class than those convicted from the slums in various cities around the land. It was why they had been transported on a merchant ship. Now, all had been violated.

Martha turned to the three younger girls and sought to comfort them. All would be physically sore and emotionally distraught. She knew how she felt after she had been attacked. A thorough wash was the first thing they needed. With no hip bath, there was the coopered keg of saltwater and a large tin basin available. She filled that with water and set it on the small hob stove the doctor used. With the doctor gone, the girls cleaned themselves as best they could.

Upon his return, Doctor Roylance checked the girls over and ensured they were not severely injured.

Sarah was still bleeding and so disconsolate that she lay on the bed, unmoving. Her baby was restless. She wept. She murmured to Martha, "How could such depraved men think they had the right to do such things?" She moaned, "Why are men such filthy dogs? Sorry, doctor, I don't mean you."

There was little more he could do for any of them. "No offence taken, miss, but this will make you a bit more comfortable." The doctor brought her a towel to sop the blood.

He had seen such carnal activities by the men on other naval voyages. Any woman who had come within arm's length of the lusty sailors was often taken by force. He did what he could for those women, but he couldn't keep them all safe at all times.

Thomas thought back to his lovely new wife, Eleanor. They had married only shortly before embarking on this voyage, and he missed her warm body lying cradled in his arms. She was so precious to him and also to her family. These girls were equally as precious to someone and needed to be kept safe. He shook his head and set about clearing a space for his mattress on the sickbay floor. Could he keep them safe?

Chapter 11 My New Friend
Jack's Journey
1819

*J*ack packed his scant possessions and was escorted to a waiting ancient carriage outside the prison. He and a fair-haired lad were the only two occupants. As Jack sat on the torn squab seats, he smiled. "Hello, I'm Jack Turner." This was the first time he introduced himself by his new name.

There was no reply until the guard twisted the key in the lock of their shackles. They were now joined at both the ankle and wrist. The young man beside him looked sad. "I'm Charles." There was no hello or last name, just Charles. He had the most incredibly blue eyes. Charles turned to gaze at the nothingness out the window. The vehicle was parked close to a brick wall, and there was nothing to see. Jack shrugged and remained quiet. If the silent man beside him were to be his cellmate, he would hopefully reveal more than his first name over time. In the meantime, he relaxed. He wondered how many more felons would be taken aboard with them.

Minutes later, the carriage rocked as a red-coated soldier climbed in with them. Rather than sit opposite and face backwards, he made them move. This would be the first of many shuffle dances the two young prisoners would need to perform. They settled on the rear-facing seat as the coach moved off. The soldier smiled at them. "Well, gentlemen, I hope you will give me no trouble. I'm Ensign Geake from the 48th regiment; four more armed guards are on the roof, and the coachman is also armed. You are being taken to the dockland, where you will be loaded on board your cruise ship for your voyage to the Antipodes." He smirked at his own joke.

Jack and Charles glared but did not respond. This was no pleasure cruise. Geake stretched his legs. Jack had to move his feet quickly as they were kicked out of the way. Thankfully, Mr Wilberforce had brought him a pair of serviceable shoes rather than the court shoes he had worn when arrested. His outfit was what he wore when in the stables. His clothing was some of Bill's old work apparel, since he owned nothing inconspicuous. The soldier asked, "Do you have any questions? I can see you are both dying with curiosity."

Jack shook his head. Charles was still mute. Jack glanced at his shackle-mate and caught another flash of blue. Charles's eyes were astounding. They were the bluest eyes he had ever seen—the colour of the sky on a hot summer day; throw in his white-blond hair, and he was a handsome man. Surprisingly, he was quite clean. He reminded him of someone, but he couldn't think who that was.

Geake chuckled again. "Fine, then I shall fill you in regardless of your wishes. You two are to be the only prisoners on the ship until we reach The Downs anchorage at Deal. There, we will collect a full load of convicts. For some reason, you two have been earmarked for quick and somewhat luxurious transportation. Most convicts are sent on open wagons." He shrugged. "Anyway, you will be cellmates for the next few months, so get used to each other."

With that comment, Charles glanced at the youth beside him. He'd taken little notice of him earlier and now realised that Jack was clean and exceptionally well-dressed. His eyes were the colour of light amber, and his hair was to match. He had the nerve to smile. How dare he be so happy with what was happening? Charles just wanted to go home. Home... somewhere he would never see again. Charles sighed in utter frustration.

Geake continued. "The rabble we are about to collect is not only Irish political prisoners, but pick-pocketers, sheep and cow stealers, vagrants, perjurers, highway robbers, those charged with assault, and some arrested in possession of forged bank notes. I presume your crimes come under one of those categories?"

Both young men nodded. Jack had decided to keep his illustrious background a secret. However, he had been charged with assault. He need not give details. Charles looked shamefaced but didn't comment. Geake's brows lifted. "Quiet, aren't you? I presume you both can talk?"

The two young men replied in unison, "Yes, sir." They fell silent again.

Geake chuckled. "I suppose that my scarlet jacket is the reason for your silence?" They both shrugged, but no reply was forthcoming from the prisoners. The soldier said, "Fine! Then settle back; our trip is only a few miles." The occupants relaxed. All three kept their eyes outside rather than meet the steely glare of each other.

The ship that came into view was a three-masted sailing vessel, as most were. Geake said, "Well, lads, that was one of the quietest trips I've had in a while. This beauty is your transport. Her name is the *Shipley*, and she was built in 1805. She was a fourteen-gun privateer for a while, then the French got hold of her and ransacked her cargo, and some of her crew died. Anyway, in 1812, she was turned into a transport ship. They did the West Indies run until then; I believe this is her third convict voyage."

Jack glanced at his new companion to gauge his interest. None.

The guard continued. "From what I can gather, her occasional cargo meant that no conversion was required to turn her into a convict transport. She's a sturdy tub, and she should make good time. Your captain on this voyage of discovery is Master Lew Moncrief, and the ship's surgeon is Doctor Henry Ryan. Nice chaps, but try not to get injured. I've heard that these ships' sawbones will hack off your leg for even a splinter, as they do on other vessels."

Dual gasps echoed in the quiet cab. The soldier chuckled. So, they were listening. The carriage stopped beside a gangplank. The soldier alighted and said, "Wait here." The two young men had little choice in the matter, so they remained where they were. For ten minutes, they watched the activity surrounding them. Jack stole a few glances at his companion. He saw that Charles' eyes were welling with unshed tears. His heart went out to him. In that instant, Jack decided that he would befriend him, whatever it took. Charles's few words sounded cultured, and that was a relief. He hoped he would respond to his offer of friendship. He also noted he didn't smell.

Geake returned and unlocked the ankle irons. "Come on, boys, this will make it easier to walk. I don't know who you two are, but I've been told I must take care of you. No roughing up and the like. Hence, your luxury carriage today" He turned to Jack and said, "Mr Wilberforce sent through something to the captain for you, laddie, so I presume you have friends in high places."

Jack gasped, then smiled. What had his friend sent? With the ankle irons gone, they were still joined by the wrist, so the young men ambled carefully towards the ship. They realised they had to rely on each other for balance. As neither young man had ever had to share anything before, sharing personal space would be different.

Jack whispered, "Ready?" Charles nodded and returned the caring question with a half smile. Jack grinned. "Come on then, let's go." A single nod was all the reply he received. They each carried a small bundle. Neither was very dirty, and both wore old, but quite fashionable attire. As Charles was shackled by the wrists to the left of Jack, he stepped onto the gangway first. Charles expected it to bounce, but it didn't. He had never previously set foot on a vessel and was extremely fearful of what lay before them.

Likewise, Jack had never seen a ship such as this, as his days had been spent in the luxury of the royal palaces. Admittedly, he had travelled on the royal barge a few times, but to venture into open waters was not something he ever expected to do. His desire for adventure and the actual implementation were different. To spend months in close proximity with many convicted souls made him fearful, to say the least. Drawing a deep breath of the fetid London air, he gingerly stepped onto the gangway and followed Charles onto the deck. Red-coated soldiers were carrying numerous crates from a pile at the top of the passageway. Another was on guard, watching. His new pillbox hat sat at a jaunty angle. His uniform was slightly different from the other soldiers'. They heard him gasp as Charles came into his line of sight. Jack noticed him grab the railing in front of him to steady his stance.

The doctor met them as they moved to the gunnels. "Ahh, our first two passengers! Follow me, gentlemen, and I shall show you where you will be housed. Captain Moncrief wishes to meet you both later." Without waiting, he paced off at great speed. He crossed the deck, and as he was about to descend through a small hatchway, he turned back to the prisoners and said, "Cover one eye and don't remove your hand until I say."

They did and stood waiting for a minute or so. The doctor said, "Okay, now follow me. As soon as you reach the lowest step, remove your hand." The order was strange, but they saw the medical man had done the same thing. As they reached the last step, both lowered their hands. Although the deck was dark, they were amazed that they could see with the eye they had covered.

The doctor chuckled. "That's a pirate's trick. I know you have seen drawings of them wearing eye patches; it's because they often need to head belowdecks quickly. The patch allows them to see immediately upon entering the darkened areas. Clever, eh?"

Two heads nodded reluctantly. They followed the doctor through a warren of corridors and past numerous cabins. The medic opened a door that led to his onboard hospital room. "Medical check first, then you can choose your berth below. You have the pick of the deck for the next few nights. Make the most of it, as the Irish are notorious for causing trouble."

Fifteen minutes later, they were following the doctor from the sick bay. Both had been given the all-clear from any medical conditions and finally had their manacles removed. Both rubbed their wrists as they walked. Their eyes had fully adjusted to the darkened deck, but they were warned to repeat the trick before they descended to the lower deck as it was even darker. Their escort, Ensign Geake, followed silently. The steep ladder-like set of steps led into a dungeon-like void. The stench of stale urine hit them first. This deck had obviously been used before this voyage, which may have been its first trip carrying convicts. Both lads wondered if slaves had been transported on the vessel. Jack knew that the East India Company traded slaves, and the cage-like facilities showed that this was indeed likely. He presumed that the trips to the West Indies were bringing them human cargo and taking back sugar cones.

The doctor confirmed Jack's supposition. "Sorry about the smell, but some of the last occupants were not used to using the facilities. They were not appreciative of what was supplied. Irish, of course. However, the cargo before them was for Dominica, I believe."

The stench worsened as they drew closer to the cages. Geake pushed past them and led the way to the stern of the ship. He reached a small cell and pulled the door open. "This is to be your home away from home, lads. This cell is typically where the most troublesome prisoners are placed. However, you two can have a bit more freedom here. You won't get knifed as you sleep, either. There used to be another bunk above, but the last occupants smashed it. Sorry, but you will need to share the slab bed. You have an entire eighteen-inch width each. Luxury!"

The cell contained one wooden slab to serve as a sleeping platform, approximately a yard wide and eight feet long, and two coopered buckets sat on the floor. One bucket was full of water, and the other was empty, to be used as a chamber pot. There was nothing else. It was stark, cold, and dark.

Both young men stood numb at what they beheld. How had

their lives come to this? The cell door slammed shut behind them, making them both jump. The sound of the key turning in the lock made them both swivel around. Footsteps faded as they remained stunned at what had befallen them. The stench made their stomachs roil. Alone in the darkness, both shivered. The only place they could sit was on the slab bed. Thankfully, a pinpoint of light came from an oil lamp at the foot of the ladder, some distance away. It was the only source of illumination, providing little light for their surroundings.

Charles plonked himself down on the hard surface with a resigned sadness. He swore, dropped his head on his hands, and wept.

Jack sat beside the distraught lad and placed a caring hand on his back. "Charles, take just one day at a time! If we stick together, we'll survive this."

A soft sob escaped from the young man. Charles nodded, then said, "I didn't even do anything wrong, Jack. I was at work, and a damned sheep strayed into my front yard at home. Mama had asked me to fix the latch, and I didn't. This is my own damned fault." He sniffed. "My mother and sister are now alone; I was their money earner." He attempted to stifle another sob but failed. "So much for being the man of the family; I'm weeping like a blooming baby." He wiped his eyes with his sleeve. "What are they going to do now? How will they cope?"

This time, Jack swore. It was not something he did often, but Charles's story elicited a response from him. "You're kidding? Would your employer not vouch for you?"

Charles shook his head and sat up a little straighter. "He did, and they did not believe him. The damned sheep was in my yard, and therefore, I was found guilty. However, I was only given seven years instead of fourteen because of his testimony." He looked around him and said, "Now this!" His long sigh showed his frustration. "What about you, Jack?"

Jack shrugged. He had already decided that no one, not even his wife, should he ever marry, would ever fully know his story. How could he possibly explain everything in a way that she would believe him? He knew that revealing his conviction without the backstory would be adequate. He said, "I got fourteen years for assault. I admitted it, so I was found guilty." Hopefully, Charles would not pry. He didn't. Jack thought that he might open up if asked. "Tell me about your family, Charles."

Charles chatted for the next two hours about his village and house. He mentioned it was in Kent but gave few details pinpointing the actual locality. He described the thatched cottage so vividly that Jack felt he could wander through the rooms blindfolded. Charles' mother and sister were named Elizabeth, but he called his sister Lilabet. He mentioned his mother's love of gardening and how the vegetable patch had kept the three of them from starvation. He and his sister helped his mother preserve the harvest, and they swapped produce for food they didn't grow. A small bequest came from his father's family, but they had no idea who supplied it.

Eventually, Charles asked about Jack's family.

Jack replied truthfully. He said, "My parents died when I was born, and a loving guardian angel brought me up, then she died. I will tell you that my guardian introduced me to Mr William Wilberforce. I think he intervened to arrange our early transportation, based on the ensign's comment. I have a feeling he chose you, as we are of an age. I listened to Mr Wilberforce speak in Parliament House about slave trading, and I befriended his son, as we are of a similar age. To find that we are now incarcerated in one of those same slave ships sends shivers up and down my spine. I was with Bill Wilberforce on the day the law passed through Parliament. Bill and I cheered loudly." All he said was true, but far more was left out than he voiced. It was no secret that he was friends with the Wilberforce family. That gave nothing away about his background. Discussions about what Parliament House looked like inside kept Charles asking too many personal questions. They would have kept talking, but a clanging sound echoed through the decking. The ship was preparing for departure, and they had not unwrapped their bundles. Their journey into the unknown was about to start. They decided to experiment with how they would sleep. Would they even fit on the small sleeping shelf side by side? It certainly didn't look very comfortable.

Charles was thawing to Jack. He asked, "Do you think we will be given blankets? I feel that the memory of my feather mattress at home is a thing of the past." He gave a half laugh that sounded more like a choke.

Jack chuckled, as well. "I already miss mine." They were trying to settle when a soldier appeared.

The lamp flame was turned up on the ladder light, which lit their area much better. However, the soldier carried another lantern. He said, "Hey, chaps, I have your convict issue: blanket, plate, spoon, and mug. Don't lose them, as they will not be replaced." He noted they were trying to lie side by side and suggested, "I hear that on other convict ships, they sleep top to tail. It's your call, but just an idea." He unlocked the grill and handed in the goods. "I would give you another blanket, but you should be warm enough if you share them. Move so your feet are at the other person's armpits."

Charles flipped around, and the guard saw them wiggle into position. As he closed and locked the gate, he said, "We go with the ebb and flow of the tide until we reach the sea." A grinding sound was echoing through the deck. Though the anchor had not been used, the anchor chain was being moved. In the dim light, the soldier saw the interest on the faces of the two young men. He explained, "There will soon be the sound of the anchor being dropped, and in about six hours, we'll haul it up with the tide change and drop it again at the next tide when we heave off to the side. It will take us four to six days to reach the sea. Then we'll head to Deal near Dover to collect your bunkmates. Settle in as best you can, because the next occupants will be just as bad as the last breathing cargo. We expect trouble from this lot, so keep your noses clean. It's why you have been put in this small cell. Only two fit in here now. Trust me, you won't want to share with them."

The pair accepted their allocation of goods and placed them on their pallet bed. Jack chuckled as he stacked the tin plates and spoons. The last plates he had helped put away were the Prince Regent's Royal Worcester mauve porcelain dinnerware. He didn't explain his mirth to Charles.

~

They fell into a routine and took turns pacing around the small cell to get some exercise. It took four days before they felt the waves underfoot, and when they did, the movement tipped them off-kilter.

On the day they hit the first wave, which tipped the sailing ship sideways, Charles cried, "Oh God, save us." His stomach was roiling.

Jack chuckled and replied, "He's the only one who can."

Charles clung tightly to the bars of their cage. He said, "What the hell do you mean? Surely you can't believe that rubbish?"

As Charles had been pacing the cell, Jack was lying on the bunk with his arms behind his head. "I do, my friend. I would not have survived to the grand old age of twenty-one without the Lord's help. Mr Wilberforce's last words to me were that I had to keep my faith. God would somehow get the glory from all this."

Charles groaned. "You are one of those religious fanatics.

Really?"

Jack laughed. "Yes! Sorry, but you're stuck with me. However, I promise you this: I will never bring it up, but if you do, prepare yourself for an earful. I will answer any question you have."

Charles groaned. "Just my blooming luck!" He vomited into the previously empty bucket. The stench of the urine, excrement and vomit mixed with the movement of the ship soon had Jack grabbing the other coopered pail. The water bucket had tipped over soon after hitting the waves. The floor sloshed with their drinking water, vomit and urine. Two miserable lads groaned and voiced their wishes to die. Another wave tilted the ship in the opposite direction. Jack slid along the slippery surface of the bunk, bucket clenched firmly in his arms.

Within an hour, the pair were lying on the cell floor, clinging tightly to the buckets and a cell bar. They were heaving their stomach contents into the coopered pails as the ship ploughed through the choppy seas.

The doctor came to see how they were faring. He discovered them prostrate on the floor, clinging to their buckets in one hand and cell bars in the other. They hardly noticed his arrival until they heard laughter. With the flick of his hand, he motioned for the guard to unlock the door. "Come on, boys. You need some fresh air. Soldier, you take the fair one; I've got this lad." The boys were hoisted onto the sides of their rescuers and helped up the ladder. As soon as they emerged into the sunshine, they covered their eyes as the sunlight blinded them. Surprisingly, the seas were reasonably calm. The fresh air soon blew away the stench of the cells below. As they collapsed to the decking, the doctor said, "I'll get something for you. Hang on."

Ensign Geake released Charles and sat near them. He said, "Well, lads. You both look a bit green around the gills." Both reeked of vomit.

They nodded. Charles wished he'd brought his bucket. He moved like lightning and reached the side before he vomited again.

Geake chuckled. "Good aim, Lockley. Come, Turner, you look green too. Let's join him at the gunnels." Jack staggered to join his new friend. He sank onto the decking beside him. His stomach was beginning to ease. The turbulent expulsion of food seemed to settle it. With the smell now absent, he took long, deep breaths of the fresh, salty air.

Geake sat beside them with his feet hanging over the edge. The salt spray gently washed over them. "I came to tell you, lads, that until we get to Deal, you won't be under lock and key. There is nowhere you can go except overboard, and I doubt that either of you can swim. With both of you hanging over the gunnels, that is where the term 'hungover' comes from, but it's usually referring to drunks, not seasickness."

Both young men shook their heads. Neither would be tempted to jump overboard.

A bucket of seawater was brought to them. Stripping off, they doused their filthy clothing in it, then donned the wet but clean attire.

The doctor arrived carrying two tin mugs and a bottle under his arm. "Get this into you, lads. It will settle your stomachs." He handed each of them a mug and filled it halfway. They expected the liquid to be alcoholic, but it was water, flavoured with lemon and a touch of honey. After a sip, they each downed the concoction. Jack nodded his thanks and held out the mug for a refill.

Charles blew out his cheeks as he realised that his stomach was not roiling as much. He watched the rolling waves and, after a while, said, "I thought the seas would be crashing over the deck. Down below, the deck was moving violently."

The doctor sat and sprawled out behind them, his feet crossed at the ankles. "No, lads, it's the stench. We couldn't bring you on deck until we cleared the land. Naval rules. It's the smell below that turns your stomach. This ship was used to transport slaves and did a couple of convict trips to Sydney. The same captain skippered them on the last voyage, but a different surgeon was on board. Robert Espie is now serving on the *Agamemnon*. Nice chap. This is my first trip on this convict transport, but I've done other naval voyages. Philip Geake here is only with us until we reach Deal. Then, he's to take a placement there."

The soldier, Philip, nodded. "Hence, I can befriend you as I'm soon to depart." He chuckled. "The doctor is in no man's land. He must treat you regardless of status."

It was the doctor's turn to laugh. "Therefore, I am now overseeing the care of two ill patients rather than sitting and enjoying the sun. Once we load the remaining felons, you will become mere numbers to me. I rarely remember faces as I treat the illness, not the person. However, I may remember you chaps, so keep out of trouble."

The two young men were beginning to feel normal again. The warm sun quickly dried their clothes. Jack asked, "Do either of you know much of what is before us?"

The doctor nodded. "I've been before, as I did the trip on the *Tyne* last year. We carried a load of Irishmen." He shook his head at the memory. He groaned at the thought of the uncouth persons on the previous voyage.

Jack wanted to know what to expect upon arrival. He knew it was unlikely he would get to chat freely again. "Would you mind telling us what we're in store for?"

With a nod, the doctor revealed more about their destination. "Well, lads, I'd love to, but let me say, you need to survive the voyage first. That means when you are offered your daily dose of lime or lemon juice, you drink it. Scurvy is one of the dangers of a long voyage, and your future travelling companions will often refuse to consume the substance. You've just had your dose today. As you have tasted, it's nice." He shrugged. "I suppose their diet doesn't include much citrus fruit, so they are not used to the bitter-sweet taste. Set an example for them, and I will appreciate that. I discovered that the Irish don't eat much meat, especially the salted stuff. They would rather fill themselves full of dried peas and potatoes. They seem to thrive on it, so I'm not too fussed as long as they arrive healthy."

Jack said, "Will do, sir. I liked it." Charles agreed.

The doctor smiled. "Good, okay then. What do you know about the colony?"

Jack and Charles looked at each other blankly. Jack said, "I know nothing, sir. Except that it's called Botany Bay. I met Sir Joseph Banks, and he told me it was a flat place. I was not told about the penal settlement. I know more about slavery than convicts."

Doctor Ryan chuckled. "Ahh, well, it looks like I must start from the beginning. The Americans are to blame, as we used to send our convicts there, but then the Boston Tea Party thing happened, and they blocked us from sending them our criminals. I can see why, as they were often the most troublesome prisoners. Anyway, roll on some years, and the old battleships were being used as prisons. They are called the hulks. You two are lucky that you had no time incarcerated in them. Part of my duty was to see to the health of the prisoners on board those stinking wrecks. Most of the vessels were in a bad state of decay and leaked like a sieve. The river rats love them; they stink worse than below here. Anyway, enough about them! Many of them hold the prisoners until the navy has a shipload of useful subjects to send to New South Wales. We're heading to Deal on the

Dover coast, but the river mouth in Portsmouth has many more hulks. Other ports have at least one each. Woolwich, Chatham, Deptford, Plymouth and Devonport."

The boys were listening, their eyes fixed on the doctor's face.

He continued. "By 1787, the hulks were so overcrowded that they had to empty them somehow. Seventeen years earlier, Lieutenant James Cook had charted the East Coast of the Great South Land, as it was called, but also known as New Holland by the Dutch. On his return, he was promoted to Captain. Even then, the English searched for places to expand, but had no plans to settle there. His orders were to observe the transit of Venus from Tahiti in June 1769. Charting the coastline was an aside. The transit observations were used to calculate the size of the solar system, which assisted in nautical navigation. About then, the English took Cape Town from the Dutch, along with numerous other places. So, when reports came back that the new land had only a few locals and no European settlements, the idea of a penal colony took shape. As you said, Jack, Sir Joseph Banks suggested it to the king. Cook arrived at Botany Bay, but only landed to bury someone named Sutherland and to replenish his water. Eighteen years later, on January 18th, Governor Arthur Phillip found the ground at Botany Bay unsuitable for farmland. He moved the settlement further north to Port Jackson. You wait until you see the harbour. It's incredible. Had he arrived two days later, the French may have claimed it."

Jack said, "So Botany Bay is not the settlement?"

The doctor's head shook. "No, the main town, Sydney Cove, is a few miles to the north. Parramatta is a few hours further west. It was all scrub when Governor Phillip and the first of the eleven ships of the First Fleet arrived in Sydney Cove on January 24, 1788. The last ship dropped anchor two days later. Scrub is what they call the low bushland over there. There are cabbage palms, towering gum trees and some strange flowers, but the foliage doesn't fall like our trees here. The vegetation is mostly evergreens. The gum trees have a scent unlike any I've smelled before. But it's also volatile. John White, the chief surgeon on the First Fleet, distilled some of the leaves and produced an incredibly pungent oil that seems to stop the putrefaction of wounds. The gum leaves burn very easily when dry; therefore, bushfires are common." He was about to describe more of the settlement when the dinner gong went. He said, "I'll finish this later."

Chapter 12 The Southern Seas
Martha's Journey

A worried frown settled on Doctor Roylance's brow; he was puzzling about how he could keep the women safe. He could not be with them at all times and knew the men would not hesitate to take them by force. If enough of them grouped together, they may force their way through the now heavily bolted door. They had added extra locks.

It had been a week since the attack, and Sarah had hardly moved from her foetal position on the bed. She had shuffled over to the furthest place from the door and remained still. This was not good for her or her baby.

Surprisingly, Doctor Roylance slept well on the floor of the sick bay.

The girls were good roommates and kept the medical facility much cleaner than usual. Their days passed uneventfully.

~

A week slid by, and now the ship ploughed through the leviathan waves that nearly turned the vessel upside-down, but they survived unscathed.

The girls were content to remain in the large room and cut bandages from some torn bed sheets that the captain and doctor had purchased in Cape Town. They had washed and boiled the first fifteen sheets, so they were ready to cut and roll them into bandages. One sheet was strung up across the area where the doctor slept to give each gender some privacy. He slept partially dressed, removing his coat, boots, and any other uncomfortable paraphernalia.

As the girls had no option but to sleep in their undergarments, they waited until he was behind his curtain before crawling into their communal bed, where they shared blankets.

With the six locked into the sick bay, the nights usually passed without incident. Occasionally, they were awoken by someone knocking on the door for treatment, but their nights were usually undisturbed.

After a week of stormy weather, the sun finally emerged from behind the clouds. Doctor Roylance realised the women had not been out of doors since their departure from Cape Town.

During his morning rounds, he left two guards at their hospital door. He went to check on the prisoners before returning to run the morning clinic for the others on board. Some of the convict men showed signs of scurvy, and he hoped the remaining miles would be traversed quickly without undue serious illness. He said nothing about his idea to sit outside with the girls.

Half an hour later, his return was met with a few crewmen seeking his medical expertise for minor cuts and bruises.

Martha assisted the doctor as he stitched a long cut, while the three young girls attended to the mess they made. The floor had trails of blood from the various injuries. By the time the last patient had departed, the room was spick and span once more.

The doctor tapped Sarah's feet. "Come on, mum, we're all going for a walk outside. The seas are as calm as they are going to get, and the sun is shining."

Sarah stirred. The thought of getting outside was enough to brighten everyone's day. She sat up and said, "Will you remain with us, sir? I don't want a repeat of their punishment. I hurt something bad."

The doctor smiled. "I certainly will. I don't trust these scoundrels as far as I can kick them. The captain awaits you on the poop deck, and you may remain outdoors for a few hours, so take something to do."

Martha jigged with delight. "Really, doctor? Oh, this is wonderful." She hastily gathered an armful of torn sheets and asked the doctor to take the scissors. They would have much more room to cut the large swathes of bedding and roll more bandages. If the rips were in awkward places, they made slings from the shorter sections. "Sir, may I ask if you really need all these turned into bandages? We are in great need of underclothing. I know you have needle and thread, and we would only need one or two of the sheets to furnish us each with a new set of garments."

The doctor shrugged. "I have more than sufficient already, so I do not see why not. Sew away merrily, Martha. I don't imagine this will be gentle on your skin, but I suppose it is better than none." He collected his sewing box as he departed.

The girls followed the doctor out of the room and up a narrow staircase they had not seen before. This led to the private cabins, which meant they did not need to go near the men in the cells. They settled themselves in the shade of the sails and set to work cutting out their new apparel.

Martha had made many garments over the years, as her father had kept bolts of fabric on board for their use. She showed the girls how to draft a pattern and mark the sheeting with a stick of chalk.

She soon had twenty panels cut out for drawer legs. The selvedge edges were carefully trimmed off to use as drawstrings for the waistbands.

Sarah's garments were problematic. She realised that her distended stomach would protrude through the gap. So she added a longer tie to the two sides of the drawers. Once she had the baby, the garment would only need to be tied tighter.

Rather than cause any problem for the captain, the girls worked industriously for nearly an hour before one of the crew brought a steaming mug of tea for his skipper.

The captain heard a groan of desire from the women behind him. He ordered that more hot tea be brought for the five women.

A billy full of hot, sweet tea arrived with a lone crewman. He had five tin mugs dangling from his sailor's belt.

James, the lad who had lost his fingers, was now aiding the cook. "Here, Miss Martha, I've not had a chance to thank you for helping save my hand." He held up his bandaged appendage. "There have been no infections set in, and the stitches are ready to come out. I get an itch in the missing ones, but I still have the two if I need to pick things up. The doctor said he would have taken my whole hand but for you. So, thank you." He gave her a mug and filled it with the steaming brew.

Martha glowed at his praise of thanks. The boy must have only been about fourteen. He was not even old enough to shave.

Even though they had been sitting in the sunshine, the wind was cold, and the hot beverage was a welcome treat.

As James passed Sarah the last mug, he dug into his pocket and pulled out a handful of sweet ship's biscuits. "The captain said you are all to have some of these. Cook made them this morning. They are sweet oat ones, and they are delicious."

The day passed in the warmth of the fresh air as they slowly nibbled the oat cakes.

Eventually, the girls had to retreat to their quarters for the convicts' evening medical check. All had a red glow on their faces, and the salty air had blown away their cobwebs. Each had finished their new undergarments, and all were eager to try them on.

~

A week later, the ship hit some gargantuan waves as it turned south to round Van Diemen's Land. Visits outdoors were unsafe, so they remained confined to quarters.

The ship was to skirt around the bottom of Van Diemen's Land before heading north to Sydney, where their journey would end.

For Martha, that could not happen fast enough.

The doctor told them that the captain intended to make haste to their destination.

With the convicts battling scurvy and some of the crew rumbling about the privileges he was giving to the women, the mood was becoming ugly. Rumours abounded that the doctor was receiving their favours once the doors to sickbay were shut.

Something was about to explode.

The seas finally quieted enough to move around the ship safely. However, the girls chose to remain locked in sickbay.

~

Three days out of Sydney, they were awoken by someone hammering on the sick bay door at midnight. Whoever it was said, "Doctor, come quickly; James has had a bad fall, and we think he has broken his leg."

The doctor pulled on his boots and jacket and left the small hospital room. "Martha, don't let anyone in but me."

She nodded wearily. "I won't, sir."

He closed the door behind him, but did not know that a cork had been pushed into the lock hole in the doorframe. The door closed, and he turned the handle to ensure it had locked, but he did not push against it. Had he done so, it would have just pushed open, for it had closed but not latched. Martha sleepily slid home the bolts, but didn't notice the screws had been loosened.

No sooner had his footsteps retreated than the door was

shouldered open. The loosened screws popped out, and a group of crewmen surged into the sickbay. The girls were surrounded by some of the same crewmen who had forced themselves on them before.

As the girls were now garbed in only their shifts, there was no resistance to the men's vile attentions. The first man to enter was the young man whose arm Martha had helped save. His arm was still in splints and was supposed to be in a sling, but it hung loosely by his side. A few crewmen followed him in. She had discovered his name was Eliot Marsh. Martha was about to cry out when he gave her a backhanded thump.

He said, "You're mine whore. I've come to finish what I wanted weeks ago. No one gives me fifty lashes and gets away unscathed." He sent her sprawling across the cabin, and, with the help of another two crewmen, they lifted her onto the operating table. After ripping off her night attire, she lay spread-eagled on the central bench. Although she tried, she was unable to fight him off.

Eliot took his turn first and finished what he had been unable to do before. Each used her as she lay sprawled on the operating bench. She protested, but others held her down. Two held her arms, and two held her legs open. The violations were bad enough, but the indignity of her nakedness was abhorrent.

As one gained relief, the next one took his turn.

Eliot gloated about how they stopped the door from locking.

Martha struggled against being held, but resistance was futile and only meant she was further injured. She received more than one punch for her efforts. However, that did not stop them. One by one, the men who held her down took their turns at her. She couldn't even see what was occurring to her friends.

The other girls suffered a similar fate; only they were violated on their sleeping platform.

Even Sarah, who was due to give birth any day, was not exempt. They repeated her humiliation by assaulting her backward while she was forced onto her hands and knees. Only this time, she received a belting first. One kicked her up the nether end to make her conform to their lustful desires. Fearful for her child's safety, she did as she was told.

Martha lost count of how many had entered and left the room, but there were far more than before. Twenty or thirty crewmen had undoubtedly been and gone; more were lined up. She knew there were more than one hundred on the manifest. She felt like most had visited the girls that night. They just kept coming. No sooner had one man finished than he was pushed aside and another violated her.

The assaults continued one after the other with hardly a let-up between men. With so many crewmen, most were unfamiliar; only one face was known to her, and Martha kept her eyes fixed on Eliot as the others used her body. Though he was supposed to be under arrest, he stayed to enjoy the carnage from the doctor's chair.

Eliot remained watching the entire time and took pleasure in watching her face as each new crewman took his turn. He egged on each of his friends. After what seemed like an hour, Eliot had another go at her before he smashed his fist into her cheek. He saw he had cut her face and chuckled. He said, "I hope that leaves a scar. I have plenty, thanks to you. Some of my chums now have ladders of welts on their backs. So we wanted to give you whores some of your own medicine before it was too late. Sadly, James had to have an accident with a bit of help from me to give us access to you. He was going to try to stop us. You have a champion in him."

She said, "We're not whores, but you have used us as such."

Eliot was angry. "You are now, girlie. You've been had by more men than even I can count. If I were here longer, I'd take you again, but the doc is due back soon."

"I'll tell him. I'll..." She went to say something again, but he gave her another backhanded slap. She shut up. She was dizzy after the hit; she heard his evil cackle. She opened her mouth to speak, and another uppercut punch knocked her out.

It was another hour before the doctor returned, and he was horrified to discover what had befallen his bunkmates.

Martha was unresponsive on the centre table, almost naked and in an indecent position. The three young girls were scantily covered in the remnants of their night attire, bruised, and two had cuts and swollen lips. They, too, had been knocked out by their attackers. Sarah was groaning with pain. As she was nearly at term, he had noted that the baby had dropped earlier that day, preparing for its arrival. He swore.

Goodness knows how many had violated them, but there was no sign of the perpetrators now. He had been gone for two hours. James had been pushed down an open hatch and fallen into the cargo hold two decks down. It took twelve soldiers and a couple of crewmen to extricate him. Then the lad required treatment for his wounds and stitches. He noted that some of the crew had come and gone, and now wondered if they had been heading down here. He managed to cover the girls before he started cleaning their wounds.

He checked Martha's vital signs and realised she had been knocked out but was otherwise okay. He left Martha on the central table, covered with a sheet. He would need to tend to the cut on her cheek, but it had almost stopped bleeding, so she was in no danger. It would require stitching.

He checked Sarah and realised that she was bleeding from the men's activities and wondered if her labour had started. The child felt large, and she was a slip of a thing. He hoped she would be able to deliver it without trouble.

James had thankfully not broken his leg, but the slash on it required twenty stitches, which he had done once James was in his hammock. Therefore, the doctor was covered in blood.

Doctor Roylance admitted how Martha's idea of using alcohol between patients certainly reduced the infections, so he washed his hands with the hard lye soap and then doused them in rum. With a new needle and some catgut, he set three tiny stitches into Martha's cut, closing the gash on her cheek.

She roused as he was cutting the last stitch.

With the bleeding now crusted, he cleansed her cheek with a damp cloth dipped in rum.

Her eyes met his, and the pain he saw etched on her face reminded him of his wife Eleanor when he told her that only weeks after their marriage, he had to leave her for more than a year. He brushed the hair from Martha's forehead. "I'm so sorry, Martha. I should have called the guard, but I was so damned tired I didn't think."

She shook her head and said, "You could not have stopped them; there were too many. Last night's guards were some of the first attackers. It wasn't just the crew this time." The tears that had flooded her eyes drained away down the sides of her bloodied face, washing a channel through the drying ooze.

The doctor swore.

She said wearily, "They blocked the hole where the door locks with something and somehow loosened the screws from the inside bolts. They boasted about it." A sob escaped her. She lifted her hand to feel her injured cheek. It hurt, as did her nether region.

He said, "Oh, my dear girl! I feel some responsibility for this. Mayhap we should have housed you in a cabin, but we felt this was safer."

The doctor's empathy undid Martha.

He helped her sit up and offered comfort. Although only draped in a sheet, she wept on his chest as he placed a caring arm around her shoulder.

She realised that her bottom hurt a lot. She sobbed in earnest. "It was that same man with the broken arm. You said his name was Eliot." She hiccoughed and said spitefully, "I should have let you cut his arm off. He had the nerve to blame me for the flogging that he received for violating us the first time. Why do men think that they can do this to us and then blame us as if it's our fault? Why do we always have to pay the price for their lusts?"

This time, he drew her into a fatherly hug while she sat on the table. She clutched the sheet tightly. Kitty handed Martha a gown, and the doctor turned her back as Martha slipped it over her head. He said, "I am so sorry, Martha, but I shall ensure that he and his friends are punished fully. The captain will not tolerate such behaviour from his crew. I will also speak to the captain of the guards. Admittedly, I thought convicts were the ones we should have been worried about, not the crew or soldiers." He was gutted. His inattention had led to this. He assisted Martha to the girls' shared bed and realised Sarah was still groaning. She was bleeding profusely from her violations and had a dark pool between her legs. This time, her abuse had triggered labour. The baby was coming. He groaned. He needed sleep.

He turned to the girl he had just sewn up and said, "Martha, I hate to say this, but we have a long night ahead of us. Sarah's baby is coming. Can you dress properly and help me?"

Martha merely nodded. She was also dog-tired and angry that this had happened, but she had survived reasonably unscathed. She was battered and bruised; however, she had managed more sleep than the doctor. They could have knifed her had they wished, and they hadn't. Thankfully, her flow had just finished, so it was unlikely she would conceive. She wasn't so sure about the others.

The three other girls had dressed while they talked and had gone to sleep in each other's arms. Martha pulled on her drawers and tied an apron over her dress. Now clad in her only clean dress, Martha tended to Sarah while the doctor prepared for the birth of a child.

~

All the following day, Christmas Day, Sarah travailed in labour. The contractions brought her no closer to birth. She was too weak to walk. Her bleeding had eased but not stopped. The baby's head was engaged for delivery, but there was little progress. The doctor and Martha helped her stand and walk around the room. The baby needed gravity to help with its arrival.

The doctor wondered if one of the men had used an implement to impale her somehow as the blood drained faster than they could sop it up.

Sarah was getting weaker and weaker.

The ship sailed on.

None in sickbay was aware that the ship had reached the magnificent harbour. The wind dropped as the vessel turned into the vast bay.

They had no idea that they had reached their final destination.

Finally, Sarah was down to a three-minute contraction. She had no energy left. She vomited and needed to push. The head was out.

They heard the anchor drop as the sound of cockerels crowing from the shore met their ears.

Sarah's breathing shallowed. She had lost so much blood that the pile of towels were dripping. She finally delivered a baby boy; however, he never breathed. His limp, grey body lay in Martha's arms as the doctor tried to stem the bleeding of his mother.

All his efforts were for naught. Sarah exhaled a shallow breath and failed to take another. Both were gone.

Martha shouted at her friend. "Sarah! Breathe! Breathe, darn you."

She didn't.

Martha's shoulders slumped. She was numb over the loss of her friend.

The doctor removed the limp baby from Martha's arms and placed him on his mother's breast.

Martha was exhausted but turned to gaze at her friend for the final time before drawing the sheet over her face. Only then did she weep. Deep hacking sobs almost made her collapse. She had only had an hour or so of sleep in the past forty-eight hours, and Doctor Roylance had managed even less.

The doctor scooped Martha up in his arms and cradled her as she cried against his chest. He had come to care for this young girl as if she were a daughter or little sister. He was more than twice her age, yet she was so full of wisdom, and to think that she had been dealt such a horrific hand in life hurt. He had served in the Navy for ages, but this lass had sailed the seas all her life. His shirt was damp with her tears, but she needed the comfort. He rested his chin on her head. Hopefully, here in the colony, she would have a better life than what had occurred for the past year. He prayed to God for her safety. He would put in a good word for her when he met with Governor Macquarie.

The other three girls had each other and wept until they slept.

After some minutes, Doctor Roylance realised Martha had fallen asleep in his arms. He carefully placed her on the slab bed beside the other girls and covered them with blankets.

Achingly tired, he retired to his mattress. It would be an hour or more before the surgeon in charge of the hospital in Sydney came aboard for his inspection. Nothing more could be done for the women. His eyes closed, and he knew no more.

Chapter 13 Arrival In Hell
Martha's Trauma
December 1818

*M*artha was numb. She was so tired that she had fallen asleep in the doctor's arms. She slept for an hour before waking and noticed the ship was hardly moving. The anchor's release again stirred her slumber. She could see that the boat was moving close to shore. Sleep overtook her again. The doctor must have laid her down at the other end of the bed from her deceased friend. She could see his shoe-clad feet under the partition sheet.

He was also ready to drop from tiredness; he knew he had more to do, but after propping a chair under the door handle. He finally slept.

The ship had moved into the cove for processing, and the Sydney doctor pounded on the sick bay door. Doctor Roylance stirred; he checked his small carriage clock. He had slept for four hours. He jumped from his bed and walked to the door. Knowing the crew were untrustworthy, he was unsure about the soldiers. He asked, "Who goes there?" On hearing it was the surgeon, he moved the chair from under the handle.

The six soldiers who remained with him to rescue James were the only men he trusted. They were from the 17th, 24th, and 34th regiments; yet, he must leave the four girls and tell the captain what had occurred. He asked two of the six crewmen to take turns watching the girls. Sarah and her child were dead and would need to be buried as soon as possible.

The four girls woke when they heard the men's voices. Martha listened for a while, then she dozed again until more men's voices woke her.

Since the second round of violations two days ago, Kitty, Vicki, and Milly had barely spoken. All were deeply distressed. Sarah's death dampened their morale even more. The ship was now anchored a short distance offshore in Sydney Cove. Doctor Roylance said he would remain with the girls whenever possible until they were taken from the ship. The two bodies were quickly removed and buried in the local cemetery.

~

Hours passed, and they attempted to repair their torn night attire.

Once twilight approached, he decided to give the girls some air. "Come, ladies, we are going for an evening stroll."

The four girls were stunned, but they willingly stood at the railing on the main deck. Kitty said, "Cor, sir, it's so blooming 'ot. 'Twas Christmas Day yesterday, and I'm meltin'. It's supposed to be cold. 'Twas at home anyhow." She wiped her arm across her damp forehead.

One of the crew passed behind them, and Vicki moved towards the doctor for protection. Milly hooked her arm through the arms of her two companions. Martha said, "But, sir, we are in port. How are we permitted on deck?"

The doctor chuckled. "Martha, have we not just sailed halfway around the globe?" She nodded. He continued, "Should you decide to jump ship, exactly where do you think you will run to?"

Understanding dawned on her. "Oh, I see. So even if we escaped the ship, we could go nowhere."

He nodded and pointed to some of the activity on shore. "Girls, that group of men is a chain gang of male convicts. They are the worst of the worst men. Yes, even worse than those we carry. Should you run away, men like Eliot inhabit the bushland in this place. Many convicted men have escaped and live beyond the law. They take what they wish, steal food, use women and cause trouble with the Aborigines. They are the indigenous people of the land. They are as black as night and are called the ghosts of the bush. However, I like all those I have met. I would trust them over any of the felons here. In this place, escaped criminals are known as bushrangers rather than highwaymen. You must never wander anywhere alone. Martha, as an educated woman, you will probably be assigned to a family as a domestic servant, so you are unlikely to see many of them." A frown followed his cocked eyebrow and tipped head. He was serious.

Martha gasped. "Cor, doctor, I've been violated often enough not to tempt that fate."

He moved her slightly away from the young trio. The doctor nodded and said, "I must warn you that Eliot will be joining them in chains soon. He is being booted from the ship along with a dozen of his friends. Martha, I refuse to tell those three traumatised girls, but you all must remain well away from the male convicts in this place."

Martha's eyes were wide in fear. "I will, sir. Are they all that bad?"

With the three girls so close, he nodded in reply. "I will put in a good word for you and see if you can be placed somewhere safe." Her tear-filled eyes broke his heart. He wished he could take her home and leave her with Eleanor. That was not possible, so the next best thing would be to try to have her placed somewhere away from such vile men. The smell of roasting meat met their noses. Martha said, "Is that fresh meat cooking?"

The doctor nodded. "Yes, it's Boxing Day, and we're celebrating as we missed Christmas yesterday."

Martha shook her head. "I can't. Sarah's cold and gone; how can we celebrate?"

The doctor said, "You must go on living, Martha. Honour her by having a good life. Strive to be happy, marry a good man and have a bevy of wonderful, adventurous children. Your term will be over before you know it. Find others to help."

She nodded. As they chatted, the chain gang marched up the hill toward a large three-story building. The twilight faded, and night engulfed them. A raucous noise reached them.

Vicky had her fingers in her ears. "Wot's that noise, doctor? It's bloomin' loud."

The doctor had thought the same thing when he was here last. "There are many varieties of cicadas here, and one has two drums on its tummy. It's the loudest one I have heard in any port in the world. Here, they have a blatantly obvious name for it. It's called a double drummer cicada. There are green bladder ones and tiny ones that sound like crickets."

~

Although Sarah and her baby had been buried the day they arrived, it took a week before the other girls were unloaded. Doctor

Roylance escorted the four girls on deck and left them with the captain. He did not trust any of the crew, and the girls had experienced enough trauma in the sick bay.

Captain Craigie promised the medic that he would ensure their safety.

Doctor Roylance had an appointment on shore, but he kept mum about who he was meeting.

The girls had sewing to do and sat behind the captain on the quarterdeck. They were trying to repair the damage to their night attire caused by the attack. Some items were beyond saving, and the doctor gave them more of the linen sheets he had in storage. They settled down to make new garments. The sewing kept the hands busy, but the four bent heads remained silent about the catastrophe that had occurred days earlier. Their apparel needed to be replaced after the attacks. An occasional wet spot appeared on the sewing and was quickly absorbed into the cotton or linen. Tears and memories were beyond control. The fear of what lay before them also worried the four girls. With Sarah dead, they were grieving her loss. The doctor told them that Reverend William Cowper hadn't asked whether the child had breathed. He buried them together in the consecrated church ground.

James was the only crewman permitted near them, except the captain.

Hours passed in silence. Their garments were now recognisable from the flat, torn sheets they had been earlier that day. There was no discussion about their violations.

~

At four that afternoon, Doctor Roylance returned to the ship. Rather than report in, he bounded up the ladder towards them. "Good afternoon, ladies! I've had an eventful day. Captain, would you care to join us?"

Captain Craigie came at his call. They may well be at anchor, but he would not leave his vessel without someone being on watch. He beckoned his first mate and handed over his duty watch. Martha thankfully did not recognise the first mate's face. He had not been one of the men to violate them. The captain ushered the ladies and doctor up onto the poop deck. "We are all ears, doctor."

The doctor inhaled deeply and released it slowly. His voice kept low, he said, "Well, I have had an interview with the governor. He has been made aware of what has occurred and has arranged a placement for each of you. You three girls will go to the government dairy. Martha, there's a farm the governor uses as a safe house near Camden. It's where you will be going. It is run by a friend of his who, until recently, served as the governor's personal security. You will be collected from the female gaol as soon as transport can be arranged."

Martha was delighted. A smile hovered around her lips, and her heart rate calmed. Then, her emotions overwhelmed her. It was just as well she was already sitting. Her sewing was forgotten as the tears flowed. She turned to Vicki, who was closest, and hugged her as she wept with delight. Kitty and Milly were already weeping with happiness at their placement. They would all be kept safe. The three young girls packed their scant possessions and tidied the medical area for the final time. A long boat took them from the ship to a waiting, tattered carriage.

Martha remained on board until the following morning. Rather than sleep alone in the sick bay with the doctor as a guard, she was moved into the cabin next to the captain. As she had to travel a couple of days to her place of assignment, she had to spend a few nights incarcerated in the old gaol. Soon after dawn, she and the doctor would travel by boat to the Parramatta prison.

As they were in the harbour, they had access to plenty of water. It was hot, and being locked in a cabin with no open window was almost unbearable. When the door closed, she threw herself backwards on the mattress in the box bed and relaxed. This cabin was similar to the one she had on her father's ship. This small room felt like home.

Half an hour later, the doctor brought her a tray of food. It had obviously been sourced from onshore, as there was fresh roast pork and a selection of roasted vegetables. Taking her time over the delicious meal, she relished every mouthful. A hot bread-and-butter pudding followed it. After she finished every skerrick of her scrumptious meal, she set the tray near the door.

A few minutes later, the doctor knocked and said, "Martha, open up; I have a surprise for you." Recognising the doctor's voice, she unlocked her door and greeted the nice man. He was holding something, and three large pitchers of water stood next to him. His grin showed her he was up to something. "I thought you would like a bath. The captain collected this when he took the girls ashore. We must return it tomorrow."

Martha was stunned. "You did this for me? I'm just a convict girl, sir." She swiped away a rogue tear.

The doctor frowned. "There is nothing insignificant about you, my dear, as the word 'just' infers. You are one extraordinary young lady. Embrace the new life ahead of you and strive to leave behind the experiences you have endured. Do not let these bad men destroy your life. As you told us earlier, be a survivor, not a victim. Hunt for a wonderful man and make a happy life for yourself. Believe that God will look after you."

Martha was now very teary. She nodded. "I will try, sir." She moved aside so he could place the tin bath in the centre of her cabin. After he shifted the three large pitchers of hot water in, he collected her empty tray and remained to ensure she locked her door. "Enjoy it, dear; I shall return in about an hour for it." Martha relished her bath; she washed all of her clothing. After she was dressed, she dragged the full bath to the door. She listened to see if anyone was nearby, then tugged it, containing the three empty jugs, into the corridor and locked herself back into the cabin. The room was draped with wet garments, but she was now clean and relaxed. Life may not have turned out as she wished, but if what she was told was true, she would be kept safe until she served her time. She would only be twenty-four by the time her term expired. Martha slept deeply.

~

She was up and dressed before the doctor knocked on her door the next morning. She had folded all her clothing as the heat of the closed room dried them. She folded them neatly and wrapped them in a remnant from one of the torn sheets, knotting the corners so she could carry it easily.

Doctor Roylance escorted her onto the main deck, and the captain waited to say farewell.

The captain apologised profusely for the abuse she and the girls had received from his crew. "Miss Martha, I wish to inform you that the dozen men who attacked you have been dealt swift justice. They were unloaded soon after docking and have already been tried and imprisoned. They have received a three-year term of hard labour and one hundred and fifty lashes each. However, I have someone here who would like to thank you personally." He stepped aside to reveal James, who was almost hidden behind him.

Martha's face brightened considerably. "James, how's your hand?"

The young crewman held up his injured hand. "It's good now,

Miss Martha. But for you, I would have a stump. As I mentioned earlier, the captain has assigned me as an assistant cook, and I can also perform other tasks on deck if required. Even the itch from the missing fingers has nearly gone."

The captain tussled his hair. "You're a good lad, James. You pull your weight with half a hand, more than the scum who have just been removed from my ship. I have word that some good crewmen are looking for work, so you might get some new friends."

James grinned, but Martha could tell he was surprised by the glowing comment. "Thank you, Captain. I try my hardest." Martha knew him to be a shy lad, but he had been so brave when they had treated his mangled hand.

The time to depart arrived. Martha and the doctor moved to the side of the ship. There was a flimsy contraption hanging over the side, with a swing-like object attached. Martha was horrified. "Sirs, must I use that to reach the longboat?"

The captain was somewhat surprised. Yesterday, the girls refused to climb the rope ladder and used the chair. He should not have been surprised that Martha would refuse. He knew that she had spent much of her childhood on the deck of a ship. He shook his head, "No, miss, but I left it there from yesterday, should you wish to make a dignified exit."

Her giggle eased his fear. "It's not that, Captain. I have fallen from one of those contraptions before. I'd rather use the ladder."

A simple, "Oh," was all the response she received. While they were speaking, the doctor had already descended the rope ladder. She descended the wobbly rope like an expert. The doctor reached out to steady her entry into the rocking longboat. No sooner was she seated than the captain carefully threw her bundle down to the boat. It landed in the doctor's arms, and he passed it to her. The captain called. "Take care, Miss Martha." She nodded and called her thanks. Her new life was about to start.

~

After a four-hour trip up the harbour westward to the blue-tinted mountains, the small boat they were in was aiming directly towards a line of mangrove trees. Martha loved the salty spray from the oars showering her. She lifted her face to catch the spray. A smile settled on her lips as she relished her surroundings. Some sailors from the ship had offered to take them on their journey, and the doctor had hand-chosen these men as he knew none were involved with

Martha's abuse. These crewmen had assisted him and some soldiers in extricating James from the hold on the night in question. These six swarthy young men wanted to keep the girls safe. They were friends of James, and they knew that their young friend would have lost his hand but for Martha's intervention. They wished to see her safely to her destination and offered to escort her. They considered this one way to repay her for her kindness to their friend.

Doctor Roylance had made this journey before, so he knew where to go. As they drew closer, an opening appeared in the trees, and a channel became visible. The doctor directed them to take the main channel. The Duck River was off to the port side. The boat continued to head upstream as the river narrowed. He said to Martha, "We have another two miles or so before we reach the entrance to the Parramatta River. Then, a mile upriver, we will reach the King's Wharf. The government store, located near the wharf, is run by a soldier from the barracks. There's a drinking hole nearby that's a shady place that you are never to venture into. I have never passed by without some drunks sleeping off the inebriation of the previous night. Never put yourself at risk, Miss Martha."

Martha blanched. "I won't, sir. I've had enough done to me to never willingly place myself in such a position again."

The doctor motioned for the men to rest. "We have about three miles to go from here, lads. Take a breather, and then we'll head off again. The tide is just changing, and the incoming water will make the row easier upstream." They sat and waited for about ten minutes. Martha scanned the bay, absorbing her surroundings.

As the tide slowly changed, they rowed the last mile to the opening in the mangroves. There they waited for the tide to turn. One crewman held onto a mangrove branch until the tide began to carry them upstream. Once the current was flowing rapidly, the boat pushed off from the muddy trees and once again travelled upstream, drawing closer to Parramatta.

Thirty minutes later, they rounded the final bend in the river. They didn't hurry. A sprawling array of cottages was visible. The final sweeping bend saw the longboat pull up at the small jetty near a dilapidated two-storey building.

The doctor explained, "This is the government barracks building. The partially built building up there on the hill is the new barracks. I was shown around town during my visit last week. Completion is still about a year away, but the facilities will be wonderful once they are finished. The same goes for other buildings in town. Governor Macquarie is turning the colony on its head, and it's now a decent place to live. The gaol building is on the immediate list for replacement, and the Female Factory, as it will be called, is also under construction up that way." He pointed to the north. "Unfortunately, you will be housed in the old timber gaol until the Duffys can make arrangements to collect you. That's the name of the family you have been assigned to."

Now out of the boat, Martha was wide-eyed and looking at everything around her. In fear, she clung to the doctor's arm. She grabbed her small bundle of apparel and held it tightly. Two of the sailors accompanied them. Both were armed with a flintlock pistol and walked a pace behind the doctor. They walked the quarter of a mile from the wharf towards the gaol. The sun was now nearly overhead, beating down upon their heads. Martha clutched her possessions and was so absorbed in everything around her that she missed the approach of a red-coated soldier behind them. The unshaven, bedraggled man in a military coat said, "I'll take the prisoner from here, sir." He grabbed her arm.

Doctor Roylance pulled Martha closer. "No, thank you, sir. I have promised to escort her myself." The man tried to tug her out of the doctor's grasp. The bedraggled soldier held her tightly.

The sailors approached and said, "Hands off Miss Martha, sir, or we'll fire." Both had their pistols primed and ready.

The soldier realised he was outnumbered. "Fine, then deliver her yourself."

Doctor Roylance paused. "I have every intention of doing just that. I am here at the governor's instruction. Lay one hand on this woman, and you will have the three of us to answer as well."

Martha had only seen him this angry twice before, and both times had been after their abuse. She shrank even closer to him.

The soldier shrugged. "Fine, then she's your problem." He swivelled where he stood and stormed off in a foul mood.

When he was out of earshot, the doctor said, "Martha, he was unlikely to take you to the gaol. His boots and trousers were not government-issued military gear but convict attire, which means the red jacket was probably stolen. This settlement is full of ne'er-do-well men who will try to trick, connive and bamboozle anyone they can. He is probably a convict who has served his time."

Martha looked at the doctor with absolute horror. "You mean

he wanted to…" She couldn't finish. Tears cascaded down her cheeks.

The doctor nodded and finished her words. "Yes, dear, I mean just that. He probably wished to carry you off to have his way with you. I brought armed men with me for a reason. This place is full of ruffians and criminals. We are now in a penal town, and no female is safe, married or not. I have made arrangements for you to be removed as quickly as possible. You must remain in the prison for only a night or two, but that can't be helped. I would have sent you with the other girls, but they only had room for three."

Knowing there was light at the end of the tunnel gave her hope, but she nodded miserably. "I'll try to stay out of their way."

After crossing a bridge, the four arrived in front of a high-fenced building constructed mainly of sandstone but hastily repaired with timber. The dilapidated building looked as though it was on the verge of collapse and certainly didn't appear very secure. She asked, "How do they restrain anyone in here? You could push it over with the help of just a few men."

The blatantly obvious comment made the doctor chuckle. "It's exactly why a new prison is planned, well, at least for the women. The building was constructed under the instruction of the Reverend Samuel Marsden, and although much may be said for his passion and verve, he is sadly lacking in building prowess. He employed novices, and the stone was not prepared properly. I believe that one wall barely lasted a year. It was completed in 1804 and needed repairs the following year. As it was a convict-built building to restrain said convicts, I wonder if the lack of skill was intentional. Four years ago, the architect Francis Greenway made derogatory comments about both the building and Marsden." The doctor gazed at the dilapidated structure before him. "I give you fair warning: do not cross Marsden. He has no liking for the criminal element in town, emancipated or still confined. Regardless of whether you stole tuppence or murdered someone, they are all tarred with the same brush for him. He gives short shifts to all. One female felon here is a titled peer but intentionally stole something to have herself convicted. It's a long story, and I will not go into it, but unless she is with her husband, the reverend gentleman ignores her. I use his title loosely, as his nickname is the flogging parson."

Martha gasped. "Are men of the cloth not supposed to be holy and forgiving?"

The doctor nodded. "Supposed to be, yes, but in this case…

well, I would not like to be him on Judgment Day before his maker. I'm not saying he does not believe in God, but I think he forgot Jesus' words to love everyone and let Him be the judge. Just stay well clear of him and keep your mouth shut if you should come across him."

Her eyes were as big as saucers. "I will, Doctor, and thank you for the warning."

They approached the big, fenced door, and the doctor knocked on the communication hatch. It opened, and after a brief conversation, they were permitted entry.

The two crewmen had to remain outside.

Martha swallowed nervously. Her fingers now dug into the doctor's arm. Rather than pull away, he drew her closer. He wished he did not have to leave her here, but she would not be safe if she remained in the cabin on board. His parting words to her were, "Martha, I want you to know that I admire you, as you have taught me much. I ask that you not give up. Stand firm in your faith and know this: I will pray for you." He left before she could reply.

The doctor ensured that she was in a solitary cell and that the guards were to ensure her safety. She wasn't sure what good his prayers would be, but she could use every one of them. He would not leave until the matron of the women checked on her latest charge. Once done, he had little choice but to say his farewells to her through the small grill on the door of her cramped prison cell.

Martha remained at the door until the sound of his footsteps faded. Alone, abandoned and afraid, she looked around the tiny room. The door to her cell seemed nearly as flimsy as the rest of the building. When it slammed shut behind the doctor, some of the stone that held the hinges chipped off the wall. The heat was not too bad, as it faced south rather than west. That meant the sun wouldn't heat the room too much. Her face was hot from the boat trip, and she was sure she had a touch of sunburn. She was used to that, as she had often been burnt when on her father's ship. However, today, she had no ointments or liniments to cool her skin. Realising she was thirsty, she noticed two buckets, one full of water and one empty. A dented tin mug hung from a hook on the full one. Thirst won, so she tasted the water. It was fresh, so she took a long drink and washed her face.

With nothing to do to while away the time, she lay on the pallet bed and closed her eyes.

The door crashing open woke her. However, it wasn't unlocked, but it was being forced open. Initially, she expected someone to bring food, so she didn't move quickly. It was not. The leery grin that met her eyes was Eliot's, and he was not alone.

He said, "Hello, Miss Alexander, we meet again." His fist flew out before she could scream. She felt her jaw crack as his fist connected with her chin. A slap followed, and while she was reeling from the punches he rained down on her, Eliot grabbed her cotton gown and tore it from neck to her knees. Moments later, he forced himself on her. His grunts as he rutted her made her feel sick. Fighting was no use; she knew that would only bring her more pain. She felt him finish his vile act, and no sooner had he pulled himself off her than another took his place… then another and another. As before, he had lined up his friends to use her. Where was the staff? Where were the guards or matron? Where was her safety? A silent tear slid down her cheek, but she remained quiet.

Eliot jeered. "Oh look, the whore is weeping again." He waited until the current man had finished with her before crashing his fist into her other cheek. "I'll teach you to tattle on me, whore. I have no job, and now I'm to work on a chain gang when my arm heals. Thanks to you, I don't even have the excuse of being maimed. If I'd lost my arm, I would have been put on light duties; now I am forced to walk on a treadmill." His hand slapped her again. After watching his friends use her, he hauled himself from where he stood to give her a kick to the ribs.

Time passed in a blur for Martha. Why did he hate her so? What had she done to him that brought his condemnation upon her so violently?

More men came and went. Between each man, Eliot punched or slapped her each time she tried to pull away. She was sore all over. Her eyes were recipients of his fists. Her face was so swollen she could hardly see. Her ribs hurt, and each breath was a chore. As Sarah had advised, she refused to fight back; she lay quietly, knowing that any resistance would bring more pain.

She had no idea how long the abhorrent situation lasted. She lost count of the men who came and went. Her last memory was Eliot approaching her and hearing his evil laugh. "Got no fight left in you, eh?" She saw his fist approaching, then she was rendered insensible.

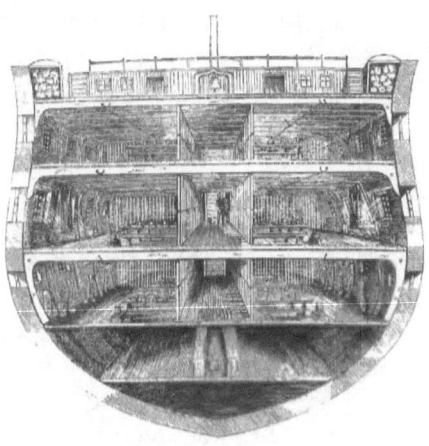

Chapter 14 New Cellmates
Jack's Journey

The boys were the only two convicts on board for the first few days. They were served whatever the cook had made for the crew and soldiers. This would stop once the other convicts were loaded. However, for the moment, they were given a meal that looked like edible food.

Charles realised that more meat was on his plate than he had seen in ages. He relished the good meal and ate every skerrick.

The cook, Jock Thurston, offered them leftovers if they did the dishes. They jumped at the chance. Having emptied their stomachs overboard, they were both grumbling loudly.

Jack compared the single plate of food with the sixteen or more courses served at the regent's table. He had often been a guest at a few of these elaborate banquets, but the staff would eat the leftovers in the kitchen. The shredded steamed cabbage, corned beef, and creamy potato mash he was served today were delicious. He didn't like the over-spiced, creamy sauces served at the royal tables, and the prince's banquets would last for hours, where the tables groaned with fancy food.

As neither lad voiced their thoughts, they just smiled at each other and tucked into the food. Hopefully, the doctor would find time to continue his narration of the colony's founding.

Once they had finished their meal, they remained at the end of the long table, listening to the conversations around them. Charles noted that one soldier, Major Edward Grace, could hardly keep his eyes off him.

Earlier that day, the man had been with Captain Moncrief on the poop deck, and Charles watched as the soldier ran to the railing and vomited. Had sea-sickness struck this man down as well?

The military man looked about the same age and had hair of a similar colour. Even their eyes were a similar stunning blue.

While Charles was in dirty clothing, the soldier was immaculately garbed in a brand-new uniform with the bright red coat signalling his rank as a major. Charles dared not speak to him unless addressed. All the man did was stare at him.

He returned the gaze with a smile and a nod, but wondered at the investigative inspection he was receiving. He gave a nod of acknowledgment and dropped his eyes to his nearly empty dinner plate.

As the soldier was halfway along the table, Charles spoke to Jack quietly and said, "He keeps watching me. Have I got mud on my nose?"

Jack had also noticed his new friend's penetrating gaze. The man had barely cast him a glance. However, Jack had gazed intently at the soldier. His almost-twin had visited the regent with his father, Lord Charles, a duke, only a few months ago.

The soldier had not been introduced to them, but Jack knew the duke and his eldest son by sight. It was the younger of those two men that Charles had reminded him of. Was this soldier a brother and, therefore, a son of a peer? If so, why was he here? He knew the peer was the Duke of Gracemere, but he didn't know their family name. The prince addressed the duke as Gracemere, and his son, David, as Marquess of Allingmere, as was his title.

Jack's gaze flicked from one face to another. Yes, these two could be brothers or cousins. However, Charles seemed not to know the soldier. That was a problem for another day.

Their meal was over, the dishes needed to be done, after which they would return to their cramped quarters below.

The weather on the somewhat short trip to Deal turned rough, but the two lads now had their sea legs.

As they were now permitted to leave the stinking cell below, they found a nook where they were out of the spray but remained safe.

The soldier kept watch on them from afar. He was a major

without men to command.

They presumed they were to be collected in Deal.

~

The doctor had not had a chance to continue his dialogue about the colony, and the two young men did not wish to sound pushy.

Dover drew closer, and the boys realised that their lives would change once the other convicts were on board. There was a sea of anchored ships in the harbour.

Charles uttered an appropriate word. "Cor!"

Jack said, "I totally agree, Charles."

The captain stood beside them and said, "As soon as the anchor drops, scram, vamoose, scoot, and stay out of sight until you are called. Unfortunately, your quarters below will become cramped and disgustingly unpleasant. You should not be out of your cell, but I won't be telling anyone."

He was instructed to permit Jack more freedom than any other felon. The other man was to accompany him where possible. So far, both had behaved impeccably. He had no idea who either man was, but he realised they were well-behaved and would cause no trouble. Both were educated to some degree.

The boys knew they should have remained locked up. They were not looking forward to the following months. The captain told them there were more than one hundred prisoners to collect, plus some more of the 48th, 53rd, and 69th regiments.

Major Grace, who was the blond soldier, would finally have some men to command.

The captain noticed that the lads had not yet left. He said, "Jack, I should have mentioned earlier, but shortly before leaving London, Mr Wilberforce had me sign for a couple of cases of things. I have one hundred spelling books and a large amount of printed matter. Most are some form of religious information. However, he also said to tell you there are fifty Bibles, slates, and chalk. He mentioned that you would like to know. He added something about teaching others to read." He looked puzzled. "As his letter mentions you with some familiarity, I gather you are literate?"

Jack nodded. "I am indeed, sir, and that information is wonderful news. I can teach anyone interested, if required. As to knowing him, his son, Bill, was my best friend. However, Mr Wilberforce was a witness to the incident that led to my arrest. It is he

I turned to when I discovered my guardian had died."

Charles had remained silent, but now added. "I can read as well, sir."

The captain grinned. "Wonderful news! I shall work something out for anyone who wishes to better themselves on the voyage. The doctor may assist you."

With a nod, he moved to take the helm. He would take his vessel to collect the cargo of men. Sometimes, he hated this job, but every now and then, he found a ray of sunshine in the darkness of human cargo.

With a long sigh, he spun the wheel to turn the ship. "Lads, head down to the main deck and get ready to hide below."

The boys slid down the railing from the quarterdeck and headed to the hatch that led to their cell. There, they waited for the captain's signal to vamoose.

From this spot, they could see the vessel manoeuvre its way past the anchored ships. Doctor Ryan, Major Grace, and Ensign Geake were on the foredeck, watching Captain Moncrief guide the ship gracefully past the plethora of anchored vessels.

It took half an hour to navigate into their designated anchorage.

As soon as the call of "Anchors aweigh" came, the boys opened the hatch door and crept below deck.

From today onwards, life would become unpleasant.

~

On June 4th, the last of the provisions were loaded aboard. Longboats were loading one hundred and forty-eight men.

They came in groups of six and were brought on board. They filled the cells below decks. Each was chained in wrist irons in pairs, and some were double-ironed by the ankles.

They had started filling the cells at the bow of the ship, and the boys were at the stern.

The soldiers were currently filling the cells halfway along the deck when Phillip Geake had escorted six new felons into a cage. After ushering them into their cell, he made his way along to see the boys and say farewell.

Charles heard a goat bleating, so he asked Ensign Geake if he could relieve her pain.

Phillip frowned. "Pain? What do you mean?"

Charles explained. "Sir, I used to work as a stable worker and farmhand. I helped milk the goats and cows. I can tell by her bleat that she needs to be milked."

With raised eyebrows in shock, Phillip said, "Fine! She's only just been brought on board. Take Jack with you, and whatever you do, do not venture on deck. Take the milk to the galley, then return to your cell. Shut the door when you get back so it looks locked."

He turned to the slightly older lad. "Charles can teach you to milk as four cows are to be loaded later this afternoon. If you're happy, I'll have you two assigned to their upkeep. However, I actually came to say my goodbyes. I am leaving on the last boat." He unlocked the cell door and followed them out of the convict deck.

Once they were out of earshot of the other convicts, he said, "This lot of criminals are rotters. Amongst them are crimes such as picking pockets, sheep and cow stealing, vagrancy, perjury, highway robbery, assault, and possession of forged bank notes. They are not the worst I've seen, but pretty darned close. I think one has a few scalps to his name, but he was only charged with theft. What's more, this lot stinks. Keep your heads down, lads. Major Ned Grace will remain on board, but there will be members of three regiments to accompany you. Two other majors will join him. Major Ned is with the 48th, and although he's new, he's a really nice chap, but he's only along for the ride as he won't take up his commission until he meets the governor. There will also be men from the 53rd and 69th regiments in charge of the prisoners. For some reason, I noted that Ned's been watching you, Charles." A cocked eyebrow followed.

Charles replied with a nod. "I noticed, sir, but I've never met him before, and I don't know him."

The soldier shrugged. "Okay, thought I'd mention it: same hair and such. So, no relation?"

Charles denied any known connection.

Geake continued. "Anyway, I must be going, lads. I'll let someone know you are here. The chaps from the 69th regiment will be overseeing your voyage; the soldiers from the 48th and 53rd are only passengers. I believe that we only have one paying passenger. She's a minister's wife heading out to rejoin her husband. Mrs Cartwright, I believe, is returning after some time in England." He saluted them and then left. Despite the denial, he wondered whether the soldier and the convict lad were related, but asking the major was not his place. He shrugged and went to collect his belongings.

The boys reached the area where the stock was housed and

heard the nanny goat's agonised bleating. No kid was in sight, so Charles had been correct.

The nanny goat was in pain and had a very distended udder.

A coopered pail hung upside-down on the bulkhead, and a three-legged stool was outside their pen. In a matter of minutes, Charles was seated next to the beast and began stripping her milk. After relieving the pressure in her udder, he asked Jack to join him in the stall. "Want to learn to milk?"

Jack grinned. "You bet! I've never had anything to do with farm animals except the odd dog. Horses don't count. I love them." He grinned, knowing how much time he had spent in the royal stables. He watched as the goat nibbled the hay in her manger.

Charles chuckled. "I worked as a farmhand as well as in the stables. I skipped school to tend to the horses. I love all farm animals." Charles moved aside and pointed for Jack to sit on the squat three-legged stool. He explained, "Goats have two teats, and cows have four, but milking them is similar. You never know when you will need this skill. One of the first things you need to know is that you must have clean, warm hands. The clean hands are obvious, but the animals won't let their milk down if your hands are cold."

After dipping his hands in a bucket of drinking water, Jack blew on his hands to warm and dry them as Charles had done. He gingerly placed his fingers on the goat's full teats and attempted to milk her. The nanny goat pulled her head out of the trough of food and turned to look at him. After giving a long bleat, she returned to nibble her hay.

Jack squeezed, and nothing came out. "It's not working."

Charles squatted beside him and placed his hands over his. "Like this, squeeze and slide."

Jack felt the subtle movement of Charles's fingers and duplicated it. Soon, he heard the milk spray hit the bucket. Charles moved away. After a while, Jack said, "This is so cathartic, Charles." The slosh, slosh of the milk was slowly filling the bucket.

A short while later, sounds were heard further along the deck. The other animals had arrived. Charles checked on the other stock: a horse and a few cows. Jack rested his head against the flank of the goat as Charles had done. "I could get used to this, my friend."

Charles chuckled. "You may have to, as they will need milking twice daily in all weathers. There are a few cows, and at least one of them may require milking, and they have four teats. The others are in calf, but one has already dropped hers. We'll need to rig up some hammocks for them, for when we get bad weather."

They finished stripping the goat of her excess milk and carried the pail to the galley.

The cook greeted them with a cheery hello and said, "Thanks, lads. The cabin-class passengers are having a roast tonight before we hit the open seas. It's cooked, and I have a treat for you both. Half an hour later, this would all be gravy, but here's a slab of bread and dripping for you both."

Charles's face lit up. "Thanks, sir."

Jack had never eaten this so-called treat before and looked dubious.

Cook soaked an inch-thick slab of fresh bread crust in the pan juices and handed it to the first young man.

Jack hung back to see what it was like. It looked edible, so he gingerly put his hand out for his morsel. Even though his stomach rumbled, he nibbled the bread and juice, and then, liking it, he took a huge bite. He said, "Oh, Charles, this is so good. I've led a somewhat sheltered existence and never had this before."

"Rather!" said his friend, grinning. "Fills the hole in a young man's tummy."

They knew not to eat in front of the unwashed masses below, so they sat in their old places at the long dining table and ate slowly.

They had just finished their treat when the cook placed a plate of off-cuts of the roast in front of them. "Hoe in lads, there are some potatoes under the meat. They busted when I dug them out of the pan."

In unison, the boys said, "Thanks, Mr Thurston."

The cook chuckled. "Jock will do, lads."

The boys made short work of the food before returning to their cell.

The crowd below were safely under lock and key. They slipped back into their cell and lay listening to the chatter.

Within hours of the bulk of the convicts being loaded, the two boys learned to stay quiet.

Phillip had been correct.

The newcomers were filthy, foul-mouthed, and uncouth. Every alternate word was riddled with blasphemy, swearing, or a tirade against the lawmakers.

The boys hardly dared whisper to each other. They had an hour to wait until the first meal was served to the masses.

A cauldron was bubbling away, and it smelled ghastly. It smelled like a gross mix of a dog's breakfast and dirty dishwater. Having just devoured the offcuts of a delicious roast dinner, the boys grinned at each other. Hopefully, they would be assigned other upper-deck duties once they left port.

They lay on their bunk and waited.

Six of the ugliest blighters were ushered into the cell adjoining theirs.

A big bald beast of a man walked in first. He saw the boys watching them. "Wot ya lookin' at, youn'ngs?" He claimed the bunk closest to theirs, turned to them, and glared. He cleared his throat, and a gooey glob of spittle landed on the cell floor. He watched the boy's faces and released an evil cackle. He said, "Name's Tom Onions, and none of the funny mouthing off from you. Want some lessons on life? 'Cause mess wit us, and that's wot you'll get."

Jack's mouth was open in horror. He had never seen such an uncouth person.

In the dim light, Jack could see half an ear missing and the jagged edge that showed it could have been bitten off. His head shook in response to the statement.

He was about to reply when Charles grabbed his arms and said, "Shh."

Jack didn't need to be told twice. He shut his mouth and nodded. He realised that offering to teach some of these convicts to read was not an option. Prayer was another matter. He promised himself that he would keep that up daily.

Their six new neighbours fought over who would sleep where. A few punches were thrown until their sleeping quarters were settled.

One ended up bloodied, with his nose bent and bleeding from Tom.

Both boys were thankful that their shared bed was on the far side of the cell.

They could hear them talking, but the men could not reach Jack and Charles unless the boys leaned against the bars dividing the cells.

Having already eaten a full meal, the boys hung back when it came to dishing out the slops the convicts were served. They held their tin plates out to Jock to get their food ration. They knew that if they didn't take their quota, it would cause questions.

They were the last in the line. However, knowing they had

eaten upstairs, he only gave them a small serving of the slop. As the cook dished up their meal, he added another slice of bread.

Rather than dumping it in the brown mess as he did with other convicts, they realised these two slices were more of the thick bread and dripping they had eaten earlier. He met their surprised faces and said, "Shh, slip it under your plates. Make the most of it, as you won't get this treat again." In a loud voice, he said, "You two will be washing up, so you go eat over there."

The boys took their portions and sat on the lowest step of the ladder leading up to the next deck. They ate in silence, listening to the cacophony of noise around them. The smell of unwashed bodies was overwhelming, but a bit of breeze was coming through the hatch above them. The stench of the buckets used as chamber pots made the aroma worse. They looked forward to the milking time when the only smell was of animal dung.

The other prisoners had to eat their swill in their cells. The boys devoured their meagre meal and washed up the serving utensils and cauldron.

Jock paused beside them before leaving and quietly said, "One of the new prisoners will be assigned as a cook, and there will be others assigned to ensure fair rationing. Keep well clear of them all, and see me after milking each time." He then said in a louder voice, "You two. Make sure everything is clean and tidy for tomorrow's meal. Them beasts will need twice daily milking and you'se going to learn to do it. Right?"

The boys said loud enough for the closest convict to hear. "Yes, sir! We will, sir."

Cook was about to leave when he turned from the third step and said, in a loud voice that carried through the cells, "We'll choose the orderlies tomorrow when the rules are read to you all. I know that lessons for reading and writing will be offered for those who wish to learn. So think about that overnight."

~

The routine of rising when their cell was unlocked and heading to the stock was a blessing. They milked the goat and cow and carried the milk to the galley in two pails.

Jock dished up a large bowl of creamy porridge, followed by two thick slices of bread, accompanied by a dribble of honey. He handed them the food and said, "A worker is worth his pay. Just make sure you eat something when you go downstairs."

The boys nodded.

Only six convicts volunteered to learn to read; one was from Tom's cell next to them.

Jack and Charles were the designated teachers. As the only reading material was the religious pamphlets Mr Wilberforce gave them or Bibles, discussions soon turned to faith. The evening milking was followed by more good fare.

The boys felt they could tolerate the conditions, including the numerous fights and squabbles, if they received decent food after completing their chores.

The first big storm hit, and many convicts succumbed to seasickness. This added to the smell but reduced the fights.

The boys had their sea legs and weathered the storm with delight. Due to the stench, they spent more time with the animals, who were now strung up in hammocks for their safety, than locked in their cell.

Charles wondered if the blond major had disembarked at Deal; however, when they were permitted to sit outside as the storm passed, the blond soldier stood watching them. Again, Charles gave him a nod of acknowledgement, knowing he was being watched, but nothing more.

Two hours of sitting in the sunshine during the day made the nights more bearable. The six in the cell next to them were brought out in pairs rather than as a group and were kept shackled to an iron ring on the deck when out of their cell.

Jack and Charles stayed well clear of them.

To date, Jack had kept quiet about his faith, but Charles noticed that Jack had a nightly time of prayer before going to sleep. He didn't admit it to Jack, but he had also started praying before sleeping. Memories of his mother's words came flooding back to him. They attended the village church when they could, but Sundays were often spent tending their vegetable garden. His maternal grandfather had been a minister, so his mother instructed her two children in the faith. Now, Charles' prayers had started in the middle of one horrendous storm, where he wondered if the ship would tip over. He never asked about Jack's faith, as he didn't want an earful of religion, but he listened hard during the reading lessons. He admired his friend's fortitude. Nothing stopped his daily prayers. Even when Tom teased him mercilessly, Jack would not stop. He chuckled when he even said a prayer aloud for Tom. The vile brute hurled abuse at Jack, but nothing else.

~

A week out of Cape Town

The convicts settled down for the night, though not everyone was asleep.

Jack was praying, and Charles waited for him to hop into bed. It was cold, so they were touching, head-to-toe, and snuggling under their double-thick blankets. The weather cooled, and they realised that body heat and double blankets were much warmer.

Since the sea was horrendous again, Charles was drowsy but clinging tightly to the base of the bed out of habit. Jack held onto a bar of their cell as he prayed in the pitch dark. The seas were so rough that all lamps were extinguished for safety. Tom and his bunkmate were still awake and whispering, but not softly enough to stop them from being overheard in the adjoining cell.

Jack was horrified at what he heard.

Charles was dozing, but Jack shook him awake and put a hand over his mouth. "Listen."

They remained silent but listened hard. The whispers of mutiny reached their ears. Jack dared not move. He was cold and wished to pull the blankets tighter. They waited and waited. Eventually, the two criminals were snoring.

Jack attempted to sleep. They knew they could not discuss what they had overheard until they did the milking.

The hours until dawn seemed endless. Jack lay awake for ages, and finally, he fell into a restless slumber not long before they had to rise.

Charles shook him awake. "Milking time, Jack. Come on."

They tidied up the cell and had put on their shoes by the time the guard came to wake them.

A soldier about their age had been assigned to them. Errol Findlay would escort them to the animals at dawn and dusk each day. They then would take the buckets of milk to Jock in the galley. A second cow had given birth last week, and her milk was now in. The heifer consumed a lot, but there was ample milk for the galley to use. The remaining two cows were ready to drop their calves at any moment.

While the boys milked their chosen animals, Errol held the calf away from its mother. They had little chance to chat about what they had overheard until they were on the way to the cook. "Who can we tell? The doctor only ever comes when we're down in our cells."

Jack said, "Phillip said that the blond soldier who keeps watching you is a nice chap. Let's see if we can grab his attention." As he finished speaking, they arrived at the cook's side.

Jock had a treat for them this morning. "Morning, lads! Get this into you." He handed them two plates filled with the end crusts of the loaves; only these had been dipped in beaten egg and fried in pork dripping.

Jack grinned. "French toast sea style. Thanks, sir. You're not wrong; this is a treat." The boys ate their breakfast while doing the dishes. They hoped that Major Grace would arrive early and ask if they could have a word with him. But the galley remained empty. They had finished their snack and returned to their cell. The porridge on the convicts' menu would fill their stomachs. The seas had eased overnight, and reading and writing classes on deck resumed for the small group. They waited until the major appeared at the poop deck rail. The man took up this position daily and oversaw the classes.

Other guards of the 69th regiment were on convict duty guarding the felons, but Ned had nothing else to do, so he watched and wondered. Who was this felon who bore such a striking resemblance to his brother? A frown settled on his brow, and his eyes hardly moved from the fair-haired convict. He listened to Jack as he subtly shared his faith with the class. They didn't even realise they were hearing the true faith shared so lovingly that he was sure even Jesus would have been pleased. Each lesson solidified his beliefs, but hearing such words from a convict left him stunned. Who was this young man? How could he get to spend more time with him?

For an hour, the boys held their class. They were fully aware of the major's observation from above but had no way to catch his attention.

When the class finally drew to a close, Ned was still watching. What he saw made his heart skip a beat. The fair-haired convict, Charles, caught his eye. He looked worried. Ned was sure he mouthed, "Help." He wondered if he had seen the action until Charles did it again. He nodded to the other lad next to him and did it a third time. Something was up, and they turned to him for help. He wondered what excuse he could use to draw them aside when they gave him one. Charles pushed Jack, and a minor squabble ensued.

As the other soldiers led the students below deck, Ned reacted. "You two, up here on the double. No fighting or we'll see you in irons." Ned nodded to the soldiers escorting the others away and said, "I'll deal with these two." The guard nodded and left with the other convicts. Once out of sight, Ned said, "Follow me, both of you and no fighting." He sounded gruff, but the boys hoped Phillip was right about him. They entered the cabins on the upper deck and followed the tall young major to a door. After checking that no one was nearby, he pushed it open and ushered the two into his own cabin. Once inside, he turned to them and said, "What's all this about?"

After a glance around the room and then at each other, Jack nodded for Charles to speak. "Sir, we overheard a conversation last night. There are talks of an attempted mutiny by Tom Onions and his friends. We would have told the doctor, but we have not been able to see him alone." Charles glanced at Jack and saw him nod. "Sir, I've noticed you were watching me, and although I don't know why, Ensign Phillip Geake said we could trust you, so we are. We don't know who else to tell."

Ned looked surprised when he realised the man's accent was similar to his own. This man was also from Kent. "Stay here and touch nothing." He left them in his cabin and returned moments later with the captain.

Jack noticed a well-used Bible beside the soldier's bed and smiled.

Ned said, "Tell him what you told me." The boys retold the story, adding more detail. This time, Jack repeated what he heard.

Captain Moncrief swore. "Major Grace, we must get these two out of the cells. I'm sure there is a spare cabin somewhere on this deck, so have their things moved there. If word spreads about a mutiny, we could be in big trouble, but that's nothing to what would happen to these two if it were discovered they had reported the conversation."

Ned nodded; he agreed. "Sir, to make it realistic, I think they may need to have a fight and then be removed. I can say they are on restricted liberty." He turned to the two young men and said, "Do you think you can make it realistic?"

Jack grinned. "Yes, sir, I think we can manage that."

Charles smiled. He would agree to a few punches if they could complete their journey in a cabin. "We certainly will, sirs."

The captain nodded. "When you two boarded in London, I wondered about the wisdom of letting you be so free on the ship. I believe that trust is now paying off. Don't let me down, lads. Mrs

Cartwright is our only passenger; the other occupants are the soldiers from three different regiments. One wrong move, and you will be back downstairs with the rabble. You will still need to keep up your duties, milking and washing up after our meals, but if you behave, you will have a much more comfortable journey than any other convict." He wished he could have moved them out of the cells earlier.

The boys nodded in unison. Jack said, "We will abide by all your rules, sir. However, what will happen to the classes?"

Ned was impressed that the young man still wished to continue with them. "If you are prepared to do them, we'll work out something." Charles smiled. He wanted to hear more about the living faith Jack shared. It was nothing like the stuffy church talks he had heard as a lad. He was absorbing all the information from the reading classes, but did not ask any questions. However, he was aware that there were many things he wished to know. He wanted to understand more of what made Jack tick. Why was he so keen on sharing his faith? He certainly lived what he believed. He only heard Jack swear once, and his actions were always gracious and appreciative. Charles looked at his friend and smiled. Yes, he'd be quite happy to be confined to a cabin for the following weeks. He could question him to his heart's content in the cloistered room.

The captain was watching him and said, "Are you all right, lad?"

Charles nodded. "Yes, sir, just deep in thought."

The captain chuckled. "Fine, let's get this fiasco underway. Major Grace, please escort these two below."

With the plan about to be set in motion, the boys followed the captain from the major's cabin. The major exited last and closed the door. They parted company at the entrance to the convict ladder. Jack descended first, with Charles hard on his heels. This was intentional: they decided to fight where most other convicts could see them, which was in the meal preparation area. Jack slowed his descent, and Charles ran into him.

"Watch where you are going, will you?" Jack said gruffly.

Charles felt like chuckling. If that were the worst Jack could come up with, he would teach him a few choice words. "Well, I wouldn't have run into you if you'd moved faster. Move along."

Jack turned on him. "I'll move as fast as I damned well wish. Go past if you're in such a hurry." Charles pushed him, and Jack pushed back. They soon scuffled, giving faux punches, but one hit home. Jack's nose was soon bleeding, adding to the realism of the fight. The cheering of the other prisoners echoed around the deck.

Tom and his mutinous friends couldn't see much, but they knew a fight was on. Some were calling Jack's name, some barracking for Charles. Ned slowly followed them into the squalid deck. He had needed to pause as the stench nearly overwhelmed him. He swallowed his bile. Ned had not descended into the hellhole before, and it took a lot of determination to do so voluntarily. It reeked.

The boys were getting tired, but they kept up the ruse, throwing the occasional punch. Thankfully, Major Ned appeared and broke it up. He waited for a few minutes halfway down the ladder and then broke up the fight. "So much for being well-behaved prisoners; I think some time in the black hole will fix you two. Move along and get your things. We'll see how long the captain gives you as punishment." He grabbed the boys by the scruff of their shirts and, keeping them apart, marched them to their cell. He didn't know which cell they were in, so he whispered to Jack, "Lead on."

Jack did. Now holding a handkerchief to his nose. They soon had their meagre possessions bundled up. Ned said loudly, "Upstairs first, and I'll get the doctor to check you before I deal with you."

Jack's nose was oozing goo down his shirt. To keep up the show, they made a fuss about who owned things like blankets and utensils.

Tom couldn't resist butting in. "So little namby-pamby boy has some fight in him after all. Who would 'a thunk?"

Charles turned to the filthy man and remarked, "Something had to give. I can only take so much." Tom and his cellmates laughed at Jack's broken nose and Charles's bleeding knuckles. An unlucky punch struck Jack's nose when the ship moved. He had no intention of connecting with his friend's face, but it certainly did the trick. He grazed his knuckles on the ladder, not on Jack, but Tom didn't know that.

Ned chuckled to himself. It certainly was a good show. The young men would now be safe in the adjoining cabin to his on the upper deck.

As Ned escorted them to sickbay, one of the students called out, "Hey, what will happen to classes? Will someone else take over?"

Ned told him to pipe down and added, "I'll let you all know later." They headed further along the deck to see the doctor. From there, they could use another ladder to climb onto the deck out of sight of the convicts.

By noon, the lads were comfortably ensconced in a small servant's cabin. Each bunk had mattresses, a feather pillow, and two blankets.

Jack and Charles grinned at each other.

Charles said, "Well, this is a bit better. I'm sorry about the punch connecting, Jack. That was an unlucky shot when the ship bucked."

Jack laughed. "A busted nose is worth getting out of that hellhole. I hope the soldiers can watch and catch Tom and his cronies before it's too late."

Chapter 15   A Place of Healing
Martha

$\mathcal{A}$ gentle hand stroked her forehead with a cool cloth. A calming voice spoke, and someone else responded. The woman's voice had a Scottish accent similar to her mother's, and it sounded distressed. "Oh, Hetty dear, how could someone do this to the wee lassie? Thankfully, Janey told you about her while you were with me."

The person holding the cool cloth said, "Elizabeth, I do not know, but I shall take her home until she is well enough to go to Mark and Cathy. She can't arrive looking like this; they can't nurse her, and I have a spare room. Can you fix that with Lachlan?"

Martha heard someone sit near her feet.

The lady with an accent said, "Of course, dear. May I suggest that we load her in my carriage and take her directly to my home now? The doctor can attend to her at my place. Is Joel with you today?"

The other lady must have shaken her head. "No, he's with the children. Hector brought me in today."

Martha heard a slight gasp. The Scottish lady asked, "Hetty, isn't he a life convict? Are you safe with him?"

The other lady, Hetty, chuckled. "Yes, Elizabeth, I trust him as much as I do my Joel. Hector is the man we need today. He's as strong as an ox and will be able to carry her with ease. We need to get her into some sort of gown. She can't be seen in this state by any man. Can you see if that bundle is clothing?"

Martha felt herself being carefully stripped and reclothed in her spare gown.

She was lapsing in and out of consciousness and had no fight left in her. These women, whoever they were, would not hurt her. She knew they would care for her, and that was all that mattered. She sighed and slept.

She roused when she felt herself lifted and carried by someone who smelled clean and masculine. For some reason, his arms brought comfort, not fear. She rested her bruised cheek against his chest as he carried her the short distance to the carriage.

His Scottish brogue murmured, "Relax, lassie. You're safe now."

His accent reminded her of her father's soft lilt. He gently placed her on the seat of the carriage, and her head rested on a lady's lap. Martha had no idea who this was, as she was unable to open her eyes.

Moments later, she felt the carriage move off smoothly.

Caring hands held her still.

The trip crossed a bridge, and the carriage climbed a hill. Every movement was agony.

She was unable to stop her groans.

Soon after it halted, the same strong arms lifted her again and carried her inside.

He noticed tears sliding down her cheeks. He asked, "Are you awake?"

She nodded against his chest. He whispered, "My name is Hector. Miss Martha, know that you are safe. These are good people. Trust them as I do."

She nodded again. The blood had congealed from the cuts on her lips, and it hurt to move them. More tears slipped from her swollen eyes. How had her life come to this? What had she done to deserve any such punishment?

They passed through a door, and voices came from a room to the side. One she recognised.

She turned towards the familiar voice, and even though moving made her almost scream with the pain, she reached out her hand. She felt the wall as they passed, then grabbed onto the doorway's frame.

Hector paused and said, "Miss, you are safe."

She shook her head. "Doctor, help me!" Her voice was but a croak, but the gasp and cry that followed meant he had heard her plea.

Doctor Roylance realised immediately who Hector held.

"Martha, is that you?"

He abandoned his meeting and followed Hector to tend to her.

Again, Martha relaxed in Hector's arms. She knew she was safe, as this man had protected her for so long. She must have passed out again.

She didn't remember being placed on the bed to get her wounds dressed. Hetty and Elizabeth Macquarie gently stripped off the cheap dress, and with the help of Mrs Macquarie's dresser, Mrs Jones, the three ladies managed to get her dressed in one of the First Lady's soft lawn night gowns.

Martha was still lapsing in and out of consciousness while the doctor worked.

Finally, she slept peacefully.

~

When she woke, the smell of brandy hit her nose. Something cold covered her eyes, and it felt wonderful. Her wrist hurt, as did her ribs. Her lips stung, and she touched them and felt that someone had stitched them.

The well-known voice said, "Yes, Martha, I cleansed the wounds with the governor's best brandy as you taught me." The doctor's hand brushed the hair from her bruised brow. "I'm so sorry this occurred."

Martha gently shook her head. After swallowing, she said, "Water!"

An arm eased her to sit, and the doctor held a cup to her bruised lips. After a long drink of water, she felt better.

Relaxing in his arms, she said, "Eliot did this." Her voice rasped the name. "I should have let you cut off his arm, as it was what he wanted. All this is because of that day."

She felt him kiss her head in a fatherly way. "Damn!"

She added, "He was not alone. His friends were all with him, and some other prisoners. They broke into my cell and enjoyed themselves thoroughly." A sob escaped her.

Martha heard gasps from the other side of the room. She didn't realise the two ladies were there as they had remained quiet.

A different Scotsman spoke, and it was not Hector. He said, "Doctor Roylance, if you are finished here, we shall go and see to the perpetrators immediately. Such vile creatures need immediate chastisement. We shall take my security detail."

The doctor reluctantly said, "Yes, sir, can you give me a

moment?"

The man at the door said, "Of course, Doctor, tend to the lassie first."

Doctor Roylance did as instructed. He removed the cool compress from Martha's eyes and realised she could see.

The medical man said, "Martha, this time, I can guarantee you are safe. You should have been safe in the cell. You shall never return there. Mrs Hetty Walker will take you to her home until you are well enough to go to Mark and Cathy Duffy's place. Mark is my friend and will care for you as if you were their daughter. Cathy's grown son and daughter, and their families, live with them. They have many children between the three couples, and they run a Government Store down south. However, you will remain here at Government House until Hetty takes you to her home tomorrow."

A tear slid down her cheek, and he thumbed it away. "Hetty, come and meet this dear girl," he said.

A rustle of gowns meant the woman he had beckoned had come.

Martha could not turn her head.

Hetty came to stand beside the doctor. "Hello, dear. I came to find a maid, but I found a dear girl who needs me as much as I need her. Will you come home with me to heal?"

Martha wept with relief. She croaked a "Yes, please, ma'am."

The doctor stood and let Hetty take his place. "She may eat or drink what she wishes, but do not let her laugh; she has at least one broken rib and probably a few cracked ones. I recommend soft food for a day or so. Her nose is broken, and I have reset it; her wrist is strained. That scum will certainly pay for what he did. But for Martha, he would have lost his arm. She has much skill in those small hands, so care for her well, Hetty."

He walked to the other side of the bed, checked the original stitches on her cheek, then kissed Martha's forehead again in a fatherly manner.

He left with the authoritative Scotsman who waited at the door. Hetty's caring hand caressed Martha's bruised cheek.

Martha saw tears trickling unheeded down the woman's cheeks. She reached out and touched the caring woman's hand. "Don't cry, ma'am. He's not worth it. I will survive because I will not let him win."

Hetty continued to weep. "He does not deserve to breathe, my dear."

The Scottish lady on the other side of the room said, "My Lachlan will deal with him. I shall keep you informed about his fate. Breathing will be his biggest problem." She knew he murmured that he would see them hanged. She didn't dare tell them that. He was so angry when he left.

Martha carefully turned towards her rescuer. "I care not, madam, but I do not want him to do this to anyone else. If I succumb, then he wins. So I will fight and survive."

Martha groaned as she moved, and she ached all over. She sighed and said softly, "I only tried to help him, yet he did this."

She fell silent, her eyes closed, and she relaxed, then slept again.

~

The following morning, Martha was able to open her eyes fully. She noticed she lay in a luxurious room with red velvet drapes. She moved to sit up and groaned in agony.

The raucous cries of some birds had woken her at dawn, and she wished to know where she was.

She carefully eased her way out of the four-post bed and padded barefoot across the room.

She pulled open the heavy drapes and sat on the nearby chair. She watched the sky colour with the morning sun's rays. The heat shimmered on the horizon, and she was already uncomfortably hot, sticky, and sore. Beads of perspiration trickled down her brow.

From the elevated bedroom window, she looked down the street. She had no idea she had been carried upstairs.

The cottages she saw were evenly spaced on both sides of the dirt track. This place was vastly different from London, and she was spellbound by its emptiness. She had seen many small or primitive places in her short life, but this was so hot, dry, and dusty. It reminded her of India but without the throng of people.

A few sick-looking, straggly sticks with leaves attempted to break the brownness of the view. Amongst them were the odd grey-green trees that Doctor Roylance said were called gum trees. They exuded an unusual scent.

This morning, the pungent odour assailed her nostrils.

She gingerly turned when she heard a soft knock on her door. "Enter."

A maid came in carrying a cup of hot chocolate. "Good morning, miss. Did you sleep well? Mrs Walker asked if you were ready for me to bring you a breakfast tray?"

Martha gingerly turned. "Thank you, miss. I slept well. I would love something to eat."

She saw the maid was about to curtsy and said, "Please don't, dear. I'm a convict and do not deserve such respect."

The girl smiled. "Miss, Governor Macquarie said everyone is worthy in God's eyes. Only some of those really bad sinners make our lives unhappy. The doctor said you tried to help the bad man, and he hurt you. The governor knows who you are and says you are still welcome here. The ship's doctor stayed overnight and said he would tend to your injuries before you leave with Mrs Walker and Hector."

The girl assisted Martha in washing her sore face and in changing out of the beautiful lace-trimmed lawn nightgown she wore. Martha had not even noticed how sheer the delicate fabric was. She donned another gown similar to the maid's. The blue drill dress was practical and bland. The maid had hers covered with a calico apron.

The maid giggled. "Sorry, miss, but this is all that the Government Stores stock. In winter, we all wear woollen serge gowns and get a choice of blue or brown." She didn't introduce herself, and Martha didn't think to ask her name.

Martha sighed. She didn't care as she was decently clad, and because her stomach was full of scrambled eggs and toast. It was the best food she had eaten in some time. It was even better than the roast meat she had on the ship. By the time the sun reached the tree line, she was carefully making her way down the curved staircase. A new day was ahead, and she would face it bravely. She reached the bottom of the stairs and had no idea where to go. Hetty Walker appeared from a doorway and ushered her into the drawing room. "Come, dear."

The doctor, the vice-regal couple, and Hector awaited her there. She gasped when she saw Hector. His shock of red hair and grizzled beard framed his face like a lion's mane. However, his beautiful smile gave her confidence. He said, "You're looking better, lassie."

She curtsied to everyone carefully before replying, "I am, thank you, sir. Although I have a fair amount of healing to do yet." She must have grimaced when she curtsied as Hetty came to her side. Two others were in the room and had yet to be introduced. The tall man stood facing the windows. The woman stood beside him and smiled. She was lovely.

Martha took a hitched breath when the man turned. She

understood why he had kept his back to her. Half of his face was melted, yet he still smiled with a lopsided grin. Martha immediately felt empathy for him. Her scars were almost invisible, but his were blatantly obvious. He was dressed immaculately, so he must have been a man of some standing.

The lady at his side said, "Welcome, dear. You are safe and amongst friends."

The governor introduced himself, then stepped forward and said, "Miss Alexander, permit me to introduce my friend Perry White and his good wife, Katy. Like you, she is serving her time. I have your file and have spoken extensively to Doctor Roylance about you. Let me assure you that you will receive no condemnation from any of us."

Hetty moved to Martha's side. "Hector is also serving time; he is a friend. Martha, my mama, Sarah, was a convict, so I really do understand." Martha smiled, then noticed that the red-haired Scotsman had moved towards the door. She gave him a small smile. He was the man who had carried her. Hetty took her hand and said, "Are you ready to leave, dear? For your comfort, Hector will need to drive slowly for much of the journey. The road to Windsor is quite good, but from there, we will be on backroads in a wagon."

Tears glistened in Martha's eyes. It was overwhelming that they cared about her comfort. What was it about these people that calmed her tormented soul? She was instantly at ease in the room full of strangers.

The other lady in the room had yet to speak. Martha figured it was the governor's Scottish wife, Elizabeth.

It was, and she now came to Hetty's side and told her about the isolation of Hetty's farm. There, she could heal in peace. Her placement had been arranged, and when she was better, she would be escorted to Camden, where she would live with more of their friends.

Elizabeth Macquarie thumbed away a tear that had escaped from Martha's blackened eyes. Her gentle caress showed she cared. "Hetty, please take our carriage. She won't survive the trip on an unsprung wagon, dearie."

Martha whispered, "Why help me, ma'am?"

Mrs Macquarie released a musical giggle. "Because you need help, dearie, and we're in a position to do just that."

The governor moved to stand beside his friend at the window. The only person in the room she knew now moved to her side.

Doctor Roylance said, "Martha, with your permission, I would like to dress your injuries again. I have asked Mrs Walker to join us so I can show her what needs to be done. She will need to remove the various stitches in a week. I had to re-suture your cheek cut."

Martha smiled nervously and nodded. She was on the verge of releasing a flood of tears, so she stayed quiet. The three left the room together. Hector followed them and went to prepare the carriage. He had to collect Mrs Walker's luggage and secure it in the luggage compartment at the back of the new vehicle. Martha had been given her allocation of convict clothing and a new blanket. Her small bundle had been vastly increased in size with the allocation from Government Stores.

Mrs Macquarie added some luxuries and new linen underclothing for her, as well as the nightgown she had worn last night. It was packed into a small carpet bag.

At the governor's instruction, more apparel had been included than the usual allocation as a form of compensation. Convicts who should have been secured in cells had caused this girl's distress. This was his way of showing how sorry he was. Ultimately, he took responsibility for the guards' absence from duty. They were men from his regiment, and they had failed in their duty.

This was not the first time this had occurred. His friend's wife, Katy White, had nearly been the recipient the last time. Thankfully, her husband, Perry, had discovered her before any violation occurred. A hardened convict had escaped his men's custody and kidnapped Katy.

Yesterday, Lachlan's heart pounded faster when he first heard of the young convict girl's situation. He had been in conference with the doctor who had filled him in about the attack on the five girls. He gasped when he heard her name, as he had been expecting her arrival. He had received notification from Mr Wilberforce in London that she was known to him.

When he heard about a third attack on Martha by the same vile men, he felt sick. A few extra clothing items were not adequate compensation, as keeping her safe was far more important. Placing her with Mark and Cathy Duffy in Camden would be the best place for her after she was well. However, staying with Hetty Walker for six months would allow the girl to heal in peace. She did not need small children crawling all over her.

~

Hector drove as carefully as he could. Thankfully, they had been permitted to borrow the governor's unmarked carriage rather than the unsprung open wagon on which they had arrived. Hector would need to make a return trip tomorrow to swap the vehicle for their farm wagon.

Hetty explained that most of the potholes on the road had been repaired, but Martha was unprepared for the agony each jolt would cause. She was white with pain, and Hetty thought she might pass out. Eventually, Hetty dug under the seat and pulled out a wrapped bundle. It was a feather pillow, and she carefully placed it on Martha's lap. "Hold it to your chest."

Although her ribs were strapped, each tiny movement was sheer hell. The doctor said that she had only one broken rib, but today, they all felt smashed. The soft pillow padded the movement and eased her discomfort. But, she was unable to stop the cascade of tears.

After six gruelling hours in the carriage, it pulled into the courtyard. The final few hundred yards down the farm road were almost unbearable. The carriage stopped in a farm compound courtyard on the Hawkesbury River's elevated banks.

Martha released a long sigh of relief. They had made some comfort stops along the way, but she knew she had to return to the coach each time. Now she didn't need to leave for months.

They had passed no one for some miles. This farm was in the middle of nowhere.

Birds sang merrily, and the peace of this beautiful place had already calmed her aching soul. As they had driven along the elevated roadway near the farm, a single tree had caught Martha's gaze. "Oh, wonderful, you have a White Willow tree," she said, pointing out the small, silvery-leafed tree to Hetty.

Hetty smiled. What was so special about this tree? "Yes, dear. I believe the previous owners brought it out from England with them. Why? Is it special?"

Martha nodded. "Yes, Mrs Walker. Have you heard of willow bark as a painkiller?" Hetty nodded this time. Martha explained, "The White Willow is one of the trees you can use. I could dearly do with some to kill the agony in my ribs. Weeping willow can be used, but I heard that the White Willow is the most potent."

Hetty was stunned that this young girl knew such things. "Really? Did Doctor Roylance teach you these things?"

Martha shook her head and explained some of her unusual childhood. "No, ma'am, I learned about this in Egypt. Mama was interested in all forms of medicine and taught me a great deal. Willow bark medicine has been used in places like Egypt for thousands of years." She recalled the day she met the doctor, and he inquired about cleansing the sick bay. He had realised the benefit of doing this, as none of the sailors had major infections after their surgeries. His instruments and operating benches were immaculately clean after that. She asked, "Would it be possible to get some of the bark? I could make something to ease my discomfort."

Hetty smiled. "I will collect some myself."

As she said this, they arrived at the back of their house.

After sitting for many miles, the two women alighted, and Hetty escorted Martha indoors through the kitchen. Next to that room was a well-appointed guest bedroom. Martha sank onto the bed and looked lovingly at her female saviour in appreciation. "Thank you so much, Mrs Walker. You have no idea how much your kindness means to me." Hetty assisted Martha in removing her shoes and then lying her back on the bed. Martha was asleep before Hetty left the room.

Hector was joined by his boss, Joel, and the three Walker children: Oliver, Ernie, and three-year-old Molly.

After greeting Joel with a long and loving kiss, Hetty and the children set off for the tree. Martha would need the pain-killing medicine as soon as she awoke. She had no idea how to make it or how much to collect, but she was sure Martha would teach her. Having been gone for nearly three days, Hetty relished time with her children. She had intended to return with a maid who could assist with the farm work; a long walk would ease the discomfort in her legs. However, she had returned with a sick girl who needed care. She smiled and gave a skip. For some reason, reaching out and helping this girl made her happy. Her mother had been a convict, and helping Martha was a way to understand what she had gone through. Although the girl would add to her work for a while, Hetty felt this poor lass might become a friend. If she could ease her pain with this bark, she would have it ready for Martha when she awoke. Doctor Roylance had filled her in a little about Martha's extraordinary background.

Martha woke in a strange room. Many things had been strange lately. She was a little confused, as the whitewashed walls were not the luxurious room she had woken in the last time. She had no idea what time it was or how long she had slept. She moved carefully and eased herself from the bed. It was a pallet bed with a horsehair mattress, but it was surprisingly comfortable. Either that, or she was merely exhausted.

Someone had obviously checked on her, as there was now a posy of strange flowers in a handmade pot next to her bed. The simple gesture put a smile on her face. She noticed her door was ajar, and a small face poked around the edge and then vanished.

Moments later, she heard the small girl call out, "Mama, she's awake."

Martha chuckled. Whoever the child was, she had obviously been told not to make a noise until their guest woke.

Hetty entered and checked on her patient. "How are you feeling, dearie?"

Martha grimaced as she stood. "As well as could be expected, ma'am, I suppose."

Hetty placed a hand on her brow to check she was not hot. "Please call me Hetty, as I wish us to be friends."

Martha was stunned. "But, ma'am, I'm a convict."

"You are, dearie, as was my mama. You are also a girl in need. I need a friend, as I'm the only woman for miles, so we can fill each other's needs in friendship. So, please call me Hetty." She pointed to a washbasin and ewer. "First, have a warm wash, and then come and see what we have in the kitchen."

Ten minutes later, Martha left her room and was greeted by a strange man. "Hello, I'm Hetty's husband, Joel. I wish to say welcome, but I shall leave you to the ministrations of my beloved wife. However, I won't go until you tell me how you use this stuff." He pointed to a basket on the kitchen table.

If she didn't hurt so much, Martha would have danced with delight when she saw what Hetty had for her. "Oh, wonderful; you collected some bark for me." She gulped. The basket held a massive amount of bark. "That's a lot of bark, though; I won't need that much, so we'll dry it to use later when required. Once dried, you can store it like cinnamon sticks and use it ground, steeped, or boiled." Martha didn't realise that Hetty had all but ringbarked the small tree to collect the medicine for her.

Hetty looked puzzled. "Can you show me?"

Martha nodded. "Certainly, ma'am. I mean Hetty. While it's fresh, I will make tea. I need some immediately. It is prepared by slowly boiling three teaspoons of willow bark in half a pint of water for about fifteen minutes. As there is so much, and I know I will need more, I'll make up a big batch. Another method is to soak the bark in cold water overnight. The liquid is then strained, and one small cupful is consumed three to four times a day. It eases pain and helps reduce inflammation. I could use some now, so may I make some tea? It is not to be used if the patient is bleeding."

Hetty found a pan and set it to boil with a few pints of water, then watched as Martha added the fresh bark.

Martha split the remaining bark into slivers and cut it into four-inch lengths.

Joel brought out a wide-mouthed ceramic jar with a large cork lid. "Will this work?"

Martha nodded, looked around the room, and then asked if they had any wax wraps. Little Molly ducked into the pantry and returned with three different sizes of wraps. Martha chose one and held it over the fire until it softened. She placed it over the mouth of the jar and then reinserted the cork. "I'll dry the remainder of the bark first, but once dry, this will keep it for as long as necessary. There should be enough tea in that brew for me for a while. It can be drunk either hot or cold and flavoured to taste."

Molly slipped out to join her brothers and Hector. It was milking time, and the children had chores to complete.

Fifteen minutes later, Martha was sipping the astringent brew.

Joel chuckled. He had not left as he said he would, but stayed to learn how to make the medicine. "I presume it is not a pleasant taste?"

Martha's screwed-up face showed that it was bitter. "No, and I have to drink a cupful three times a day."

Hetty handed her some honey. "This might help. It's from our hive."

Martha nodded, took the jar, scooped in a spoonful, and stirred well. "Mama used to add cinnamon or pineapple juice, but honey should work well. Thank you all so much. I feel quite spoiled."

Hetty came to her side and said, "Sweet girl, you have had far too much trauma in your short life. We hope this will begin a new and much happier start."

Joel waved a farewell and followed their daughter.

With each carrying a mug of tea, Hetty led Martha out through the house and onto the front verandah. The house was elevated well above the highest flood level. The view westward was incredible. As the sun headed towards the horizon, Martha realised she must have slept for a few hours. She gasped at the glorious sight before her.

The house was halfway up the hillside, overlooking the Hawkesbury River. The two-hundred-degree views were incredible. "Oh, Hetty, this is so beautiful."

Hetty led her to a rustic rocking chair and suggested she sip her bitter brew while resting.

Martha's slight exertion had worn her out. She did as suggested. She relaxed and watched the river flow in its path.

The young girl's sweet nature had already won Hetty over. It astounded her that so much had happened to the lass, yet she was not bitter.

In the hours Martha slept, Hetty had filled her husband and children in on why she brought back an injured girl instead of a maid. Her compassion had been stirred when she accompanied Elizabeth Macquarie to the gaol to select a new staff member. Janey Brien had met her on arrival and taken her to see the state she had just discovered Martha in.

Hetty told Joel that they had found Martha unresponsive and stripped naked. Bootprints marred the magnolia skin of her body. Her freckled face was black and blue, and oozing blood from various places. "I could not leave her there, Joel. I had to bring her home to heal."

Joel hugged his beloved wife. He knew Hetty's mother, Sarah, had arrived as a felon. Had she experienced this as well?

Sarah married three times before she found happiness. Past memories of another girl washed over him. As a small child, he had witnessed such an attack as this girl experienced, but had been unable to help his friend's sister. Carly had died. In a way, it was why he had come to Australia. Memories of her washed over him anew. He said, "Love, bring as many needy girls as you wish. We have room, and they need sanctuary. Hector and I will ensure that they remain safe."

That day, a seed was sown that would grow in later years.

In the meantime, Martha settled in and began to heal.

~

A week after her arrival, the smell of something baking met the family's noses.

Martha had taken a week to allow the majority of the cuts and bruising to reduce in size and colour. The willow bark tea was working well, and the pain was bearable.

Hetty had taken the stitches out of her lip and cheek, and the puckering of the cuts' itch eased. Martha presumed they would leave scars, but life was full of things that left their mark. If Perry White could cope with half his face melted, then a few scars were nothing in comparison. She had survived, and the governor said Eliot would not. The governor had sent a note to say that Eliot and his friends would be hanged for their diabolical abuse of her and the other girls on the ship.

As a thank-you to Hetty, Martha baked some bread for the household. Hetty's effort was edible, but only just.

Without telling Hetty, Martha had set a basin of dough to rise the night before. She rose some hours before dawn, knocked the dough down, kneaded it and put it in tins to rise. When she rose at daybreak, she placed the three fluffy-topped loaves in the hot oven and then dressed. Breakfast would be different this morning. French toast was on the menu as the chickens had laid a basket of eggs.

The stale bread would sop up the herbed egg mixture and disguise the dense, heavy consistency of Hetty's loaf.

Chapter 16 Heart and Soul
Martha

*M*artha settled in well. Her ribs still pained her if she overexerted herself. Hector was always on hand to carry any heavy loads, but he never made any inappropriate moves. He was like a protective shadow.

One day, about a month after she arrived, Martha had to call him for morning tea. She had made him some special treacle and oat cakes.

He adored them and complimented her after nearly every bite.

His overwhelming appreciation made her giggle, and her ribs ached. She was not usually a silly girl, but around Hector, she seemed to lose the ability to speak sensibly. She was not attracted to him romantically, but something made him stand apart from the Walkers. She realised he had done this intentionally, and each time she laughed, more of her stress eased.

Today, she had been knitting socks for the children when Hetty asked her to call Hector for tea. It was over tea that Joel would discuss the jobs that needed to be done.

Oliver and Ernie looked after the chickens that they had been given from Bentley's farm, further up the hill. The addition of fresh eggs to the family's menu was a wonderful treat. Before this, the only source of animal produce that they ate was if Hector or Joel shot something, or if someone caught any fish from their small jetty.

However, occasionally, fresh food would mysteriously appear.

Hetty never said where it came from, but she would hurriedly bag up some flour or sugar and leave to walk up to the big rock platform above the house.

With the arrival of six new hens, Hector constructed a new chicken coop. It had an egg-laying box, so no one needed to enter the enclosure to collect the delicious oval globes.

Molly called them cackle berries as the hens cackled when an egg was laid.

The Walkers' neighbours, Fanny and Phil Bentley, were almost hermits. They and their small son lived a secluded life on their isolated farm on the hill above the Walkers.

Martha met them once or twice and liked Fanny. After one chance meeting, Hetty revealed that Fanny was also a convict and she had been sold in a wife swap market; however, the community had paid for her freedom. Phil kept her safe, and they had not long had their first child, which was not ideal, but Phil was determined to marry her legally when he could. For the moment, Fanny was his common-law wife.

Hector had heard the discussion and said, "Ooch, in bonny Scotland, they would only have to say they were man and wife in front of at least two witnesses to make it legal. The English complicate matters so much and then spend a fortune celebrating the day with a lavish feast, when that money could have been put towards setting up the new family. It's not about the wedding, but the marriage is the thing that's important. The permanent commitment to each other and a firm and faithful promise in the sight of God." He knocked back the rest of his tea and left before anyone could comment.

Joel heard his farmhand mention his belief in God on several occasions. He watched his retreating back and frowned. How could a man like Hector believe in a higher power? He knew the man was serving life for murder. Too many bad things happen to good people, and Joel always blamed God for bad things. He sighed a quick huff of resignation and turned back to Martha. "The man is an enigma. He leaves me mid-sentence regularly and rarely stays around to explain himself."

Martha had already spoken with the Scotsman and had more questions. Joel's comment added another topic to her list. Her opportunity came after luncheon. Hetty took the children aside to do some schoolwork while Martha made bread and set a stew to bake. Two dingos had killed two hens at Bentley's farm, but not eaten them. Phil scared off the wild dogs and rescued the dead birds that they dropped as they ran. As there were only the two of them, they couldn't eat two chickens. They gave Hector a dead hen.

Having just one chicken wasn't enough to roast for seven people, but it would make a delicious baked dish.

Martha first plucked and boned the bird, then removed most of the meat. She kept the bones for a soup and set them to boil. Then, she diced the meat into big chunks. She added an assortment of fresh vegetables to the baking dish with the chicken, which she had tossed in some flour. She then added some parsley, diced some onion tops to both pots. She raided the pantry and found an old bottle of wine.

After checking with Hetty that she could use it, she added a good slosh of white wine to the baking tray.

The dish had a base of sliced potatoes, and she added a layer of mashed pumpkin with an egg glaze to the top. The one-pot baking tray was mainly filled with vegetables. All the ends of the vegetables she added to the soup pot. Nothing was wasted. Even the feathers were kept for stuffing pillows. They had plenty of duck feathers, as Fanny and Phil seemed to have a ready supply of fresh wild ducks.

Martha discovered they had befriended some of the Aboriginal women. Fanny assured her that they were lovely. Martha knew that women the world over were similar. Only their skin colour and facial features varied. She had not seen any signs of them near the house, but Hetty and Joel had an area where they left food for the local tribe, and they would often find gifts of other edibles in return. It was where the occasional kangaroo tail or fish came from.

With dinner cooking, she carried a mug of tea out to Hector. He had been working on his small blacksmith's fire since he left them, and she heard him quenching the coals. She knew he would need a drink once he was finished.

Having delivered her meagre offering, Hector rested against the wagon and sipped the potent brew. He liked it black and sweet, so Martha had added a large dollop of honey. "Ooch, lassie, this is just perfect." He drank deeply and released a groan of satisfaction.

Martha was unsure of how to broach the subject that was eating at her. She hoped Hector would elaborate on a comment he had made to her the previous day. Eventually, she turned to walk away, too fearful to voice her concerns.

Hector could tell she was hesitant. He chuckled. "I'm being a bit mean to ye lassie; spit out what you wish to ask me."

Martha turned to him. "Hector, why do bad things happen to good people if your God is supposed to be a loving deity?"

Hector's face lit up with delight. "And here I was thinking you were going to ask me about why I was here. This question I will answer."

Martha shook her head. "Why you are here is not my business, Hector; if you wanted me to know, you would have already told Mr Joel and Hetty your past. I don't know anyone else to ask about God stuff, and you mention Him often enough for me to think you believe. I mean, really believe. I asked Fanny, but she doesn't know much either. Phil has only mentioned bits to her."

Hector shuffled himself onto the flatbed of the wagon he had been leaning against. "I do, lassie, I believe in God. I believe wholeheartedly. Settle back, for this may take a bit of time. Answering a question like that is not a yes-no answer, but I have a feeling you know that."

Martha nodded. "I've never had much time or opportunity for church, and although my parents believed in God, they never took the time to teach me what they believed. Papa would cry out for God's help when sailing through the enormous seas, and I know he prayed regularly until Mama died. But how can an invisible God help a person on a ship in the middle of a storm at sea? Papa even asked Him to send the storm away. I still don't know how we survived that hurricane, but we did, so I suppose God answered Papa's plea. He told me that Jesus calmed a sea, and he believed God could do the same with an ocean."

Hector chuckled and said, "The most powerful weapon in the world is the word of God. With Him on your side, you will have all the support you need. Your Papa did the right thing in calling upon the earth's maker to calm the storm. You are right; Jesus did that once in front of his disciples. They were caught in a violent storm on the Sea of Galilee. Jesus slept through it until one of his men woke him and begged Him to save them. Jesus then banished the storm, just as your Papa asked."

Martha sat listening wide-eyed. "Why do you talk of God and then switch to Jesus in the same breath? Are they not two different people?"

Hector smiled. Realising she understood nothing, he said, "Ahh, I think I shall start at the very beginning. If I don't, I don't think it will make any sense at all. Now, I will say that one conversation will not be enough to answer all your questions, but as neither of us is going anywhere, we have all the time in the world."

Martha nodded and settled herself on the lower step to listen. Dinner was cooking, so she had time.

Hector took another swig of his tea and said, "The prologue to the beginning is a bit of an explanation about the Bible. There are sixty-six books in the Bible; thirty-nine are dated before Jesus, and twenty-seven are from the time of Jesus' birth and some years afterwards. These books cover a vast period of time; I'm not talking lifetimes, but many generations, spanning thousands of years. Each author did not write a new story from scratch; rather, they continued the narrative, contributing to a single story. It's now 1819, and we date our calendar from the birth of Jesus. We're not quite sure how accurate that is, but that's really irrelevant. Jesus was born, and that changed the entire world. Now, having said that, I shall ask you, who was Jesus?"

Martha had no idea. She shrugged. "I've heard some people use his name to swear. I know that's wrong."

Hector nodded. "That's true, it's one of the Ten Commandments. *'Thou shalt not take His name in vain.'* However, we are here, living in a penal colony with an assortment of people who have broken every single one of those ten rules given to us by God. Even so, the laws of this land and our motherland are centred on those ten simple rules. We can't even keep them. Okay, the prologue is over; we shall start before Adam is made. Ready?"

She nodded.

Hector took another sip. "The first words in the Bible, in Genesis, are pretty descriptive. Genesis, chapter one, verses one to five, says,

'In the beginning God created the heaven and the earth. And the earth was without form and void, and darkness was upon the face of the deep. And the Spirit of God moved upon the face of the waters. And God said, Let there be light: and there was light. And God saw the light, that it was good: and God divided the light from the darkness. And God called the light Day, and the darkness he called Night. And the evening and the morning were the first day'."

Martha was impressed that Hector knew the passage by heart.

He continued, but was not quoting the bible. "The Angels were made before mankind, but mankind was not made until some days later in verse twenty-six. We have no idea how long it took to get to that stage. Some say it happened in the blink of an eye, while others say it took thousands of years; whatever the case, it is irrelevant, for God made it happen. His days are not our days. It was then that the trouble really started."

Martha gasped but didn't interrupt.

He cleared his throat and said, "At the beginning of the story, there was only one rule for Adam and Eve, not ten. They broke that, too. God put them in a beautiful garden. We call it the Garden of Eden. In the centre of this fragrant and productive wonderland were two trees. One was the Tree of Everlasting Life, and the other was the Tree of Knowledge. God had told them to eat of any tree except the Tree of the Knowledge of Good and Evil. That was their only law. Just one small rule, and they could not obey even that."

Martha was listening and motioned for him to continue.

Hector leaned forward and looked directly at her. "Martha, God made everything good, and by that, I mean perfect. The angels and mankind were given free will. But we and the angelic realm were given the option to obey God. First, one of the angels rebelled. One whom we know as Lucifer defied God's will, and along with a third of the angels, he was cast out of heaven. That was the first sin. It was driven by pride, greed, and ego. But Lucifer did not stop there. He was jealous of God's relationship with the man and his wife, so he took the form of a snake and slid up into the tree that held the fruit God had told them not to eat. Once there, he tempted Eve to disobey God. She did and then offered Adam the forbidden fruit. That one small act of disobedience brought sin into the world."

She was about to interrupt, but he asked, "Can you hold your questions?" She nodded and relaxed to listen.

Hector smiled at her and continued. "God knew, as he is all-knowing. I won't go into all the details, but the couple appeared covered in fig leaves, whereas before, they had been naked. They had gained knowledge. God knew instantly. They were cast out of the garden and, therefore, separated from access to Him. However, God did not completely cut them off. He promised a way back, but not immediately. He promised that He would open a special doorway back into their lost perfection."

Martha could not help but say, "Really? He wants us back?"

Hector nodded. "Once out of the garden, they entered Lucifer's world. It is this that we still live in today. If you read the Bible, you will read of the prophets, kings, and the sagas of what happened to God's people as they refused to follow Him. However, each prophet was another step closer to entering a new relationship with God. The kings follow the prophets until we reach the pivotal point in our time. Jesus was born to a virgin girl called Mary. Martha, you are probably only a year or so older than she was. She loved God and listened when He spoke to her. She accepted her special role in God's plan. She was to give birth to God's son and name him Jesus. This baby was the son of a man, but also the Son of God. The Creator had made this young girl conceive and bear this special child without a man being involved in the conception. Jesus is God's son. He is fully man because Mary was human and fully God, as He has no earthly father. He is also the fulfilment of God's promise to Eve. Jesus is the pathway back to a relationship with God, as He promised when He cast Adam and Eve out of Eden. I say 'is' instead of 'was' because, when He rose again at the time we celebrate as Easter, Jesus never died again. He is still alive, but not as his disciples knew Him."

Martha frowned but remained silent. She had many questions.

Hector said, "Jesus grew as a normal boy, yet he was perfect, even when young, He did not sin. However, Jesus had to wait thirty years before His ministry began. Then, in three short years, His teaching changed the world. Jesus taught repentance and how to follow God. He taught that sin is real and denying it will not stop it from happening. He taught his twelve chosen friends about what God had sent Him to say. He didn't choose royals, dukes or politically important people. No, he chose ordinary men and women, too. Peter, Andrew, James and John were fishermen. Matthew was a tax collector, Mary Magdalene was a prostitute, and others were from equally lowly positions. Although Jesus preached to thousands, He challenged His close friends, just twelve men, to spread His teachings to every corner of the world. We are aware of this because some of them wrote down their stories. They are included in the Bible and called the Gospels."

Martha listened to them being read when she was young. She said, "That's Matthew, Mark, Luke, and John, isn't it? But they each tell a different story. They contradict each other sometimes."

Hector drained the last of his tea and said, "Very true, but say we were to go into the three children inside and ask each what they did today. We know they did not leave the house, but I bet all three stories would differ. Each writer of the Bible told their own story as God put it on their hearts. Even the Apostle Paul bemoaned being sent to gaol for his beliefs, but because of that unfortunate situation, we have Paul's amazing words in writing nearly two thousand years later. Had he not been imprisoned, then he would have had no need to write his letters." He fell silent for a while. Sometimes, he was challenged by those very thoughts. Why was he here?

Martha's brow went from furrowed to clear as each bit of the story fell into place. She could identify with Paul and being locked up. With her eyes filled with unshed tears, she said, "So it's God's will what happened to me? That I was vilely attacked four times by horrible men who thought nothing but to slake their lusts and anger on my body?" A sob escaped her lips. "If so, then I hate Him!"

Hector shook his head. "No, Martha, don't hate. God did not and does not condone the bad things done to you or to me. That all goes back to free will and sin. Many refuse to believe in God and the forgiveness He offers when we repent, as Jesus taught, and truly say sorry for our actions. Only then do we return to fellowship with God. Bad people do things to good people, dragging them and us down into the mire they've created. We are truly the innocent victims."

By now, Martha's tears were flowing. "So it wasn't my fault?"

Again, Hector shook his head. "No, you were an innocent victim of evil men. They followed their base desires and violated you horrifically. How you cope will either make you or break you. I know that you have already refused to allow yourself to succumb to that vile oppression, and that is good, but what I am going to say will be hard to hear."

He came and stood beside her, then knelt in the shed's dirt. Looking at her with his face filled with loving care, he said, "Martha, you must forgive them. They harmed you dreadfully, but hating them will only eat you from the inside out. They will not even know of your feelings, so it matters little to them, but it will harm you dreadfully."

Martha sucked back a sob. "How? Why do they get off free, and the girls and I have to live with the pain of what they did to us? They were responsible for Sarah having her baby early, and then she died, as did her son." Her anger was building. "Why shouldn't they pay?"

Hector reached out and took her hand. "Martha, dear girl, they will pay. Each one of us must stand before God on Judgement Day. We are told that in the Bible. God is just and knows the heart of every person, not just what others know. They will not escape His eternal punishment, and it will be far more effective than anything you could do to them or even say to them. We know that the governor ensured that Eliot and his close friends have already been hanged, so they will already be judged."

She thought, "Good." Another sob choked her words. "Fine, what do I have to do?"

Her weeping broke his heart. Hector sat next to her on the step and slipped an arm along her shoulder in a comforting way, and not in any way threatening or sexual. He explained, "Believe that God loves you; trust that and ask for forgiveness for any sins you have committed and accept that Jesus has already wiped them clean. He will judge your abusers appropriately, and the hardest thing is, you must forgive them. Once done, leave it to God. Move on with your life and seek the peace that loving God and walking in his path will bring."

Hetty had come to call them for dinner some time ago. She stood, watching and listening as they talked. Hector had seen her and had cut short his talk. It was only after she arrived that he had touched the girl. "Martha, Mrs Walker will care for your physical wounds; let God tend the spiritual ones. Go with her now."

Martha nodded and went to Hetty for a big, but gentle hug.

As she was leaving, she turned and said, "Thank you, Hector. I have more questions, but I will consider what you said."

Hector's face lit up. He'd not yet had the opportunity to speak to Joel or Hetty, as something held him back each time. One day, he was sure God would open that door. He had a feeling Hetty knew a lot more than she let on.

Hetty had come to tell them that dinner was ready. She had taken the dish from the oven for Martha. The unusual meal was cooked, and it was Martha's turn to serve.

The two women now alternated cooking at night, which gave each a break from the routine.

Martha still had to be careful of her ribs, but only kneading the bread hurt.

Martha quickly discovered that Hetty had been born in the colony to a woman who had been a convict, as she had claimed. Her father, a Frenchman, was her mother's second husband. After he died in a race, Sarah remarried an emancipated convict. Consequently, Hetty had no hesitation in befriending Martha.

Under Hetty's loving care, Martha blossomed. Her confidence returned, as did her laugh.

Over the weeks she had been there, they had sat on the verandah and spun yarn when all the chores were done.

~

As the weeks turned into months, Martha knew she was well enough to work a full day. Her time on the farm was drawing to a close. Her ribs had healed, and her scars had faded. It was hard to believe that she had been with Hetty and Joel for over six months.

The freckles from her childhood once again appeared on her nose and cheeks. A cheery smile accompanied a healthy glow.

More conversations with Hector had brought peace to Martha's troubled heart. He had walked her through the path of being able to forgive her attackers. Knowing that they were all dead made that easier. God will have judged them already.

Governor Macquarie had sent a lengthy letter the week after her arrival, saying that all had been confined in irons.

A month later, another screed was received to say all had been condemned to death. This had occurred only days before Martha's first talk with Hector. However, guilt racked her because they were dead because of her.

Day by day, Hector prayed with her and walked her through understanding forgiveness and being washed clean by God's grace.

She was finally able to release her hatred.

~

June 1819

At the end of June, Joel returned from Parramatta on his monthly run to collect the food stores, accompanied by a document and instructions. Hector was to take her to Camden as soon as possible.

The next stage of Martha's life was about to start.

Both women wept, but the parting of the firm friends was inevitable.

As Hector helped Martha onto the wagon's front seat, Hetty stood by weeping. "Promise you will write, Martha. I want to know how you are." Hector gee'd up the horse, and they pulled away.

Martha called back to her friend, saying, "I promise, and once I'm free, I'll come back to see you."

Once out of sight, Martha wept silently. She was petrified at what was before her. She had been so happy at *Loganberry Farm* that she wished she could have stayed.

She hardly noticed their route and unintentionally ignored Hector when he spoke to her. Her misery was pitifully obvious.

She knew they had passed *Bentley's Farm*, but didn't look up to see if Fanny was waving.

Hector gave her some time to cry before saying, "Martha, I know we've had many long chats, but I wish to tell you about the Duffys' place. Captain Mark Duffy arrived with the Macquaries and fell in love on the journey out. Cathy Callan and her daughter were on the way out to join her convict son. They are a love match and married in Cape Town."

Martha had been told that by Hetty.

Hector saw her nod and continued. "Cathy had not long given birth to twins before they moved to Camden. They were a big surprise, but their arrival meant they had four bairns under six. Add to that Josh and Alice's children and Jenny and Drew's bairns, and you will have your hands full of little ones. Mark's eldest lad, Gideon, would only be nine now." He heard her hitch a breath.

Hector took a glance at his travelling companion to gauge her interest. "I got to know Captain Duffy when the governor came to the gaol. I discovered through Mr Joel that they all have a strong faith, even though Cathy and Mark both grew up in the slums of London. He's the one who saved Fanny."

Martha was listening, but wondered why he was telling her all this.

Hector revealed his reason moments later. "Hetty has been wonderful for you, but you need to be with Cathy. She has experienced what you have. She was sold at a young age and used poorly. She will understand as Hetty never could. Trust her, Martha; trust the entire family, for they are all Godly people."

Martha's misery lifted a little. Could she trust God enough to believe He would place her somewhere as good? "You really believe that I'll be safe?"

Hector didn't take his eyes off the narrow track as it wound its way along the river. "I do, Martha. I know you will be safe, and I believe you need to be with them. You are not alone. We are all here to help you."

They chattered for a while until they reached the main road at

Penrith. Here, he could pick up speed.

However, it would still be a two-day trip each way.

Chapter 17 A Nod to Ned
Jack

The two boys remained inside their cabin while the other convicts were permitted on deck. After five hours, Captain Moncrief, Lieutenant Windsor, and Major Ned unexpectedly visited them.

Ned saw them jump to attention and chuckled. He said, "You're not in trouble; we just need some information. Can you give us every skerrick of the conversation you overheard?"

Jack nodded. He had heard much more of the mutiny conversation than Charles, so he answered the question. "Sir, Tom Onions has a small group of better-behaved prisoners who are all set to take the ship when we near Cape Town. They plan to storm the day watch and release Tom and his cellmates. From there, I presume they will release the rest of the prisoners and take the ship. I heard some of the crew would join them, but I didn't hear who." As Jack revealed the plan, Ned realised that their mutiny could have worked if the young felon had not reported the conversation. Ned did not know that Onions had recruited some of the well-behaved convicts. Ned nodded and smiled at Jack, but he kept his eye on Charles Lockley. Reporting the mutiny could mean instant release for these two convicts upon arrival in the colony. However, they would be marked and need to be kept safe. This pleased Ned, as he wanted to ensure their safety. He had been surprised to learn that Jack was two years older than he was, and Charles was a year younger; that meant he was the same age as his brother Paul. Paul's twin, also Charles, and named after his father, had died soon after birth, but he would have been precisely the same age as this man. Ned shivered with the coincidence. For them to share the same last name confused him.

His Majesty's Pageboy

In the remaining months ahead, Ned planned to get to know both lads well. Lieutenant Windsor was in charge of the 69th Regiment, which was on guard for the convicts. Ned was in the 48th regiment and was only a passenger on this voyage. He would not take up his commission until he arrived in the colony, so he could spend some quality time getting to know these two. He had volunteered to be their personal guard, more to stave off boredom, but it allowed him to befriend the two unusual convict men.

They were both well-spoken and surprisingly well-mannered. Ned noted that Jack even thanked God for his food before eating. His family also did this. The fact that Jack was not hiding his faith intrigued him. That was one more thing they had in common.

As Ned had only purchased his commission a few weeks before departure, he had just enough time to complete his basic training before the ship sailed. He had never done anything like this before, and everything was foreign to him. He had even needed to learn to dress himself. He and his brothers had always had valets. Even when they were sent to school, one had joined them to care for their clothing.

Having shut the door to his previous life, Ned was determined to make his own way. He was not the heir; his snobbish big brother, David, was. So he knew he and his two younger brothers would need to make their own way. Ned had not expected to be thrust into this new situation so quickly. Within just one short year, he had gone from attending his presentation at a Levée in London to being engaged soon afterwards and then thrown aside by the cuckolding shrew. She laughed in his face after being caught in a compromising position with his own elder brother; she threw Ned over.

Ned would have fled if she had insisted he marry her, but he would have exposed her philandering somehow. He would rather be charged with breach of promise than be tied to an immoral virago. He should have outed her at the ball when he caught her in a compromising position. Unfortunately, that was not enough for her. She had already captured David. They had married by special licence the week it all exploded. David was a marquess and the heir to the dukedom, so Elouise set a snare for him. Ned had tried to warn David what she was like, but he accused him of jealousy. He had all but banished him, so Ned left. He released a long sigh of resignation.

Ned had been pleased to leave, but he had nowhere to go. He owned no land and had little inheritance until he turned twenty-one.

192

Joining the military was his only option. Now he was free, but his nearly twenty-year-old heart hurt. It would be his birthday next week. He had no one to bring him hot chocolate and wake him with a hug, as had occurred every other year. Friendship with two convict lads about the same age was enough to ease his loneliness. If these two lads could read as well as they boasted, they might be interested in reading his books. He had found a tiny bookshop in Deal that stocked an excellent selection of novels. He had Walter Scott's *Rob Roy*, *Waverley*, *The Antiquary*, *The Bride of Lammermoor*, and, most excitingly, *Ivanhoe*, a brand-new release. He also picked up copies of *Frankenstein*, *Childe Harold*, and *Swiss Family Robinson*. These should pass the time well.

With the mutiny foiled, Cape Town was bypassed. The soldiers on board all but lauded the two convict boys for their bravery in standing against such a villainous plot. Once the various convict groups had gone below decks, the lads were given the freedom of the ship. They continued milking the animals and caring for them. Their evening meals were once again taken in the galley mess with the rest of the ship's complement. After the meals, they helped Jock clean up.

The sails caught the strong winds of the roaring forties, and the ship travelled eastwards, braving the mountainous seas. Jack and Charles spent many of the roughest days holed up in their cabin, clinging to their bunks, trying to read Ned's books.

When calm, Ned joined them, as few of the other soldiers on board were permitted such off-duty time. As Ned was travelling to Sydney to meet his new commander, he had as much time as he wished. He used it to get to know these two unusual convicts. This would be worth the ridicule from his peers, so he offered to take special guard duty of them.

~

December 16th 1819

By the time the *Shipley* reached their destination, the three young men were comfortable with their unusual friendship. Ned had grown close to Charles. He planned to ensure they were assigned to safe places far from the ruffians below. On arrival, Ned hoped to disembark and report to his new commanding officer, Governor Lachlan Macquarie; however, the governor was unavailable. Ned returned to the ship.

Shortly before embarking in England, Ned met with his distant cousin, Vice Admiral John Hunter. Nearly twenty years earlier, the now elderly man had been the second governor of New South Wales, and John had met with Lachlan Macquarie before he assumed the leadership role. Ned heard from John that the current governor was a fair and just commander and a man of faith.

His first meeting with the governor was on board the convict vessel, later the same afternoon. Ned saluted them on arrival. Governor Macquarie, the Colonial Secretary, John Campbell, and the Chief Surgeon came to vet the latest batch of convicts. After receiving the medical clearance to head below deck, Captain Moncrief mentioned that there were two special convicts in a cabin.

Rather than wait for names, Governor Macquarie's bushy black eyebrows lifted. "One wouldn't be a lad named Turner, would it?"

A frown flashed across Ned's brow. The lieutenant didn't respond, so Ned did. "Yes, sir, one is. He and his cellmate reported that a mutiny was being planned. It was thwarted because of their bravery and actions."

Macquarie nodded. "I'll meet them later. I need to speak with Turner privately. After you arrange their paperwork, send him to me. I gather from your uniform that you are assigned to me. Are you Grace?"

Ned nodded, then remembered this man was his superior. In his previous life, he had never had to salute or bow to anyone, and he only needed to bow to dukes and royalty at home. Such was the privilege of being a duke's child. He said, "I am, sir; I have only recently enlisted."

Lachlan nodded. "So, first posting? No active service?"

Ned's reply affirmed the comment, as he shook his head nervously.

Lachlan said, "Fine, I'll have you in charge of the female convicts as well as working with me when required. They should like that, but you won't." He saw Ned's brow lift. "Hunter mentioned you. Come see me for orders." The governor chuckled. "For those two, I will have a Ticket Of Leave awaiting them." He dismissed Ned with a salute and followed the surgeon below to meet the rabble. Ned followed.

The stench from below deck was enough to make Lachlan gag. Thankfully, the hatches had been opened for a while, and the deck below was somewhat aired. The governor muttered something unintelligible to the doctor before covering one eye. Ned understood the Gaelic expression and smirked. Lachlan knew he had to follow the doctor into the darkened bowels of filth that held over one hundred and forty tortured souls. Releasing a long sigh and a deep breath, Lachlan descended into hell.

Ned ducked into his servant's cabin to see his two friends. He said nothing but gave them a thumbs-up. Jack and Charles smiled and relaxed.

~

Three days later, Ned settled into his new quarters in Parramatta. This was a shared cottage with two other officers. Each of the existing majors had a female convict who came to clean and warm their beds. He wasn't keen about that but knew it was his right as an officer to claim whatever convict female he wished. He would think about that later. He had no intention of taking a bedfellow, but someone to wash his clothes would be good. Ned knew that Jack and Charles would be brought to his office the following day, and he thought he might as well familiarise himself with the bookwork. His father had insisted that he learn how the estate ledgers were kept in case he ever needed to assist his brother in running the ducal estates. Unlike David, he liked the monotony of doing the figures in preference to being fawned over by society's primped and preened spoiled misses, so he focused on the task, but David loved being known and seen. He presumed that the convict ledgers were similar. He hoped that all the names, convict numbers, and vessels on which they arrived were recorded. If so, Charles's record may give him some information about his background. If the surgeon had done his job correctly, there would be a physical description of the prisoner. Knowing his role here was to care for the women, he would do his best. Surely, there were women who, like Jack and Charles, deserved a better situation than being thrown in with the rabble. How would he determine who they were? He would need help from the inside to reveal the needy girls. He also had to figure out what to do with the females once they were separated from the rabble. John Hunter had told him there were many such women if he looked hard enough. John's first rescue had been Helena Rosedale. She married Crispin Milroy, the head of his security detail. Ned wanted to meet the Rosedale family as soon as he could. He had also met John's honorary nephew, Rudi Greenwood. Rudi and his wife had only recently returned from the colony and assisted Lachlan in the production of the new coinage.

He dropped his head in his hands and prayed. He heard noises from another bedroom and knew one woman had not yet left. Their carousing was not quiet. He groaned and emitted a long sigh. Such was his life now.

Having put away his clothing. Ned left his bedroom to investigate his new office at the front of the cottage. Thankfully, he did not have to share his room or office with anyone. A letter awaited him. When opened, it contained the two Ticket of Leave documents and a summons from the governor. He had to report to Governor Macquarie at Government House immediately. Relief flooded over him. He could leave the carnal noises for a while. The official residence was a short walk away, and he wandered up to meet his commanding officer. John Hunter had described this building well. Though he had not seen them, John mentioned the addition of the two side wings soon after this governor arrived. Since then, other outbuildings have been constructed.

As Ned was not expected at any particular time, he dawdled. He absorbed what he passed to familiarise himself with his new hometown.

A surprise awaited him in the governor's office. A friend and childhood mentor was sitting with the governor. Perry White had been his senior mentor at school in England and was one of the last people he expected to find in New South Wales. It was unmistakably him, but half his face had melted some years ago in a fire. Ned knew him years before his burns, but it was undoubtedly Perry.

The burned man gasped when he saw Ned. Perry was just about to welcome him by his real name. Ned quickly said, "Hello, sir, I am Major Edward Grace. Newly arrived in the colony." He saw Perry's stunned face and, while the governor was not watching, mouthed, "Later," to him.

Perry replied with a subtle nod. He left soon after Ned arrived.

After the official documents were signed, Ned was dismissed. On exiting, Ned saw his friend waiting for him.

Perry said, "What's with the sham moniker, Ned?"

Ned knew the guards were within earshot. "Shh, can we talk later? I saw a log on the river's edge just down from the barracks. Meet me there tonight at seven." Perry nodded and then returned home. Ned walked with him. He had to meet the warders at the gaol. He had seen the new two-storey mansion on the main street and discovered it belonged to Perry and his wife, Katy.

Once he had completed the official work, Ned returned to his office. He spent several hours rearranging his workplace and then returned to his room. After his evening meal, such as it was, he went to meet Perry. To have a friend from home in the wilds of a penal colony was sheer bliss. He lifted his eyes heavenward and gave thanks to God.

The men went for an evening stroll, and Ned revealed why he was there. He discovered that Perry and Katy were already assisting the female convicts, and their cousin, Janey Brien, had already sorted out many girls who were now in safe houses. Perry then dropped the bombshell that Katy was serving time herself. They parted with further meetings assured.

Ned could always have a seat at their table if he desired. He also had to find a woman to assist him with his washing. Perry and Katy agreed to house her as he needed a part-time maid.

Ned refused the offer of a comfort woman, so Perry's suggestion of a part-time maid suited them both well. Whoever she would be, she would clean his room and tend to his clothing, but nothing else. She would live in Perry's household. He said goodnight to his friend and walked towards his cottage. God had indeed been working before he arrived.

Janey was already picking out the girls who needed help. He could now find a safe place for them. God would also need to open doors there. The governor mentioned a secret farm on the Hawkesbury River that was being used for the purpose.

Ned found that he was also required to assist with the governor's security when needed. For the first time in months, Ned smiled. He realised he was happy. Considering the luxury he had left behind, he was amazed. He didn't even miss his valet very much.

The January heat was sapping, and he finally collapsed onto his bed in nothing but his drawers. It was too hot for a nightshirt.

Ned had his initial morning convict muster at seven. Realising he would need to wash a shirt to wear tomorrow, he bemoaned his lack of a valet. He really needed someone to wash and iron his clothing.

~

Ned was startled awake at six by the raucous birdcall outside his window. He managed to shave without nicking himself. Thankfully, his fair whiskers were sparse.

He was dressed and breakfasted before his fellow officers. He made tea and waited for them to rise.

One of the other officers' women prepared a breakfast of burnt fried eggs and overcooked thick chunks of toast. He ate because he was hungry, filling up on creamy porridge, followed by more toast with a tart, ambiguous mixed fruit citrus marmalade. No French toast here, but his stomach was full. He sighed. He would need to get used to the heat as he was already perspiring, and it was not even seven o'clock. Duty called.

The convict muster was soon over, and Ned was followed away from the gathering by Jack and Charles. They had been brought up from the ship the evening before and housed with the general population of convicts in the rickety gaol.

He apologised, but there were no other options until they were processed. "Come, I need to get a laundry maid."

Ned needed to divert to the female prisoner muster to choose a maid for Perry, as a group of women was being assigned that morning.

As he neared the line-up of felons, a gasp from behind him pulled him up short. Jack and Ned turned and saw that Charles had stopped walking. His eyes were focused on something, or rather, someone.

Ned followed his gaze and saw a beautiful woman in the line of convict women.

The woman had also seen them and paused in her momentum. Unlike all the other filthy convict females, she was clean. Her fair hair shone like a beacon, and her face was unmarked.

Ned smiled. He was sure he had found the perfect maid.

Charles only realised he was immobile and staring when Ned spoke to him for the second time. Ned asked, "Charles, what's wrong?"

Charles turned to the major and said, "Sir, can you save her?"

With a nod, Ned pointed out the chosen convict woman to the sergeant. He said, "Bring her, the blonde one, to my office." He pointed out the clean convict female.

Ned and his two friends waited to ensure they selected the right woman. He looked at Charles to ensure he had the right convict.

Charles gave an imperceptible nod.

The three men turned and walked back towards his office.

The guard and the blonde woman followed, carrying her pitifully small bundle of possessions.

Charles checked a few times to ensure she was coming.

Ned smiled. This was his first rescue, and hopefully, there would be many more. He had yet to speak to her, but she certainly stood out from the others.

An hour later, Charles and Ned accompanied Sal McCarthy to Perry's house. Both convicts had been assigned to his friend.

Sal was to work part-time at his cottage, but she would live at Perry's house. She would do Ned's laundry and cleaning.

Charles would take over as Perry's groom-cum-footman, if they had such a thing in this land.

Ned knew nothing of Jack's background as he had remained mum about his past. He was well-educated and had good manners. The governor informed Ned that he was to take responsibility for Jack's unique placement should anyone ask. However, Ned knew Macquarie had Jack's assignment prearranged before his arrival. Who was this lad? Surprisingly, Jack was assigned to Macquarie's friend Mark Duffy down near Camden. Ned had no idea who Duffy was, but knew Jack had a secret, probably illustrious past. Was he a peer incognito as well? Ned knew that the governor wanted to see Jack privately, so he supplied a written pass to permit him to wander through the colony as he pleased.

Jack had figured out who Ned was soon after they met. If the soldier wanted to remain incognito, that was his choice. Did the old duke know his son was here under an assumed name? He had his own secrets, so he would keep Ned's identity quiet. Jack received his paperwork and a pass to access Government House for his appointment with the governor. He said nothing but "Thank you."

Jack opened his Ticket of Leave and grinned. Enclosed with it were instructions to see the governor immediately and a sketch map for directions.

Ned pointed him to the large house on the hill and gave him a gate pass to enter the official property. Jack said farewell to Charles and Ned, then left. Most convicts required an escort, but the governor and Major Grace had signed his pass. It permitted him to go where he wished. Jack chuckled. With this being issued, he was sure that Prinny had written to the governor. He wondered what had been said. Should he say more? He hoped the governor would ask, if not tell him, what he knew.

Jack's assignment and interview with Macquarie after Ned's office were eye-opening. The first thing he noticed was that the governor stood when he entered.

Lachlan Macquarie waited until the door closed before he said, "Lord John Templestowe-Meade is what I believe you were called until recently?"

Jack nodded and gave a half-bow. He wondered what else the governor had been told. He was sure that would be revealed. "I'm just Jack Turner now, sir. I'm here to serve my time and start a new life."

Jack realised that he could reveal everything if required.

The governor asked him to take a seat, then explained that he had received two letters. "The one from William Wilberforce was received first, about two felons who were due to arrive. I must say that as letters of introduction go, these are corkers. I greatly admire Mr Wilberforce's work and thoroughly support his fight to stop slavery. For you to be a friend of his lifts you high in my esteem. However, it was followed by a lengthy letter from the Prince Regent himself. Admittedly, I am confused about Lord Clive's intentions, but his demise draws his betrayal to a close. However, that leaves you in an uncertain situation, as not all of his cohort of traitors have been arrested yet. I was informed that you need to keep your head down and stay out of public view. I don't believe that they know what name you are now living under, but we must take care to keep it that way."

Jack was unaware of this, but should have expected that more traitors would need to be uncovered. Their deception ran deep. He released a long sigh.

Lachlan continued. "I will not let you read the prince's letter, as it contains further unrelated instructions for me. Suffice to say, your assignment is safe as it's in the middle of nowhere at the moment. There are plans to build a town nearby, but for now, it's quite a solitary settlement. In theory, you shall be all but free, and Mark Duffy knows this. He said he would write again later. I am to let him know how you fare and to keep him informed should you need anything at all."

Lachlan lifted his eyes from the documents in front of him. This confident young man was very different from any other felon he had met.

Jack grinned. He wondered if he should explain more of his situation, but the governor knew more than he had hoped anyone would ever discover. If Mr Wilberforce knew about Charles, why had his friend not mentioned that? A frown flashed across his brow.

Lachlan continued. "This is a very unusual situation for a

convict to be in, but I believe you will be happier here than amongst the bigoted peers at home."

Jack was stunned. This was not the response he expected. He nodded. "Um, indeed, sir. I do believe you to be correct. I feel the peers of the realm would not have forgiven me for parading as one of them for nigh on twenty years. I am a nothing, sir. Born to peasants, who were some of Lord Clive's first victims. I am an orphan with nothing at all but a name."

Lachlan smiled and said, "At least the name you use now is your own. Some do not even have that. Many here need help, and although I have worked hard, so many arrive that we are constantly overwhelmed."

Jack agreed. Mr Wilberforce said he would send on his possessions when he was settled. Did that mean after he was assigned or later? It was not as if he would need any of the clothing he wore in the palaces. He hoped that his mentor would sell those clothes and send some books.

An idea came to him. "Sir, would it be possible to have some paper and write back to my supporters? Mr Wilberforce has my possessions in his care and has said he will send them to me. Also, I would like to thank the prince and his family for their support over the past years. Things were a mess, and I didn't have that chance before I left, as it all came to a head on the day of the queen's funeral."

As they were sitting on the settees, Lachlan waved to his desk. "Go to it, lad."

Although Lachlan had work to do himself, a few minutes to permit the young man to pen his thanks would not go astray.

After supplying the parchment, Lachlan walked to his office window and looked out over his dusty realm.

This was not the view he had first seen from the window. Ten years ago, it was filthy, with derelict, wattle-and-daub shacks. Now, the town had grown quickly, encouraging more people to settle and farm. Elspeth's gardening prowess had converted the back of the official residence into a lovely perfumed garden. It was at the end of a long walk from the house, but somewhere to sit in the spring and soak in the sweet scents during the warm evenings. Sadly, he couldn't see it from his office. So yes, the vista before him had changed vastly over the past decade.

The scratch of the quill finally stopped.

Jack sanded the second letter. "I appreciate your generosity, sir." He gave a nod of thanks, then grinned and added, "I bet no other convict has sat at your desk and penned letters to a member of parliament and the crown?"

Lachlan roared with laughter. "No, laddie, you are right there. However, you are no ordinary convict, are you?"

Jack released a soft chuckle and shook his head.

A thought occurred to the governor. "There is another well-educated convict lad you should consider befriending, at some point in the future. He's also reasonably new here. Bill Miller, who, with my support, has recently opened the *Royal Admiral Duncan Inn*. Although his background is not as illustrious as yours, it's not far off. His education is beyond belief." He paused, then added, "Oh, and he met Bonaparte on the way out here. I shall tell you why he is here, as he assaulted the son of his boss, as the vile fellow made a pass at the lass who is now Bill's wife. His boss sent his son to Canada and cut him off. The family are of good stock. Mrs Miller's mother, Mrs Ross, has a boarding house in Sydney where many of my senior officers live."

Why Jack needed to know this was beyond him. He smiled and stood.

Jack returned to the settee, leaving the two letters on the governor's desk. In private, Jack had called the prince by his nickname of Prinny, but the regent's secretary would read this missive, so Jack wrote it more officially, but he signed it as: Little Lord John.

Lachlan took the young man's place at the desk. He noticed that the two letters were written in the most elegant handwriting, with not a single smudge, a difficult feat at the best of times. He should have expected this if the lad had grown up in a royal palace.

Jack saw his glance and said, "Sir, please feel free to read them. There is nothing there that has not already been discussed today."

Lachlan gave a nod and set them aside to peruse later. He said, "Now, we must discuss your assignment. The man you are going to was my personal security guard. He lives with his extended family. I shall give you a brief of them. I am sure you will be happy. Mark was shot in the arm during a bushranger raid, and his stepson-in-law, Drew, had a similar experience a year or so earlier, but at the tollgate here. Josh Callan, Mark's stepson, is the only able-bodied man there. You will like him. Josh used to be my groom, but, like you, is, or was, a convict. Mark wrote begging for an able-bodied man to assist them, but he asked for someone trustworthy. I decided to send you there as soon as I received the first letter about you."

Lachlan still missed the lad. He sighed and continued. "Mark's farm hand, George, an older man, has only one eye. Jack, I will add that Josh is also my friend. I trust him implicitly, and I don't say that often. He arrived as a child and left my care as a worthy young man. He and his sister Jenny lost their father in tragic circumstances. He had to step in to provide for his family. He is one of many petty criminals in this parched place with similar fates. I hope my own son grows up to be like Joshua Callan." Lachlan fell silent, thinking about the boy who had become a confidant to many of the settlement's secrets.

The governor released another long sigh. "It is Wilberforce's mention of your strong faith that I have chosen this family to host your term. They are also believers. They have a few young women who have had bad experiences *en route* here. The girls were placed there by Perry White and his cousin. I believe the latest lass was sent there six months ago. Wilberforce heard of her story and wrote to me about the injustice she suffered in London. She would have gone earlier, but she was set upon so violently that we were not sure if she would even live. Believe it or not, Martha's crime could have been the same as yours: assaulting a peer, but she was only charged with break and enter."

Jack smiled. The name evoked fond memories of a beautiful girl at a ball in London. She spent most of the evening talking to him. His eyes turned to the window, but his mind went back to that magical night. He was aware that she had been assaulted by her prospective groom, who then accidentally killed her father. He wondered what had happened to her. Had she eventually been forced to marry him?

Jack's smile caught the governor's attention. Lachlan watched his expressive face soften as a happy memory surfaced. He interrupted his reverie with one word. "Son?"

Jack chuckled. He turned back to the governor and explained. "I met a girl in London named Martha Alexander, and I was thinking back to that magical evening at the ball. That is part of my old life. I shall never see her again." He gave a long, forlorn sigh.

Lachlan's face lit up. He felt like cheering, but chuckled. God had gone before both of these young folk. He had seen the state she was in after her assault, and he had come to know Martha when she accompanied Hetty on the occasional visit over the last months that she lived with the Walkers. Mark wrote that Hector had spoken to her about his faith, and she was a vastly different lass from the one Lachlan had written to him about.

For now, Lachlan said, "Never say never, laddie. God works in mysterious ways." He stood. "Give it a week at Duffy's, and let me know how you settle."

Jack sighed. He felt he had encroached on the vice-regal gentleman long enough.

There was a tap on the door. His training kicked in, and Jack jumped up to open it.

The housekeeper brought in the tea tray, and she asked, "Is there anything else I can get for the young gentleman?"

Lachlan waited for a moment and said, "That will be all, thank you, Mrs Eccles."

Jack took his seat and was served tea by the governor.

The brew was hot, sweet, and black. He was astonished by how this interview had gone. Governor Macquarie was well aware of his past. Jack found it hard to believe that the Prince Regent and Mr Wilberforce had both written to the viceregal gentleman requesting that the governor oversee his well-being. The prince had done what he said. He smiled, glanced heavenward and gave thanks.

Lachlan saw the small action, and a smile also settled on his lips.

When they finished tea, another knock on the office door brought news that Jack's ride had arrived. He was to be taken to his accommodation by wagon with a delivery of produce for Duffy's store.

Jack felt like hugging the governor, but he gave him a regal bow and departed with a grin planted on his lips.

Chapter 18 Serendipitous Meeting
Jack and Martha
January 1820

By the time Martha had been at Duffy's store for six months, she had settled in and learned to love the three families she was now assigned to. She helped run the shop and set up a new product display. Cathy Duffy reminded her of her mother, only this dear lady had a cockney London accent rather than her mother's cultured Scottish one. Cathy was petite and very capable, being able to turn her hand to almost anything. Her husband, Mark, had been shot by bushrangers and had full use of only one arm. Something similar had occurred to Cathy's son-in-law, Drew, when they all ran the southern tollgate in Parramatta. Cathy's son Josh was the only able-bodied man at the store. Between the three men, they had four good arms. An elderly man named George lived in the outback barn with his beloved dairy animals. Martha rarely saw him, which suited her perfectly.

The store was, in reality, a mini Government Bond Store. It supplied items similar to those she was allocated upon arrival; it also stocked a large selection of building supplies. The Duffys' store had been placed close to John Macarthur's new farm to surreptitiously oversee his political activities. This man was an ex-soldier and was one of the main forces behind the Rum Rebellion and the military coup in 1808. His friends had managed to oust Governor Bligh, but when Governor Macquarie arrived, things began to change. John Macarthur and some of the other military personnel involved had already returned to England, giving the new governor a free hand to rearrange the colony. This troublesome man had been absent for nine years and only recently returned.

Martha heard from Mark about their early days in the colony, as he had been the governor's personal security guard. Ten years ago, as newlyweds, Mark and Cathy had lived in Government House in Parramatta with Jenny and Josh before moving to the Parramatta tollgate to get it started. The Duffys had met on the ship out and married in Cape Town in September 1809.

Cathy was accompanied by her young daughter, Jenny, now married to Drew. They came to join Josh, who was to follow them as a convict. Josh had been convicted of theft. He was assigned to Mark. Though young, Josh became Governor Macquarie's groom. The unlikely pair bonded, and from there, options for the family opened up beyond their wildest dreams.

After the double wedding of Jenny and Drew, and Josh and Alice, the two young couples took over the tollgate while Mark, Cathy, and their four small imps moved to Camden at the governor's request. The governor wanted the new government store established before John Macarthur returned from England, so he needed someone totally honest and trustworthy.

When Cathy discovered Martha's eclectic education, she asked her to teach the gaggle of children who lived in the two residences. The four ladies, Cathy, Jenny, Alice, and Martha, then rearranged the shop to empty the upstairs storeroom and to prepare the empty room for Martha to use as a classroom.

The next wagon load of goods included boxes of educational materials, including slates, chalk, and a small pile of well-read books. Martha set to work with the new schoolroom. Two of the nearby farmers' children came when they could.

Martha loved teaching the children. As a girl who had been expected to marry well, she and her eclectic education, along with many adventures, captivated the children on days when they were not keen on reading, writing, or doing arithmetic. She would tell the children a story about her childhood adventures and then ask them to write a journal entry about what they had heard. The youngest ones drew pictures. The older boys loved the pirate story, as well as other adventures and experiences, but there were many other snippets of history she snuck into the stories. This also sparked their interest in geography, as she would have them locate the incident's location. That would lead to learning about the country, its produce, language, and the people living there.

~

The days quickly rolled into weeks.

Martha realised she had been in the colony for nearly a year. Christmas in the newly named Australia was vastly different to the chill in England. Martha had experienced many such hot Christmases in various countries in her youth. These hot days brought memories of her parents to mind. Although she missed them dearly, she barely noticed the passing of time. However, she loved her new home. Everything here was new, and the animals in this land were unique to the point of being strange. There were giant birds, called emus, that were taller than a man, and strange bouncing animals that kept their babies in a pouch on their stomachs. The grunting of the possums at night made her think a herd of rutting wild pigs was surrounding them, so Martha asked for a gun to protect the family.

After giggles from Cathy at her request, she showed Martha the cute creatures making the horrible noise.

Cathy took out some fruit scraps and placed them on a table outside. Cathy said, "Stand and watch as they come down and eat."

Two fluffy grey-brown animals with black brush-tails were soon munching on the fruit.

Martha could not help but exclaim, "Oh, Cathy, they are so cute."

Cathy hooked her arm through Martha's. "Wait until you see the ones in the trees. They are called koalas, and some people refer to them as bears. Now, they are really cute. They look nothing like any picture of a bear I have ever seen, but you would know more about that. I presume you have seen a real bear."

Martha nodded. "I have, ma'am. There are numerous sorts: black, brown, panda, polar, and sun bears. I've seen all of these, and none would I class as cute, and all are downright fearsome. The pandas could be classed as cuddly, I suppose. They only eat bamboo, but they are quite large." They stood watching the brush-tailed possums until the fruit was gone.

Martha wondered why Cathy had drawn her aside until the possums went.

Cathy turned and took Martha's hands. "Dear, we need to have a little chat." She swallowed nervously before saying, "Martha, dear girl, Mark wrote to Lachlan for more help. I wanted to tell you before he sent the letter, but I didn't know how. Sweet girl, another young man will be coming to assist the men. George is getting old and needs a little help with moving things, as he keeps tripping over. Drew and

Mark each have only one good arm, so Josh needs an able-bodied man to help with some of the work. We need a fit man to assist with the store."

Martha's heart fell, and then soared when Cathy first spoke. "Oh, ma'am, I thought you wished me to leave. This is your place. You can have whoever you need. I am a convict lass who can read and write; nothing more, nothing less. Do not consider me in your needs."

Cathy drew her into a hug. "Of course, we will consider you, Martha. You have had a horrible experience, and we do not wish to add any trauma to that. Trust me, I know exactly what you went through. I know the fear of meeting a new man."

Martha was relieved. "Ma'am, Cathy, if I can stay here with you, that is all I wish." She unexpectedly teared up. "Please don't make me leave. I presume the new man will be outside with George or in the house with you in the back servant's room?"

Cathy nodded.

Martha swallowed bravely. "Then I shall be fine. My room, next to Drew and Jenny's children, is almost impenetrable to any raider. I have survived the worst at the hands of a pack of vile men. I should be able to handle one young man if he tries to overstep the line. I'm sure Mark will speak to him should that occur."

~

The usual driver was not alone when the government stores wagon arrived the first week in January. A young man sat next to the regular driver.

Martha was at work, teaching, and missed the crunch of the wheels on the gravel roadway; the children did not.

The sound of a new voice made the children stop working. They initially fell silent, ensuring that it was not bushrangers. They had a small escape hatch at the back of the room, in case the undesirable criminals attacked again. Both Drew and Mark had been shot in similar raids, so they had reason to be fearful. However, this morning, the voice was met with a laugh from Mark. All the occupants of the room exhaled a long sigh, and chatter resumed. Whoever it was, they were all safe.

Lessons continued for the next half hour, and then Martha released the children as the room was too hot to work in. She took half an hour to tidy the room and write the lessons for the following day on the blackboard. Then she checked the children's work before joining the family for their noon meal. They all ate at the kitchen's long table in the rear residence.

The luncheon was in the main house at the back of the store. Mark, Cathy and their children lived there, sharing it with Josh, Alice and their little ones. The main house had three small staff rooms at the back. Martha had refused one of these rooms as they backed onto the courtyard. She felt vulnerable, and Cathy understood her anxiety when she heard her story. She preferred her tiny, windowless, secure room upstairs above the shop.

Jenny and Alice had cooked a roast piglet for everyone for lunch. The new man had unpacked his small bag and was standing with his back to her. He was waiting to carry the platter to the table when he turned. The sight that met his eyes stunned him. The girl with the adorable freckles from the ball stood before him. He whispered, "Martha!"

Martha's jaw dropped open. She nearly called him by his title, but he interrupted her. She mouthed, "Lord John." She saw him give an imperceptible shake of his head.

Jack said, "Hello, miss. My name is Jack Turner. I'm pleased to meet you." He put his finger to his lips for her to say no more.

Martha quickly gathered her confused thoughts and welcomed him. "I'm Martha Alexander, and I've been here for six months. I am sure you will love it here, sir." They needed to have a long talk later. Why was Lord John Templestowe-Meade here as a convict? Her heart sang with delight. A big smile lit her whole face.

Jack said, "Thank you, miss. I am sure that this placement will be all I desire." He winked at her.

Martha nodded and smiled. Who could believe that the only young man ever to move her heart would be a convict and assigned to the same place as her on the other side of the globe? Her smile went right up to her eyes.

He noticed and grinned back. His heart was singing. He remembered the governor's comment and now understood what he meant by "never say never." He knew! Had Wilberforce's letter mentioned something? Bill knew of his attraction to this girl. Was she the second felon Mr Wilberforce mentioned? He gasped, remembering the governor's comment. He had missed the connection he had briefly mentioned.

Getting through that meal was one of the most demanding chores Martha had ever had. She had to keep her lips shut and refrain from questioning him. His handsome face had seared itself in her memory during their two dances, but if what he said was true, he was the king's pageboy. If so, what had he done to become a convict? She decided to keep him at arm's length until she had some answers. Having grown up in the palace, he could be untrustworthy, a liar and another scoundrel. Time would hopefully reveal the answers to her questions.

In the summer heat, the small children were sent off for their naps, while the older ones were tasked with finding a cool spot and reading for an hour. Martha had just made herself a mug of tea when the back door opened. It was Jack.

Seeing she was alone, Jack said, "Miss Martha, we need to talk. Is there somewhere we can do so without others hearing? I need to explain the name change, amongst other things."

Martha nodded. "There's a table out front under the big tree. We can sit there and still be visible but not overheard." She refused to go anywhere private with this young man until he explained himself. "Tea?"

After he nodded, she handed him a steaming mug of hot, sweet black tea and led the way outside. They skirted the shop without talking and seated themselves in silence.

She took a sip, then said, "Everyone drinks it like this, so you may as well start now, as this is how you will be served it. There will be no dainty Chinese eggshell porcelain teacups here, sir."

Jack chuckled and said, "Thank goodness for that." He followed her to the table. As they walked, he said, "I searched for you after the ball, but you never appeared at any other function."

His words were not what Martha expected. Martha gasped. "You did?"

Jack nodded. "I did, but back then, I could not have courted you anyway, and that is what I must explain. It's also why I am here, as they are related."

They settled themselves at the table in the shade.

Martha sipped her hot brew and waited.

Jack said, "I'm here because I thumped the man who called himself my uncle. He swapped me at birth for Lady Victoria's daughter, for his own nefarious reasons. He was a spy for the French and did not wish to become an earl at that time, as it would have compromised his cover. I knew nothing about this until I was nine years old. Until then, I knew him as my uncle, and I didn't like him.

However, he was my legal guardian, and I had to do what he said. All was revealed to Lady Victoria and Her Majesty, Queen Charlotte, in an overheard conversation. I was to be murdered shortly before I reached my majority, which occurred just over twelve months ago. My so-called Uncle was Lord Clive Templestowe, and I know he was known to you as your father's business partner."

She gasped, having recognised the name.

Jack paused and took her hand as she nodded. "Miss Martha, we have more than just a connection through him. It was he who arranged for the murder of your grandfather, Malcolm McFarlane, in Calcutta. That was one of the discoveries overheard at the same time. He befriended your father and used him as a source for untraceable gemstones. I believe your father had no idea what they were used for. Clive admitted he was completely ignorant of his need for them. However, your grandfather began to suspect there was an ulterior motive. So Clive got rid of him."

Martha knew that story, but she had never been told it was outright murder. "I was told that pirates killed Grandpapa. Papa always wondered, as none had been reported in the area."

Jack shook his head. "That's what Lord Clive wanted everyone to think. His murder was one of seven we discovered that led directly back to Lord Clive. There were probably more, but they will remain unsolved. Lady Victoria never knew her maid, Rachel, was another victim, as she vanished without a trace the day Lady Victoria gave birth. She was one of the bodies found in the submerged coach with my parents. She was apparently my aunt. My real parents, the Turners, and an older female sibling of mine, their coachman, another lady, who is now sure to be the missing maid, as well as Lady Victoria's baby daughter, Jennifer, were all murdered at Uncle Clive's instruction. Lady Victoria, he killed with his own hand. He received six life sentences for their deaths, but that's a moot point. He was hanged for treason on the day of the trial."

Martha knew none of this. "Oh, Lord John, I'm so sorry."

He shushed her. "Miss Martha, I have no title and never did. I'm just Jack Turner. I use John as my name by default. I have no idea what my parents named me, but Lady Victoria called me John Clarence. The palace part of my life is behind me. I have learned to cope as best I can with the hard side of things and must survive. I could say nothing to you at the ball, but even then, I knew about my history."

Martha squeezed his hand. "Oh, Mr John, that's all so horrible! But how did you get here? What happened?"

Jack had a big lump in his throat as he'd not spoken of that day for months. "Lord Clive attacked Lady Victoria and had his way with her on the day of Queen Charlotte's funeral. He kicked her in the ribs and rearranged her face. She drowned in her own blood as a broken rib punctured her lung. I found her just before she died. She named Clive as her attacker. I found him downstairs and punched the living daylights out of him in front of the Regent and numerous other members of the royal family and aristocracy."

Martha squeezed his hand in sympathy.

Jack was moved by her compassion. He swallowed. "The Prince Regent and his group of friends watched my attack, but the prince sided with me. A decade earlier, the queen had informed her son of the overheard conversation, and the government used that knowledge to plant false information in Napoleon's ear through Lord Clive. However, he was, in truth, an earl and had been all my life. I knew this when we met, but I couldn't tell anyone. I told you as much as I could safely do. As such, I injured a peer of the realm. Even though he was disgraced, it was against the law. That was enough to see me arrested and sent here."

Martha nodded in understanding. She knew that rule all too well.

Jack continued. "Unbeknownst to me, Mr Wilberforce and the palace sent the governor letters of introduction, and they preceded my arrival. I was summoned on landing and met with the governor. Therefore, I have been assigned to the Duffys rather than elsewhere. I believe Mark and Josh are trusted friends of the vice-regal gentleman."

Martha nodded. "So I believe. It's why I'm here. Only I came at the recommendation of the doctor from my convict ship. My friends and I had a rough time on the way out. And…" She revealed some of her traumatic journey, expecting to be shunned. Her eyes filled with tears, but they remained unshed.

Jack interrupted. "Don't say more, Martha. The governor told me enough to know why you are here. Plus, I read the newspaper article in London about your papa's death. I know what happened to you the night before the church incident and what occurred there. Martha, that news about the earl killing your father spread through the palace like quicksilver. I know all that occurred and also your response to that vile creature." He gave her a smile that melted her heart. "Mr Wilberforce told me he was on the dock when you were dragged away with your papa. When he wrote to the governor about me, he must have mentioned you as well."

Jack caressed her hand.

She panicked. "So you know about…"

He nodded. "I do, and I know you had no choice in what occurred. You are a victim. Innocent of any intent. I am not a judge, but I do hope to become a good friend." He swallowed nervously. "Will you permit that?"

She nodded, but remained quiet.

The silence hung awkwardly for a few moments, and then he asked, "Martha, do you believe in God?"

That was not the question she expected. She replied honestly. She heaved a long sigh and said, "I didn't, but then after I was horribly abused in Parramatta, things changed. My attackers were the sailors booted from my ship, and they repaid said crime on board with a repeat of the violations in gaol. Only I was alone this time, and by the time they were all finished with me, I was insensible. Although I was already assigned here, I was sent to a wonderful place on the Hawkesbury River to heal. I spent six months there recovering before being brought here." She took a drink of her cooling tea. "That place, *Loganberry Farm*, had another convict. His name is Hector Macdougal, and he taught me about God and forgiveness. He's one of those fierce-looking red-headed Scottish highlanders. But, Jack, he's a gentle giant with a heart of gold. He taught me about God and my need to forgive my attackers. What he told me made sense. They are now all dead. They were arrested the day I left Parramatta. The governor saw they dangled on the gibbets some weeks after my attack. So, in answer to your question. I didn't, but I do now. Why?"

Jack didn't directly answer her question but said, "Because I believe in repentance, forgiveness, and being washed clean. I believe I have been given a fresh start in life, and I wish to start anew. I also believe in God-incidents, and finding you here is truly miraculous. Martha, the past is behind us. The future is unmade and for us to work at…" He paused before adding, "…possibly being together, but it's too early for that yet. However, I have been looking for you for over a year. You must remember that nothing that occurred to you was your fault. You are the same wonderful girl I met at the ball; only now I can do something about that – if you wish."

Martha had expected rejection, but Jack was offering the possibility of a life together and redemption. A single nod was all she could muster. Her eyes welled with tears of happiness. Of all the men she had ever met in the many countries she had been to, Lord John, or Jack as she now had to call him, was the man she begged her father to allow her to marry. Hector had told her about repentance and forgiveness. She had recently confessed her stubbornness and stupidity to God. Jack had just voiced his absolution. Now, they could start afresh together.

The emotions played on her beautiful face as Jack stroked her hand lovingly. He said, "You don't need to make any decisions now, Martha. Just know I am here for you if you wish."

Martha managed to give him a wan smile. "I wish, Lord John, more than you could ever know. I never forgot you either. I begged Papa to let me wed you. In my darkest days, that one night at the ball gave me the courage to fight and survive. I could imagine nothing nicer than having you near."

Her gaze dropped to their hands. Rather than pull away, she entwined her fingers with his, and she clung tightly.

The handsome young man across the table from her glowed with delight. Jack grinned. Mr Wilberforce had told him to trust God. If today were the outcome of his conviction, he would be content. He had found his heart's desire. "Lord John is dead and buried, Martha. I'm just Jack; your Jack if you will have me."

Another squeeze of her fingers was followed by, "Willingly, Jack." Her eyes caught movement from the shop, but she did not drop his hand. She never wished to let go of him again. Finally, she was no longer alone.

Unbeknownst to them, Cathy had watched their interaction from the moment they sat down. When she saw Martha's slight movement and realised the touch was mutual, she knew she needed to find out what was going on. She quietly exited through the front door and walked to join them. When she arrived at the table, they did not break the clasp. Cathy raised an eyebrow and looked at Martha for an explanation.

With her free hand, Martha brushed the leaves from the seat beside her. "Please join us, Cathy."

Cathy took a seat and waited. She saw Jack's caring glance at the girl and wondered what would follow.

Jack spoke first. "Mrs Duffy, the governor assigned me here

due to a letter of introduction he received prior to my arrival. I don't know what he told you, but the writer knew my conviction to be a technicality. It was more for my protection. Here, in this land, I could start afresh."

Cathy nodded. "I know about a letter, but we were not told who it was from."

Jack smiled and said, "And I hope that the sender remains unknown for some time. I may tell you one day, when I receive the all clear."

His glance at Martha told Cathy that she knew who it was. However, she waited for him to finish his story.

Jack did. "Ma'am, those details are irrelevant, except to inform you that Martha and I knew each other in London. I was not in a position to pursue a relationship with her at the time, but I looked for her. By the time I tried to find her, she had already been arrested. It was the man who called himself my uncle who had her grandfather murdered. So our family connection is long-standing."

Cathy gasped. Martha had mentioned nothing about him. She looked at the girl beside her.

Martha's face turned to Cathy. "I never knew my mama's papa had been murdered. I thought pirates had killed him. Cathy, his death was how my parents met. Jack's uncle weaselled his way into my father's life and became a business partner. Papa married Mama soon after her father's death and began their voyages of discovery, and they had a very happy marriage. Lord Clive was present when Papa was killed and paid for Papa's burial. Jack has just filled me in on the situation."

Jack's subtle shake of his head made her refrain from saying more.

She gave an imperceptible nod of understanding.

Cathy was stunned. "So, did either of you know that you were both convicts?"

Both shook their heads.

She continued. "By the look of your hands, I'm guessing that you wish this to be more than just a friendship?"

They had forgotten their hands were intertwined, and both immediately pulled their hands back into their laps.

Jack said, "It's early days, Mrs Duffy, but that would be my goal if Martha wished. I wanted to court her in London, but that was not possible."

Martha added, "I begged my father to permit me to marry Jo… Jack, but I had been promised elsewhere. I never saw him again. Then things went haywire."

Cathy caught Martha's nod and grin. She chuckled. "Jack Turner, if God sees fit to reunite you after such a traumatic start for you both, who are we to stand in His pathway? Ensure you remain within the confines of propriety; she has had enough trauma in her short life to receive more."

Martha's face lit up. "Thank you, Cathy. I have already told him of the horrific details that brought me to this point, but he already knew most of them. Additionally, Hector MacDougal discussed repentance and forgiveness. Jack knows none of it was consensual, but the repercussions will remain. I shall always remain fearful of groups of men. When you told me a new man was coming, I admit I panicked for a moment, but then a wave of peace washed over me. It was like God was saying, 'Trust me.' So I did, and He brought me Jack."

Both Jack and Cathy noticed her long, contented sigh.

Jack caught her eye and smiled.

Martha's lips replied with the biggest grin she had given since the ball.

Cathy had said her piece, so she left them to finish their tea.

Jack gazed lovingly at Martha, taking in her adorable freckles. She had lost a lot of weight, but not so much that her curvaceous form didn't look nice even in a hideous drill convict gown. He wondered what had happened to her pearls. Had his Uncle Clive stolen them?

That was a question for another day.

Chapter 19 The Way Forward
1820
Jack and Martha

$\mathcal{A}$fter Jack's explanation, Cathy permitted them regular time off. Rather than find somewhere private to go, they remained in sight and respectful at all times, often at the table in front of the shop.

Jack settled into his new quarters and quickly made himself indispensable. He could lift heavy loads easily, and together, he and Josh could handle anything really large. He treated Martha as the lady he knew her to be. Although she may not have had a title, she was worthy in his eyes as a gentlewoman. She also never asked Jack to be alone with her.

Martha was still somewhat in awe of the young man who had grown up in the royal palaces of London in the presence of the king and queen.

He occasionally forgot she was listening and dropped a nickname of one of the royal family.

They had promised each other that his past would never be mentioned in anyone's hearing, and it wasn't. But with her, he could talk freely. This was something he never expected to be able to do.

He shared his childhood experiences, noting that he witnessed far too much immorality at court after Prinny became the Regent. "Martha, I never wanted one of the society girls. I saw the shallowness of them. They primped and preened but lacked substance. They were born to breed the next generation of equally shallow society peers."

He harrumphed in frustrated anger. "Thankfully, I also saw good men like the Duke of Gracemere and the new Duke of Cheatham. They are good men and incorruptible. Their friends are like them."

When anyone asked about their relationship, she replied that they had met each other in London. This was true, but they did not mention any details.

~

Some weeks after his arrival, the household had settled down to dinner when the neigh of horses was heard.

Cathy, Alice and Jenny grabbed the children and fled from the kitchen.

The pantry had a hidden room where they could remain undetected by robbers.

Unfortunately, that was who had come. Bushrangers needed to eat, and that meant stealing food.

It was during the very first raid that Mark had been shot and lost most of the use of his arm. Although he could lift nothing heavy, his hand still worked.

Drew had been shot in the shoulder when the family lived at the tollgate. He had been a soldier back then and had been medically discharged on half pay.

Tonight, George had taken his meal to the stable accommodation, leaving Martha and the men at the table. She did not understand why the women and children fled.

There had been no bushranger raids since her arrival, so she was not aware of the protocol. It was too late to hide now as the front door crashed open.

Mark stood and turned to face the approaching raiders.

Heavy boot steps approached, as did the odour of unwashed bodies. Five others followed the lead man.

Mark sighed and said, "Hello, gentlemen. The door was unlocked. You did not need to smash it."

Martha nearly gagged at the stench of the filthy men, and memories of her assaults washed over her. Their convict apparel was almost threadbare, and their faces blackened with dirt. She was sure they were alive with lice. Three were scratching their hair.

The leader had a gun pointed at Mark's chest. He said, "Shut it, mister! We'll do what we want and take some vitals. You lad, you're about the same size, so go get us some of your clobber, and I don't mean that convict garbage we got issued." He was looking at Jack.

Determined not to cause a fight, Jack said, trying to disguise his posh accent, "Sorry, but all I got is my convict clobber." He subtly reached out for Martha's hand under the table.

A string of expletives was thrown at Jack.

Unfazed, Mark said, "I have a stock of clothing that will fit you. A new shipment arrived last week, and I haven't had a chance to unpack it yet. The clothes are in one of the supply rooms. They are stored with the food outside."

The muzzle of the gun waved sideways.

Mark took that as an instruction to lead the way to the storeroom. "We'll need a lamp," he said, picking up an oil lamp and leading the way to the storeroom furthest from the shop and residence.

Three of the uncouth fellows followed, and the three younger, itchy men remained. All had guns.

The odour did not leave with the first men. These three were as on-the-nose as the others. One must have fouled his trousers as he stank.

Jack found it hard not to gag.

This foul-smelling scoundrel approached Martha and lifted his hand to her cheek. "Well, ain't you a pretty morsel? If I had more time, I'd like to taste your wares."

Martha slid closer to Jack on the bench seat.

The vile felon said, "Oh, so that's how the wind blows, eh? Maybe he'd like to watch you get ridden here on the table."

He continued to stroke the slight scar on Martha's face. "Me friends can hold me barking irons on you while we have a little play." He bent down to kiss her.

She shook her head to pull away, so he grabbed her chin. He dragged her to her feet and into his arms.

Jack jumped up, but had a gun directed at him.

One of the younger men said, "If the boss sees ya, he'll skin ya alive. Otherwise, we'd all take turns." He paused and added, "Then again, maybe we will all share her anyway. The boss ain't back yet, so we could have a quickie with her. Pity we can't hang around for a good play."

An evil chuckle was followed by, "Well, a peck will have to do for today, but next time, I'll make sure we have some hay to tumble in when I come again. I want to grind my wiffles into you, my pretty lass." He grabbed a handful of her hair and forcibly kissed her.

Thankfully, it was only a quick one, but it was disgusting.

His blackened teeth and rotten breath made Martha gag.

She pulled away and ran to the safety of Jack's arms. She hid her face against Jack's shoulder. The bushranger tasted worse than he smelled.

The youngest intruder said, "Leave her be, you stupid idiot."

Jack slid his arm around her and drew her close.

It was only then that he noticed the other two muskets were pointing at Drew and Josh. Drew's face dripped with perspiration, and he was sheet-white. He had wondered why they had remained silent, but then Jack caught a subtle movement of Josh's head.

He saw one of the crooks had Drew by his injured shoulder. Knowing how painful it was, he must be in agony. He remembered Drew had been injured by raiders in Parramatta.

With minimal movement, Josh's eyes dropped to the table, then to the back door. With the bushranger behind him, they could not see his face. Josh mouthed the words, "Ready to run!"

Jack gave a subtle nod in the guise of consoling Martha; he whispered, "Run when I say."

Martha nodded against his chest and whispered, "Be careful."

Jack replied with words he never thought he'd say. "I love you!"

Martha was unable to reply as she wished, but her heart sang. She whispered, "Me too!"

Josh distracted the young man. "What food do you want? I can get you some of whatever you need."

In reply, the man with the gun shoved four empty sugar bags at Drew. He said, "You two, fill those with sugar, rice, and flour, and we also want a barrel of salted meat."

However, he waved his weapon at Jack and Josh rather than Drew.

While Jack was distracted, the man grabbed Martha, but she pulled away and went to kick his shin. "Feisty pullet, aren't you?" The man went to grab her again and tried to pull her in for another kiss.

She twisted from his arms, but another man caught her and held her against him.

He took his time kissing her until she pulled away.

Rather than head to the pantry, the boys made for the large tin of flour against the side wall. They made as if to fill the bag, but both grabbed handfuls of flour, turned quickly, and threw it into the three men's eyes.

Martha saw where they were heading, and although she had nowhere to run, she quickly turned her head into the crook's shoulder.

Strangled howls filled the kitchen. All abandoned their guns and tried to brush out the stinging, abrasive powder from their eyes. They were unable to see and were clawing at their faces.

She kneed the man holding her.

He doubled over.

Then, rather than running from the room, Martha grabbed a spool of strong twine from the drawer on the table where she had been sitting. They used this thin but very strong string to truss roasts and tie garden plants to stakes.

Before the three invaders realised, they were tied to chairs and gagged.

Martha had run to tie Drew's captive first, as he only had one good arm to restrain him.

Jack and Josh had the strength to hold the other two ruffians while she worked.

Drew grabbed a second spool and tied up the second raider while Jack and Martha dealt with the third one.

Dirty dishcloths and used tea towels made very effective gags, and these were also tied tightly *in situ* with lots more twine.

Mark's voice was heard approaching, and rather than call a warning, Josh, Jack, and Drew took the abandoned muskets and waited for the raiders to enter via the back door.

Mark led the way in, and when he saw the three bushrangers firmly trussed, he attempted to block the view of the returning thieves.

As each robber entered, a muzzle poked them in their ribs. Soon, all six were bound, gagged, and very angry.

Mark, however, kept his voice low and said, "There will be more outside. Drew, cover them. Martha, do you know how to fire a flintlock pistol?"

She nodded.

He handed her a loaded weapon that he had tucked down the back of his trousers.

The three men crept out the back door again.

Martha felt ill. The last time she had held a weapon, her father was teaching her how to shoot. They were at sea, and he wanted her to feel the kickback of the exploding weapon. A lone masked gannet had landed near their ship, and her father had her aim at it. Thankfully, the bird escaped unscathed, if not somewhat frightened, but it showed her the power of the recoil. Her father's lesson was not finished. He had said, "False bravado is your greatest weapon. You have one shot, and you are unlikely to hit anything. However, if you look as though you are very familiar with handling a weapon, you should not need to fire it. Holding it confidently will do the trick, so no shaking." He then chuckled as her hands had been shaking so hard she nearly dropped the pistol into the sea. "Hold it firmly and with determination to intimidate. You will have more use of this if you hold the muzzle and thump them with the butt end."

This incident had occurred a short time after pirates had boarded them, and she used the head pirate's gun and pulled the trigger. Unfortunately, being a matchlock, not a flintlock pistol, the wick was not alight. Her father taught her more about guns after that. Using her father's flintlock pistol, she could easily hit a target at a hundred yards. Now, years later, those lessons resurfaced. With that thought, she took a deep breath and held the gun as still as she could. Amazingly, it was steady in her hands, and she waved it towards the lead bushranger who was trying to stand up.

His gaze held hers, and he saw that she held it with confidence.

She waved it at the crook and said, "Never underestimate a woman with a gun. My papa taught me to shoot after we were boarded by pirates. I was a child back then, so I have had years to perfect my aim. Are you game to risk that I miss?" He sat down again and harrumphed. He had no idea she was quaking in her boots.

Outside, Mark led Jack and Josh to the front of the store. Eight horses were visible, and two men were holding them, watching the front entrance.

With some elaborate hand signals, Mark motioned for Josh and Jack to move to the rear of the horses while he approached the lookouts directly.

Rather than walk straight up to them, Mark slipped back around the other side of the house.

The sound of someone dry retching followed an audible groan. Mark staggered drunkenly towards them, and he slurringly said, "In the dog house again, chaps. Don't go in for any grog, as they just hut up spot…" He staggered and hiccoughed. "No, I mean shut up shop. Yes, that's it! That's what I mean."

He faked another hiccough and swayed. "Turfed out and not a penny to my name. Can't lend a poor fellow a dump or a penny, can ya?" He hiccoughed again and then pretended to fake-vomit once more.

The closest guard said, "Leave us alone, you drunken sot." He tried to move away, but found his path blocked by Josh and Jack.

Moments later, both lookouts were being forced inside by a very sober Mark and a chuckling pair of young men behind him.

The boys had quickly flicked the reins over the railing to stop the horses from wandering away.

Jack said, "Quick thinking, Mark. Good job!"

The crooks' arms were twisted behind their backs. They soon joined their compatriots at the table and were trussed to match their friends. The thin twine cut into their wrists. The more they wiggled, the more it hurt.

Martha kept her gun trained on those seated at the table.

With the bushrangers captured, Mark went to report to Cathy and the girls. "Stay out of sight until we move them to the store room, but it's now safe. The storeroom is built of stone, and they won't be able to escape. The new major is due here tomorrow for a break, and he's coming with a big delivery, so there should be some extra hands. There should be a few soldiers and some convict workers with them."

Within thirty minutes, the dry-goods store had been prepared for overnight occupants.

Mark hoped they would all get rolling drunk; if so, they would be less likely to cause trouble.

Martha prepared two loaves of sliced and buttered bread, a hunk of cheese, and some oranges while the crooks watched. All this was left on one of the full barrels in the storeroom. Mark took a firkin of potent cider that had been left to brew too long, along with some tin mugs for them to drink from.

The cider was in a nine-gallon keg that had been overlooked during the previous season. It had a kick like a mule and, hopefully, would knock them out quickly. It was probably over ten per cent alcohol.

The first three taken over were the white-faced crooks who wished to clean the flour from their eyes.

When Mark prepared the storeroom, he placed two empty buckets for use as a privy. Finding the bucket of water, with their hands still bound in front of them, the first three men were still using the water to scour the flour off their faces when the next group of felons arrived.

Drew stood guard outside the storeroom with a pistol while Mark and Josh moved the thieves one by one.

Jack remained in the kitchen with Martha, guarding the others.

Following the floury men, the lookouts followed, still tied up, and, finally, the three ringleaders. The eight prisoners resisted all the way to their night's accommodation until Josh held a pistol to their heads.

As the last man was forced in the door, Mark said, "There's food and drink for you now; the buckets are your privy. There is a nine-gallon firkin of cider to drink. If you behave, you will get breakfast tomorrow. Sleep well, my friends. An armed guard will be on watch all night, so do not attempt to escape." Mark chuckled. His laugh was the last thing they heard as the opening was sealed. The thunk of the solid door, which even rats had not managed to chew through, sealed their fate for the night.

The slamming door made the leader groan. They were still gagged and tied, but Mark had loosened the hands of the youngest lookout. It would take them some time to untie each other in the dark, but it was safer than doing it before locking them in.

Mark and Josh turned back to the house, leaving Drew on guard.

The clunk of the door brought George to the door of his room. "Hello, boss, something up? I thought I heard voices."

Mark explained what had occurred. With the bushrangers secured, Josh went to release his wife and family.

George said, "Cor, boss. Would you like me to work a shift tonight guarding them? Sorry, I heard nothing out the back."

Mark nodded, "We all will, George. Stay here for a while and relieve Drew while we release the girls."

George nodded and took the pistol.

Cathy and the family were released from the pantry safe room and set about putting the sleepy children to bed.

They quickly arranged a rotating guard through the night. Each would take a two-hour shift until the soldiers arrived sometime the next day.

Cathy waited until they had left the room before gathering Martha in her arms. "I'm so sorry, Martha. I intended to tell you about what we do when such things occur."

Martha hugged her mistress back. She was in awe that the children had not made a peep. "How did you keep them all so quiet?"

Cathy glanced at her husband. "That's not hard; they all knew Drew and Mark were shot by such men and know fear. They know the consequences of making a noise." Cathy caressed the girl's face and asked, "Are you all right? Did they hurt you?"

Surprisingly, Martha found that she was not even shaking. "Two kissed me but mentioned their wish to do more. Jack and Josh threw flour in their eyes before they had the opportunity." She explained that her second pirate adventure had been much worse. The first time she met a blackguard was when she was a child, and she had no idea what to do with a pistol. "I'm okay, Cathy. Jack held my hand for most of the time."

Jack had followed the last crook outside. She turned as he entered. She glanced at the young man, who had hardly taken his eyes off her through the ordeal. Her smile and glance brought Jack to her side. Jack held his arms open to her, and she walked into them. He asked, "Martha, is anything wrong?" Her beautiful smile touched his heart.

She shook her head. "No, I'm fine, thanks to you." She rested her head on his chest. She wanted to say that she had heard his words of endearment, but had no chance to do so that night. Her eyes were only for him. Martha hoped her inappropriate action would go unnoticed by Cathy as she was drawn into Mark's arms. Josh and Drew did likewise to their wives.

Cathy did notice Martha's action and was stunned. This girl had been violated, abused, and beaten so severely that it had taken six months for her to heal, and yet she trusted this new young man implicitly. There was obviously truth in their meeting in London.

Jack released Martha quickly, but she took his hand. He grinned when he looked at their entwined fingers.

Mark's brows rose in amazement. A cocked eyebrow at Jack was Mark silently questioning their stance.

Jack leaned in and whispered something to Martha. She nodded in reply. They reluctantly dropped hands as they parted. He then said good night. He was on the next watch, so he needed some sleep. Both were smiling.

Martha needed to put more bread on to rise. She set about doing that while the others settled the last of the children.

The household finally settled down for the night.

~

The following day, the wagon of supplies arrived late morning.

The now drunk prisoners had been fed scalding porridge and then shut back in the sealed black hole. Major Ned Grace and his men waved to Jack upon arrival.

Mark realised this was the new soldier who had come for a week to do his first survey of the area. A dozen of his men mounted and guarded the small gang of six convicts, who quickly offloaded the stores.

The new stock was unpacked. Some clothing and building materials were piled on the grass outside the stone storeroom. Josh and Jack would sort them out after the wagon departed. The wagon was prepared to transport the newest shackled convicts, along with the Ticket of Leave felons who had arrived as labourers. The crew usually stayed overnight before returning, but today, they had a quick meal and then prepared for the return trip with extra prisoners. Their destination would be the lock-up in Liverpool.

The six soldiers would escort the prisoners. This gang of bushrangers had been terrorising many of the outlying farms for a while. Ned and most of the soldiers had ridden, so he would remain for the week as planned, as he had other people to meet. He also wished to catch up with Jack.

The wagon typically had room for a dozen men and stores, but now twenty would need to squeeze on board. The six convicts who had come with the wagon were good workers and were in their final months of servitude. They would not risk their freedom to help the bushrangers. After unloading, they remained unshackled. Two would need to travel with the driver. All the new prisoners would have their wrists and ankles shackled and locked onto the iron rings in the wagon's deck. They were not friends of the well-behaved convicts. The bushrangers' future did not look good. Hanging would be the most likely outcome for the leaders, while flogging would be the punishment for the younger lookouts.

Shortly before their planned departure, Ned's bulky six-foot-plus form filled the storeroom's doorway. Piles of convict irons waited next to the armed soldiers. Ned fully expected to be almost crash-tackled when he opened the door, and he wasn't wrong. Josh and Jack stood on either side.

Although nursing headaches from the cider, three charged at Ned. He stepped aside and let them pass. They stopped short when they noticed a dozen red-coat soldiers with muskets pointed at them. The crooks froze. Knowing the strong likelihood of being shot, they halted their attempted escape. Blue language filled the air.

Soon, all were shackled and locked onto the flatbed wagon. The last three were permitted to wash the remaining flour from their faces. Their eyes were red and weeping, and they were cursing the boys over the cheap trick pulled on them.

Josh, Jack, and Drew grinned, slapped hands with a high clap and chuckled.

Ned watched his friend's interaction with the young lass. On the voyage out, Jack had mentioned a girl he had met at a ball. Was this really her? Jack had said nothing could ever come of that evening, but God worked in mysterious ways. According to Lachlan, God had brought them together again.

While the soldiers fed the quickly sobering criminals, Ned had a chance to catch up with Jack. He asked, "How are you settling in?" He noticed that the young convict's eyes had hardly left Martha Alexander's smiling face.

"Fine, thanks, Ned." He released a long sigh of contentment.

Ned followed his gaze. "How is she coping, Jack? The governor mentioned you met her in London." For some reason, Lachlan had told Ned not to update anyone on Jack's whereabouts or what he was doing. He was even forbidden to tell Charles where Jack was. Charles was recently married to the maid he had rescued on his first day on the job. Sal had been accosted but not violated, and she turned to Charles for protection. Their mutual friend proposed that day, and Samuel Marsden married them soon afterwards. Ned figured that Jack would ask if he wished to know, so he remained silent about Charles.

Jack grinned. "I did, sir. I'm settling very well now, thanks. We are fine. Martha had many long discussions with a man named Hector at Walker's farm. He led her to faith, and the Lord led her back to me. Ned, she is the girl I met in London before all this happened." He waved his hand over the area. He gave her another smile. "I plan to propose."

Martha gave them both a shy smile and turned to head indoors.

Ned grinned back, leaned close to Jack and whispered, "I would do it sooner than later, Jack. I can even fast-track the paperwork if you wish. She is safer married than single. The governor told me to ask about your reunion. He knows more than he has let on, doesn't he?" Ned saw Jack's face light up.

Jack nodded. "He knows most of my background as well as hers. He even knows we met in London, if his expression when I mentioned her name is anything to go by. However, I think I'll ask her for a walk now."

Without waiting to be dismissed, Jack went to seek his lady love. He had no ring, no home, no income, and no likelihood of any of that changing anytime soon. His possessions had not arrived, as he had nowhere to store them. He found Martha cleaning out the storeroom where the prisoners had been kept.

Rather than ask her for a walk, he pitched in and helped clean the stinking room. The first things he tended to were the two full buckets of excrement. At least the filthy criminals had not used the floor as a toilet. However, the smell was so bad that it made him gag. He appreciated the palace maids even more now. He had never thought of the stench when using his porcelain facility in special lidded chairs in his room in the palace. Hopefully, with the buckets gone, the odour would not taint the contents.

Contrary to what Mark had told Jack, this room was used to store barrels of non-perishables, not bags of flour and dry goods. Crates of government-rationed clothing and building products were housed here.

When the storeroom was clean and the new products were put away, Jack asked Martha for a walk.

Rather than saying yes immediately, she asked Cathy for permission.

Jack followed her into the kitchen.

As Ned had already spoken to Cathy while they were working, she replied, "You may, Jack, but I wish you to stay in sight. You are both off duty for the next hour."

They wandered out of the kitchen with Martha's arm hooked through Jack's as though they were heading off on a stroll through Hyde Park in London. Cathy chuckled quietly and walked into the front sitting room to watch them as a chaperone. The other adults followed.

When the courting couple were well away from the store but still visible, Jack dropped to one knee.

The three resident couples and Ned stood at the sitting room window, watching as Martha replied yes to Jack's question. They could tell as they saw her nod, then she threw herself into his arms, and they embraced, but he did not kiss her.

When the hug occurred, the seven adults inside turned away to give them some privacy.

Alice and Jenny decided to whip up a batch of scones with jam and whipped cream for the afternoon tea. Unfortunately, they didn't have time to make a cake to celebrate, but the scones would be ready when the newly engaged couple returned to the store.

~

An hour later, the children were called, and Mark told them that Jack had proposed and that Martha had accepted. The celebration relieved the tension of the past twenty-four hours.

For Martha, Jack was everything she thought he was. He treated her with adoration and respect, courting her as if she were a princess.

To him, she was just that.

With Martha's approval, Jack asked Ned to apply for permission to marry as soon as possible. Only then could he protect her as he wished.

Martha knew that her future was with Jack. He would keep her safe, honour her, and cherish her all of her life. She adored him and often dreamed about him.

Now engaged, when they were alone, Jack opened up to her about his life at court. She had already asked him for more details about the letters of recommendation, and he confirmed that one had indeed been from the regent rather than a generic one from the palace. He told her of his reply while sitting at the governor's desk and using the monogrammed governor's stationery and his eagle's quill.

A giggle followed her gasp. "I bet that won't occur often."

Jack confessed, grinning, "I said the same to the governor."

His retelling of the palace antics would often have her laughing. He told her about the conversations he had overheard, the speakers forgetting that he could hear them. Listening to some of these vile propositions made him reject the disgusting bed-hopping that often occurred in the palace with the Prince Regent's blessing. He was pleased Queen Charlotte knew nothing about her son's antics.

~

Ned remained for the week and did daily inspections of the outlying farms. He returned to Parramatta with the request for the marriage of two convicts. He would hand this to the governor personally, as he had been instructed to give this young convict as much lenience as he could. Also, keeping it from going through other hands would keep Jack safe.

Ned realised there was much about this young man he didn't know. He hoped that one day, Jack would confide in him. The governor's personal interest showed Jack was not a normal felon. Ned was surprised that the governor trusted him with these details, but Perry and John Hunter had vouched for him, saying he was trustworthy. The fact that the governor had asked Ned to hide any involvement from the official channels was eye-opening. All that Lachlan Macquarie would tell him is that he had received two letters of introduction from London and that Jack Turner was totally trustworthy. He had been convicted on a technicality, but was not a criminal. He had struck a peer who had hurt someone close to him.

For some reason, Lachlan had asked Ned to tell Charles that he had arranged the placement and not the governor. Who was this young man?

~

Only two weeks later, at the end of January, a visitor arrived unexpectedly. He carried a letter in response to the marriage request. This man was a travelling minister.

Jack and Martha's wedding ceremony was performed with little fuss. Both knew what sort of palaver would have occurred if they had married in London, but this was all they wanted. They were both saddened that their loved ones would never know, but the future ahead of them looked bright. They were married in the front room of the Duffys' house. Only the family attended, but as neither the bride nor the groom had any other relations, the Duffys were as close as they could be.

Mark gave Martha away, which she thought was funny, as she would be moving from her tiny room in the shop building to the back room of their house. She was nearly nineteen, and Jack was twenty-three.

Alice, Jenny and Cathy dressed Martha in the wedding gown Jenny had worn. Like Martha, Alice had been a convict and had nothing when she wed. The two girls bonded and often spoke about how their faith sustained them as they coped with the aftermath of the trauma. Alice had found Josh, and now Martha had Jack. He knew everything about her past, yet he still loved her.

Before the newlyweds arose the following morning, the minister had left for other appointments. They had been given a week off duty.

Jack's expression was one of adoration. He opened doors and pulled out chairs for her. He always offered her his arm when they walked. The children and others quickly copied Jack's excellent manners. Both Mark and Cathy had grown up in the very poorest part of London, known as the Rookeries, so they looked to this unusual couple for etiquette lessons. Their rough edges had been smoothed during the years living in Government House, but Jack and Martha's manners showed the family how much they didn't know.

Soon, dancing lessons were held, as George could hold a tune by tapping two spoons together. The children were taught elocution, grooming, deportment, and manners.

~

A week after their wedding, Martha's story unfolded to Cathy. She confessed that the Earl of Oxenborough-Thorpe had ravished her the night before their planned wedding and then described the horrific day that followed. Up until then, she had only told Cathy about the abuse on the ship and gaol. She was amazed to discover that the earl's debauched ways were known to both of the Duffys. The earl and his appalling friends, one of whom was Lord Wiskhamford, who had run over Cathy's first husband, James. These two peers had a reputation for buying the youngest children possible for their disgusting activities. They were not fussy if they were boys or girls, but the younger, the better. They were known to both sexually abuse the innocent mites and also inflict cruel punishments on them. Many were marked with facial cuts after such treatment, if they even survived.

When that link was revealed, Cathy winced. Her reaction was to embrace Martha and weep with her, but Martha was strong; she refused to let that man have power over her.

Cathy had escaped the earl's trap when a child, but not his friends. The earl had only been a young man at the time. She revealed her father had sold her virginity to a filthy peer who had deflowered her for money when she was only thirteen. Cathy had told Alice her story, but had never mentioned the details to her children. Mark knew everything.

Cathy said, "Martha, I had been used and discarded, like rubbish. I was only just a woman when I was sold to a madam by the man who had purchased me from my father after he found someone younger. They called her 'The Abbess' in the Rookeries. The peer vilely used me for weeks before he found a younger child. Men like the Earl of Oxenborough-Thorpe and his cronies took their pleasure with us. They were not just looking for carnal pleasure, but they also loved cruelty. They took delight in watching one another whip us and then rape us. They took their pleasures by watching their friends use us. Sometimes there were more than one working us over at a time. Each act was more horrific than the one before. We were powerless. It was nothing to them if one of the little children died at their hands. We were merely pawns for their entertainment, disposable beings with no value." The faces of both women were wet with tears.

Martha now realised that this was probably how the earl's first three wives died. Her gasp of horror made her tears flow again.

Cathy reached out and took her hand. "Martha, you will receive no condemnation from me, my dear. Both Mark and I know him and his type. For him to still be engaging in his disgusting, lustful activities at his age is revolting. I wonder how many children he killed in the pursuit of satisfying his gross lusts. You did well to escape reasonably unscathed. I know for a fact that he likes cutting and marking his human victims. He probably would have taken great joy in marking you with a cut on your cheek each time after he had violated you. I heard that his first wife's body was covered in such scars."

Martha gasped again when she heard the word human. "Cathy, rumours abounded that they didn't like only children. Was that true?"

"If you mean animals?" Cathy nodded. She couldn't voice her knowledge of the bestiality of such men to Mark. She whispered, "Large dogs were a favourite of this vile group, but other animals were used. Horses were known to shy away from Lord Wiskhamford." Cathy wondered if this was why one had run down James. Martha didn't need to hear the gruesome details of her first husband's death or of the man who did it.

Martha was horrified to discover an evil connection between them. She hugged Cathy after she told her story. However, it did mean she could discuss things with Alice and Cathy that Jenny could never understand. Drew had lived on the streets in Sydney, but his experiences were vastly different.

Cathy added, "At age ten, Jenny had been noticed by this group of carnal peers, and this was the main reason we left London. I really don't know how we kept her away from them. After James was killed, it became impossible to keep her safe any longer. I had heard a whisper that they were planning to take her by force. Had Josh not been arrested, we still would have come here."

Martha clasped Cathy's hand. "You don't need to tell me, Cathy."

Cathy shook her head. "I do, for I can't tell anyone else. You understand the danger more than anyone in the family. Even Alice."

Martha nodded. "Go on then."

Cathy drew a long breath and continued. "Josh and Jenny are unaware of this, and they don't need to know. Mark and I decided never to let Jenny know, but I think she guessed something had prompted our departure from London so quickly. It wasn't Josh's arrest. However, Josh's gaoler and his wife found us in our refuge at the church and fed us until our ship left."

Cathy sighed and thought back to that horrific week. She continued her story. "After Josh was arrested, we were alone in the Rookeries. Josh's prison guard, whom I knew from church, was the one who brought word that the earl and his friends were looking for Jenny. The day after Josh was arrested, we packed up and left our room. Many orphaned children lived in a church crypt. The ministers there were the ones who saved both Mark and my first husband, James. I knew we would be safe there for a week or so. The crypt is at St John's in Hackney. I realised we needed to follow Josh very quickly. We sailed before Josh did. I met Mark on the way here." Cathy had seen Martha's tears as she told her story.

When Martha had dried her eyes, she said, "We are survivors, Cathy, not victims. I intend to assist other girls like us who have been forced to do things against their will."

Cathy caressed her downy cheek. "Dear, that is why you are here. Thanks to Perry and Katy White, Lachlan has realised that many women are forced into petty crimes against their will, only to face far worse consequences once convicted. Lachlan has placed Major Ned in charge of the female placements because he's a friend of Perry's and can be trusted. Thankfully, Katy escaped such abuse, but she saw much of it. The good Lord has placed us here as a safe house for such girls. Joel and Hetty Walker's place, where you healed, is perfect for more girls. We sent Ned to meet them. I heard that one girl went there soon after you left. Hetty has already taken on two more girls. One is a maid, the other was in a similar state to you. I met Hetty in town a few times when they came to meet the Macquaries, so we write often. I'm quite sure others will follow. Phil Bentley, who lives behind them, saved Fanny, as you know. Mark was involved in that: Fanny was sold by her husband at the market; Mark had the felon arrested, as the sale was illegal. It was one of his last arrests before he took over the tollgate. His last duty was much more pleasant. He was the master of ceremonies for a community concert. There, the Parramatta tanner's musical ability was revealed. George Ellis should have appeared on the stage in Europe rather than tanning kangaroo hides in a penal colony. But that story is for another day. There is much to be done in this settlement, and we need as many helpers as we can."

Martha nodded. "If the Lord sees fit, then one day we will as well. I'm sure He will already have those plans in motion."

Chapter 20 News from Home
1821

Only weeks after their marriage, Martha realised she had not had her monthly bleed since their wedding. After all the abuse and violation she received, she wondered if she could conceive. She had been surprised that she had not contracted the sailor's curse of the clap, but she hadn't. Of that small mercy, she gave thanks to God.

Jack was everything good, kind and considerate in the marriage bed.

Before their first night together, Cathy had taken her aside and given her some hints about how to make that side of marriage enjoyable.

Mark had done the same to Jack and reminded him not to use the burning, harsh lye soap on his nether regions.

Josh took Jack aside after the quick service and gave him some hints on keeping his wife contented.

Jack had never been with a woman that way, so their first time was somewhat awkward. For Martha to know more of the workings of procreation than her husband was a little embarrassing.

Now, a month after their wedding, Martha did not tell Jack about her suspicions until she was sure.

~

Confirmation came some weeks later when she had to throw up on waking.

Jack was concerned about her being poorly and was greatly surprised when she giggled in response.

After they consummated their marriage that first night, they enjoyed a very happy union.

They delighted in discovering the joys they could bring to each other. The relaxed and loving state in which said activity left them was delightful. They would fall asleep contented, sated and safe. Jack was in seventh heaven.

~

Two months after they married, Jack rolled over after their morning lovemaking. Martha said, "Jack, you know you said that you had no known blood family?"

He nodded absentmindedly.

She giggled. "Well, we've been working hard to fix that, and now I can tell you that you are not."

Jack frowned. "Not what, love?" He rested on an elbow while gazing at her luscious breasts. They seemed perkier in the last few weeks. Desire surged through him again.

"...Not alone any more, my belovéd." She reached out to caress his prickly cheek, turning his eyes to hers rather than her sumptuous breasts.

She picked up his hand and placed it on her stomach. "Jack, we're having a baby. You are going to be a father. We are starting a family. That's why I was sick. It should be here by October or early November."

Jack almost catapulted out of the bed as though she had struck him. "What? But we... I mean, can we... You know, what we just did?" He stood gazing at her stomach, as she was naked.

Martha giggled again. Before she retired to bed last night, she asked Cathy if they could continue their pleasurable activities while expecting a child.

Cathy explained they could, but they had to be more careful as her baby grew. Consequently, rather than reply, she reached out to him. "Yes, my darling Jack, and I will want it more often until the child comes. After that, you will have to wait for about six weeks, so we had better make up for that now."

Jack needed no second invitation. He climbed into their bed and drew her to him.

Another loving embrace followed the delightful news.

Although he adored Martha, this child was of his blood.

Having never known his birth parents or his sister, he was thrilled.

Hopefully, more children would follow. For the first time in many years, Jack realised he was happy.

Martha fell asleep in his arms.

Jack fell to thinking about why he had gone to the ball where they met. Boredom had been his motivation.

Even surrounded by an overabundance of wealth all of his life, he had been unsettled. He had only known luxury.

From the age of nine, his every whim had been fulfilled, and he had never had to purchase any clothing as the palace had supplied every item he wore.

Even Lady Victoria needed to buy her own apparel, but the king ordered that he should have a new outfit every month. This occurred when he was a child, growing fast; however, the king's order had never been rescinded.

He hoped William Wilberforce would have the good sense not to send all the fancy attire. He should have said that in his letter.

Jack quickly tired of the velvet silks and embroidered damasks. As he grew, his outfits became almost plain, as he refused the fribbles and furbelows of his peers.

His outfits were an untrimmed version of the royal attendants' livery. His white breeches and stockings were paired with the finest linen shirts, white damask vests, and a deep burgundy long coat with golden-thread frog fastenings. A Venetian lace cravat was his typical necktie.

As he grew, the outfits varied little until he turned eighteen. As he had reached his full height at seventeen, he asked if he could have some everyday clothing that was not livery.

His wish was granted when an entire wardrobe of clothing was delivered over the following two weeks.

His new wardrobe included casual shoes rather than court garb. For once, he had clothing that he could wear outside of the palace. However, this new wardrobe also included items suitable for his sporting prowess and evening wear. It was then that he received his blue-and-gold outfit, which he wore to the ball where he met Martha.

Now, a new future and a new family were growing in his beloved wife. He drew his sleeping bride closer and closed his eyes.

~

Martha had befriended a local Dharawal woman soon after her arrival, but had been too frightened to tell Cathy. With a child on the way, Martha wanted their ancient wisdom when it was time to deliver her baby. She had quickly picked up some words of their complicated language and then discovered that this woman spoke English quite well.

After much giggling, the two became firm friends.

Martha realised that the various native peoples she had met over her life had much more knowledge about birthing than those in her household.

Martha's new friend, known as Peggoty, was to attend the birth.

Cathy had given her blessing, but insisted that the women wear a calico shift while at the house or store. This was more for their safety than anything.

Farmers frequented the shop, and not all of them were trustworthy.

The women at the store ran up some simple gowns that they could slip on quickly.

Peggoty agreed with another giggle.

Over the weeks, other new friends from the tribe were made. While other farmers had trouble with things going missing, this new friendship protected the store rather than causing trouble.

Peggoty arrived twice to warn them of bushrangers in the area.

Mark was able to send a message and have soldiers waiting for them.

Mark and Josh built a small cupboard at the back of the stables to hold the calico dresses. Other food items were frequently left here for visiting members of the tribe who often snuck in at night.

Cathy found gifts of fish or an occasional kangaroo tail left as a thank-you on the kitchen table.

The tribal women had crept into the house in the middle of the night and placed the food where it could not be missed.

Fresh ducks were a delight, and Peggoty promised to bring six when the governor arrived for a visit.

~

In September, the governor wrote and mentioned that he would be in the area in mid-October. He hoped Mark would have a room for him and his entourage.

Mark and the boys set about preparing for the official visit.

The household was already preparing for the arrival of the Turners' first child.

Martha's baby was due any day. However, she was tireless. She had already prepared for the arrival of their baby, and Peggoty and another older woman promised they would come when her time arrived. Peggoty said their word for woman was *duba* and for child was *gurung*.

Martha probed her new friend for more information about their people and their customs. She and Jack would often be seen sitting under the trees, talking to the local folk.

~

October came and went. Lachlan sent a letter with the weekly order. An issue had arisen, and he would explain when he arrived.

Marcus John George Turner arrived on the last day of October 1820. His arrival coincided with a second letter from Lachlan Macquarie.

The governor confirmed the new dates of his visit and mentioned that he had mail for Jack and Martha.

Marc was a placid baby and soon became used to being passed to whoever had empty arms.

A tribe of children often followed Josh and Jack as they worked, and little Marc was added to the masses of children carried everywhere.

~

The governor's entourage finally came in early November. Lachlan's delay was due to an unexpected visitor at Government House.

In early October, Howard Marlow, the senior housemaster at the orphanage in Sydney, had been kidnapped and beaten up.

Howard and another man arrived on the doorstep of Government House in Parramatta the day before Lachlan was planning to leave.

The trip was delayed.

The young convict teacher was bedraggled and in need of medical care. He had been assaulted and had broken ribs.

However, this situation revealed who had been behind the importation of illegal spirits and the large amount of missing funds from the orphanage.

Eventually, Lachlan's small black unmarked carriage arrived with Major Ned Grace at the reins.

Lachlan brought news from home in the form of letters from the Wilberforce men for Jack that also carried a message for Martha.

Jack realised that his letter would have only just reached them, but it was nice to know he had not been forgotten.

When Ned heard about the birth of their son, he chuckled.

He didn't tell Jack much, but he mentioned that Charles and his wife, Sal, were expecting a happy event any day.

Jack hadn't heard about his friend's marriage and asked Ned about it. He had been with them when Charles first saw Sal.

Soon after the carriage was loaded, Lachlan had a quick word with Ned. "You may discuss Lockley with Jack, but keep silent about Jack and Martha to your friend in town. While you are chatting, you may hand him this."

Ned nodded in agreement and wished he knew why there was all this secrecy.

With permission to talk, the pair sat at the table in the front yard and caught up on all the news from town.

Jack tried to hide a letter he had been reading.

Ned filled Jack in on their mutual friend's assignment. He was still puzzled about Jack's presence, if not existence, and that it had to remain almost secret. Ned didn't ask why, but he knew by now that Jack was someone very special. He had realised that when studying in his cabin on the way out to the colony. His exquisite handwriting was not something that would have been taught in a charity Sunday school.

Jack asked Ned about how his prayer life was going, as he often did when he visited.

Ned often had to accompany the governor and make various visits in the area. He tried to catch up with Jack on each visit.

He had often carried Jack's mail to the governor, but this time, Ned brought a letter from England.

Ned recognised the handwriting on the unstamped letter Jack was trying to hide. He sucked in a deep breath. That letter was from the new king. He had delivered another letter to the governor shortly before being told they were leaving that day.

For Lachlan to read it and then wish to high-tail it to Jack was telling. Few would have associated the two things, but Ned was a duke's son and knew the handwriting of the new king well. He was aware that King George III had died early in the year, and the Prinny was now the king. But why would he write to Jack?

He lifted his stunned gaze and looked a the convict sitting with him.

Who was this man?

Would he ever find out?

Would Jack ever tell him?

Casting all thoughts of the private letter aside, Ned filled in the last months and how he had settled into his new abode in Parramatta.

Jack plied him with questions, none of which gave Ned any clue to Jack's identity.

~

Eight months later, April 1821

Martha asked Jack for a walk while little Marc was asleep.

She revealed that she suspected that she was carrying their second child and was due in December, shortly before Christmas.

Jack was delighted and swung her around excitedly.

Life was wonderful at the Duffys' store, but the happy couple knew it could not last.

They had to make way for others who needed help.

They knew it would not be long before they had to move on and make a life for themselves elsewhere… but to where and do what?

They turned to God in prayer. He knew best.

Having one small child in their tiny room was fine, but two would be problematic.

Jack had still not heard that all the spies from his so-called uncle's circle of traitors had been caught.

It was that news that the governor came to tell him on his last visit.

The king's missive said that there was one more felon to catch before he would be safe.

Sir Robert Chesterfield and Lord Montgomery had sung like birds and named every person involved with their treason; however, one man was yet to be arrested.

Jack knew he had to stay hidden until he received the all clear from Prinny. He had not even told Martha that he was still in danger, but he asked that she never speak of their time in England or ask to leave the store alone.

Jack was surprised that he had not heard from Bill or William Wilberforce for some time, or that Martha had not received her luggage from the Tuddenhams.

Surely their friends would have received their letters by now.

He sighed in frustration.

Neither was too concerned, as they had sufficient attire, a roof over their heads, and they were safe. They also had each other, so they were content.

They would stay put until the Lord opened a door elsewhere.

Chapter 21 A Fresh Start
January 1822

Word of the Macquaries' departure came as a shock to everyone at the store when it arrived shortly before Christmas. Lachlan had said nothing on his visit only weeks earlier.

Soon after the news arrived, so did Lachlan. He visited the store to introduce the replacement governor, Sir Thomas Brisbane, to the area's key figures.

He came to say farewell to the Duffy household, but particularly to Josh and Jack.

The night of their arrival, they gathered in the main house for a family meal. The new governor and Lachlan discussed the state of the farmers in the area. Some of the more controversial owners were agitating again. The colony did not need a third uprising.

The first had been the Castle Hill Irish Rebellion in 1804. This was a precursor to the Rum Rebellion, which occurred four years later. Both were due to the New South Wales Corps' unjust and greedy behaviour. The English soldiers treated the Irishmen and women like dirt. That attitude had caused the first uprising. Behind both upsets were the militia, who disliked authority and distrusted the governor.

Governor Phillip Gidley King chose five emancipated convicts as his personal bodyguards rather than those in the military, as he trusted none of them. He believed having such untrustworthy soldiers guarding him would be a danger to him and his family. One of those emancipated guards, Charles Whalan, was retained by Lachlan.

The second uprising was related but had been brewing since

the first militia arrived, before Governor Phillip departed. The same soldiers had run an illicit rum trade and taken in the money.

Even in Governor Hunter's days, John had problems with his secretary, who had been running the sales in Sydney. John Hunter's private scribe, Nathaniel Franklyn, shot himself soon after he was exposed as the frontman of the illegal trade.

Phillip Gidley King had similar issues. Governor Bligh walked into a ticking time bomb, which he set alight by siding with the farmers in Windsor over the ex-military settlers.

John Hunter had warned Lachlan to trust few. John had listed those whom he excluded from the blanket comment. He had only fifteen trusted men, and some had already resigned from the military. John named each one.

A firm hand was needed to quell the military settlers' greed. Lachlan's arrival had brought a semblance of peace, but trouble was not far below the surface. Lachlan, the dour Scotsman, had been like oil on troubled waters. He had listened to the wisdom of previous governors. It was why he had placed Mark in this isolated store while John Macarthur was in London. The government's presence in the area brought stability. Trusted officers patrolled the area regularly, and peace reigned.

When John Macarthur returned after nine years of exile in England because of his involvement in the coup, Mark had already befriended all of Macarthur's neighbours and also his wife, Elizabeth. Macarthur's wings were severely clipped. London forbade him from participating in politics at all, but he still had a cohort of military men willing to do his bidding.

This trip had already been exhaustive. Lachlan needed to introduce the new governor to the many settlers and familiarise him with the area. However, he needed to have several conversations before he left the store. As Sir Thomas retired to bed early, Lachlan and Mark enjoyed a long catch-up at the kitchen table. They were unlikely to meet again, and they had much to discuss.

Cathy buzzed around, and as they were occasionally interrupted, nothing private could be discussed. Not that they had much to talk about, but reminiscences.

Eventually, everyone retired to bed, and the house fell silent.

~

Martha and Jack's newest son, Alexander Willoughby Turner, woke his parents just after dawn. Martha fed him. Then Jack took him out of their room so he would not wake everyone else. He also wanted to make Martha a cup of tea. She had been up twice to him during the night and was exhausted. Knowing Martha, she would be hard on his heels anyway, so he planned to stoke the fire and put the kettle on. The day ahead would be busy, and Martha was already tired. Jack made his way to the kitchen and was surprised to find it occupied.

Two men were enjoying a mug of tea. Josh had beaten him to the kitchen and sat with Lachlan Macquarie. They beckoned for him to enter.

Jack cradled baby Alex while trying to stoke the fire for the morning's cooking.

Josh had added some wood to boil the kettle earlier, so it didn't take much for Jack to coax a flame once he stirred the coals, added more kindling, and then a couple of small logs.

Martha dressed and came to the kitchen to help prepare breakfast for the guests. The door was closed, which was unusual. She knocked and was also beckoned inside.

Josh and Lachlan had obviously been up for some time, as the teapot needed a refill, and they had both finished their mugs of strong brew.

When Josh offered to take the baby and leave the couple to talk to Lachlan, Jack realised something was afoot.

Lachlan had asked to see them before he left, and this opportunity was a Godsend. Lachlan looked at the adorable baby with a hint of jealousy. Before sailing from England, they had lost their daughter at only a few weeks old, and Elspeth had carried only one of her nine confinements to term, delivering a living child. Little Lachie was the apple of their eye and somewhat spoiled.

This little boy, Alex, had his father's honey-gold eyes and a crop of unruly, light-brown hair. His surprisingly toothy grin took in the governor, but he reached out for Josh. His big brother, Marcus, was equally adorable. Thankfully, he was still asleep.

Jack passed the baby over to Josh with relief. He knew a serious conversation with a babe in arms was nigh impossible.

Josh nodded and took the mischievous imp for a walk.

Now alone in the kitchen, Lachlan greeted the young convict couple but addressed Jack, patting the seat next to him. "Jack, sit for a while. I have news for you." Lachlan proceeded to fill them in on his plans. "When you arrived, I read of your bravery in reporting the rabble on board. However, as you know, I was already expecting you. I realised, when we met, that there was far more to you than what I had read. Our first interview revealed much more, as have the occasional letters from London. You have done what was asked of you here and more."

He turned and looked at Martha. "I'm glad you now have each other. William Wilberforce wrote to me about you as well, my dear. He was in church the day your father died. He knew of a great injustice being done to you and your family, but could do nothing over there."

He heard her gasp of surprise, but continued talking. "When I received his second letter about you, Jack, I decided to place you both here. I had no idea you had already met until Jack mentioned your name. Anyway, because of William Wilberforce's letter, I expected you both. That is all beside the point. I have a project to run by you. Jack, this would not have been possible earlier, as the regent, now King George IV, had to ensure that the remaining members of the spy gang in the palace were caught. The last of them was rounded up shortly before the old king died. The last of Lord Clive's peers has been dealt with, and the other two men are still under permanent house arrest. My boy, you are now safe."

Relief washed over Jack's face. His shoulders sagged as the news swept over him.

Martha's brow creased in puzzlement. Had Jack been in danger all this time? Was that why he did not permit her to leave the store? She took a seat beside him and reached for his hand. "Jack?"

He said, "Shh, love, I'll explain all later." However, he was grinning.

She nodded. She could see the final cloud had lifted from Jack's past.

Lachlan explained, "As I am leaving, I have been righting a few last-minute wrongs. Therefore, Mark and Josh now own this store. I told Mark last night and gave him the deeds; I also informed Josh this morning that he is to inherit it after Mark passes away. It's what his father James would have wanted for him. This was at Mark's request, but I had to think long and hard before deciding whether to grant it. I now have." He sighed. "Now, Perry and Katy White are returning to England with us, along with their household. Jack, your friend Charles Lockley will run Government Stores in Parramatta as well as manage a refurbished inn next door to the King's Wharf. He is to gain ownership when such a thing is permitted, and that is just a matter of time."

Martha stood, stoked the fire, and stirred the porridge, but listened.

Jack grinned. "Thank you, sir. I'm glad for him, sir."

Lachlan smiled. "So, that leaves the need for a reward of equal value for you." He heard Martha let out a slight noise of surprise, which was almost a squeak. He smiled and continued, "If you and Martha are willing, I would like you to move to Emu Ford and open an accommodation inn there. The king assured me that there is no longer any need for you to remain hidden, and I wish to see you established as soon as possible. I have been to Bathurst, and this land will open thousands of acres of new farmland there. However, staging houses and inns will be required. I would like to know if you are interested?

Jack's heart was racing. He nodded. This is just what Mr Wilberforce suggested he do. He would be following in his father's footsteps, though the Turners were unknown to him.

Lachlan pulled a bulky envelope from his coat and handed it to Jack. "This is the title document for some land in Emu Ford, and the foundations of the inn have already been started, well, in truth, it's nearly finished. It should be ready for you to move into soon. You will need to construct the stables and outbuildings, but you have plenty of time before the road traffic picks up. This contains £10 reward money from the government to tide you over until it's a paying concern. In case you are wondering, Charles Lockley received the same for reporting the mutiny."

Jack accepted the governor's thanks with a nod. "I'm overwhelmed, sir."

Lachlan was still not done. "I also have another letter for you. One that I have had in my possession until it could be delivered personally. When we first met, I mentioned that there was a promise of more to come. I believe this may well be a fulfilment of said promise by a person well known to you. I gather you will recognise the handwriting. I received a letter from the same person in the government despatch bag. He mentioned your safety in that missive." Lachlan handed two envelopes to Jack.

Jack was lost for words. He took the letters and gave the esteemed gentleman a nod of thanks. He recognised Mr Wilberforce's handwriting on the bottom franked letter and smiled. The top one only had his name on it in a scrawly script. He broke the seal and pulled out the paperwork for the land grant. He read the legal transfer of four acres of prime farmland into his name. His hands dropped to his lap. Should he accept this? This was the governor's reward.

By now, Martha was too intrigued to remain at the stove. She stood behind Jack's chair and read over his shoulder. With a good-hearted chuckle, Martha leaned over and took the document from his hand, leaving him with the unopened letter and the money. She was fearful he would hand it back. "On behalf of us both and our sons, I will accept willingly, sir. We will do as you ask and help whomever we can, just as I promised Mrs Fry and Hetty Walker. Mr Perry's cousin, Janey Brien, saved my life when she brought in Hetty and Mrs Macquarie to help me. If this is how we can repay both you and them, then we are thrilled to do so. Major Ned is now doing the same for other girls." She slid the legal parchment into her apron pocket.

Jack grinned at her but remained silent. He was thrilled she was not angry that he had not revealed the danger to his life. Although she didn't often get into a miff, she had a volatile temper when someone crossed her loved ones. He had discovered that when a thief came into the store and tried to light-finger some of Cathy's stock. She had the thief in an armlock before he realised he had been seen. Her upbringing on a ship certainly stood her in good stead for running an accommodation inn. He was in awe of his clever and very talented wife.

Lachlan chuckled at the marital interchange. He had the same excellent rapport with Elspeth. He slid another letter face down across the table to Jack.

Jack glimpsed the letter's writing and released a small gasp when he recognised Prinny's script. He had already been given a livelihood; what more could this contain? His mind was blank as to what this could hold. He picked up the envelope and cracked the royal seal from the back with a flick of his finger. This time, he unfolded the paper. He gingerly flattened the enclosed screed written on the familiar royal parchment. After three deep breaths, Jack dropped his gaze to the letter. He looked at it almost fearfully. His hands shook slightly as he read the king's words.

Lachlan watched the emotions wave across his face. The young man's face showed that the memories were flowing over him. He waited.

Jack's friends, if one dared call the new King that, had not forgotten him. Mr Wilberforce had instructed him to help people, and this letter and the other documents provided a way to do so.

Knowing that the governor recognised the writing on the second letter, he glanced at the governor with a cocked eyebrow. "Do you know what this contains, sir?"

Lachlan smiled in his lopsided manner and said, "I have a fair idea, laddie, it is why I wished to hand-deliver it."

Finally, after far too long, Jack dropped his gaze to the handwritten screed. Prinny wrote to him as a friend, not a convict. The salutation was to 'Little Lord John.' The king assured him that should Jack ever wish his children to be presented at court, they would be welcomed with open arms. Future monarchs would be advised of his part in keeping the country safe. The governors who would follow Macquarie were all to be informed that they were to assist him should he ever need such help. He glanced at Martha, then Lachlan and read on. Yes, Jack could and would run the inn as all danger had been dealt with. He was safe.

Jack slumped in his chair. He had not realised how this dark cloud hung over his head. The final felon was named. He had been hanged quietly after a short trial. He looked at his beloved Martha with glassy eyes. She was his world. But he now had friends, good friends, and some were in high places. Jack had already dropped names because of the conversation with Mr Wilberforce. One such man sat with him now.

Jack sighed. If the gentleman sitting across from him approved, their new inn would be called the *Arms of Australia Inn*.

Mark had already found another teacher, so Martha was at a loose end. They would leave as soon as could be arranged. He smiled at his wife lovingly.

She knew all was well.

Martha turned to prepare for the morning meal. She was making French toast for everyone this morning. The bacon and onions were already sliced and cooking. The smells emanating from the hob stove were delicious.

Lachlan looked at the young woman in awe. She could turn her very skilful hand to almost anything. Doctor Roylance from her ship had told him, but he had not realised just how skilled she was.

Jack knew that King George III had died two years earlier on January 29th, 1820. Prinny, as Jack thought of him, had hand-written this missive himself.

The second page of this lengthy letter contained astounding information. King George IV had sent some funds from the Earl of Templestowe-Meade's estate, which, as Jack knew, had reverted to the crown.

Jack checked the date on the first page. The letter was dated only months after the prince had ascended to the throne. This letter contained many paragraphs of profuse thanks for the ongoing care of his father and, later, his mother. Prinny had given him the nickname "Little Lord John." It was how he addressed this screed.

The king sent his personal thanks for Little Lord John's loving care of Queen Charlotte. Jack was stunned that even though Prinny knew his story, the king still called him "Lord John."

Because of Jack's loyal service to the crown, the screed carried the information that one hundred pounds would be awaiting them when his time was up or when it was needed. Governor Macquarie already had it in trust for Jack. Then, fifty pounds would be paid annually for the next ten years.

Jack released a long sigh. It was over, and now their life could begin in safety.

Lachlan looked worried. "Are you all right, son?"

Jack nodded and gasped. He had no right to that money or the estate. "Why?" Would the governor be able to enlighten him? Jack was astounded, but he would not refuse it. After a few moments, he chuckled and passed the letter to Lachlan. In this land, ten pounds would make a man wealthy. However, one hundred pounds was a fortune, and the funds would ensure their future until the inn was on its feet and well beyond.

Lachlan read the illuminated letter and grinned. "Good, that will help with your future. I knew you had been close to them, but not that close. He truly gave you a nickname?"

Jack nodded.

Lachlan smiled. "I was instructed to keep the sealed envelope in a safe place until you require it. Sir Thomas knows it's for you. It's why he wished to meet you. He has also been shown where your possessions are. I shall have them sent to your new house, along with Martha's luggage that I have in storage. Mr Wilberforce sent them in the new governor's ship. I didn't send them earlier as it would take too much explanation."

Jack grinned. He had never admitted to anyone, except Martha, just how close he was to the royal family. Though Martha knew it was now time to reveal all to Lachlan Macquarie.

In the quietness of the country kitchen, over another mug of tea, he did. "Sir, I can now tell you just how close to the family I became. I was His Majesty, King George the Third's only personal pageboy. I slept in his room and tended to the ageing king's every need. Through the early days of his illnesses, I stayed when others were not permitted to approach him. He was the grandfather figure I never had, and I loved him dearly. When he became too ill for even my care, Prinny, now King George IV, let me stay with Queen Charlotte. Lady Victoria Templestowe was her personal attendant. I called her my mother. I had been swapped for her daughter, Jennifer, at birth. We didn't know that until I was nine." He turned to his wife. "Martha, love, should we have a daughter, I wish to name her so."

He saw Martha nod.

Lachlan felt his jaw drop open. He clenched it closed again.

Jack continued. "I was educated with the royal grandchildren and on first-name terms with all of the family. As the queen neared her time of death, Mother and I were the only two she trusted. Lord Clive, my so-called uncle, was growing anxious as I neared my majority. Though he was known to others as my uncle, we were not related. When I came of age, he would no longer have access to funds from the estate. I was to be removed." He swallowed, then continued. "The royal family drew me even closer, knowing the danger I was in. Uncle Clive was a traitor to crown and country and as evil a man as the worst criminal here. He was the real Earl of Templestowe and also a spy for the French. This came about as the Frenchwoman he loved had been caught passing information and executed. Clive's hatred of the crown was deeply embedded. Clive was hanged on the day I turned twenty-one. I watched him dance on the gibbet as I promised and turned away in disgust. However, that was a few weeks after the Queen's passing."

Jack uttered a groan, then shook his head. Remembering how the death of the two beloved royals had hit him. "After many years watching the attendants comfort the king, I knew how to make Her Majesty comfortable and ease her pain. I was with her and four of her children when she died. Even Mother and the medical staff were outside."

Lachlan gasped.

Jack's eyes had filled with unshed tears. "I loved her dearly."

Martha came to his side and placed a caring hand on his

shoulder.

He nodded in acknowledgment of her loving action. He hitched a breath, wiped his eyes and continued. Jack smiled and rested his head on her arm.

He had never been able to speak of that horrible day; now he could. "Sir, as I said, the royal couple were like grandparents to me, and I loved them so much. I grieved for them as family. I carried the queen's crown in front of her coffin. Seen, but invisible as usual. The guest list was restricted to family, court officials, such as the Ladies of the Bedchamber, of which my mother should have been the leader, and the queen's other attendants. Only Lady Victoria was missing from the procession. A reduced guest list of fifty-four members of the general public attended the service at the royal family's invitation. The funeral was at eight in the evening, as the king would be asleep by then. However, the flagstones were covered with straw, so the carriage wheel sound would be muffled; therefore, he could not hear if he was awake. I believe that His Majesty died just over a year later, without knowing she had already passed on. Prinny told me that he had no plans to tell his father." Jack sniffed and blew his nose.

Lachlan's gaze never left his face.

Jack inhaled deeply and said, "On return to *Frogmore House*, I went to look for Mama. I found her on the floor of her bedroom. She had been ravished and was brutally beaten. Some of her final words were to name Uncle Clive as her attacker. She died in my arms minutes later."

He wiped away some of the tears cascading unchecked down his cheeks. Reliving that day had never been easy; voicing it now was even harder. "I was covered in her blood and stormed out of her room, determined to find my 'uncle' and extract due punishment." He sniffed. "I laid him out flat, ensuring he had a busted-up face and a mangled visage. I accused him of everything from murdering Martha's grandfather in India to swapping me at birth. He confessed it all in the presence of the guests. I wouldn't have stopped hitting him, but Prinny placed his hand on my shoulder. Uncle Clive was arrested for murder, but before he was, he said he wanted me charged with hitting a peer. Knowing that more traitors were yet to be uncovered, I was sent here for my own safety; otherwise, I would have been kept in the royal cell in the Tower of London, where I was incarcerated. Hence, the letters you received. I will add that I have no idea why Charles Lockley was chosen to accompany me, but I'm glad he was. I learned that he is trustworthy. Ned will vouch for that." He still wondered if there was a relationship between his friends, but both denied any knowledge of it.

Lachlan nodded. He had never heard a story like this.

After releasing a long sigh, Jack said, "Mr Wilberforce drew me away and helped clean me up. The clothes I wore when I was arrested were some of his son's old garments. Bill and I are friends. Because of my connections, I was not locked up with the rabble but in a private cell in the Tower of London, where my friends often came to see me. Prinny asked Mr Wilberforce to escort me to Uncle Clive's hanging."

Jack reached out for Martha's hand and kissed the back of it. He lifted his gaze to Lachlan and said, "Lord Clive, Sir Robert Chesterfield, Lord Montgomery Sharp and another co-conspirator arranged the murder of Martha's grandfather, my parents, sister, and others. Sir, the royal family protected me. I should have been hanged or incarcerated for twenty-five years for assaulting a peer, but the spies could not reach me in a penal colony. Prinny arranged for a term of only fourteen years for me. We knew others in Lord Clive's spy group were still at large, but they are now all captured." He tapped the letter.

Martha took a seat beside him and rested her head on his shoulder. "So it's over now. You are sure?"

Jack nodded, saying, "Yes, love. We are now safe." He paused and swallowed. "So, sir, yes, I grew up in the royal court and was on first-name terms with them all. But I'm a nothing, a peasant masquerading as an earl. The senior members of the royal family all knew and treated me as an equal. My birth parents, the Turners, were simple folk who ran a stable. Now, I shall do likewise. Prinny's thanks to me marks the end of that part of my life. I will tell him that, should we have daughters, I will accept his offer to present them at court. Our sons, too, should they wish. They have been offered a presentation at a royal levée when they are old enough. Eventually, I will tell them all, but I will be old and grey by then, unless the need arises. When the royal family discovered the reality of my birth, they packed around me rather than cast me out as a peasant imposter."

Jack's admission took Lachlan's breath away. Lachlan had no idea this lad was so close to the throne of England. He knew he had lived at the palace, but he had no idea just how close he was to the monarch. For Jack to personally see the king and queen to the point of sleeping and working in their bedrooms. He was in awe that he had even been present when Queen Charlotte died.

Lachlan's mouth opened, then closed again. Jack even called the current king by his nickname. He finally said, "Son, I'm stunned."

Jack had the courtesy to look embarrassed. "Sorry, sir, but I could not reveal everything to you earlier. They were still searching for the remaining spies. A loose word to anyone, and my life could have been forfeited. Hence, the secrecy of where I was. This was also why I refused to permit Martha to visit her friends on *Loganberry Farm*."

Lachlan had long ago revealed that the regent had written to him before his arrival. However, he had never told Jack that it also contained information that, in *lieu* of Jack's service, the lad would be given a lifetime bequest from the Templestowe-Meade Estate. Lachlan was pleased Jack's royal friend had come good on his promise.

Martha knew Jack's story and, after stirring the porridge, she came to his side again. "This is good news, Jack."

Jack nodded and gave her a loving smile. "Our family is safe, my love. Our life can now begin in earnest. We can leave here in safety."

Lachlan smiled and said, "I'm sure he will tell you anything else later, Martha."

She nodded and went back to the pot of boiling porridge.

Jack wiped his eyes and blew his nose, then gave the viceregal gentleman a shy smile. He said, "Now, sir, I'm soon to be a convict innkeeper. I was thinking of calling it *The Arms of Australia.*' What do you think? Inns and hostelries with 'arms' in their title indicate loyalty to the monarch. I think I qualify." Jack grinned mischievously.

Lachlan animatedly said, "I think it's perfect. I presume you were thinking of Martha's Alexander Coat of Arms and your background."

Jack shook his head. "No, sir. The Alexander motto is 'By land, by sea,' and while that is how we both arrived, it's not after that. No, this is in honour of the royal family, you, and the Turners. The Turner motto is 'To be, rather than seem to be.' I am no longer hiding, so I can now truly be myself. I will hide no more. However, you called this land Australia, and without you, we would not have a future here. By joining the Arms and Australia, I feel I am honouring both my past and our future. You did not need to follow my friends' requests. You even permitted me to pen letters to them from your desk when I arrived. Sir, we owe our future to you and the good Lord." He sighed, smiled, and added, "Mr Wilberforce first suggested that I turn my skills towards an inn of some sort. I willingly admit I never thought it possible."

Lachlan glanced at Martha. "I presume Martha knew all this before you met here?"

Both young people nodded.

Jack's face softened when he looked at his wife. "Yes, sir, well, much of it. I told her the pertinent bits the night we met in London, not about my birth and the baby swap, as that would have put her in danger. Back then, I was in no position to court her, but I still wished to. She pleaded with her father to permit us to be together. It was not God's time. I looked for her, but she had vanished. Then I read of her father's death and what the disgusting earl did to her. The paper spared nothing but her name; they wrote "Miss A" and "Captain W.A." Knowing her background, I filled that in. However, it said nothing of her arrest or prosecution, let alone transportation here."

He held his hand out to his beloved Martha as she came to his side again. "Even had the title and wealth been mine in truth, I would have given it all up just to have her beside me."

Martha slid her arm along his shoulder. She looked at Lachlan and explained. "It's true, sir. I begged my father to permit me to marry Lord John, as I knew him then, soon after we met. I knew there was more to his story, but I did not care."

Silence fell in the kitchen as the three thought back to the changes that had occurred over the past years.

Lachlan heard noises from the house. He realised that the conversation had become a lot more emotional than he had planned. He said, "Oh, I know what I need to tell you, Martha. Janey Brien asked me to let you know that she will return to England with Perry and his family. They are travelling with our entourage. I think you know, Janey is their cousin."

Martha nodded.

Lachlan said, "Therefore, I have assigned her to them for her life. I didn't say where that was to be served. Like your husband, she deserves her reward. She too assaulted a peer, but unfortunately, he died. He was trying to molest her. All she did was push him away. He fell and hit his head. Her life has not been easy, but with Perry and Katy, she will find happiness, so she is returning home to England with us. She will have a good life with them."

Martha gave a long sigh of happiness. "Thank you, sir. She deserves so much."

She had come to know Janey during those six months at Hetty's place. Once she was well enough, Hetty, Hector and Martha used to go to town for their shopping trips. It was Janey who had discovered her and called Hetty to help. Martha wished to thank her for her rescue.

Elizabeth Macquarie came with them to the gaol. It was Hetty who knew Janey. Through Hetty's friendship with Elizabeth Macquarie, Janey was placed in charge of weeding out needy girls. She had told them about the attack on Martha when Hetty had come to find a maid.

Lachlan gave Martha a nod of acknowledgement. "At last count, I believe there are nearly eighty girls who have been saved from further vile abuse thanks to her. She has placed them at many of the safe houses we have scattered around the colony. Ned Grace will carry on that work and keep an eye on you both. He holds instructions from London that overrule any given here. He will watch over you. As you suggested to Janey, Joel, and Hetty Walkers' farm has taken on many such brutalised women. When you left, a lassie named Fran was rescued. She was in a state much as you were and is now making baskets and has turned the finances of the farm around." He chuckled at the girl's ingenuity.

Martha was delighted. "I'm so glad. Hetty was so nice to me. She treated me as a friend. Did you know her mother, Sarah, was a convict?"

Lachlan grinned and nodded. He knew Sarah's story. John Hunter had mentioned her as trustworthy. Sadly, she died soon after he arrived.

Jack smiled to himself. He had worked out who Ned was soon after meeting him on the ship. Charles was still an enigma, but that was not his business. Was he another brother of Ned's, possibly born out of wedlock? Maybe one day he would find out. For now, his own past could be buried deep. A new life was ahead of them. Jack reclined in his chair and fully relaxed. Something he had not been able to do for many years.

Lachlan finished the last of his sweet tea. He said, "Jack, as I said, I have your new place under construction; however, the roof should be completed soon. I suggest you prepare to leave as soon as you can, as a new batch of girls will need your rooms here. Your new building will be habitable by the end of this month, but I suggested to Mark that you go and see what is being built. You will need to sleep rough, but I'm sure you will cope for a night or two."

Duffy's store was changing personnel again.

A crying child broke the morning silence.

Jack folded the letters and stuffed them into the pocket inside his jacket so the others would not see them.

Moments later, Josh returned with Alex, followed by their toddler, Marcus.

The private conversation was now over as the rest of the household was stirring.

Little Marcus ran in, climbed onto his father's lap, and wrapped his arms around his neck.

~

The two governors and their entourage took their leave an hour later.

As Lachlan exited the front door, he handed Martha a bulky envelope. "Wait until I've gone to open it. It arrived with your other things."

Lachlan passed another letter to Josh as he climbed into his carriage and repeated the instruction he'd given to Martha.

As the carriage rattled down the dusty road, Mark and Cathy came to stand beside Jack and Martha.

Mark slung his good arm around his wife's shoulder and said to Jack, "Lachlan suggested that you have a few days off and go to Emu Ford to view your new home."

Jack's face lit up. "Really, Mark? But what of the work here?"

Mark chuckled. "Well, while you are away, we shall move you into the guest room that Lachlan has been occupying. You see, new faces are arriving the day after tomorrow. So spend today packing, and you can sleep in the governor's room tonight. Create a list of the furnishings you will need during your stay, and we can place an order with the store's wagon upon your return. Lachlan mentioned you have access to funds, and he would take the cost from what he holds for you."

Jack nodded. "More than sufficient, thank you."

Mark chuckled. "Ahh, well, I bet he didn't tell you that two consignments arrived for you shortly before Christmas. They are in storage at the Government House in Parramatta. Martha, Lachlan said he had given you something from Mrs Tuddenham in London."

She smiled. Remembering the minister's wife, who helped her in London. Martha was astonished. The governor had hinted, but not confirmed, that her things had arrived. She had wondered about her luggage. She tore open the bulky envelope the governor had given her. It contained a sizeable green velvet bag that caught her attention. She could feel what it contained. She untied the ribbons and tipped the contents into her hand. The long rope of perfectly matched pea-sized pearls poured out of the bag to the gasp of all but Martha and Jack.

Mark and Cathy were in awe of the milky orbs, but Jack grinned.

Martha turned to her husband and chuckled. It was because of these gems that Jack had first spoken to her. She wore them tied in a double knot, as her mother had, rather than as most women did. Debutantes usually wore a small choker of seed pearls, not a king's ransom of pea-size sea gems.

Jack, as Lord John, had muttered, "Sacrilege!" when he saw how she wore them, and she had chuckled in reply. That was while they were dancing, and her pert reaction had sparked their unconventional conversation. They were together now because of that conversation.

She lifted her blue eyes and met Jack's amber gaze. He was watching with a big, cheesy grin on his lips.

She slipped on the pearls and naughtily tied another double knot into the long strand of priceless sea-gems, then grinned at her husband. The strand of pearls looked quite incongruous with her convict attire.

She and Jack turned to the house to tend to their sons. They paused halfway back and gave thanks to God for how things had turned out.

Josh was left in the courtyard, with his wife, Alice, at his side.

His mother and Mark watched as the dust ball of the departing carriage faded away, then went to join them.

Lachlan had handed Josh a letter and left, and told him to read it after he was gone. Well, he now had.

Martha and Jack heard a gasp as Josh opened the letter. They didn't wait to hear what it said. They would be told if they needed to know.

In the almost empty courtyard, Jack bent down and pecked her lips with a gentle kiss. "Martha, the night at the ball, you stood out like a beacon of purity in a surging sea of immorality. You and only you were all I could see that night. I never forgot you. I even mentioned you to Lachlan before I arrived here for my assignment. To find you waiting for me here was an answer to prayer."

Martha threw her head back at Jack's chuckle. "Me? Why? I had an adventurous childhood, and all I wanted to do was to settle down and have a family with you."

Her belly laugh set the tone of their future. She continued. "Jack, I meant what I said that night. I never cared for what you were or had. I only saw a kind man who cared for me. You never wished me to change, and you didn't even mind my freckles or my unusual, adventurous past."

Martha gave a skip of delight. She was content. No, she was more than content; she was happy.

As the pearls landed with a bang on her chest, the strand snapped. She caught one large, loose pearl from the broken, knotted opera-length rope of pearls and glanced at Jack with a stunned look.

The pair gazed at the milky orbs, then Martha laughed. "Jack, can we sell these and build our future with what we get from them rather than the blood money from your uncle's estate? We can do much good with that, but I don't want our future to be tainted by the past. We can use that to help others. I'm sure many more like us will arrive with nothing."

Jack removed the broken pearls from her neck and pocketed them. "My beloved, I do like the way you think. Here's to a new future and washing away our pasts. I hope never to mention again what I told the governor this morning."

Martha drew her beloved Jack into her arms and said, "Here's to the future, my beloved grown-up royal pageboy."

Cathy turned in time to see her young friends crushed in a passionate embrace. Their kiss made Cathy blush.

She and Mark drew closer to them. They would soon be walking on the path to a new future.

Eventually, Jack lifted his lips from Martha's and noticed Cathy watching them. They both lifted a hand to wave, then turned into the house, hand in hand.

They had packing to do.

The Duffys had started their lives in the squalor of London, and Martha and Jack had wanted for nothing in the wealth of the upper echelons of society. Here, the tables had turned.

Martha's past was on the oceans, Jack's in the palaces of

London. Now, they would work for the benefit of the less fortunate girls in a penal colony.

God had a new plan for them, which would begin next month. The future awaited.

Jack's bountiful blessing enabled them to have more children and help more people. They would make their inn the best they could and help whoever needed them.

Martha hoped she would quickly conceive the longed-for daughter they would name Jennifer.

Jack ushered his belovéd indoors, and they walked through the cool corridor towards their new room. As they stripped Lachlan's bed, it was like stripping away the last vestiges of their pasts.

They had to pack to start their new life.

Leaving Duffy's would not be the end but a new beginning for them both.

The *Arms of Australia Inn* in Emu Plains, NSW.
Run as a Cobb & Co. staging inn by Thomas and Betsy Ellison
and later, their daughter, James and Sara Hunter.
Today, it is a museum in Emu Plains.

For more of Jack and Martha's story through the years, read
"Amelia's Tears "and
"The Lockleys of Parramatta" *Series.*

Charles' identity is revealed in **"Hands Upon the Anvil."** *As well as who
Turner's daughter, Jennifer "Jenna," marries.*

Mark and Cathy Duffy's story is in **"Tuppence to Pass."**

Hetty Walker's story is in **"The Vine Weaver"**

Historical Note

Author's note about dates.

I have kept the history of the royal family and palaces as accurate as possible, based on historical records. Many of the princesses and the crown prince (Prinny) had somewhat dubious morals. It is against this background that I have set this story of a young man's coming of age amid the immorality of palace intrigues.

Buckingham Palace was known as *Buckingham House* at the time. Prinny enlarged it and renamed it a palace. All the other residences are historically accurate.

Most of the voyage information is true, except for that of the *Shipley*. Although she did carry a convoy of stores and convicts as stated, she sailed much later in the year. When I started researching my first book in 2020, the exact arrival dates were not a priority. However, as the **Lockleys of Parramatta** series grew, my error became apparent. The dates didn't tally. The *Shipley* actually arrived on September 26, 1820, not late December 1819, as is in this story and others.

The claim that *Hadlow* collected five women in Cape Town is true; the women may have been female stowaways, not convicts (though this is debated). I have not been able to find any other names besides the expectant mother's. Her name was Sarah Holloway. I have incorporated the abuse of the girls to align with Martha's story in other books. (The Vine Weaver, and Amelia's Tears)

Having said that, according to research via the Parramatta Female Factory. Supposedly 80% of convict women who were transported to New South Wales were abused. While it was rarely recorded, it occurred often. Many of our female ancestors were violated in such a way, but they became survivors, not victims.
(Statistics from Parramatta Female Factory)

I write these stories to honour the brave women who rose above their abuse. Not all were convicts. Many of the free women were abused by their husbands. At the time, domestic violence was neither against the law nor uncommon. It was, in essence, unacknowledged. Charles and Sal Lockley were modelled on my ancestors, John and Sarah Ellison, who ran the *Jolly Sailor Inn* at the wharf in Parramatta. They had the first known 'safe room' for abused women. This came to light when John was prosecuted for serving spirits after hours (on a Sunday) and running a brothel. Both Reverends Marsden and Cowper confessed in court that both clergymen knew the Ellisons had a safe room for abused women. To say I'm proud of them is an understatement.

Twenty per cent of Australians can still claim convict heritage. I claim four convicts, and my husband has three. In Australia, we term having convicts in our family tree as being *"Australian Royalty."*

The *Arms of Australia Inn* still stands in Emu Plains, but it now serves as a museum. My Great-Great-Grandparents, Thomas and Betsy Ellison, lived there and ran it for many years. My grandfather, Norman A. Hunter, was born there in 1879. It remained in the family until 1968, when it was sold in an almost derelict state. It was completely refurbished to become the museum it is today.

The Arms of Australia Inn in 1968.

Characters

Martha's Story

Willoughby Alexander d 1818

m **Heather** McFarlane d 1817 (father Malcolm - murdered d 1796 in India)

    Child 3

    2 babies died at birth, one boy, one girl. Cords around their necks

    3 Martha b 1802, a convict on the *Hadlow,* Dec 26th 1818 *(sentenced 7 yrs)*

    4+ more children lost as miscarriages.

Lord Edgar, Earl of Oxenborough-Thorpe, tries to marry Martha.

Sir Robert Chesterfield (Lord Edgar and Clarence's 'friend')

Lord Montgomery Sharp, Viscount of Rathsharp

The Beattie and Johnson families on a merchant ship.

Jack's Story (sentenced 14 years)

Lord Clarence Templestowe, Earl of Templestowe-Meade, Meade House

b 1770 d 1797

M Lady Victoria Nichols

b 1777 d 1818

    Children (2 daughters, both dead)

    1 Elizabeth Catherine b 1796

    2 Jennifer Victoria - died 1797 - drowned at Lord Clive's instructions

    1 **John (Jack)** Clarence **Turner**/Templestowe-Meade b Dec 1797 d 1886

    Changeling son (14-year sentence). Arrived on Shipley Dec 24th 1819

  M 1820 **Martha** Turner (née Alexander), *Arms of Australia,* Emu Plains,

  b 1802 d 1886   (Arrived on the *Hadlow* 1819)

      Children 7

      1 Marcus (called **Marc**) John George Turner, b Oct 31, 1820

      2 Alexander (**Alex**) Willoughby b Dec 1821

      3 Jennifer Martha (**Jenna**) b1823 *(marries Charles Lockley's son, Eddie)*

      4 Victoria (Vicky) Heather b 7/1825

      5 Catherine (Cathy) Charlotte b June 24 1827 *(m Charles's 3rd son, Wills)*

      6 Nicholas (Nicky) John b late April 1830

      7 Malcolm (Calum) William b 1832 bapt Jan 1833

Lord Clive Templestowe, Earl of Templestowe-Meade, b 1772, was arrested & hanged in late 1818 on Jack's 21st birthday.

On the Journey to Australia

Charles Lockley - Jack's friend (7 years)(Charles' family is the core of the *Lockleys of Parramatta* series)

M Sarah (**Sal**) McCarthy Feb 1820 Children 6

Major Ned Grace, blond soldier on the *Shipley (3). (NB Ned appears in most of my other books - See "Unshackled Lives" - free with newsletter signup.)*

Ensign Phillip Geake - London to Cork on *Shipley (3)*

In Australia
Mark and Cathy Duffy
Cathy's son and daughter, Josh and Jenny and their families.
Joel and Hetty Walker - *Loganberry Farm* (see *The Vine Weaver*)
Hector Macdougal - convict worker, (see *The Vine Weaver & Scotch at The Rocks*)
Phil & Fanny Bentley - see *Far From the Whispering Sheoaks (2027)*
Janey Brien
Perry and Katy White see *A Lady in Irons*
Linus Rosedale. See *When Upon Life's Billows*
Crispin Milroy and wife Helena.
Howard Marlow See *Bound Down in Iron Chains (2027)*

Real People
In London
King George III b 1738- d 1820
Queen Charlotte b 1744 - d Nov 1818
The Prince Regent (Prinny)- later King George IV
Princess Amelia (died young) - Other royal siblings
Sir Charles and Lady Oakeley - in India
William Wilberforce and his son William Jr

On ships or on Foreign shores
Sarah Hallowell - a convict girl in Cape Town - four others were with her - unnamed. She was heavily pregnant on boarding and delivered a stillborn child and succumbed shortly afterwards.
Charles Blomfield, chaplain to Bishop of London.
Doctor Thomas Roylance & wife Eleanor on *Hadlow*.
Captain Craigie of the *Hadlow*.
Captain Lewis W Moncrief on *Shipley (3rd trip)*
Surgeon Henry Ryan *Shipley (3)*
Lieutenant Windsor of the 69th commands the Guard, consisting of a party of the 48th Regiment and some soldiers of the 53rd Regiment.
Mrs Cartwright, wife of the Reverend Mr Cartwright, free passenger.
48th, 53rd, 69th Reg aments - soldiers

In Australia
Governor Lachlan and Elizabeth Macquarie
Governor, later Vice Admiral John Hunter
Governor Thomas Brisbane

NB Details about the **Shipley**
The *Shipley* left the Downs on 5 June 1820 (not 1819).
She arrived at Port Jackson on 26 September. (not 24 Dec 1819) and carried 150 male convicts, four of whom died en route - all true.

Bibliography

History of sugar
https://en.wikipedia.org/wiki/History_of_sugar
East India Company
https://en.wikipedia.org/wiki/East_India_Company
Sir Charles Oakeley
https://en.wikipedia.org/wiki/Sir_Charles_Oakeley,_1st_Baronet
Qing dynasty
https://en.wikipedia.org/wiki/Qing_dynasty
Newgate Prison
https://en.wikipedia.org/wiki/Newgate_Prison

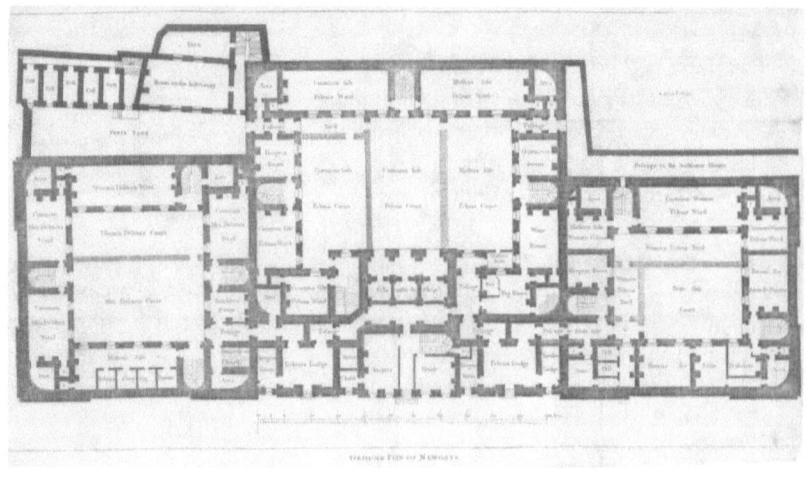

Newgate 1808

Convict ships
Charles Bateson's **"The Convict Ships"** - book ISBN 0908120516
https://catalogue.nla.gov.au/catalog/947602
https://vandemonian.info/convict-ships-alternative
https://convictrecords.com.au/ships?page=5
http://www.blaxland.com/ozships/index.htm
Shipley
https://www.freesettlerorfelon.com/henry_ryan_surgeon.html
NB the *Shipley*, 3rd voyage arrived 26th Sept 1820 *(Jack, Charles and Major Ned) (NOT 23rd Dec 1819, as mentioned in The Lockleys of Parramatta)*
Hadlow
https://freesettlerorfelon.com/convict_ship_hadlow_1818.htm

If you loved this book, you may also enjoy these similar titles.
(*All are stand-alone stories*)

First Fleet Convict Era Trilogy 1788-1800

Gentle Annie Soames

Her dreams lead to unexpected outcomes. An Australian First Fleet story.
A First Fleet story with the descriptions taken directly from the Journal of
Doctor Arthur Bowes Smith was the doctor on board the Lady Penrhyn.

Annie Soames is a girl beloved by the community but not afraid to voice her desires. That leads to trouble, illicit love, and a world turned upside down.

Oliver Quilpie, the newly married Marquess, finds his arranged marriage unsatisfactory; he is irresistibly drawn to his wife's companion. Unfortunately, he can't keep his hands off her. In retaliation, Annie copies his every move while riding, dressed as a highwayman. However, she has now fallen in love with him. This ultimately leads to her arrest and banishment to a distant land.

After some years, Oliver's wife dies, and his thoughts turn to Annie. He seeks to find her, but she has vanished. He is horrified to discover she was transported to New South Wales as a convict on the *Lady Penrhyn*. Will Annie want to see him?

ISBN 9780645441574   ISBN ebook 9781923097063   LP ISBN 978-1923097346
https://mybook.to/GentleAnnieSoames

Long-listed in the Historical Fiction Company Competition 2024

The Emancipated Potter

Sydney Cove 1788 to Parramatta 1795
Not all felons are convicts, and not all convicts are felons.

Colin Osborne's serene life as a talented potter is crushed by a self-important peer. A single punch sends Colin across to the other side of the globe.

Aggie Gibbs is a young convict girl being hunted by a wayward soldier. The two find themselves in a town of criminals and lecherous men.

Captain John Hunter is Colin's mentor, and he paves the way for a new life for his young friends. Then disaster strikes, and he must leave.

Can Colin keep Aggie safe? Will they fulfil Captain Hunter's wishes to build a decent life for the convicts destined to live out their lives in the penal town? Will John ever return to New South Wales? Paperback ISBN 9781923097476   ISBN ebook 9781923097483

Paternity Unknown

Sydney 1788 - 1800 The Aftermath of the First Fleet landing.
Can forgiveness be that easy?

Connie Waterson is traumatised after she became one of the victims of the attack when the convict women were landed on February 6th, 1788. She finds herself expecting an unwanted child. Along with her friends, she must learn to cope with the challenges of their new environment while protecting the life growing within her.

Nigel Bray is a young convict who almost instantly regrets his carnal actions on the day the prisoners from the *Lady Penrhyn* landed. Knowing that Connie is the unwilling recipient of his base desires, Nigel does what he can to ease her path. He is racked with questions: is the child his? Will she ever forgive him? What must Nigel do to win Connie's trust?

ISBN 9781923097438   ISBN ebook 9781923097445   LP ISBN 978-1923097452

The Hunter to Macquarie Collection 1795-1822

When Upon Life's Billows

Sydney 1795-1821 - Governor John Hunter
Keep your friends close, and your enemies closer.

John Hunter loved his life at sea. The wind blows where no man knows, and John is caught in a storm. His ship, the *HMS Sirius,* was wrecked in 1790. Five years later, he became the second governor of the rough and filthy penal settlement of New South Wales. From a place he once loved, he now seems to be in the wrong place at the wrong time, trusting the wrong people.

Helena Rosedale is not your typical female convict. She fiercely battles to prevent the men from abusing her, earning her the nickname "*Helena the Hellcat.*"

Crispin Milroy, alone in the world, serves on the new governor's security detail. Can he win the fair lady's heart? Life in 1795 in Sydney Cove was harsh at best. Food is scarce, and disease often ravages the settlement. Life throws everything at these times, yet somehow, they manage to survive. Why does John trust this young couple when others betray him? What trials must Helena and Crispin endure to make their new lives in this unforgiving town bearable? How can John ease their path?

ISBN: 9780645783339   ebook ISBN: 9780645783346

The Saddler's Song
London 1790s to Parramatta 1840s
The Strains of Starting Again.

George Ellis is the son of a tanner, living on the outskirts of London. Alone and hurting after a disease takes his family, he seeks a new life, setting up a business in New South Wales. His beloved violin is his most treasured possession, and his talent for making music is hidden from all but a select few. **Ben Parker,** a saddler, is also heading to the colony. Combining their skills to start afresh in a new world, the young men find accommodation with a family. Two of the daughters steal their hearts — but how will the business survive in a stock-starved land where access to leather is limited? What is the saddler's song, and why is it so special?   ISBN: 9780645783353   eISBN: 9780645783360

Tuppence to Pass
London 1800s to Parramatta 1820s
An Unlikely Partnership

Josh Callan never expected much from life—just enough to get by in the gritty backstreets of London. But when he's caught stealing from the very man who murdered his father, Josh finds himself branded worthless by a sneering judge and sentenced to a distant, brutal world: the penal colony of Sydney.

Arriving just as **Governor Lachlan Macquarie** takes charge, Josh steps into a colony on the cusp of change—and into opportunities he never dreamed possible. As he earns the respect of the powerful governor and becomes a trusted confidante, Josh begins to forge a new path not just for himself, but also for his family and his beloved. Can a boy dismissed as nothing rise to become something more? And what will his unexpected friendship with the governor cost or gain him in the end?   ISBN : 9781923097070   eISBN: 9781923097087

His Majesty's Pageboy
London to Emu Plains, Australia, in the 1800s

Jack Turner, raised in privilege and known as Lord John. However, at age nine, his true identity is revealed. He struggles with society's immorality and shallowness. He finally meets a pure young woman he feels he could love, but because of his chequered background, he is unable to pursue her. Then, his life takes another turn.

Martha Alexander, daughter of a wealthy shipping merchant, met Lord John while at a society ball in London. She is expected to marry well, and she has feelings for John. But her father's drunkenness led to the loss of everything he owned, including Martha, dooming her to a forced marriage. How do these two young people end up as convicts in Australia?
       Paperback ISBN 9781923097308   eISBN 978192309792
Coming 2026

A Fist Full of Holey Dollars
Sydney Cove 1810+

Captain **Rudi Greenwood** is a solitary man trapped in a job without a purpose in a land where alcohol is the currency and rules are frequently ignored in the pursuit of wealth.
Bethany Edwards is a grieving widow expecting her late husband's child. Rudi's attraction to the lovely widow compels him to reassess his views and contemplate someone new. She seeks Rudi's help and support, but is that all she truly feels?
When **Governor Lachlan Macquarie** asks Rudi for help improving the roads, a casual remark alters Rudi's life and affects the entire colony. To tackle the alcohol issue, he proposes creating a new currency. With Bethany by his side, will he rise to the governor's challenges? What actions led to him being despised by the exclusives and free settlers in the colony?
       Paperback ISBN 9781923097407   eISBN 9781923097414
Coming 2026

Far From the Whispering Sheoaks
Set in Australia in 1817+

Fanny Little was in the wrong place doing something she thought was legal. Her actions led to her arrest, trial, and banishment. She was assigned from the female prison to ex-soldier Gordon McKenzie and soon found herself in the despicable and humiliating situation of being sold in the public marketplace.
Phil Bentley is a man running from his jealous uncle. He is seeking safety on a secluded farm half a world away. With the community backing them, can Phil save Fanny from Gordon's vile abuse? Why is their relationship destined to spark controversy? And who is Jas? Why does Gordon wish to harm the child? Will they ever escape the shadows pursuing them?   Paperback ISBN 9781923097315   eISBN9781923097322
Coming 2026

Bound Down in Iron Chains

An Australian Historical Tale, set in the Boys' Orphanage in Sydney in 1818+

Smuggling, Rum and Ructions

A gripping tale of betrayal, courage, and survival in colonial Australia.

When honest London bookkeeper **Howard Marlow** is wrongly convicted and sent to New South Wales, he's assigned to the **Sydney Boys' Orphanage**, where corruption runs deep and the accounts don't add up.

There he meets **Naomi Buckingham**, a convict girl hoping for safety—but facing danger instead. As the two uncover coded ledgers and a smuggling ring tied to the colony's elite, they must risk everything to expose the truth.

In a brutal world built on power and fear, can two convicts bring justice to those who have none?

Paperback ISBN 9781923097353   eISBN9781923097360

Coming 2026

Buddy's Promise

From the Shadows of London to the shade of the gumtrees

Raised on the streets of London, **Obadiah "Buddy" Jensen** hides a fierce loyalty behind a tough facade. When a dying boy begs him to protect his little sister, **Emily Bolt**, Buddy vows to keep her safe—never expecting she'll become the love he can't have.

Exiled to Australia as a convict, Buddy builds a new life, but when Emily reappears years later, everything has changed. He is married with a child.

She was six when he found her. She was lost when he left. Torn between past promises and present choices, can they find their way back to each other—or will fate keep them apart forever?

An emotional historical romance of love, loss, and redemption across the seas.

ISBN 9780645783384   eISBN 9780645783391

Coming 2027

Unlikely Convict Ladies Trilogy 1792-1840s

Dancing to Her Own Tune

Co-authored by Sheila Hunter and Sara Powter

Sydney 1790s to England 1830s

Annie White is released after serving seven years as a convict in Sydney. She has a visitor who helps her start a baking business. Annie is then asked to assist another ailing man, **Sam Corbett**. She nurses him back to health, and a relationship blossoms between them. They settle into a life together, barely making ends meet, when she realises she's expecting a child. Sam's past is laid bare, and he must come to terms with the revelations. They both must confront their accusers and discover that the answers to their questions are not what they anticipated. Their life experiences seem to cling to them, and, unable to shake them off, they end up back in England. They must face their ghosts and recognise they are not who they think they are. How can they transform their anger and spite into love and forgiveness? The Dance of Life goes on.

ISBN 9780645110715   ISBN9780645110722

Long-listed for the Historical Fiction Company Competition 2022

Amelia's Tears

Parramatta 1828 – England 1840s

From Tears of Sadness to Tears of Joy.

Amelia Westaweller awaits her assignment in the Parramatta Female Prison. Forced to leave the relative safety of gaol, she is assigned and now faces her worst nightmare. A foul man claims her and makes her life a living hell. Then, her world goes black. A glimmer of hope arises when she hears from her brother, Jim, who has enlisted a friend to help her. She writes to Jim, pouring out her heart and telling him of the horrors of her new life. He encourages her to stay firm in her faith. All she can do is pray. When Major **Ned** Grace, her brother's friend, enters her life in Parramatta, he starts to ease her path. Things have changed, as now she has a child in tow. How can Amelia forge a new life for herself? What man could want her with her background and a child at her side? Who is the gentleman who turns her tears of sadness into tears of great joy?

ISBN: 9780645110739   eISBN: 9780645110746 Hard Cover ISBN 9798420617953

A Lady in Irons
England 1800s - Parramatta 1808+

Katy Harrington is mourning the death of her husband after he died in a shooting accident. Barely coping, she awaits the birth of their child. If it's a girl, she must hand the family home to her husband's brother. The day after giving birth to a daughter, she and her daughter are left on the side of a road. She collapses and is found by someone she thought had died in a fire ten years before. **Perry White**, badly scarred himself, nurses her back to health. They marry and move in with her widowed friend, Mary.

After some years, she discovers her husband and friend in each other's arms. Now living in a love triangle, she flees. Grasping the only straw available, she intentionally gets arrested and is sent to a colony far away. By doing this, her marriage can be annulled.

What happens in the Colony is different from what she expects. Governor Macquarie comes to her rescue, but what of Perry and her children?

ISBN: 9780645110784   eISBN:9780645441505

The Convict Birthstain Collection 1820-1840s

NO MORE, MY Love
Hunter Valley, NSW, 1820s

Jess Elkin is distraught when tragedy ravages her family. Now widowed, she becomes the victim of a carriage accident and is nursed back to health by the driver.

Marcus Ryan, a hard-headed woollen mill owner, was not expecting to fall in love. Yet, when Jess's fortunes suddenly turn for the worse, Marcus must decide how far he will go to pursue her. Years after following her to Newcastle, Australia, Marcus vanishes. Jess is left wondering if he will keep his promise to return to her… Will she ever see him again?

ISBN: 9780645441536   eISBN 9780645441581

Long-listed in the Historical Fiction Company Competition 2023

The Vine Weaver
Hawkesbury River area 1820s+
New Beginnings and Old Threats

In the 1820s, **Joel and Hetty Walker** lived on a secluded farm on the Hawkesbury River, which became a haven for the protection of young convict women. A series of events brings **Fran Rea** to Hetty's attention, and she is taken to the farm. Fran and Hetty develop a cottage industry under the compassionate eye of farmhand **Hector Macdougal;** Hector's loving words change lives. It is to him that Fran turns when threatened.

The vines now must draw them close to survive the future revelations, and of those, there are many.

ISBN: 9780645441512   eISBN: 9780645441529

Long-listed in the Historical Fiction Company Competition 2023

https://amazon.com/dp/0645441511   https://amazon.com/dp/B0C6Z552Y2

The story continues in "Scotch at The Rocks"…

Scotch at The Rocks
Glasgow, Scotland, early 1800s to The Rocks, Sydney 1830s

Orphaned children Brodie Stewart and Heather Anderson live on Glasgow's streets. Although hungry, they somehow manage to survive and stay out of trouble. Heather finds a job and looks to be settled; things go pear-shaped for them both. Eventually, they marry by declaration, but even that gets complicated, and they are both arrested soon after exchanging their vows. In 1838, they were transported to Sydney as convicts. Heather arrives within weeks of Brodie, and they are assigned close to each other. They are now living in the docklands of Sydney, known as The Rocks. They now have to forge a new life halfway across the world from their homeland.

Adventures abound, and Brodie gets press-ganged. While he's away, Heather's life changes and soon, she's officially selling Scotch Whisky at a shop in The Rocks.

You can take a Scot out of Scotland, but where did the Scotch come from?

ISBN 9780645441550 ebook 9781923097001 Large Print 9781923097254

Waiting at the Sliprails
The Bathurst Road 1830s
A Convict's Tale

Bea Dawes's term of conviction nears an end, and she has few options other than marriage to a stranger or going on the street.

Jack Barnes, the hired drover, wants a wife. Bea accepts his offer; then, she discovers that he could be gone for months, leaving her alone with **Billy and Netty,** part of the tribe of an Aboriginal tribe who live on his secluded farm. Bea learns to love her husband and also this wonderful Aboriginal couple. Drought ravages the farm, and Jack must hit the long paddock with the flock. In his absence, a visitor arrives, threatening to destroy everything she has worked so hard for. Can Bea touch her heart? Can she cope? Will the drought ever end? And when will Jack return?

ISBN: 9780645441543   eISBN: 9781923097032

PenCraft Award Winner for Literary Excellence, Christian Historical Fiction 2024

Convict Shadows of the Past
Two Jennifers, two hundred years apart

When she discovers her convict family history, eight-year-old Jenny Kellow learns that she was named after a convict from nearly two hundred years ago. Inspired by her grandfather's stories, she delves into her ancestors' convict past. From him, she hears tales of bushrangers, convicts, and life in the early colony of Parramatta. She embarks on a journey to retrace the footsteps of her convict great-great-great-grandmother to honour her. Jenny's quest begins with microfiche in the 1960s, where she discovers a small tin mining town in Cornwall and the production of a cheese that set London alight. She uncovers that her ancestor, **Jennifer Kellow,** brought her cheese-making skills to Parramatta, where she taught others the craft. Echoes of the past can still be heard if you know where to listen. Who was the first Jennifer, and what does she have to do with cheese? Why is she so elusive? Did Jenny's ancestor, Jennifer, ever see those two small crosses carved into the bricks of the Female Factory? Would Jenny ever uncover her ancestor's story?

ISBN: 9780645783315   ISBN ebook 9780645783322

A NaNoWriMo 2022 book winner

In Defence of Her Honour
London 1800s to Parramatta 1819
Will the real man of quality please stand up?

Bill Miller was raised and educated with the sons of the family. The youngest, Bert Edison-Browne, had been his best friend. However, jealousy intervenes when Bill's excellent schoolwork begins to curtail their friendship. He wins a scholarship and enters Oxford University. When Bill's father dies unexpectedly, Bert insists that Bill take over as butler, but it's more to oppress him. Bert's jealousy grows and festers. He is now looking for a way to rid themselves of their new butler. A ruckus ensues, and Bill is arrested for assaulting Bert.

Molly Ross, the housekeeper's daughter, will vouch for him. It's too late; Bill has been arrested and is soon to be sentenced and transported. With Bill gone, Molly now fights to defend herself from Bert. After hitting him with a pan, she, too, is arrested and sent to Sydney. Bill and Molly arrive with letters of introduction and compensation from Bert's father. Soon, they will be running the best inn in Parramatta with an endorsement from the governor.

ISBN 9780645441567   ISBN ebook 9781923097049

Long-listed in the Historical Fiction Company Competition 2024

I Can't Stop Tomorrow
Irish Famine 1840s to Avoca Beach, Australia

Escaping bigotry and prejudice in Ireland, the O'Shane family lives on a secluded farm on the west coast of Ireland. The potato blight soon decimated their farm. It's always darkest before dawn, and the two remaining girls cling to the hope of a new life. With the kindness of strangers, the eldest girls, **Clare** and **Kerry O'Shane,** head to their cousin, Sal Lockley, in Parramatta, Australia.   A new, wonderful life awaits them both. **Shéamus Connor** is the annoying teenage boy who reluctantly draws Clare's affection. However, living in a convict town means ruffians abound.

John Moore is a bad-tempered and troubled Irishman who is content to live alone on another secluded farm until he discovers Clare and two other lads need rescuing.

Can John protect her from the pain inflicted by an evil world?

Can Shéamus find his lost love, who has fled?

ISBN: 9780645441598   ISBN ebook 9781923097056

Madeline's Boy

England 1830s to New South Wales 1840

The race to protect an Orphaned Boy

All is not straightforward when money and titles are involved.

Orphaned, afraid and on the run, Chip must flee.

Madeline was his mother's best friend. Maddie now needs to keep her charge safe and alive. She must give up her life to protect the boy she has loved since birth.

Months after Chip's parents' demise, Maddie sets out to deliver Chip to his Uncle Humphrey, who lives in Sydney. Through him, she meets Chip's uncle's friend, Tim, who falls for Maddie —but will they find happiness?

The menacing presence soon finds Chip, and Maddie needs to hide him again. They are relocated from hidden farms to secret valleys, ultimately ending up in an Aboriginal encampment.

Can Tim find a way to be with Maddie? And if so… Will Chip ever be safe?

ISBN: 9780645783308   ISBN ebook 9781923097094

Long-listed in the Historical Fiction Company Competition 2024

Jam or Marmalade for Tea

England 1820s to New South Wales 1825 *(Governor Brisbane Era)*

Martha Hamilton is the eldest of four orphans struggling to survive on their own. She is caught stealing, tried, convicted, and transported to New South Wales. With her family gone, she becomes despondent. Life holds no meaning for her, and the ocean waves look inviting.

Captain Guy Manning is a frustrated and injured redcoat soldier returning to Sydney for a new assignment. He notices Martha trying to jump overboard and rescues her. How do two cats bring them together?

A convict ship is no place for romance, and she's far too young anyway, isn't she?

Can Guy save her and forge a life together for them? What connections does he have to try to save her siblings? Why is marmalade important for their future?

Paperback ISBN 9781923097933   eISBN9781923097285

A NaNoWriMo 2023 book winner

https://mybook.to/JamorMarmaladeforTea

A prequel to 'The Lockleys Parramatta' series

(Free novella with newsletter signup)

Unshackled Lives

Set in England *& Australia in the 1800s*

Australian historical fiction of early colonial days

Ned Lockley is the second of four sons of the Duke and Duchess of Gracemere. As his mother's favourite, his childhood years were blissful, but he needed to grow up, and quickly.

A whirlwind romance is followed by a loved one's betrayal. The following emotional turmoil is particularly challenging for Ned to cope with, especially amid a collapsing and immoral society.

Ned can't stay as his family is falling apart. His mother's words to remain true to himself and his faith make him leave everything he knows. How did Ned end up in New South Wales in charge of placing female convicts? Will he ever find happiness or discover who Charles is?

ISBN 9781923097377   eISBN 9781923097384   LP ISBN: 9781923097391

A 100-year, six-part Australian Colonial series

The Lockleys of Parramatta 1800-1900

Hands upon the Anvil

A blacksmith's life and love are more than work

Parramatta 1830s

Eddie Lockley's parents were transported for their crimes. Can a steadfast lad rise above his origins and guide others to succeed in a land of opportunity?

Ten-year-old Eddie longs to help his mum and dad. Living in a convict town with his family, the keen youngster has been working with the local blacksmith since his sixth birthday. But when a lieutenant doesn't stop abusing his older brother, the young boy yearns for the day when he can stand up and end the torment. Though he's thrilled when his mentor offers to send him off to learn his letters, Eddie fears he won't be around to watch his siblings' backs. But as he takes on the biggest adventure of his life, the brave believer soon discovers that God is looking out for everyone he loves. Does this young man in the making have what it takes to change everything for the better?

ISBN 9780994578235 Ebook ISBN 978-0-9945782-5-9 Hardcover 9798496177368

Out Where The Brolgas Dance

Gold is found, and so is love

Parramatta 1840s

How can a question change so many people?

It's the 1840s, and discoveries across the Blue Mountains continue. Major Mitchell's new road is complete, and towns are planned and being built. Abundant land is available for those who want it. Eighteen-year-old **William "Wills" Lockley** has laid a solid foundation for a respectable career as a blacksmith, but the Lockley lust for adventure flows deeply within his veins. He dreads the monotony of work at the blacksmith's forge and yearns for adventure in a new frontier. Wills meets six Englishmen (*Coping with what is now known as PTSD*) who have the means to make his dreams come true. What they discover changes the Colony and their lives forever. Gold fever ensues. While in the West, Wills must deal with an uncertain romance. Does Cathy even want him?

ISBN 9780994578242 Ebook ISBN 978-0-9945782-6-6 Hardcover ISBN 9798755445504
LP ISBN 9781923097155
https://mybook.to/OutWhereTheBrolgas

Diamonds in the Dirt

Diamonds, love and money… but there is much more to life.

Parramatta 1850s

The youngest Lockley son, **Luke Lockley**, has completed his university education, and his life lacks direction. No job, no money, and no love. Desperately alone, he prays for guidance. How can Luke trust that God has a plan for him if he can't even find a job? He does the only thing he can … he prays. Within a week, life has changed … oh, how it has changed as his brother Wills turns up with a suggestion. Would Luke be interested in joining the expedition with John Evans? **Reverend William Clarke** needs assistance with a government mineral survey. The challenges, adventures and finds are life-changing for many. However, it gives Luke meaning, purpose and direction. The condition of his heart problems also takes a turn. Can he walk away? Will she wait for him?

ISBN: 9780994578273 Ebook ISBN: 978-0-9945782-8-0 Hard cover ISBN 979-8788011141
https://mybook.to/DiamondsintheDirt

The Earl's Shadow

Who or what is the 'shadow'? How does it affect so many?

Parramatta 1860s

Charles Lockley, the Earl of Coxheath, spent his youth as a convict in Parramatta, unaware of his noble birth, with limited education and few social skills. Now, after a near-death experience, Charles must decide how to live the rest of his life. He is thrust out of his comfort zone in London. There, Charles discovers his purpose. He delivers a speech in parliament—an action that will reshape the empire.

His eldest son, **Charlie**, shares many of his father's shortcomings. However, the past continues to haunt Charlie.

But how does **Jim Leslie,** the Cobb and Co. coach driver, fit into their story? And what exactly is 'The Earl's Shadow' that he mentions?

ISBN: 9780645110708 Ebook ISBN 978-0-9945782-9-7
Released June 2022
https://mybook.to/TheEarlsShadow

Once a Jolly Swagman

An old black Billy Can contains the secrets of an incredible life

An Australian Historical Novel Inspired by the songs of The Seekers

Set in 1870s Parramatta and Kent, UK

Rick Lockley, struggling to escape his family's expectations, runs away to find himself. **Jack**, a jolly swagman, takes him under his care. Even after years together, Rick knows little about the old man.

On his death, Jack leaves Rick his precious billy can; the contents reveal Jack's identity. Stunned, Rick must travel to England to finalise Jack's wishes. There, he uncovers Jack's life of love, betrayal and a link to his own family. Rick also discovers there is much more to learn about this enigmatic man.

ISBN 9780645110753   Ebook ISBN 978-0-6451107-6-0
Released Sept 2022
https://mybook.to/OnceaJollySwagman

Jonty's Journey

Gems, Love, Artists and a Golden Lion
Australia and South Africa 1880-1902

Sydney Jeweller **Jonty Evans's** passion for gems takes him to Africa at a volatile time. There, he finds the diamonds he wants and is given a lion cub. However, Jonty is all but kidnapped. His experiences in the Transvaal plunge him into questioning everything he knows about life. Soon, nightmares haunt him. (This is now known as PTSD.)

Upon returning home, he nearly ruins his chance with **Lottie Lockley** before it even begins, and he finds adjusting hard. Lottie's father, **Luke** Lockley from Parramatta, takes him under his wing and directs him to someone who can assist.

Jonty is then called back to Africa as a liaison and reunites with his lion, Chimbu, after saving the life of his security detail. His life journey introduces him to remarkable artists, politicians, poets, rebels, and the scapegoat soldier, Harry Breaker Morant. Can Jonty lay the past to rest and find his lost peace?

ISBN 9780645110777   HC ISBN 9781923097124   Ebook ISBN: 978-0-6451107-9-1
Released Feb 2023

More books are planned for a new trilogy, but they won't be released until 2027

Fools Gold Trilogy
The Breeze Gently Shifts
The Silver Thimble
Knots behind the Tapestry

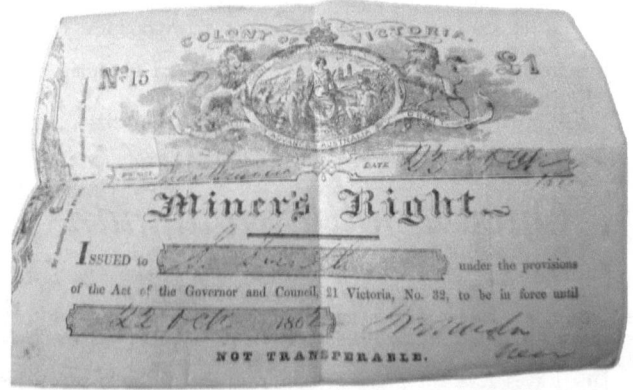

Sheila Hunter's Australian Colonial Trilogy 1840s

Co-Winner of 1999 NSW Senior Citizen of the Year, In the Year of the Senior Citizen

Mattie

The Story of an Australian Convict Child
An Australian Historical Story inspired by real Life.

An orphaned child, Mattie, is convicted of petty theft, sentenced to seven years, and sent to Australia. She meets another convict woman who, at her death, gives Mattie a chance for a new life. She makes the most of everything that comes her way, earning her freedom, falling in love, marrying, and becoming a mother. But life is not kind to her.

She meets bushrangers, moves to Bathurst's gold fields, and opens a store. Yet, she is the kind of woman who made Australia what it is today. Can she survive alone in a man's world? She is a remarkable woman who breaks down all her barriers.

(Mattie's story continues in The Lockleys of Parramatta - bk 4 & 6)

ISBN 9781503252370 & ebook AISN BOOTTEDBTO

(The story continues in The Earl's Shadow & Once a Jolly Swagman)
https://mybook.to/Mattie_sh

Ricky

A boy in Colonial Australia

Ricky English and his mother immigrated from England to join his father in the new Colony of Sydney. Upon arrival, there was no sign of his father. Ricky's mum uses the tiny amount of money they brought to get lodgings in a run-down building. Things go from bad to worse when his mother dies; he is thrown out of the hired rooms, and the caretakers confiscate all their possessions.

Ricky lives on the streets of Sydney Town as a street waif. Ricky finds safe places to sleep and befriends freed convicts who can help him survive. One day, he encounters a lost child and helps reunite her with her family. These people try to help him, but he insists on doing things his way because of his stubbornness. However, he has found a mentor and confidante. The story follows him through his life. He survives and turns his life around, helping others along the way. ***(Will's story continues in Jonty's Journey)***

Paperback ISBN 9781500770570   Kindle ASIN: B00MLYN6IG
https://mybook.to/Ricky_sh

The Heather to The Hawkesbury

Four Scottish families brave a new life in a strange land.

Torn from their homeland by starvation, four Scottish families are forced to leave the Isle of Skye and seek a new life in Australia. **Mary Macdonald**, her husband **Murd**, and their family, her brother **Fergus** MacKenzie, sister-in-law **Caro** MacLeod, cousin **Alex** Fraser, and all their loved ones are compelled to emigrate from Scotland because of the Potato famine and Clearances.

The story follows these families as they journey from Scotland to the New South Wales colony in the 1850s. Mary struggles to cope with the changes and losses in the first months of settlement. Although the other women rely on her, she is nearly overwhelmed. Mary can't settle in this fierce land and pines for home.

Together, the families endure hardships such as accidents, loss, floods, and relentless work, ultimately forging a strong bond with their new homeland. Trials, tribulations, and triumphs mark their saga as they establish themselves in Australia.

Will Mary ever find peace and contentment where danger and sickness have taken loved ones? Can her love for Murd sustain her through the turmoil of life? And what becomes of the brooch given to Mary as she leaves her mother?

ISBN 9781503251434   ebook 9781923097025   Large Print ISBN1533473641

Available on Amazon/Kindle & Large Print
https://mybook.to/TheHeathertTHawkesbury

Sara's Author Bio

Sara Powter
PACIFIC WANDERLAND PUBLICATIONS

Sheila Hunter and Sara Powter were a passionate mother-and-daughter team of amateur genealogists. While working together on their family tree, they made many captivating discoveries. Our most significant discovery was finding four convicts who held very different perspectives on life in the colony from the military. These four felons were transported to Australia between 1792 and 1814, during the height of the convict transportation era. Before her passing in 2002, Sheila adapted some of these histories into enchanting stories, known as her Australian Colonial Trilogy. Sara later had these published. Sheila left a fourth unfinished story, inspiring Sara to complete it. However, before she did, **the Lockleys of Parramatta** were created to see if she could do justice to her mother's work. The first two in the series were completed before attempting to finish **Dancing to Her Own Tune** for her mother. (*Sheila wrote the first 30k words*)

Vividly living through the Colonial Era, these books delve further into the theme of overcoming adversity in Colonial Australia, and how it developed, the demise of the Convict system and the discovery of mineral wealth.

Sara skilfully intertwines precise archival data with a captivating narrative to craft a collection of stories about faith, love, loss, and redemption.

Two hundred years after her family arrived in Australia, Sara continues the Australian Colonial stories that start with **Gentle Annie Soames**, a saga about the First Fleet. Her **First Fleet Trilogy** is now complete. Following this chronologically are the **Hunter to Macquarie Collection,** the **Unlikely Convict Ladies Trilogy,** and The **Lockleys of Parramatta. The Convict Birthstain Collection**, set in the mid-1800s, follows. All the stories are stand-alone novels. There is a chronological list of her books on her web page.

Amazon Aus QR

See Sara's web page to keep up to date with more stories.
An online store is available for a signed copy of Sara's books.
https://www.sarapowter.com.au/ *(Australian Postage only)*

Feel free to email her at
saragpowter@gmail.com

BOOK BUB
https://partners.bookbub.com/authors/6273615/edit

FACEBOOK https://www.facebook.com/profile.php?id=100063887262514

Would you like to receive **a free copy of the book *"Unshackled Lives"*** ?
Download from Book Funnel after you sign up.

FREE Newsletter signup
From my web page.